# Twenty Thousand Leagues Under The Sea

# Twenty Thousand Leagues Under The Sea

## An Underwater Tour of the World

Jules Verne

Trans
Atlantic
Press

This is a Transatlantic Press book

This edition published in 2012

Transatlantic Press

Sky House, Raans Road, Amersham, Bucks, HP6 6JQ, UK

Jules Verne asserts the moral right to be identified as the author of this work.

Cover image © Mary Evans Picture Library

Author biography © Transatlantic Press

A catalogue record is available for this book from the British Library

ISBN 978-1-908533-29-6

Printed and bound by CPI Group (UK) Ltd, Croydon, CR0 4YY

# JULES VERNE

B orn in Nantes in 1828, Jules Verne appeared destined
to follow his father and forge a legal career. He went to
Paris to pursue a law degree, but his studies took second
place as he determined to establish himself as a writer.
His early literary efforts were as a dramatist and librettist,
but in the 1850s he began to publish short stories,
supplementing his income by working as a stockbroker.
The breakthrough in terms of commercial success came
with the publication in 1863 of *Five Weeks in a Balloon*.
It was the first of his celebrated "*Extraordinary Journeys
into the Known and Unknown Worlds*", a tag coined by his
publisher Pierre-Jules Hetzel. He followed it with *Paris in
the 20th Century*, but Hetzel considered the book's dark
futuristic vision too depressing, and it would remain
unpublished until 1994. That rejection may have helped
persuade Verne to focus on stories more upbeat in tone.
A *Journey to the Centre of the Earth* appeared in 1864,
followed by *From the Earth to the Moon* (1865), one of
the earliest space adventures. Verne established himself
as one of the founding fathers of science fiction, though
the term would not enter the language until long after
his death. His other enduringly popular works include
*Twenty Thousand Leagues Under the Sea* (1869), *Around
the World in Eighty Days* (1872) and *The Mysterious
Island* (1874), while he continued the tale of his space
travellers in *Around the Moon* (1869). Verne's later books
were tinged with foreboding, showing his concerns
regarding the onward march of science and technology,

and regarding those holding the levers of power. He was widely acclaimed, a recipient of the *Légion d'honneur*, though he said he was "considered of no account in French literature". He spent the latter years of his life in Amiens, where he died on 24 March 1905, aged 77.

# TWENTY THOUSAND LEAGUES UNDER THE SEA

"Strike, mad vessel! Shower your useless shot!
And then, you will not escape the spur of the Nautilus!"

Following a spate of maritime attacks and numerous reported sightings of a giant creature, the United States government dispatches the *Abraham Lincoln* to hunt down the ocean menace—whatever it is. The expedition party includes renowned scientist Pierre Aronnax and his trusty manservant, along with expert harpooner Ned Land. When the ship finds its target, all three are tossed overboard and swallowed up in the ensuing battle. But this sea-dwelling "monster" has a metal skin and is driven by human desires: the submarine *Nautilus*, commanded by the mysterious, volatile Captain Nemo. The prisoners are well treated, and Aronnax relishes the wondrous sights they encounter on their travels: extraordinary marine life, wrecks of ancient galleons and the chance to gaze upon the lost city of Atlantis. But battles with giant squid and polar ice show that mortal jeopardy is never far away, and the greatest danger of all lies in a deranged captain who has cut himself off from civilization and is waging a revenge-driven personal war.

# CONTENTS

# FIRST PART

# CHAPTER 1

### A Runaway Reef

THE YEAR 1866 was marked by a bizarre development, an unexplained and downright inexplicable phenomenon that surely no one has forgotten. Without getting into those rumors that upset civilians in the seaports and deranged the public mind even far inland, it must be said that professional seamen were especially alarmed. Traders, shipowners, captains of vessels, skippers, and master mariners from Europe and America, naval officers from every country, and at their heels the various national governments on these two continents, were all extremely disturbed by the business.

In essence, over a period of time several ships had encountered "an enormous thing" at sea, a long spindle-shaped object, sometimes giving off a phosphorescent glow, infinitely bigger and faster than any whale.

The relevant data on this apparition, as recorded in various logbooks, agreed pretty closely as to the structure of the object or creature in question, its unprecedented speed of movement, its startling locomotive power, and the unique vitality with which it seemed to be gifted. If it was a cetacean, it exceeded in bulk any whale previously classified by science. No naturalist, neither Cuvier nor Lacépède, neither Professor Dumeril nor Professor de Quatrefages, would have accepted the existence of such a monster sight unseen—specifically, unseen by their own scientific eyes.

Striking an average of observations taken at different

times—rejecting those timid estimates that gave the object a length of 200 feet, and ignoring those exaggerated views that saw it as a mile wide and three long—you could still assert that this phenomenal creature greatly exceeded the dimensions of anything then known to ichthyologists, if it existed at all.

Now then, it did exist, this was an undeniable fact; and since the human mind dotes on objects of wonder, you can understand the worldwide excitement caused by this unearthly apparition. As for relegating it to the realm of fiction, that charge had to be dropped.

In essence, on July 20, 1866, the steamer *Governor Higginson*, from the Calcutta & Burnach Steam Navigation Co., encountered this moving mass five miles off the eastern shores of Australia.

Captain Baker at first thought he was in the presence of an unknown reef; he was even about to fix its exact position when two waterspouts shot out of this inexplicable object and sprang hissing into the air some 150 feet. So, unless this reef was subject to the intermittent eruptions of a geyser, the *Governor Higginson* had fair and honest dealings with some aquatic mammal, until then unknown, that could spurt from its blowholes waterspouts mixed with air and steam.

Similar events were likewise observed in Pacific seas, on July 23 of the same year, by the *Christopher Columbus* from the West India & Pacific Steam Navigation Co. Consequently, this extraordinary cetacean could transfer itself from one locality to another with startling swiftness, since within an interval of just three days, the *Governor Higginson* and the *Christopher Columbus* had observed it at two positions on the charts separated by a distance of more than 700 nautical leagues.

Fifteen days later and 2,000 leagues farther, the *Helvetia* from the Compagnie Nationale and the *Shannon* from the Royal Mail line, running on opposite tacks in that part of the Atlantic lying between the United States and Europe, respectively signaled each other that the monster had been sighted in latitude 42° 15' north and longitude 60° 35' west of the meridian of Greenwich. From their simultaneous observations, they were able to estimate the mammal's minimum length at more than 350 English feet; this was because both the *Shannon* and the *Helvetia* were of smaller dimensions, although each measured 100 meters stem to stern. Now then, the biggest whales, those rorqual whales that frequent the waterways of the Aleutian Islands, have never exceeded a length of 56 meters—if they reach even that.

One after another, reports arrived that would profoundly affect public opinion: new observations taken by the transatlantic liner *Pereire*, the Inman line's *Etna* running afoul of the monster, an official report drawn up by officers on the French frigate *Normandy*, dead–earnest reckonings obtained by the general staff of Commodore Fitz–James aboard the *Lord Clyde*. In lighthearted countries, people joked about this phenomenon, but such serious, practical countries as England, America, and Germany were deeply concerned.

In every big city the monster was the latest rage; they sang about it in the coffee houses, they ridiculed it in the newspapers, they dramatized it in the theaters. The tabloids found it a fine opportunity for hatching all sorts of hoaxes. In those newspapers short of copy, you saw the reappearance of every gigantic imaginary creature, from "Moby Dick," that dreadful white whale from the High Arctic regions, to the stupendous kraken whose tentacles could entwine a 500–ton craft and drag it into the ocean depths. They even reprinted reports from ancient times: the views of Aristotle and Pliny accepting the existence of such monsters, then the Norwegian stories of Bishop Pontoppidan, the narratives of Paul Egede, and finally the reports of Captain Harrington—whose good faith is above suspicion—in which he claims he saw, while aboard the *Castilian* in 1857, one of those enormous serpents that, until then, had frequented only the seas of France's old extremist newspaper, *The Constitutionalist*.

An interminable debate then broke out between believers and skeptics in the scholarly societies and scientific journals. The "monster question" inflamed all minds. During this memorable campaign, journalists making a profession of science battled with those making a profession of wit, spilling waves of ink and some of them even two or three drops of blood, since they went from sea serpents to the most offensive personal remarks.

For six months the war seesawed. With inexhaustible zest, the popular press took potshots at feature articles from the Geographic Institute of Brazil, the Royal Academy of Science in Berlin, the British Association, the Smithsonian Institution in Washington, D.C., at discussions in The Indian Archipelago, in *Cosmos* published by Father Moigno, in Petermann's *Mittheilungen*, and at scientific chronicles in the great French and foreign newspapers. When the monster's detractors cited a saying by the botanist Linnaeus that "nature doesn't make leaps," witty writers in the popular periodicals parodied it, maintaining in essence that "nature doesn't make lunatics," and ordering their contemporaries never to give the lie to nature by believing in krakens, sea serpents, "Moby Dicks," and other all-out efforts from drunken seamen. Finally, in a much-feared satirical journal, an article by its most popular columnist finished off the monster for good, spurning it in the style of Hippolytus repulsing the amorous advances of his stepmother Phædra, and giving the creature its quietus amid a universal burst of laughter. Wit had defeated science.

During the first months of the year 1867, the question seemed to be buried, and it didn't seem due for resurrection, when new facts were brought to the public's attention. But now it was no longer an issue of a scientific problem to be solved, but a quite real and serious danger to be avoided. The question took an entirely new turn. The monster again became an islet, rock, or reef, but a runaway reef, unfixed and elusive.

On March 5, 1867, the *Moravian* from the Montreal Ocean Co., lying during the night in latitude 27° 30' and longitude 72° 15', ran its starboard quarter afoul of a rock marked on no charts of these waterways. Under the combined efforts of wind and 400–horsepower steam, it was traveling at a speed of thirteen knots. Without the high quality of its hull, the *Moravian* would surely have split open from this collision and gone down together with those 237 passengers it was bringing back from Canada.

This accident happened around five o'clock in the morning, just as day was beginning to break. The officers on watch rushed to the craft's stern. They examined the ocean with the most scrupulous care. They saw nothing except a strong eddy breaking three cable lengths out, as if those sheets of water had been violently churned. The site's exact bearings were taken, and the *Moravian* continued on course apparently undamaged. Had it run afoul of an underwater rock or the wreckage of some enormous derelict ship? They were unable to say. But when they examined its undersides in the service yard, they discovered that part of its keel had been smashed.

This occurrence, extremely serious in itself, might perhaps have been forgotten like so many others, if three weeks later it hadn't been re-enacted under identical conditions. Only, thanks to the nationality of the ship victimized by this new ramming, and thanks to the reputation of the company to which this ship belonged, the event caused an immense uproar.

No one is unaware of the name of that famous English shipowner, Cunard. In 1840 this shrewd industrialist founded a postal service between Liverpool and Halifax, featuring three wooden ships with 400–horsepower paddle wheels and a burden of 1,162 metric tons. Eight years later, the company's assets were increased by four 650–horsepower ships at 1,820 metric tons, and in two more years, by two other vessels of still greater power and tonnage. In 1853 the Cunard Co., whose mail–carrying charter had just been renewed, successively added to its assets the *Arabia*, the *Persia*, the *China*, the *Scotia*, the *Java*, and the *Russia*, all ships of top speed and, after the *Great Eastern*, the biggest ever to plow the seas. So in 1867 this company owned twelve ships, eight with paddle wheels and four with propellers.

If I give these highly condensed details, it is so everyone can fully understand the importance of this maritime transportation company, known the world over for its shrewd management. No transoceanic navigational undertaking has been conducted with more ability, no business dealings have been crowned with greater success. In twenty–six years Cunard ships have made 2,000 Atlantic crossings without so much as a voyage canceled, a delay recorded, a man, a craft, or even a letter lost. Accordingly, despite strong competition from France, passengers still choose the Cunard line in preference to all others, as can be seen in a recent survey of official documents. Given this, no one will be astonished at the uproar provoked by this accident involving one of its finest steamers.

On April 13, 1867, with a smooth sea and a moderate breeze, the *Scotia* lay in longitude 15° 12' and latitude 45° 37'. It was traveling at a speed of 13.43 knots under the thrust of its 1,000–horsepower engines. Its paddle wheels were churning the sea with perfect steadiness. It was then drawing 6.7 meters of water and displacing 6,624 cubic meters.

At 4:17 in the afternoon, during a high tea for passengers gathered in the main lounge, a collision occurred, scarcely noticeable on the whole, affecting the *Scotia*'s hull in that quarter a little astern of its port paddle wheel.

The *Scotia* hadn't run afoul of something, it had been fouled, and by a cutting or perforating instrument rather than a blunt one. This encounter seemed so minor that nobody on board would have been disturbed by it, had it not been for the shouts of crewmen in the hold, who climbed on deck yelling:

"We're sinking! We're sinking!"

At first the passengers were quite frightened, but Captain Anderson hastened to reassure them. In fact, there could be no immediate danger. Divided into seven compartments by watertight bulkheads, the *Scotia* could brave any leak with impunity.

Captain Anderson immediately made his way into the hold. He discovered that the fifth compartment had been invaded by the sea, and the speed of this invasion proved that the leak was considerable. Fortunately this compartment didn't contain the boilers, because their furnaces would have been abruptly extinguished.

Captain Anderson called an immediate halt, and one of his sailors dived down to assess the damage. Within moments they had located a hole two meters in width on the steamer's underside. Such a leak could not be patched, and with its paddle wheels half swamped, the *Scotia* had no choice but to continue its voyage. By then it lay 300 miles from Cape Clear, and after three days of delay that filled Liverpool with acute anxiety, it entered the company docks.

The engineers then proceeded to inspect the *Scotia*, which had been put in dry dock. They couldn't believe their eyes. Two and a half meters below its waterline, there gaped a symmetrical gash in the shape of an isosceles triangle. This breach in the sheet iron was so perfectly formed, no punch could have done a cleaner job of it. Consequently, it must have been produced by a perforating tool of uncommon toughness—plus, after being launched with prodigious power and then piercing four centimeters of sheet iron, this tool had needed to withdraw itself by a backward motion truly inexplicable.

This was the last straw, and it resulted in arousing public

passions all over again. Indeed, from this moment on, any maritime casualty without an established cause was charged to the monster's account. This outrageous animal had to shoulder responsibility for all derelict vessels, whose numbers are unfortunately considerable, since out of those 3,000 ships whose losses are recorded annually at the marine insurance bureau, the figure for steam or sailing ships supposedly lost with all hands, in the absence of any news, amounts to at least 200!

Now then, justly or unjustly, it was the "monster" who stood accused of their disappearance; and since, thanks to it, travel between the various continents had become more and more dangerous, the public spoke up and demanded straight out that, at all cost, the seas be purged of this fearsome cetacean.

# CHAPTER 2

## The Pros and Cons

DURING THE PERIOD in which these developments were occurring, I had returned from a scientific undertaking organized to explore the Nebraska badlands in the United States. In my capacity as Assistant Professor at the Paris Museum of Natural History, I had been attached to this expedition by the French government. After spending six months in Nebraska, I arrived in New York laden with valuable collections near the end of March. My departure for France was set for early May. In the meantime, then, I was busy classifying my mineralogical, botanical, and zoological treasures when that incident took place with the *Scotia*.

I was perfectly abreast of this question, which was the big news of the day, and how could I not have been? I had read and reread every American and European newspaper without being any farther along. This mystery puzzled me. Finding it impossible to form any views, I drifted from one extreme to the other. Something was out there, that much was certain, and any doubting Thomas was invited to place his finger on the *Scotia*'s wound.

When I arrived in New York, the question was at the boiling point. The hypothesis of a drifting islet or an elusive reef, put forward by people not quite in their right minds, was completely eliminated. And indeed, unless this reef had an engine in its belly, how could it move about with such prodigious speed?

Also discredited was the idea of a floating hull or some other enormous wreckage, and again because of this speed of movement.

So only two possible solutions to the question were left, creating two very distinct groups of supporters: on one side, those favoring a monster of colossal strength; on the other, those favoring an "underwater boat" of tremendous motor power.

Now then, although the latter hypothesis was completely admissible, it couldn't stand up to inquiries conducted in both the New World and the Old. That a private individual had such a mechanism at his disposal was less than probable. Where and when had he built it, and how could he have built it in secret?

Only some government could own such an engine of destruction, and in these disaster–filled times, when men tax their ingenuity to build increasingly powerful aggressive weapons, it was possible that, unknown to the rest of the world, some nation could have been testing such a fearsome machine. The Chassepot rifle led to the torpedo, and the torpedo has led to this underwater battering ram, which in turn will lead to the world putting its foot down. At least I hope it will.

But this hypothesis of a war machine collapsed in the face of formal denials from the various governments. Since the public interest was at stake and transoceanic travel was suffering, the sincerity of these governments could not be doubted. Besides, how could the assembly of this underwater boat have escaped public notice? Keeping a secret under such circumstances would be difficult enough for an individual, and certainly impossible for a nation whose every move is under constant surveillance by rival powers.

So, after inquiries conducted in England, France, Russia, Prussia, Spain, Italy, America, and even Turkey, the hypothesis of an underwater *Monitor* was ultimately rejected.

And so the monster surfaced again, despite the endless

witticisms heaped on it by the popular press, and the human imagination soon got caught up in the most ridiculous ichthyological fantasies.

After I arrived in New York, several people did me the honor of consulting me on the phenomenon in question. In France I had published a two–volume work, in quarto, entitled *The Mysteries of the Great Ocean Depths*. Well received in scholarly circles, this book had established me as a specialist in this pretty obscure field of natural history. My views were in demand. As long as I could deny the reality of the business, I confined myself to a flat "no comment." But soon, pinned to the wall, I had to explain myself straight out. And in this vein, "the honorable Pierre Aronnax, Professor at the Paris Museum," was summoned by *The New York Herald* to formulate his views no matter what.

I complied. Since I could no longer hold my tongue, I let it wag. I discussed the question in its every aspect, both political and scientific, and this is an excerpt from the well–padded article I published in the issue of April 30.

"Therefore," I wrote, "after examining these different hypotheses one by one, we are forced, every other supposition having been refuted, to accept the existence of an extremely powerful marine animal.

"The deepest parts of the ocean are totally unknown to us. No soundings have been able to reach them. What goes on in those distant depths? What creatures inhabit, or could inhabit, those regions twelve or fifteen miles beneath the surface of the water? What is the constitution of these animals? It's almost beyond conjecture.

"However, the solution to this problem submitted to me can take the form of a choice between two alternatives.

"Either we know every variety of creature populating our planet, or we do not.

"If we do not know every one of them, if nature still keeps

ichthyological secrets from us, nothing is more admissible than to accept the existence of fish or cetaceans of new species or even new genera, animals with a basically 'cast-iron' constitution that inhabit strata beyond the reach of our soundings, and which some development or other, an urge or a whim if you prefer, can bring to the upper level of the ocean for long intervals.

"If, on the other hand, we do know every living species, we must look for the animal in question among those marine creatures already cataloged, and in this event I would be inclined to accept the existence of a giant narwhale.

"The common narwhale, or sea unicorn, often reaches a length of sixty feet. Increase its dimensions fivefold or even tenfold, then give this cetacean a strength in proportion to its size while enlarging its offensive weapons, and you have the animal we're looking for. It would have the proportions determined by the officers of the *Shannon*, the instrument needed to perforate the *Scotia*, and the power to pierce a steamer's hull.

"In essence, the narwhale is armed with a sort of ivory sword, or lance, as certain naturalists have expressed it. It's a king-sized tooth as hard as steel. Some of these teeth have been found buried in the bodies of baleen whales, which the narwhale attacks with invariable success. Others have been wrenched, not without difficulty, from the undersides of vessels that narwhales have pierced clean through, as a gimlet pierces a wine barrel. The museum at the Faculty of Medicine in Paris owns one of these tusks with a length of 2.25 meters and a width at its base of forty-eight centimeters!

"All right then! Imagine this weapon to be ten times stronger and the animal ten times more powerful, launch it at a speed of twenty miles per hour, multiply its mass times its velocity, and you get just the collision we need to cause the specified catastrophe.

"So, until information becomes more abundant, I plump for a sea unicorn of colossal dimensions, no longer armed with a mere lance but with an actual spur, like ironclad frigates or those warships called 'rams,' whose mass and motor power it would possess simultaneously.

"This inexplicable phenomenon is thus explained away—unless it's something else entirely, which, despite everything that has been sighted, studied, explored and experienced, is still possible!"

These last words were cowardly of me; but as far as I could, I wanted to protect my professorial dignity and not lay myself open to laughter from the Americans, who when they do laugh, laugh raucously. I had left myself a loophole. Yet deep down, I had accepted the existence of "the monster."

My article was hotly debated, causing a fine old uproar. It rallied a number of supporters. Moreover, the solution it proposed allowed for free play of the imagination. The human mind enjoys impressive visions of unearthly creatures. Now then, the sea is precisely their best medium, the only setting suitable for the breeding and growing of such giants—next to which such land animals as elephants or rhinoceroses are mere dwarves. The liquid masses support the largest known species of mammals and perhaps conceal mollusks of incomparable size or crustaceans too frightful to contemplate, such as 100–meter lobsters or crabs weighing 200 metric tons! Why not? Formerly, in prehistoric days, land animals (quadrupeds, apes, reptiles, birds) were built on a gigantic scale. Our Creator cast them using a colossal mold that time has gradually made smaller. With its untold depths, couldn't the sea keep alive such huge specimens of life from another age, this sea that never changes while the land masses undergo almost continuous alteration? Couldn't the heart of the ocean hide the last–remaining varieties of these titanic species, for whom years are centuries and centuries millennia?

But I mustn't let these fantasies run away with me! Enough of these fairy tales that time has changed for me into harsh realities. I repeat: opinion had crystallized as to the nature of this phenomenon, and the public accepted without argument the existence of a prodigious creature that had nothing in common with the fabled sea serpent.

Yet if some saw it purely as a scientific problem to be solved, more practical people, especially in America and England, were determined to purge the ocean of this daunting monster, to insure the safety of transoceanic travel. The industrial and commercial newspapers dealt with the question chiefly from this viewpoint. The Shipping & Mercantile Gazette, the Lloyd's List, France's Packetboat and Maritime & Colonial Review, all the rags devoted to insurance companies—who threatened to raise their premium rates—were unanimous on this point.

Public opinion being pronounced, the States of the Union were the first in the field. In New York preparations were under way for an expedition designed to chase this narwhale. A high-speed frigate, the Abraham Lincoln, was fitted out for putting to sea as soon as possible. The naval arsenals were unlocked for Commander Farragut, who pressed energetically forward with the arming of his frigate.

But, as it always happens, just when a decision had been made to chase the monster, the monster put in no further appearances. For two months nobody heard a word about it. Not a single ship encountered it. Apparently the unicorn had gotten wise to these plots being woven around it. People were constantly babbling about the creature, even via the Atlantic Cable! Accordingly, the wags claimed that this slippery rascal had waylaid some passing telegram and was making the most of it.

So the frigate was equipped for a far-off voyage and armed with fearsome fishing gear, but nobody knew where to steer it. And impatience grew until, on June 2, word came that the

*Tampico*, a steamer on the San Francisco line sailing from California to Shanghai, had sighted the animal again, three weeks before in the northerly seas of the Pacific.

This news caused intense excitement. Not even a 24-hour breather was granted to Commander Farragut. His provisions were loaded on board. His coal bunkers were overflowing. Not a crewman was missing from his post. To cast off, he needed only to fire and stoke his furnaces! Half a day's delay would have been unforgivable! But Commander Farragut wanted nothing more than to go forth.

I received a letter three hours before the *Abraham Lincoln* left its Brooklyn pier; the letter read as follows:

Pierre Aronnax
Professor at the Paris Museum
Fifth Avenue Hotel
New York

Sir:
If you would like to join the expedition on the *Abraham Lincoln*, the government of the Union will be pleased to regard you as France's representative in this undertaking. Commander Farragut has a cabin at your disposal.

Very cordially yours,
J. B. HOBSON,
Secretary of the Navy.

# CHAPTER 3

### As Master Wishes

THREE SECONDS before the arrival of J. B. Hobson's letter, I no more dreamed of chasing the unicorn than of trying for the Northwest Passage. Three seconds after reading this letter from the honorable Secretary of the Navy, I understood at last that my true vocation, my sole purpose in life, was to hunt down this disturbing monster and rid the world of it.

Even so, I had just returned from an arduous journey, exhausted and badly needing a rest. I wanted nothing more than to see my country again, my friends, my modest quarters by the Botanical Gardens, my dearly beloved collections! But now nothing could hold me back. I forgot everything else, and without another thought of exhaustion, friends, or collections, I accepted the American government's offer.

"Besides," I mused, "all roads lead home to Europe, and our unicorn may be gracious enough to take me toward the coast of France! That fine animal may even let itself be captured in European seas—as a personal favor to me—and I'll bring back to the Museum of Natural History at least half a meter of its ivory lance!"

But in the meantime I would have to look for this narwhale in the northern Pacific Ocean; which meant returning to France by way of the Antipodes.

"Conseil!" I called in an impatient voice.

Conseil was my manservant. A devoted lad who went with me on all my journeys; a gallant Flemish boy whom I genuinely liked and who returned the compliment; a born stoic, punctilious on principle, habitually hardworking, rarely startled by life's surprises, very skillful with his hands, efficient in his every duty, and despite his having a name that means "counsel," never giving advice—not even the unsolicited kind!

From rubbing shoulders with scientists in our little universe by the Botanical Gardens, the boy had come to know a thing or two. In Conseil I had a seasoned specialist in biological classification, an enthusiast who could run with acrobatic agility up and down the whole ladder of branches, groups, classes, subclasses, orders, families, genera, subgenera, species, and varieties. But there his science came to a halt. Classifying was everything to him, so he knew nothing else. Well versed in the theory of classification, he was poorly versed in its practical application, and I doubt that he could tell a sperm whale from a baleen whale! And yet, what a fine, gallant lad!

For the past ten years, Conseil had gone with me wherever science beckoned. Not once did he comment on the length or the hardships of a journey. Never did he object to buckling up his suitcase for any country whatever, China or the Congo, no matter how far off it was. He went here, there, and everywhere in perfect contentment. Moreover, he enjoyed excellent health that defied all ailments, owned solid muscles, but hadn't a nerve in him, not a sign of nerves—the mental type, I mean.

The lad was thirty years old, and his age to that of his employer was as fifteen is to twenty. Please forgive me for this underhanded way of admitting I had turned forty.

But Conseil had one flaw. He was a fanatic on formality, and he only addressed me in the third person—to the point where it got tiresome.

"Conseil!" I repeated, while feverishly beginning my preparations for departure.

To be sure, I had confidence in this devoted lad. Ordinarily, I never asked whether or not it suited him to go with me on my journeys; but this time an expedition was at issue that could drag on indefinitely, a hazardous undertaking whose purpose was to hunt an animal that could sink a frigate as easily as a walnut shell! There was good reason to stop and think, even for the world's most emotionless man. What would Conseil say?

"Conseil!" I called a third time.

Conseil appeared.

"Did master summon me?" he said, entering.

"Yes, my boy. Get my things ready, get yours ready. We're departing in two hours."

"As master wishes," Conseil replied serenely.

"We haven't a moment to lose. Pack as much into my trunk as you can, my traveling kit, my suits, shirts, and socks, don't bother counting, just squeeze it all in—and hurry!"

"What about master's collections?" Conseil ventured to observe.

"We'll deal with them later."

"What! The archaeotherium, hyracotherium, oreodonts, cheiropotamus, and master's other fossil skeletons?"

"The hotel will keep them for us."

"What about master's live babirusa?"

"They'll feed it during our absence. Anyhow, we'll leave instructions to ship the whole menagerie to France."

"Then we aren't returning to Paris?" Conseil asked.

"Yes, we are . . . certainly . . . ," I replied evasively, "but after we make a detour."

"Whatever detour master wishes."

"Oh, it's nothing really! A route slightly less direct, that's all. We're leaving on the *Abraham Lincoln*."

"As master thinks best," Conseil replied placidly.

"You see, my friend, it's an issue of the monster, the notorious narwhale. We're going to rid the seas of it! The author of a two-volume work, in quarto, on *The Mysteries of the Great Ocean Depths* has no excuse for not setting sail with Commander Farragut. It's a glorious mission but also a dangerous one! We don't know where it will take us! These beasts can be quite unpredictable! But we're going just the same! We have a commander who's game for anything!"

"What master does, I'll do," Conseil replied.

"But think it over, because I don't want to hide anything from you. This is one of those voyages from which people don't always come back!"

"As master wishes."

A quarter of an hour later, our trunks were ready. Conseil did them in a flash, and I was sure the lad hadn't missed a thing, because he classified shirts and suits as expertly as birds and mammals.

The hotel elevator dropped us off in the main vestibule on the mezzanine. I went down a short stair leading to the ground floor. I settled my bill at that huge counter that was always under siege by a considerable crowd. I left instructions for shipping my containers of stuffed animals and dried plants to Paris, France. I opened a line of credit sufficient to cover the babirusa and, Conseil at my heels, I jumped into a carriage.

For a fare of twenty francs, the vehicle went down Broadway to Union Square, took Fourth Ave. to its junction with Bowery St., turned into Katrin St. and halted at Pier 34. There the Katrin ferry transferred men, horses, and carriage to Brooklyn, that great New York annex located on the left bank of the East River, and in a few minutes we arrived at the wharf next to which the *Abraham Lincoln* was vomiting torrents of black smoke from its two funnels.

Our baggage was immediately carried to the deck of the frigate. I rushed aboard. I asked for Commander Farragut. One of the sailors led me to the afterdeck, where I stood in the presence of a smart-looking officer who extended his hand to me.

"Professor Pierre Aronnax?" he said to me.

"The same," I replied. "Commander Farragut?"

"In person. Welcome aboard, professor. Your cabin is waiting for you."

I bowed, and letting the commander attend to getting under way, I was taken to the cabin that had been set aside for me.

The *Abraham Lincoln* had been perfectly chosen and fitted out for its new assignment. It was a high–speed frigate furnished with superheating equipment that allowed the tension of its steam to build to seven atmospheres. Under this pressure the *Abraham Lincoln* reached an average speed of 18.3 miles per hour, a considerable speed but still not enough to cope with our gigantic cetacean.

The frigate's interior accommodations complemented its nautical virtues. I was well satisfied with my cabin, which was located in the stern and opened into the officers' mess.

"We'll be quite comfortable here," I told Conseil.

"With all due respect to master," Conseil replied, "as comfortable as a hermit crab inside the shell of a whelk."

I left Conseil to the proper stowing of our luggage and climbed on deck to watch the preparations for getting under way.

Just then Commander Farragut was giving orders to cast off the last moorings holding the *Abraham Lincoln* to its Brooklyn pier. And so if I'd been delayed by a quarter of an hour or even less, the frigate would have gone without me, and I would have missed out on this unearthly, extraordinary, and inconceivable expedition, whose true story might well meet with some skepticism.

But Commander Farragut didn't want to waste a single day, or even a single hour, in making for those seas where the animal had just been sighted. He summoned his engineer.

"Are we up to pressure?" he asked the man.

"Aye, sir," the engineer replied.

"Go ahead, then!" Commander Farragut called.

At this order, which was relayed to the engine by means of a compressed-air device, the mechanics activated the start-up wheel. Steam rushed whistling into the gaping valves. Long horizontal pistons groaned and pushed the tie rods of the drive shaft. The blades of the propeller churned the waves with increasing speed, and the *Abraham Lincoln* moved out majestically amid a spectator-laden escort of some 100 ferries and tenders.

The wharves of Brooklyn, and every part of New York bordering the East River, were crowded with curiosity seekers. Departing from 500,000 throats, three cheers burst forth in succession. Thousands of handkerchiefs were waving above these tightly packed masses, hailing the *Abraham Lincoln* until it reached the waters of the Hudson River, at the tip of the long peninsula that forms New York City.

The frigate then went along the New Jersey coast—the wonderful right bank of this river, all loaded down with country homes—and passed by the forts to salutes from their biggest cannons. The *Abraham Lincoln* replied by three times lowering and hoisting the American flag, whose thirty-nine stars gleamed from the gaff of the mizzen sail; then, changing speed to take the buoy-marked channel that curved into the inner bay formed by the spit of Sandy Hook, it hugged this sand-covered strip of land where thousands of spectators acclaimed us one more time.

The escort of boats and tenders still followed the frigate and only left us when we came abreast of the lightship, whose two signal lights mark the entrance of the narrows to Upper New York Bay.

Three o'clock then sounded. The harbor pilot went down into his dinghy and rejoined a little schooner waiting for him to leeward. The furnaces were stoked; the propeller churned the waves more swiftly; the frigate skirted the flat, yellow coast of Long Island; and at eight o'clock in the evening, after the lights of Fire Island had vanished into the northwest, we ran at full steam onto the dark waters of the Atlantic.

# CHAPTER 4

### Ned Land

COMMANDER FARRAGUT was a good seaman, worthy of the frigate he commanded. His ship and he were one. He was its very soul. On the cetacean question no doubts arose in his mind, and he didn't allow the animal's existence to be disputed aboard his vessel. He believed in it as certain pious women believe in the leviathan from the Book of Job—out of faith, not reason. The monster existed, and he had vowed to rid the seas of it. The man was a sort of Knight of Rhodes, a latter-day Sir Dieudonné of Gozo, on his way to fight an encounter with the dragon devastating the island. Either Commander Farragut would slay the narwhale, or the narwhale would slay Commander Farragut. No middle of the road for these two.

The ship's officers shared the views of their leader. They could be heard chatting, discussing, arguing, calculating the different chances of an encounter, and observing the vast expanse of the ocean. Voluntary watches from the crosstrees of the topgallant sail were self-imposed by more than one who would have cursed such toil under any other circumstances. As often as the sun swept over its daily arc, the masts were populated with sailors whose feet itched and couldn't hold still on the planking of the deck below! And the *Abraham Lincoln*'s stempost hadn't even cut the suspected waters of the Pacific.

As for the crew, they only wanted to encounter the unicorn, harpoon it, haul it on board, and carve it up. They surveyed the sea with scrupulous care. Besides, Commander Farragut had mentioned that a certain sum of $2,000.00 was waiting for the man who first sighted the animal, be he cabin boy or sailor, mate or officer. I'll let the reader decide whether eyes got proper exercise aboard the *Abraham Lincoln*.

As for me, I didn't lag behind the others and I yielded to no one my share in these daily observations. Our frigate would have had fivescore good reasons for renaming itself the *Argus*, after that mythological beast with 100 eyes! The lone rebel among us was Conseil, who seemed utterly uninterested in the question exciting us and was out of step with the general enthusiasm on board.

As I said, Commander Farragut had carefully equipped his ship with all the gear needed to fish for a gigantic cetacean. No whaling vessel could have been better armed. We had every known mechanism, from the hand–hurled harpoon, to the blunderbuss firing barbed arrows, to the duck gun with exploding bullets. On the forecastle was mounted the latest model breech–loading cannon, very heavy of barrel and narrow of bore, a weapon that would figure in the Universal Exhibition of 1867. Made in America, this valuable instrument could fire a four-kilogram conical projectile an average distance of sixteen kilometers without the least bother.

So the *Abraham Lincoln* wasn't lacking in means of destruction. But it had better still. It had Ned Land, the King of Harpooners.

Gifted with uncommon manual ability, Ned Land was a Canadian who had no equal in his dangerous trade. Dexterity, coolness, bravery, and cunning were virtues he possessed to a high degree, and it took a truly crafty baleen whale or an exceptionally astute sperm whale to elude the thrusts of his harpoon.

Ned Land was about forty years old. A man of great height—over six English feet—he was powerfully built, serious in manner, not very sociable, sometimes headstrong, and quite ill–tempered when crossed. His looks caught the attention, and above all the strength of his gaze, which gave a unique emphasis to his facial appearance.

Commander Farragut, to my thinking, had made a wise move in hiring on this man. With his eye and his throwing arm, he was worth the whole crew all by himself. I can do no better than to compare him with a powerful telescope that could double as a cannon always ready to fire.

To say Canadian is to say French, and as unsociable as Ned Land was, I must admit he took a definite liking to me. No doubt it was my nationality that attracted him. It was an opportunity for him to speak, and for me to hear, that old Rabelaisian dialect still used in some Canadian provinces. The harpooner's family originated in Quebec, and they were already a line of bold fishermen back in the days when this town still belonged to France.

Little by little Ned developed a taste for chatting, and I loved hearing the tales of his adventures in the polar seas. He described his fishing trips and his battles with great natural lyricism. His tales took on the form of an epic poem, and I felt I was hearing some Canadian Homer reciting his *Iliad* of the High Arctic regions.

I'm writing of this bold companion as I currently know him. Because we've become old friends, united in that permanent comradeship born and cemented during only the most frightful crises! Ah, my gallant Ned! I ask only to live 100 years more, the longer to remember you!

And now, what were Ned Land's views on this question of a marine monster? I must admit that he flatly didn't believe in the unicorn, and alone on board, he didn't share the general conviction. He avoided even dealing with the subject, for which one day I felt compelled to take him to task.

During the magnificent evening of June 25—in other words, three weeks after our departure—the frigate lay abreast of Cabo Blanco, thirty miles to leeward of the coast of Patagonia. We had crossed the Tropic of Capricorn, and the Strait of Magellan opened less than 700 miles to the south. Before eight days were out, the *Abraham Lincoln* would plow the waves of the Pacific.

Seated on the afterdeck, Ned Land and I chatted about one thing and another, staring at that mysterious sea whose depths to this day are beyond the reach of human eyes. Quite naturally, I led our conversation around to the giant unicorn, and I weighed our expedition's various chances for success or failure. Then, seeing that Ned just let me talk without saying much himself, I pressed him more closely.

"Ned," I asked him, "how can you still doubt the reality of this cetacean we're after? Do you have any particular reasons for being so skeptical?"

The harpooner stared at me awhile before replying, slapped his broad forehead in one of his standard gestures, closed his eyes as if to collect himself, and finally said:

"Just maybe, Professor Aronnax."

"But Ned, you're a professional whaler, a man familiar with all the great marine mammals—your mind should easily accept this hypothesis of an enormous cetacean, and you ought to be the last one to doubt it under these circumstances!"

"That's just where you're mistaken, professor," Ned replied. "The common man may still believe in fabulous comets crossing outer space, or in prehistoric monsters living at the earth's core, but astronomers and geologists don't swallow such fairy tales. It's the same with whalers. I've chased plenty of cetaceans, I've harpooned a good number, I've killed several. But no matter how powerful and well armed they were, neither their tails or their tusks could puncture the sheet–iron plates of a steamer."

"Even so, Ned, people mention vessels that narwhale tusks have run clean through."

"Wooden ships maybe," the Canadian replied. "But I've never seen the like. So till I have proof to the contrary, I'll deny that baleen whales, sperm whales, or unicorns can do any such thing."

"Listen to me, Ned—"

"No, no, professor. I'll go along with anything you want except that. Some gigantic devilfish maybe . . . ?"

"Even less likely, Ned. The devilfish is merely a mollusk, and even this name hints at its semiliquid flesh, because it's Latin meaning, 'soft one.' The devilfish doesn't belong to the vertebrate branch, and even if it were 500 feet long, it would still be utterly harmless to ships like the *Scotia* or the *Abraham Lincoln*. Consequently, the feats of krakens or other monsters of that ilk must be relegated to the realm of fiction."

"So, Mr. Naturalist," Ned Land continued in a bantering tone, "you'll just keep on believing in the existence of some enormous cetacean . . . ?"

"Yes, Ned, I repeat it with a conviction backed by factual logic. I believe in the existence of a mammal with a powerful constitution, belonging to the vertebrate branch like baleen whales, sperm whales, or dolphins, and armed with a tusk made of horn that has tremendous penetrating power."

"Humph!" the harpooner put in, shaking his head with the attitude of a man who doesn't want to be convinced.

"Note well, my fine Canadian," I went on, "if such an animal exists, if it lives deep in the ocean, if it frequents the liquid strata located miles beneath the surface of the water, it needs to have a constitution so solid, it defies all comparison."

"And why this powerful constitution?" Ned asked.

"Because it takes incalculable strength just to live in those deep strata and withstand their pressure."

"Oh really?" Ned said, tipping me a wink.

"Oh really, and I can prove it to you with a few simple figures."

"Bosh!" Ned replied. "You can make figures do anything you want!"

"In business, Ned, but not in mathematics. Listen to me. Let's accept that the pressure of one atmosphere is represented by the pressure of a column of water thirty-two feet high. In reality, such a column of water wouldn't be quite so high because here we're dealing with salt water, which is denser than fresh water. Well then, when you dive under the waves, Ned, for every thirty-two feet of water above you, your body is tolerating the pressure of one more atmosphere, in other words, one more kilogram per each square centimeter on your body's surface. So it follows that at 320 feet down, this pressure is equal to ten atmospheres, to 100 atmospheres at 3,200 feet, and to 1,000 atmospheres at 32,000 feet, that is, at about two and a half vertical leagues down. Which is tantamount to saying that if you could reach such a depth in the ocean, each square centimeter on your body's surface would be experiencing 1,000 kilograms of pressure. Now, my gallant Ned, do you know how many square centimeters you have on your bodily surface?"

"I haven't the foggiest notion, Professor Aronnax."

"About 17,000."

"As many as that?"

"Yes, and since the atmosphere's pressure actually weighs slightly more than one kilogram per square centimeter, your 17,000 square centimeters are tolerating 17,568 kilograms at this very moment."

"Without my noticing it?"

"Without your noticing it. And if you aren't crushed by so much pressure, it's because the air penetrates the interior of your body with equal pressure. When the inside and outside pressures are in perfect balance, they neutralize each other and allow you to tolerate them without discomfort. But in the water it's another story."

"Yes, I see," Ned replied, growing more interested. "Because the water surrounds me but doesn't penetrate me."

"Precisely, Ned. So at thirty-two feet beneath the surface of the sea, you'll undergo a pressure of 17,568 kilograms; at 320 feet, or ten times greater pressure, it's 175,680 kilograms; at 3,200 feet, or 100 times greater pressure, it's 1,756,800 kilograms; finally, at 32,000 feet, or 1,000 times greater pressure, it's 17,568,000 kilograms; in other words, you'd be squashed as flat as if you'd just been yanked from between the plates of a hydraulic press!"

"Fire and brimstone!" Ned put in.

"All right then, my fine harpooner, if vertebrates several hundred meters long and proportionate in bulk live at such depths, their surface areas make up millions of square centimeters, and the pressure they undergo must be assessed in billions of kilograms. Calculate, then, how much resistance of bone structure and strength of constitution they'd need in order to withstand such pressures!"

"They'd need to be manufactured," Ned Land replied, "from sheet-iron plates eight inches thick, like ironclad frigates."

"Right, Ned, and then picture the damage such a mass could inflict if it were launched with the speed of an express train against a ship's hull."

"Yes . . . indeed . . . maybe," the Canadian replied, staggered by these figures but still not willing to give in.

"Well, have I convinced you?"

"You've convinced me of one thing, Mr. Naturalist. That deep in the sea, such animals would need to be just as strong as you say—if they exist."

"But if they don't exist, my stubborn harpooner, how do you explain the accident that happened to the *Scotia*?"

"It's maybe . . . ," Ned said, hesitating.

"Go on!"

"Because. . . it just couldn't be true!" the Canadian replied, unconsciously echoing a famous catchphrase of the scientist Arago.

But this reply proved nothing, other than how bullheaded the harpooner could be. That day I pressed him no further. The *Scotia*'s accident was undeniable. Its hole was real enough that it had to be plugged up, and I don't think a hole's existence can be more emphatically proven. Now then, this hole didn't make itself, and since it hadn't resulted from underwater rocks or underwater machines, it must have been caused by the perforating tool of some animal.

Now, for all the reasons put forward to this point, I believed that this animal was a member of the branch Vertebrata, class Mammalia, group Pisciforma, and finally, order Cetacea. As for the family in which it would be placed (baleen whale, sperm whale, or dolphin), the genus to which it belonged, and the species in which it would find its proper home, these questions had to be left for later. To answer them called for dissecting this unknown monster; to dissect it called for catching it; to catch it called for harpooning it—which was Ned Land's business; to harpoon it called for sighting it—which was the crew's business; and to sight it called for encountering it—which was a chancy business.

# CHAPTER 5

## At Random!

FOR SOME WHILE the voyage of the *Abraham Lincoln* was marked by no incident. But one circumstance arose that displayed Ned Land's marvelous skills and showed just how much confidence we could place in him.

Off the Falkland Islands on June 30, the frigate came in contact with a fleet of American whalers, and we learned that they hadn't seen the narwhale. But one of them, the captain of the *Monroe*, knew that Ned Land had shipped aboard the *Abraham Lincoln* and asked his help in hunting a baleen whale that was in sight. Anxious to see Ned Land at work, Commander Farragut authorized him to make his way aboard the *Monroe*. And the Canadian had such good luck that with a right–and–left shot, he harpooned not one whale but two, striking the first straight to the heart and catching the other after a few minutes' chase!

Assuredly, if the monster ever had to deal with Ned Land's harpoon, I wouldn't bet on the monster.

The frigate sailed along the east coast of South America with prodigious speed. By July 3 we were at the entrance to the Strait of Magellan, abreast of Cabo de las Virgenes. But Commander Farragut was unwilling to attempt this tortuous passageway and maneuvered instead to double Cape Horn.

The crew sided with him unanimously. Indeed, were we likely to encounter the narwhale in such a cramped strait? Many of our sailors swore that the monster couldn't negotiate this passageway simply because "he's too big for it!"

Near three o'clock in the afternoon on July 6, fifteen miles south of shore, the *Abraham Lincoln* doubled that solitary islet at the tip of the South American continent, that stray rock Dutch seamen had named Cape Horn after their hometown of Hoorn. Our course was set for the northwest, and the next day our frigate's propeller finally churned the waters of the Pacific.

"Open your eyes! Open your eyes!" repeated the sailors of the *Abraham Lincoln*. And they opened amazingly wide. Eyes and spyglasses (a bit dazzled, it is true, by the vista of $2,000.00) didn't remain at rest for an instant. Day and night we observed the surface of the ocean, and those with nyctalopic eyes, whose ability to see in the dark increased their chances by fifty percent, had an excellent shot at winning the prize.

As for me, I was hardly drawn by the lure of money and yet was far from the least attentive on board. Snatching only a few minutes for meals and a few hours for sleep, come rain or come shine, I no longer left the ship's deck. Sometimes bending over the forecastle railings, sometimes leaning against the sternrail, I eagerly scoured that cotton-colored wake that whitened the ocean as far as the eye could see! And how many times I shared the excitement of general staff and crew when some unpredictable whale lifted its blackish back above the waves. In an instant the frigate's deck would become densely populated. The cowls over the companionways would vomit a torrent of sailors and officers. With panting chests and anxious eyes, we each would observe the cetacean's movements. I stared; I stared until I nearly went blind from a worn-out retina, while Conseil, as stoic as ever, kept repeating to me in a calm tone:

"If master's eyes would kindly stop bulging, master will see farther!"

But what a waste of energy! The *Abraham Lincoln* would change course and race after the animal sighted, only to find an ordinary baleen whale or a common sperm whale that soon disappeared amid a chorus of curses!

However, the weather held good. Our voyage was proceeding under the most favorable conditions. By then it was the bad season in these southernmost regions, because July in this zone corresponds to our January in Europe; but the sea remained smooth and easily visible over a vast perimeter.

Ned Land still kept up the most tenacious skepticism; beyond his spells on watch, he pretended that he never even looked at the surface of the waves, at least while no whales were in sight. And yet the marvelous power of his vision could have performed yeoman service. But this stubborn Canadian spent eight hours out of every twelve reading or sleeping in his cabin. A hundred times I chided him for his unconcern.

"Bah!" he replied. "Nothing's out there, Professor Aronnax, and if there is some animal, what chance would we have of spotting it? Can't you see we're just wandering around at random? People say they've sighted this slippery beast again in the Pacific high seas—I'm truly willing to believe it, but two months have already gone by since then, and judging by your narwhale's personality, it hates growing moldy from hanging out too long in the same waterways! It's blessed with a terrific gift for getting around. Now, professor, you know even better than I that nature doesn't violate good sense, and she wouldn't give some naturally slow animal the ability to move swiftly if it hadn't a need to use that talent. So if the beast does exist, it's already long gone!"

I had no reply to this. Obviously we were just groping blindly. But how else could we go about it? All the same, our chances were automatically pretty limited. Yet everyone still felt confident of success, and not a sailor on board would have bet against the narwhale appearing, and soon.

On July 20 we cut the Tropic of Capricorn at longitude 105°, and by the 27th of the same month, we had cleared the equator on the 110th meridian. These bearings determined, the frigate took a more decisive westward heading and tackled the seas of the central Pacific. Commander Farragut felt, and with good reason, that it was best to stay in deep waters and keep his distance from continents or islands, whose neighborhoods the animal always seemed to avoid—"No doubt," our bosun said, "because there isn't enough water for him!" So the frigate kept well out when passing the Tuamotu, Marquesas, and Hawaiian Islands, then cut the Tropic of Cancer at longitude 132° and headed for the seas of China.

We were finally in the area of the monster's latest antics! And in all honesty, shipboard conditions became life-threatening. Hearts were pounding hideously, gearing up for futures full of incurable aneurysms. The entire crew suffered from a nervous excitement that it's beyond me to describe. Nobody ate, nobody slept. Twenty times a day some error in perception, or the optical illusions of some sailor perched in the crosstrees, would cause intolerable anguish, and this emotion, repeated twenty times over, kept us in a state of irritability so intense that a reaction was bound to follow.

And this reaction wasn't long in coming. For three months, during which each day seemed like a century, the *Abraham Lincoln* plowed all the northerly seas of the Pacific, racing after whales sighted, abruptly veering off course, swerving sharply from one tack to another, stopping suddenly, putting on steam and reversing engines in quick succession, at the risk of stripping its gears, and it didn't leave a single point unexplored from the beaches of Japan to the coasts of America. And we found nothing! Nothing except an immenseness of deserted waves! Nothing remotely resembling a gigantic narwhale, or an underwater islet, or a derelict shipwreck, or a runaway reef, or anything the least bit unearthly!

So the reaction set in. At first, discouragement took hold of people's minds, opening the door to disbelief. A new feeling appeared on board, made up of three-tenths shame and seven-tenths fury. The crew called themselves "out-and-out fools" for being hoodwinked by a fairy tale, then grew steadily more furious! The mountains of arguments amassed over a year collapsed all at once, and each man now wanted only to catch up on his eating and sleeping, to make up for the time he had so stupidly sacrificed.

With typical human fickleness, they jumped from one extreme to the other. Inevitably, the most enthusiastic supporters of the undertaking became its most energetic opponents. This reaction mounted upward from the bowels of the ship, from the quarters of the bunker hands to the messroom of the general staff; and for certain, if it hadn't been for Commander Farragut's characteristic stubbornness, the frigate would ultimately have put back to that cape in the south.

But this futile search couldn't drag on much longer. The *Abraham Lincoln* had done everything it could to succeed and had no reason to blame itself. Never had the crew of an American naval craft shown more patience and zeal; they weren't responsible for this failure; there was nothing to do but go home.

A request to this effect was presented to the commander. The commander stood his ground. His sailors couldn't hide their discontent, and their work suffered because of it. I'm unwilling to say that there was mutiny on board, but after a reasonable period of intransigence, Commander Farragut, like Christopher Columbus before him, asked for a grace period of just three days more. After this three-day delay, if the monster hadn't appeared, our helmsman would give three turns of the wheel, and the *Abraham Lincoln* would chart a course toward European seas.

This promise was given on November 2. It had the immediate effect of reviving the crew's failing spirits. The ocean was observed with renewed care. Each man wanted one last look with which to sum up his experience. Spyglasses functioned with feverish energy. A supreme challenge had been issued to the giant narwhale, and the latter had no acceptable excuse for ignoring this Summons to Appear!

Two days passed. The *Abraham Lincoln* stayed at half steam. On the offchance that the animal might be found in these waterways, a thousand methods were used to spark its interest or rouse it from its apathy. Enormous sides of bacon were trailed in our wake, to the great satisfaction, I must say, of assorted sharks. While the *Abraham Lincoln* heaved to, its longboats radiated in every direction around it and didn't leave a single point of the sea unexplored. But the evening of November 4 arrived with this underwater mystery still unsolved.

At noon the next day, November 5, the agreed–upon delay expired. After a position fix, true to his promise, Commander Farragut would have to set his course for the southeast and leave the northerly regions of the Pacific decisively behind.

By then the frigate lay in latitude 31° 15′ north and longitude 136° 42′ east. The shores of Japan were less than 200 miles to our leeward. Night was coming on. Eight o'clock had just struck. Huge clouds covered the moon's disk, then in its first quarter. The sea undulated placidly beneath the frigate's stempost.

Just then I was in the bow, leaning over the starboard rail. Conseil, stationed beside me, stared straight ahead. Roosting in the shrouds, the crew examined the horizon, which shrank and darkened little by little. Officers were probing the increasing gloom with their night glasses. Sometimes the murky ocean sparkled beneath moonbeams that darted between the fringes of two clouds. Then all traces of light vanished into the darkness.

Observing Conseil, I discovered that, just barely, the gallant lad had fallen under the general influence. At least so I thought. Perhaps his nerves were twitching with curiosity for the first time in history.

"Come on, Conseil!" I told him. "Here's your last chance to pocket that $2,000.00!"

"If master will permit my saying so," Conseil replied, "I never expected to win that prize, and the Union government could have promised $100,000.00 and been none the poorer."

"You're right, Conseil, it turned out to be a foolish business after all, and we jumped into it too hastily. What a waste of time, what a futile expense of emotion! Six months ago we could have been back in France—"

"In master's little apartment," Conseil answered. "In master's museum! And by now I would have classified master's fossils. And master's babirusa would be ensconced in its cage at the zoo in the Botanical Gardens, and it would have attracted every curiosity seeker in town!"

"Quite so, Conseil, and what's more, I imagine that people will soon be poking fun at us!"

"To be sure," Conseil replied serenely, "I do think they'll have fun at master's expense. And must it be said . . . ?"

"It must be said, Conseil."

"Well then, it will serve master right!"

"How true!"

"When one has the honor of being an expert as master is, one mustn't lay himself open to—"

Conseil didn't have time to complete the compliment. In the midst of the general silence, a voice became audible. It was Ned Land's voice, and it shouted:

"Ahoy! There's the thing in question, abreast of us to leeward!"

# CHAPTER 6

## At Full Steam

AT THIS SHOUT the entire crew rushed toward the harpooner—commander, officers, mates, sailors, cabin boys, down to engineers leaving their machinery and stokers neglecting their furnaces. The order was given to stop, and the frigate merely coasted.

By then the darkness was profound, and as good as the Canadian's eyes were, I still wondered how he could see—and what he had seen. My heart was pounding fit to burst.

But Ned Land was not mistaken, and we all spotted the object his hand was indicating.

Two cable lengths off the *Abraham Lincoln*'s starboard quarter, the sea seemed to be lit up from underneath. This was no mere phosphorescent phenomenon, that much was unmistakable. Submerged some fathoms below the surface of the water, the monster gave off that very intense but inexplicable glow that several captains had mentioned in their reports. This magnificent radiance had to come from some force with a great illuminating capacity. The edge of its light swept over the sea in an immense, highly elongated oval, condensing at the center into a blazing core whose unbearable glow diminished by° outward.

"It's only a cluster of phosphorescent particles!" exclaimed one of the officers.

"No, sir," I answered with conviction. "Not even angel-wing clams or salps have ever given off such a powerful light.

That glow is basically electric in nature. Besides . . . look, look! It's shifting! It's moving back and forth! It's darting at us!"

A universal shout went up from the frigate.

"Quiet!" Commander Farragut said. "Helm hard to leeward! Reverse engines!"

Sailors rushed to the helm, engineers to their machinery. Under reverse steam immediately, the *Abraham Lincoln* beat to port, sweeping in a semicircle.

"Right your helm! Engines forward!" Commander Farragut called.

These orders were executed, and the frigate swiftly retreated from this core of light.

My mistake. It wanted to retreat, but the unearthly animal came at us with a speed double our own.

We gasped. More stunned than afraid, we stood mute and motionless. The animal caught up with us, played with us. It made a full circle around the frigate—then doing fourteen knots—and wrapped us in sheets of electricity that were like luminous dust. Then it retreated two or three miles, leaving a phosphorescent trail comparable to those swirls of steam that shoot behind the locomotive of an express train. Suddenly, all the way from the dark horizon where it had gone to gather momentum, the monster abruptly dashed toward the *Abraham Lincoln* with frightening speed, stopped sharply twenty feet from our side plates, and died out—not by diving under the water, since its glow did not recede gradually—but all at once, as if the source of this brilliant emanation had suddenly dried up. Then it reappeared on the other side of the ship, either by circling around us or by gliding under our hull. At any instant a collision could have occurred that would have been fatal to us.

Meanwhile I was astonished at the frigate's maneuvers. It was fleeing, not fighting. Built to pursue, it was being pursued, and I commented on this to Commander Farragut. His face, ordinarily so emotionless, was stamped with indescribable astonishment.

"Professor Aronnax," he answered me, "I don't know what kind of fearsome creature I'm up against, and I don't want my frigate running foolish risks in all this darkness. Besides, how should we attack this unknown creature, how should we defend ourselves against it? Let's wait for daylight, and then we'll play a different role."

"You've no further doubts, commander, as to the nature of this animal?"

"No, sir, it's apparently a gigantic narwhale, and an electric one to boot."

"Maybe," I added, "it's no more approachable than an electric eel or an electric ray!"

"Right," the commander replied. "And if it has their power to electrocute, it's surely the most dreadful animal ever conceived by our Creator. That's why I'll keep on my guard, sir."

The whole crew stayed on their feet all night long. No one even thought of sleeping. Unable to compete with the monster's speed, the *Abraham Lincoln* slowed down and stayed at half steam. For its part, the narwhale mimicked the frigate, simply rode with the waves, and seemed determined not to forsake the field of battle.

However, near midnight it disappeared, or to use a more appropriate expression, "it went out," like a huge glowworm. Had it fled from us? We were duty bound to fear so rather than hope so. But at 12:53 in the morning, a deafening hiss became audible, resembling the sound made by a waterspout expelled with tremendous intensity.

By then Commander Farragut, Ned Land, and I were on the afterdeck, peering eagerly into the profound gloom.

"Ned Land," the commander asked, "you've often heard whales bellowing?"

"Often, sir, but never a whale like this, whose sighting earned me $2,000.00."

"Correct, the prize is rightfully yours. But tell me, isn't that the noise cetaceans make when they spurt water from their blowholes?"

"The very noise, sir, but this one's way louder. So there can be no mistake. There's definitely a whale lurking in our waters. With your permission, sir," the harpooner added, "tomorrow at daybreak we'll have words with it."

"If it's in a mood to listen to you, Mr. Land," I replied in a tone far from convinced.

"Let me get within four harpoon lengths of it," the Canadian shot back, "and it had better listen!"

"But to get near it," the commander went on, "I'd have to put a whaleboat at your disposal?"

"Certainly, sir."

"That would be gambling with the lives of my men."

"And with my own!" the harpooner replied simply.

Near two o'clock in the morning, the core of light reappeared, no less intense, five miles to windward of the *Abraham Lincoln*. Despite the distance, despite the noise of wind and sea, we could distinctly hear the fearsome thrashings of the animal's tail, and even its panting breath. Seemingly, the moment this enormous narwhale came up to breathe at the surface of the ocean, air was sucked into its lungs like steam into the huge cylinders of a 2,000–horsepower engine.

"Hmm!" I said to myself. "A cetacean as powerful as a whole cavalry regiment—now that's a whale of a whale!"

We stayed on the alert until daylight, getting ready for action. Whaling gear was set up along the railings. Our chief officer loaded the blunderbusses, which can launch harpoons as far as a mile, and long duck guns with exploding bullets that can mortally wound even the most powerful animals. Ned Land was content to sharpen his harpoon, a dreadful weapon in his hands.

At six o'clock day began to break, and with the dawn's early light, the narwhale's electric glow disappeared. At seven o'clock the day was well along, but a very dense morning mist shrank the horizon, and our best spyglasses were unable to pierce it. The outcome: disappointment and anger.

I hoisted myself up to the crosstrees of the mizzen sail. Some officers were already perched on the mastheads.

At eight o'clock the mist rolled ponderously over the waves, and its huge curls were lifting little by little. The horizon grew wider and clearer all at once.

Suddenly, just as on the previous evening, Ned Land's voice was audible.

"There's the thing in question, astern to port!" the harpooner shouted.

Every eye looked toward the point indicated.

There, a mile and a half from the frigate, a long blackish body emerged a meter above the waves. Quivering violently, its tail was creating a considerable eddy. Never had caudal equipment thrashed the sea with such power. An immense wake of glowing whiteness marked the animal's track, sweeping in a long curve.

Our frigate drew nearer to the cetacean. I examined it with a completely open mind. Those reports from the *Shannon* and the *Helvetia* had slightly exaggerated its dimensions, and I put its length at only 250 feet. Its girth was more difficult to judge, but all in all, the animal seemed to be wonderfully proportioned in all three dimensions.

While I was observing this phenomenal creature, two jets of steam and water sprang from its blowholes and rose to an altitude of forty meters, which settled for me its mode of breathing. From this I finally concluded that it belonged to the branch Vertebrata, class Mammalia, subclass Monodelphia, group Pisciforma, order Cetacea, family . . . but here I couldn't make up my mind. The order Cetacea consists of three families, baleen whales, sperm whales, dolphins, and it's in this last group that narwhales are placed. Each of these families is divided into several genera, each genus into species, each species into varieties. So I was still missing variety, species, genus, and family, but no doubt I would complete my classifying with the aid of Heaven and Commander Farragut.

The crew were waiting impatiently for orders from their leader. The latter, after carefully observing the animal, called for his engineer. The engineer raced over.

"Sir," the commander said, "are you up to pressure?"

"Aye, sir," the engineer replied.

"Fine. Stoke your furnaces and clap on full steam!"

Three cheers greeted this order. The hour of battle had sounded. A few moments later, the frigate's two funnels vomited torrents of black smoke, and its deck quaked from the trembling of its boilers.

Driven forward by its powerful propeller, the *Abraham Lincoln* headed straight for the animal. Unconcerned, the latter let us come within half a cable length; then, not bothering to dive, it got up a little speed, retreated, and was content to keep its distance.

This chase dragged on for about three–quarters of an hour without the frigate gaining two fathoms on the cetacean. At this rate, it was obvious that we would never catch up with it.

Infuriated, Commander Farragut kept twisting the thick tuft of hair that flourished below his chin.

"Ned Land!" he called.

The Canadian reported at once.

"Well, Mr. Land," the commander asked, "do you still advise putting my longboats to sea?"

"No, sir," Ned Land replied, "because that beast won't be caught against its will."

"Then what should we do?"

"Stoke up more steam, sir, if you can. As for me, with your permission I'll go perch on the bobstays under the bowsprit, and if we can get within a harpoon length, I'll harpoon the brute."

"Go to it, Ned," Commander Farragut replied. "Engineer," he called, "keep the pressure mounting!"

Ned Land made his way to his post. The furnaces were urged into greater activity; our propeller did forty-three revolutions per minute, and steam shot from the valves. Heaving the log, we verified that the *Abraham Lincoln* was going at the rate of 18.5 miles per hour.

But that damned animal also did a speed of 18.5.

For the next hour our frigate kept up this pace without gaining a fathom! This was humiliating for one of the fastest racers in the American navy. The crew were working up into a blind rage. Sailor after sailor heaved insults at the monster, which couldn't be bothered with answering back. Commander Farragut was no longer content simply to twist his goatee; he chewed on it.

The engineer was summoned once again.

"You're up to maximum pressure?" the commander asked him.

"Aye, sir," the engineer replied.

"And your valves are charged to . . . ?"

"To six and a half atmospheres."

"Charge them to ten atmospheres."

A typical American order if I ever heard one. It would have sounded just fine during some Mississippi paddle-wheeler race, to "outstrip the competition!"

"Conseil," I said to my gallant servant, now at my side, "you realize that we'll probably blow ourselves skyhigh?"

"As master wishes!" Conseil replied.

All right, I admit it: I did wish to run this risk!

The valves were charged. More coal was swallowed by the

furnaces. Ventilators shot torrents of air over the braziers. The *Abraham Lincoln*'s speed increased. Its masts trembled down to their blocks, and swirls of smoke could barely squeeze through the narrow funnels.

We heaved the log a second time.

"Well, helmsman?" Commander Farragut asked.

"19.3 miles per hour, sir."

"Keep stoking the furnaces."

The engineer did so. The pressure gauge marked ten atmospheres. But no doubt the cetacean itself had "warmed up," because without the least trouble, it also did 19.3.

What a chase! No, I can't describe the excitement that shook my very being. Ned Land stayed at his post, harpoon in hand. Several times the animal let us approach.

"We're overhauling it!" the Canadian would shout.

Then, just as he was about to strike, the cetacean would steal off with a swiftness I could estimate at no less than thirty miles per hour. And even at our maximum speed, it took the liberty of thumbing its nose at the frigate by running a full circle around us! A howl of fury burst from every throat!

By noon we were no farther along than at eight o'clock in the morning.

Commander Farragut then decided to use more direct methods.

"Bah!" he said. "So that animal is faster than the *Abraham Lincoln*. All right, we'll see if it can outrun our conical shells! Mate, man the gun in the bow!"

Our forecastle cannon was immediately loaded and leveled. The cannoneer fired a shot, but his shell passed some feet above the cetacean, which stayed half a mile off.

"Over to somebody with better aim!" the commander shouted. "And $500.00 to the man who can pierce that infernal beast!"

Calm of eye, cool of feature, an old gray–bearded gunner—I

can see him to this day—approached the cannon, put it in position, and took aim for a good while. There was a mighty explosion, mingled with cheers from the crew.

The shell reached its target; it hit the animal, but not in the usual fashion—it bounced off that rounded surface and vanished into the sea two miles out.

"Oh drat!" said the old gunner in his anger. "That rascal must be covered with six-inch armor plate!"

"Curse the beast!" Commander Farragut shouted.

The hunt was on again, and Commander Farragut leaned over to me, saying:

"I'll chase that animal till my frigate explodes!"

"Yes," I replied, "and nobody would blame you!"

We could still hope that the animal would tire out and not be as insensitive to exhaustion as our steam engines. But no such luck. Hour after hour went by without it showing the least sign of weariness.

However, to the *Abraham Lincoln*'s credit, it must be said that we struggled on with tireless persistence. I estimate that we covered a distance of at least 500 kilometers during this ill-fated day of November 6. But night fell and wrapped the surging ocean in its shadows.

By then I thought our expedition had come to an end, that we would never see this fantastic animal again. I was mistaken.

At 10:50 in the evening, that electric light reappeared three miles to windward of the frigate, just as clear and intense as the night before.

The narwhale seemed motionless. Was it asleep perhaps, weary from its workday, just riding with the waves? This was our chance, and Commander Farragut was determined to take full advantage of it.

He gave his orders. The *Abraham Lincoln* stayed at half steam, advancing cautiously so as not to awaken its adversary. In midocean it's not unusual to encounter whales so sound asleep they can successfully be attacked, and Ned Land had harpooned more than one in its slumber. The Canadian went to resume his post on the bobstays under the bowsprit.

The frigate approached without making a sound, stopped two cable lengths from the animal and coasted. Not a soul breathed on board. A profound silence reigned over the deck. We were not 100 feet from the blazing core of light, whose glow grew stronger and dazzled the eyes.

Just then, leaning over the forecastle railing, I saw Ned Land below me, one hand grasping the martingale, the other brandishing his dreadful harpoon. Barely twenty feet separated him from the motionless animal.

All at once his arm shot forward and the harpoon was launched. I heard the weapon collide resonantly, as if it had hit some hard substance.

The electric light suddenly went out, and two enormous waterspouts crashed onto the deck of the frigate, racing like a torrent from stem to stern, toppling crewmen, breaking spare masts and yardarms from their lashings.

A hideous collision occurred, and thrown over the rail with no time to catch hold of it, I was hurled into the sea.

# CHAPTER 7

A Whale of Unknown Species

ALTHOUGH I WAS startled by this unexpected descent, I at least have a very clear recollection of my sensations during it.

At first I was dragged about twenty feet under. I'm a good swimmer, without claiming to equal such other authors as Byron and Edgar Allan Poe, who were master divers, and I didn't lose my head on the way down. With two vigorous kicks of the heel, I came back to the surface of the sea.

My first concern was to look for the frigate. Had the crew seen me go overboard? Was the *Abraham Lincoln* tacking about? Would Commander Farragut put a longboat to sea? Could I hope to be rescued?

The gloom was profound. I glimpsed a black mass disappearing eastward, where its running lights were fading out in the distance. It was the frigate. I felt I was done for.

"Help! Help!" I shouted, swimming desperately toward the *Abraham Lincoln*.

My clothes were weighing me down. The water glued them to my body, they were paralyzing my movements. I was sinking! I was suffocating . . . !

"Help!"

This was the last shout I gave. My mouth was filling with water. I struggled against being dragged into the depths. . . .

Suddenly my clothes were seized by energetic hands, I felt myself pulled abruptly back to the surface of the sea, and yes, I heard these words pronounced in my ear:

"If master would oblige me by leaning on my shoulder, master will swim with much greater ease."

With one hand I seized the arm of my loyal Conseil.

"You!" I said. "You!"

"Myself," Conseil replied, "and at master's command."

"That collision threw you overboard along with me?"

"Not at all. But being in master's employ, I followed master." The fine lad thought this only natural!

"What about the frigate?" I asked.

"The frigate?" Conseil replied, rolling over on his back. "I think master had best not depend on it to any great extent!"

"What are you saying?"

"I'm saying that just as I jumped overboard, I heard the men at the helm shout, 'Our propeller and rudder are smashed!' "

"Smashed?"

"Yes, smashed by the monster's tusk! I believe it's the sole injury the *Abraham Lincoln* has sustained. But most inconveniently for us, the ship can no longer steer."

"Then we're done for!"

"Perhaps," Conseil replied serenely. "However, we still have a few hours before us, and in a few hours one can do a great many things!"

Conseil's unflappable composure cheered me up. I swam more vigorously, but hampered by clothes that were as restricting as a cloak made of lead, I was managing with only the greatest difficulty. Conseil noticed as much.

"Master will allow me to make an incision," he said.

And he slipped an open clasp knife under my clothes, slitting them from top to bottom with one swift stroke. Then he briskly undressed me while I swam for us both.

I then did Conseil the same favor, and we continued to "navigate" side by side.

But our circumstances were no less dreadful. Perhaps they

hadn't seen us go overboard; and even if they had, the frigate—being undone by its rudder—couldn't return to leeward after us. So we could count only on its longboats.

Conseil had coolly reasoned out this hypothesis and laid his plans accordingly. An amazing character, this boy; in midocean, this stoic lad seemed right at home!

So, having concluded that our sole chance for salvation lay in being picked up by the *Abraham Lincoln*'s longboats, we had to take steps to wait for them as long as possible. Consequently, I decided to divide our energies so we wouldn't both be worn out at the same time, and this was the arrangement: while one of us lay on his back, staying motionless with arms crossed and legs outstretched, the other would swim and propel his partner forward. This towing role was to last no longer than ten minutes, and by relieving each other in this way, we could stay afloat for hours, perhaps even until daybreak.

Slim chance, but hope springs eternal in the human breast! Besides, there were two of us. Lastly, I can vouch—as improbable as it seems—that even if I had wanted to destroy all my illusions, even if I had been willing to "give in to despair," I could not have done so!

The cetacean had rammed our frigate at about eleven o'clock in the evening. I therefore calculated on eight hours of swimming until sunrise. A strenuous task, but feasible, thanks to our relieving each other. The sea was pretty smooth and barely tired us. Sometimes I tried to peer through the dense gloom, which was broken only by the phosphorescent flickers coming from our movements. I stared at the luminous ripples breaking over my hands, shimmering sheets spattered with blotches of bluish gray. It seemed as if we'd plunged into a pool of quicksilver.

Near one o'clock in the morning, I was overcome with tremendous exhaustion. My limbs stiffened in the grip of intense cramps. Conseil had to keep me going, and attending to our self–preservation became his sole responsibility. I soon heard the poor lad gasping; his breathing became shallow and quick. I didn't think he could stand such exertions for much longer.

"Go on! Go on!" I told him.

"Leave master behind?" he replied. "Never! I'll drown before he does!"

Just then, past the fringes of a large cloud that the wind was driving eastward, the moon appeared. The surface of the sea glistened under its rays. That kindly light rekindled our strength. I held up my head again. My eyes darted to every point of the horizon. I spotted the frigate. It was five miles from us and formed no more than a dark, barely perceptible mass. But as for longboats, not a one in sight!

I tried to call out. What was the use at such a distance! My swollen lips wouldn't let a single sound through. Conseil could still articulate a few words, and I heard him repeat at intervals:

"Help! Help!"

Ceasing all movement for an instant, we listened. And it may have been a ringing in my ear, from this organ filling with impeded blood, but it seemed to me that Conseil's shout had received an answer back.

"Did you hear that?" I muttered.

"Yes, yes!"

And Conseil hurled another desperate plea into space.

This time there could be no mistake! A human voice had answered us! Was it the voice of some poor devil left behind in midocean, some other victim of that collision suffered by our ship? Or was it one of the frigate's longboats, hailing us out of the gloom?

Conseil made one final effort, and bracing his hands on my shoulders, while I offered resistance with one supreme exertion, he raised himself half out of the water, then fell back exhausted.

"What did you see?"

"I saw . . . ," he muttered, "I saw . . . but we mustn't talk . . . save our strength . . . !"

What had he seen? Then, lord knows why, the thought of the monster came into my head for the first time . . . ! But even so, that voice . . . ? Gone are the days when Jonahs took refuge in the bellies of whales!

Nevertheless, Conseil kept towing me. Sometimes he looked up, stared straight ahead, and shouted a request for directions, which was answered by a voice that was getting closer and closer. I could barely hear it. I was at the end of my strength; my fingers gave out; my hands were no help to me; my mouth opened convulsively, filling with brine; its coldness ran through me; I raised my head one last time, then I collapsed. . . .

Just then something hard banged against me. I clung to it. Then I felt myself being pulled upward, back to the surface of the water; my chest caved in, and I fainted. . . .

For certain, I came to quickly, because someone was massaging me so vigorously it left furrows in my flesh. I half opened my eyes. . . .

"Conseil!" I muttered.

"Did master ring for me?" Conseil replied.

Just then, in the last light of a moon settling on the horizon, I spotted a face that wasn't Conseil's but which I recognized at once.

"Ned!" I exclaimed.

"In person, sir, and still after his prize!" the Canadian replied.

"You were thrown overboard after the frigate's collision?"

"Yes, professor, but I was luckier than you, and right away I was able to set foot on this floating islet."

"Islet?"

"Or in other words, on our gigantic narwhale."

"Explain yourself, Ned."

"It's just that I soon realized why my harpoon got blunted and couldn't puncture its hide."

"Why, Ned, why?"

"Because, professor, this beast is made of boilerplate steel!"

At this point in my story, I need to get a grip on myself, reconstruct exactly what I experienced, and make doubly sure of everything I write.

The Canadian's last words caused a sudden upheaval in my brain. I swiftly hoisted myself to the summit of this half-submerged creature or object that was serving as our refuge. I tested it with my foot. Obviously it was some hard, impenetrable substance, not the soft matter that makes up the bodies of our big marine mammals.

But this hard substance could have been a bony carapace, like those that covered some prehistoric animals, and I might have left it at that and classified this monster among such amphibious reptiles as turtles or alligators.

Well, no. The blackish back supporting me was smooth and polished with no overlapping scales. On impact, it gave off a metallic sonority, and as incredible as this sounds, it seemed, I swear, to be made of riveted plates.

No doubts were possible! This animal, this monster, this natural phenomenon that had puzzled the whole scientific world, that had muddled and misled the minds of seamen in both hemispheres, was, there could be no escaping it, an even more astonishing phenomenon—a phenomenon made by the hand of man.

Even if I had discovered that some fabulous, mythological creature really existed, it wouldn't have given me such a terrific mental jolt. It's easy enough to accept that prodigious things can come from our Creator. But to find, all at once, right before your eyes, that the impossible had been mysteriously achieved by man himself: this staggers the mind!

But there was no question now. We were stretched out on the back of some kind of underwater boat that, as far as I could judge, boasted the shape of an immense steel fish. Ned Land had clear views on the issue. Conseil and I could only line up behind him.

"But then," I said, "does this contraption contain some sort of locomotive mechanism, and a crew to run it?"

"Apparently," the harpooner replied. "And yet for the three hours I've lived on this floating island, it hasn't shown a sign of life."

"This boat hasn't moved at all?"

"No, Professor Aronnax. It just rides with the waves, but otherwise it hasn't stirred."

"But we know that it's certainly gifted with great speed. Now then, since an engine is needed to generate that speed, and a mechanic to run that engine, I conclude: we're saved."

"Humph!" Ned Land put in, his tone denoting reservations.

Just then, as if to take my side in the argument, a bubbling began astern of this strange submersible—whose drive mechanism was obviously a propeller—and the boat started to move. We barely had time to hang on to its topside, which emerged about eighty centimeters above water. Fortunately its speed was not excessive.

"So long as it navigates horizontally," Ned Land muttered, "I've no complaints. But if it gets the urge to dive, I wouldn't give $2.00 for my hide!"

The Canadian might have quoted a much lower price. So it was imperative to make contact with whatever beings were confined inside the plating of this machine. I searched its surface for an opening or a hatch, a "manhole," to use the official term; but the lines of rivets had been firmly driven into the sheet-iron joins and were straight and uniform.

Moreover, the moon then disappeared and left us in profound darkness. We had to wait for daylight to find some way of getting inside this underwater boat.

So our salvation lay totally in the hands of the mysterious helmsmen steering this submersible, and if it made a dive, we were done for! But aside from this occurring, I didn't doubt the possibility of our making contact with them. In fact, if they didn't produce their own air, they inevitably had to make periodic visits to the surface of the ocean to replenish their oxygen supply. Hence the need for some opening that put the boat's interior in contact with the atmosphere.

As for any hope of being rescued by Commander Farragut, that had to be renounced completely. We were being swept westward, and I estimate that our comparatively moderate speed reached twelve miles per hour. The propeller churned the waves with mathematical regularity, sometimes emerging above the surface and throwing phosphorescent spray to great heights.

Near four o'clock in the morning, the submersible picked up speed. We could barely cope with this dizzying rush, and the waves battered us at close range. Fortunately Ned's hands came across a big mooring ring fastened to the topside of this sheet-iron back, and we all held on for dear life.

Finally this long night was over. My imperfect memories won't let me recall my every impression of it. A single detail comes back to me. Several times, during various lulls of wind and sea, I thought I heard indistinct sounds, a sort of elusive harmony produced by distant musical chords. What was the secret behind this underwater navigating, whose explanation the whole world had sought in vain? What beings lived inside this strange boat? What mechanical force allowed it to move about with such prodigious speed?

Daylight appeared. The morning mists surrounded us, but they soon broke up. I was about to proceed with a careful examination of the hull, whose topside formed a sort of horizontal platform, when I felt it sinking little by little.

"Oh, damnation!" Ned Land shouted, stamping his foot on the resonant sheet iron. "Open up there, you antisocial navigators!"

But it was difficult to make yourself heard above the deafening beats of the propeller. Fortunately this submerging movement stopped.

From inside the boat, there suddenly came noises of iron fastenings pushed roughly aside. One of the steel plates flew up, a man appeared, gave a bizarre yell, and instantly disappeared.

A few moments later, eight strapping fellows appeared silently, their faces like masks, and dragged us down into their fearsome machine.

# CHAPTER 8

### "Mobilis in Mobili"

THIS BRUTALLY EXECUTED capture was carried out with lightning speed. My companions and I had no time to collect ourselves. I don't know how they felt about being shoved inside this aquatic prison, but as for me, I was shivering all over. With whom were we dealing? Surely with some new breed of pirates, exploiting the sea after their own fashion.

The narrow hatch had barely closed over me when I was surrounded by profound darkness. Saturated with the outside light, my eyes couldn't make out a thing. I felt my naked feet clinging to the steps of an iron ladder. Forcibly seized, Ned Land and Conseil were behind me. At the foot of the ladder, a door opened and instantly closed behind us with a loud clang.

We were alone. Where? I couldn't say, could barely even imagine. All was darkness, but such utter darkness that after several minutes, my eyes were still unable to catch a single one of those hazy gleams that drift through even the blackest nights.

Meanwhile, furious at these goings on, Ned Land gave free rein to his indignation.

"Damnation!" he exclaimed. "These people are about as hospitable as the savages of New Caledonia! All that's lacking is for them to be cannibals! I wouldn't be surprised if they were, but believe you me, they won't eat me without my kicking up a protest!"

"Calm yourself, Ned my friend," Conseil replied serenely.

"Don't flare up so quickly! We aren't in a kettle yet!"

"In a kettle, no," the Canadian shot back, "but in an oven for sure. It's dark enough for one. Luckily my Bowie knife hasn't left me, and I can still see well enough to put it to use. The first one of these bandits who lays a hand on me—"

"Don't be so irritable, Ned," I then told the harpooner, "and don't ruin things for us with pointless violence. Who knows whether they might be listening to us? Instead, let's try to find out where we are!"

I started moving, groping my way. After five steps I encountered an iron wall made of riveted boilerplate. Then, turning around, I bumped into a wooden table next to which several stools had been set. The floor of this prison lay hidden beneath thick, hempen matting that deadened the sound of footsteps. Its naked walls didn't reveal any trace of a door or window. Going around the opposite way, Conseil met up with me, and we returned to the middle of this cabin, which had to be twenty feet long by ten wide. As for its height, not even Ned Land, with his great stature, was able to determine it.

Half an hour had already gone by without our situation changing, when our eyes were suddenly spirited from utter darkness into blinding light. Our prison lit up all at once; in other words, it filled with luminescent matter so intense that at first I couldn't stand the brightness of it. From its glare and whiteness, I recognized the electric glow that had played around this underwater boat like some magnificent phosphorescent phenomenon. After involuntarily closing my eyes, I reopened them and saw that this luminous force came from a frosted half globe curving out of the cabin's ceiling.

"Finally! It's light enough to see!" Ned Land exclaimed, knife in hand, staying on the defensive.

"Yes," I replied, then ventured the opposite view. "But as for our situation, we're still in the dark."

"Master must learn patience," said the emotionless Conseil.

This sudden illumination of our cabin enabled me to examine its tiniest details. It contained only a table and five stools. Its invisible door must have been hermetically sealed. Not a sound reached our ears. Everything seemed dead inside this boat. Was it in motion, or stationary on the surface of the ocean, or sinking into the depths? I couldn't tell.

But this luminous globe hadn't been turned on without good reason. Consequently, I hoped that some crewmen would soon make an appearance. If you want to consign people to oblivion, you don't light up their dungeons.

I was not mistaken. Unlocking noises became audible, a door opened, and two men appeared.

One was short and stocky, powerfully muscled, broad shouldered, robust of limbs, the head squat, the hair black and luxuriant, the mustache heavy, the eyes bright and penetrating, and his whole personality stamped with that southern-blooded zest that, in France, typifies the people of Provence. The philosopher Diderot has very aptly claimed that a man's bearing is the clue to his character, and this stocky little man was certainly a living proof of this claim. You could sense that his everyday conversation must have been packed with such vivid figures of speech as personification, symbolism, and misplaced modifiers. But I was never in a position to verify this because, around me, he used only an odd and utterly incomprehensible dialect.

The second stranger deserves a more detailed description. A disciple of such character-judging anatomists as Gratiolet or Engel could have read this man's features like an open book. Without hesitation, I identified his dominant qualities—self-confidence, since his head reared like a nobleman's above the arc formed by the lines of his shoulders, and his black eyes gazed with icy assurance; calmness, since his skin, pale rather than ruddy, indicated tranquility of blood; energy, shown by the swiftly knitting muscles of his brow; and finally courage, since his deep breathing denoted tremendous reserves of vitality.

I might add that this was a man of great pride, that his calm, firm gaze seemed to reflect thinking on an elevated plane, and that the harmony of his facial expressions and bodily movements resulted in an overall effect of unquestionable candor—according to the findings of physiognomists, those analysts of facial character.

I felt "involuntarily reassured" in his presence, and this boded well for our interview.

Whether this individual was thirty-five or fifty years of age, I could not precisely state. He was tall, his forehead broad, his nose straight, his mouth clearly etched, his teeth magnificent, his hands refined, tapered, and to use a word from palmistry, highly "psychic," in other words, worthy of serving a lofty and passionate spirit. This man was certainly the most wonderful physical specimen I had ever encountered. One unusual detail: his eyes were spaced a little far from each other and could instantly take in nearly a quarter of the horizon. This ability— as I later verified—was strengthened by a range of vision even greater than Ned Land's. When this stranger focused his gaze on an object, his eyebrow lines gathered into a frown, his heavy eyelids closed around his pupils to contract his huge field of vision, and he looked! What a look—as if he could magnify objects shrinking into the distance; as if he could probe your very soul; as if he could pierce those sheets of water so opaque to our eyes and scan the deepest seas . . . !

Wearing caps made of sea-otter fur, and shod in sealskin fishing boots, these two strangers were dressed in clothing made from some unique fabric that flattered the figure and allowed great freedom of movement.

The taller of the two—apparently the leader on board— examined us with the greatest care but without pronouncing a word. Then, turning to his companion, he conversed with him in a language I didn't recognize. It was a sonorous, harmonious, flexible dialect whose vowels seemed to undergo a highly varied accentuation.

The other replied with a shake of the head and added two or three utterly incomprehensible words. Then he seemed to question me directly with a long stare.

I replied in clear French that I wasn't familiar with his language; but he didn't seem to understand me, and the situation grew rather baffling.

"Still, master should tell our story," Conseil said to me. "Perhaps these gentlemen will grasp a few words of it!"

I tried again, telling the tale of our adventures, clearly articulating my every syllable, and not leaving out a single detail. I stated our names and titles; then, in order, I introduced Professor Aronnax, his manservant Conseil, and Mr. Ned Land, harpooner.

The man with calm, gentle eyes listened to me serenely, even courteously, and paid remarkable attention. But nothing in his facial expression indicated that he understood my story. When I finished, he didn't pronounce a single word.

One resource still left was to speak English. Perhaps they would be familiar with this nearly universal language. But I only knew it, as I did the German language, well enough to read it fluently, not well enough to speak it correctly. Here, however, our overriding need was to make ourselves understood.

"Come on, it's your turn," I told the harpooner. "Over to you, Mr. Land. Pull out of your bag of tricks the best English ever spoken by an Anglo–Saxon, and try for a more favorable result than mine."

Ned needed no persuading and started our story all over again, most of which I could follow. Its content was the same, but the form differed. Carried away by his volatile temperament, the Canadian put great animation into it. He complained vehemently about being imprisoned in defiance of his civil rights, asked by virtue of which law he was hereby detained, invoked writs of habeas corpus, threatened to press charges against anyone holding him in illegal custody, ranted, gesticulated, shouted, and finally conveyed by an expressive gesture that we were dying of hunger.

This was perfectly true, but we had nearly forgotten the fact.

Much to his amazement, the harpooner seemed no more intelligible than I had been. Our visitors didn't bat an eye. Apparently they were engineers who understood the languages of neither the French physicist Arago nor the English physicist Faraday.

Thoroughly baffled after vainly exhausting our philological resources, I no longer knew what tactic to pursue, when Conseil told me:

"If master will authorize me, I'll tell the whole business in German."

"What! You know German?" I exclaimed.

"Like most Flemish people, with all due respect to master."

"On the contrary, my respect is due you. Go to it, my boy."

And Conseil, in his serene voice, described for the third time the various vicissitudes of our story. But despite our narrator's fine accent and stylish turns of phrase, the German language met with no success.

Finally, as a last resort, I hauled out everything I could remember from my early schooldays, and I tried to narrate our adventures in Latin. Cicero would have plugged his ears and sent me to the scullery, but somehow I managed to pull through. With the same negative result.

This last attempt ultimately misfiring, the two strangers exchanged a few words in their incomprehensible language and withdrew, not even favoring us with one of those encouraging gestures that are used in every country in the world. The door closed again.

"This is outrageous!" Ned Land shouted, exploding for the twentieth time. "I ask you! We speak French, English, German, and Latin to these rogues, and neither of them has the decency to even answer back!"

"Calm down, Ned," I told the seething harpooner. "Anger won't get us anywhere."

"But professor," our irascible companion went on, "can't you see that we could die of hunger in this iron cage?"

"Bah!" Conseil put in philosophically. "We can hold out a good while yet!"

"My friends," I said, "we mustn't despair. We've gotten out of tighter spots. So please do me the favor of waiting a bit before you form your views on the commander and crew of this boat."

"My views are fully formed," Ned Land shot back. "They're rogues!"

"Oh good! And from what country?"

"Roguedom!"

"My gallant Ned, as yet that country isn't clearly marked on maps of the world, but I admit that the nationality of these two strangers is hard to make out! Neither English, French, nor German, that's all we can say. But I'm tempted to think that the commander and his chief officer were born in the low latitudes. There must be southern blood in them. But as to whether they're Spaniards, Turks, Arabs, or East Indians, their physical characteristics don't give me enough to go on. And as for their speech, it's utterly incomprehensible."

"That's the nuisance in not knowing every language," Conseil replied, "or the drawback in not having one universal language!"

"Which would all go out the window!" Ned Land replied. "Don't you see, these people have a language all to themselves, a language they've invented just to cause despair in decent people who ask for a little dinner! Why, in every country on earth, when you open your mouth, snap your jaws, smack your lips and teeth, isn't that the world's most understandable message? From Quebec to the Tuamotu Islands, from Paris to the Antipodes, doesn't it mean: I'm hungry, give me a bite to eat!"

"Oh," Conseil put in, "there are some people so unintelligent by nature . . ."

As he was saying these words, the door opened. A steward entered. He brought us some clothes, jackets and sailor's pants, made out of a fabric whose nature I didn't recognize. I hurried to change into them, and my companions followed suit.

Meanwhile our silent steward, perhaps a deaf-mute, set the table and laid three place settings.

"There's something serious afoot," Conseil said, "and it bodes well."

"Bah!" replied the rancorous harpooner. "What the devil do you suppose they eat around here? Turtle livers, loin of shark, dogfish steaks?"

"We'll soon find out!" Conseil said.

Overlaid with silver dish covers, various platters had been neatly positioned on the table cloth, and we sat down to eat. Assuredly, we were dealing with civilized people, and if it hadn't been for this electric light flooding over us, I would have thought we were in the dining room of the Hotel Adelphi in Liverpool, or the Grand Hotel in Paris. However, I feel compelled to mention that bread and wine were totally absent. The water was fresh and clear, but it was still water—which wasn't what Ned Land had in mind. Among the foods we were served, I was able to identify various daintily dressed fish; but I couldn't make up my mind about certain otherwise excellent dishes, and I couldn't even tell whether their contents belonged to the vegetable or the animal kingdom. As for the tableware, it was elegant and in perfect taste. Each utensil, spoon, fork, knife, and plate, bore on its reverse a letter encircled by a Latin motto, and here is its exact duplicate:

MOBILIS IN MOBILI
N

Moving within the moving element! It was a highly appropriate motto for this underwater machine, so long as the preposition in is translated as within and not upon. The letter "N" was no doubt the initial of the name of that mystifying individual in command beneath the seas!

Ned and Conseil had no time for such musings. They were wolfing down their food, and without further ado I did the same. By now I felt reassured about our fate, and it seemed obvious that our hosts didn't intend to let us die of starvation.

But all earthly things come to an end, all things must pass, even the hunger of people who haven't eaten for fifteen hours. Our appetites appeased, we felt an urgent need for sleep. A natural reaction after that interminable night of fighting for our lives.

"Ye gods, I'll sleep soundly," Conseil said.

"Me, I'm out like a light!" Ned Land replied.

My two companions lay down on the cabin's carpeting and were soon deep in slumber.

As for me, I gave in less readily to this intense need for sleep. Too many thoughts had piled up in my mind, too many insoluble questions had arisen, too many images were keeping my eyelids open! Where were we? What strange power was carrying us along? I felt—or at least I thought I did—the submersible sinking toward the sea's lower strata. Intense nightmares besieged me. In these mysterious marine sanctuaries, I envisioned hosts of unknown animals, and this underwater boat seemed to be a blood relation of theirs: living, breathing, just as fearsome . . . ! Then my mind grew calmer, my imagination melted into hazy drowsiness, and I soon fell into an uneasy slumber.

# CHAPTER 9

The Tantrums of Ned Land

I HAVE NO IDEA how long this slumber lasted; but it must have been a good while, since we were completely over our exhaustion. I was the first one to wake up. My companions weren't yet stirring and still lay in their corners like inanimate objects.

I had barely gotten up from my passably hard mattress when I felt my mind clear, my brain go on the alert. So I began a careful reexamination of our cell.

Nothing had changed in its interior arrangements. The prison was still a prison and its prisoners still prisoners. But, taking advantage of our slumber, the steward had cleared the table. Consequently, nothing indicated any forthcoming improvement in our situation, and I seriously wondered if we were doomed to spend the rest of our lives in this cage.

This prospect seemed increasingly painful to me because, even though my brain was clear of its obsessions from the night before, I was feeling an odd short-windedness in my chest. It was becoming hard for me to breathe. The heavy air was no longer sufficient for the full play of my lungs. Although our cell was large, we obviously had used up most of the oxygen it contained. In essence, over an hour's time a single human being consumes all the oxygen found in 100 liters of air, at which point that air has become charged with a nearly equal amount of carbon dioxide and is no longer fit for breathing.

So it was now urgent to renew the air in our prison, and no

doubt the air in this whole underwater boat as well.

Here a question popped into my head. How did the commander of this aquatic residence go about it? Did he obtain air using chemical methods, releasing the oxygen contained in potassium chlorate by heating it, meanwhile absorbing the carbon dioxide with potassium hydroxide? If so, he would have to keep up some kind of relationship with the shore, to come by the materials needed for such an operation. Did he simply limit himself to storing the air in high–pressure tanks and then dispense it according to his crew's needs? Perhaps. Or, proceeding in a more convenient, more economical, and consequently more probable fashion, was he satisfied with merely returning to breathe at the surface of the water like a cetacean, renewing his oxygen supply every twenty–four hours? In any event, whatever his method was, it seemed prudent to me that he use this method without delay.

In fact, I had already resorted to speeding up my inhalations in order to extract from the cell what little oxygen it contained, when suddenly I was refreshed by a current of clean air, scented with a salty aroma. It had to be a sea breeze, life–giving and charged with iodine! I opened my mouth wide, and my lungs glutted themselves on the fresh particles. At the same time, I felt a swaying, a rolling of moderate magnitude but definitely noticeable. This boat, this sheet–iron monster, had obviously just risen to the surface of the ocean, there to breathe in good whale fashion. So the ship's mode of ventilation was finally established.

When I had absorbed a chestful of this clean air, I looked for the conduit—the "air carrier," if you prefer—that allowed this beneficial influx to reach us, and I soon found it. Above the door opened an air vent that let in a fresh current of oxygen, renewing the thin air in our cell.

I had gotten to this point in my observations when Ned and Conseil woke up almost simultaneously, under the influence of this reviving air purification. They rubbed their eyes, stretched their arms, and sprang to their feet.

"Did master sleep well?" Conseil asked me with his perennial good manners.

"Extremely well, my gallant lad," I replied. "And how about you, Mr. Ned Land?"

"Like a log, professor. But I must be imagining things, because it seems like I'm breathing a sea breeze!"

A seaman couldn't be wrong on this topic, and I told the Canadian what had gone on while he slept.

"Good!" he said. "That explains perfectly all that bellowing we heard, when our so-called narwhale lay in sight of the *Abraham Lincoln*."

"Perfectly, Mr. Land. It was catching its breath!"

"Only I've no idea what time it is, Professor Aronnax, unless maybe it's dinnertime?"

"Dinnertime, my fine harpooner? I'd say at least breakfast time, because we've certainly woken up to a new day."

"Which indicates," Conseil replied, "that we've spent twenty-four hours in slumber."

"That's my assessment," I replied.

"I won't argue with you," Ned Land answered. "But dinner or breakfast, that steward will be plenty welcome whether he brings the one or the other."

"The one and the other," Conseil said.

"Well put," the Canadian replied. "We deserve two meals, and speaking for myself, I'll do justice to them both."

"All right, Ned, let's wait and see!" I replied. "It's clear that these strangers don't intend to let us die of hunger, otherwise last evening's dinner wouldn't make any sense."

"Unless they're fattening us up!" Ned shot back.

"I object," I replied. "We have not fallen into the hands of cannibals."

"Just because they don't make a habit of it," the Canadian

replied in all seriousness, "doesn't mean they don't indulge from time to time. Who knows? Maybe these people have gone without fresh meat for a long while, and in that case three healthy, well-built specimens like the professor, his manservant, and me—"

"Get rid of those ideas, Mr. Land," I answered the harpooner. "And above all, don't let them lead you to flare up against our hosts, which would only make our situation worse."

"Anyhow," the harpooner said, "I'm as hungry as all Hades, and dinner or breakfast, not one puny meal has arrived!"

"Mr. Land," I answered, "we have to adapt to the schedule on board, and I imagine our stomachs are running ahead of the chief cook's dinner bell."

"Well then, we'll adjust our stomachs to the chef's timetable!" Conseil replied serenely.

"There you go again, Conseil my friend!" the impatient Canadian shot back. "You never allow yourself any displays of bile or attacks of nerves! You're everlastingly calm! You'd say your after-meal grace even if you didn't get any food for your before-meal blessing—and you'd starve to death rather than complain!"

"What good would it do?" Conseil asked.

"Complaining doesn't have to do good, it just feels good! And if these pirates—I say pirates out of consideration for the professor's feelings, since he doesn't want us to call them cannibals—if these pirates think they're going to smother me in this cage without hearing what cusswords spice up my outbursts, they've got another think coming! Look here, Professor Aronnax, speak frankly. How long do you figure they'll keep us in this iron box?"

"To tell the truth, friend Land, I know little more about it than you do."

"But in a nutshell, what do you suppose is going on?"

"My supposition is that sheer chance has made us privy to

an important secret. Now then, if the crew of this underwater boat have a personal interest in keeping that secret, and if their personal interest is more important than the lives of three men, I believe that our very existence is in jeopardy. If such is not the case, then at the first available opportunity, this monster that has swallowed us will return us to the world inhabited by our own kind."

"Unless they recruit us to serve on the crew," Conseil said, "and keep us here—"

"Till the moment," Ned Land answered, "when some frigate that's faster or smarter than the *Abraham Lincoln* captures this den of buccaneers, then hangs all of us by the neck from the tip of a mainmast yardarm!"

"Well thought out, Mr. Land," I replied. "But as yet, I don't believe we've been tendered any enlistment offers. Consequently, it's pointless to argue about what tactics we should pursue in such a case. I repeat: let's wait, let's be guided by events, and let's do nothing, since right now there's nothing we can do."

"On the contrary, professor," the harpooner replied, not wanting to give in. "There is something we can do."

"Oh? And what, Mr. Land?"

"Break out of here!"

"Breaking out of a prison on shore is difficult enough, but with an underwater prison, it strikes me as completely unworkable."

"Come now, Ned my friend," Conseil asked, "how would you answer master's objection? I refuse to believe that an American is at the end of his tether."

Visibly baffled, the harpooner said nothing. Under the conditions in which fate had left us, it was absolutely impossible to escape. But a Canadian's wit is half French, and Mr. Ned Land made this clear in his reply.

"So, Professor Aronnax," he went on after thinking for a

few moments, "you haven't figured out what people do when they can't escape from their prison?"

"No, my friend."

"Easy. They fix things so they stay there."

"Of course!" Conseil put in. "Since we're deep in the ocean, being inside this boat is vastly preferable to being above it or below it!"

"But we fix things by kicking out all the jailers, guards, and wardens," Ned Land added.

"What's this, Ned?" I asked. "You'd seriously consider taking over this craft?"

"Very seriously," the Canadian replied.

"It's impossible."

"And why is that, sir? Some promising opportunity might come up, and I don't see what could stop us from taking advantage of it. If there are only about twenty men on board this machine, I don't think they can stave off two Frenchmen and a Canadian!"

It seemed wiser to accept the harpooner's proposition than to debate it. Accordingly, I was content to reply:

"Let such circumstances come, Mr. Land, and we'll see. But until then, I beg you to control your impatience. We need to act shrewdly, and your flare-ups won't give rise to any promising opportunities. So swear to me that you'll accept our situation without throwing a tantrum over it."

"I give you my word, professor," Ned Land replied in an unenthusiastic tone. "No vehement phrases will leave my mouth, no vicious gestures will give my feelings away, not even when they don't feed us on time."

"I have your word, Ned," I answered the Canadian.

Then our conversation petered out, and each of us withdrew into his own thoughts. For my part, despite the harpooner's confident talk, I admit that I entertained no illusions. I had no faith in those promising opportunities that

Ned Land mentioned. To operate with such efficiency, this underwater boat had to have a sizeable crew, so if it came to a physical contest, we would be facing an overwhelming opponent. Besides, before we could do anything, we had to be free, and that we definitely were not. I didn't see any way out of this sheet-iron, hermetically sealed cell. And if the strange commander of this boat did have a secret to keep—which seemed rather likely—he would never give us freedom of movement aboard his vessel. Now then, would he resort to violence in order to be rid of us, or would he drop us off one day on some remote coast? There lay the unknown. All these hypotheses seemed extremely plausible to me, and to hope for freedom through use of force, you had to be a harpooner.

I realized, moreover, that Ned Land's brooding was getting him madder by the minute. Little by little, I heard those aforesaid cusswords welling up in the depths of his gullet, and I saw his movements turn threatening again. He stood up, pacing in circles like a wild beast in a cage, striking the walls with his foot and fist. Meanwhile the hours passed, our hunger nagged unmercifully, and this time the steward did not appear. Which amounted to forgetting our castaway status for much too long, if they really had good intentions toward us.

Tortured by the growling of his well-built stomach, Ned Land was getting more and more riled, and despite his word of honor, I was in real dread of an explosion when he stood in the presence of one of the men on board.

For two more hours Ned Land's rage increased. The Canadian shouted and pleaded, but to no avail. The sheet-iron walls were deaf. I didn't hear a single sound inside this dead-seeming boat. The vessel hadn't stirred, because I obviously would have felt its hull vibrating under the influence of the propeller. It had undoubtedly sunk into the watery deep and no longer belonged to the outside world. All this dismal silence was terrifying.

As for our neglect, our isolation in the depths of this cell, I was afraid to guess at how long it might last. Little by little, hopes I had entertained after our interview with the ship's commander were fading away. The gentleness of the man's gaze, the generosity expressed in his facial features, the nobility of his bearing, all vanished from my memory. I saw this mystifying individual anew for what he inevitably must be: cruel and merciless. I viewed him as outside humanity, beyond all feelings of compassion, the implacable foe of his fellow man, toward whom he must have sworn an undying hate!

But even so, was the man going to let us die of starvation, locked up in this cramped prison, exposed to those horrible temptations to which people are driven by extreme hunger? This grim possibility took on a dreadful intensity in my mind, and fired by my imagination, I felt an unreasoning terror run through me. Conseil stayed calm. Ned Land bellowed.

Just then a noise was audible outside. Footsteps rang on the metal tiling. The locks were turned, the door opened, the steward appeared.

Before I could make a single movement to prevent him, the Canadian rushed at the poor man, threw him down, held him by the throat. The steward was choking in the grip of those powerful hands.

Conseil was already trying to loosen the harpooner's hands from his half–suffocated victim, and I had gone to join in the rescue, when I was abruptly nailed to the spot by these words pronounced in French:

"Calm down, Mr. Land! And you, professor, kindly listen to me!"

# CHAPTER 10

### The Man of the Waters

IT WAS THE ship's commander who had just spoken.

At these words Ned Land stood up quickly. Nearly strangled, the steward staggered out at a signal from his superior; but such was the commander's authority aboard his vessel, not one gesture gave away the resentment that this man must have felt toward the Canadian. In silence we waited for the outcome of this scene; Conseil, in spite of himself, seemed almost fascinated, I was stunned.

Arms crossed, leaning against a corner of the table, the commander studied us with great care. Was he reluctant to speak further? Did he regret those words he had just pronounced in French? You would have thought so.

After a few moments of silence, which none of us would have dreamed of interrupting:

"Gentlemen," he said in a calm, penetrating voice, "I speak French, English, German, and Latin with equal fluency. Hence I could have answered you as early as our initial interview, but first I wanted to make your acquaintance and then think things over. Your four versions of the same narrative, perfectly consistent by and large, established your personal identities for me. I now know that sheer chance has placed in my presence Professor Pierre Aronnax, specialist in natural history at the Paris Museum and entrusted with a scientific mission abroad, his manservant Conseil, and Ned Land, a harpooner of Canadian origin aboard the *Abraham*

*Lincoln*, a frigate in the national navy of the United States of America."

I bowed in agreement. The commander hadn't put a question to me. So no answer was called for. This man expressed himself with perfect ease and without a trace of an accent. His phrasing was clear, his words well chosen, his facility in elocution remarkable. And yet, to me, he didn't have "the feel" of a fellow countryman.

He went on with the conversation as follows:

"No doubt, sir, you've felt that I waited rather too long before paying you this second visit. After discovering your identities, I wanted to weigh carefully what policy to pursue toward you. I had great difficulty deciding. Some extremely inconvenient circumstances have brought you into the presence of a man who has cut himself off from humanity. Your coming has disrupted my whole existence."

"Unintentionally," I said.

"Unintentionally?" the stranger replied, raising his voice a little. "Was it unintentionally that the *Abraham Lincoln* hunted me on every sea? Was it unintentionally that you traveled aboard that frigate? Was it unintentionally that your shells bounced off my ship's hull? Was it unintentionally that Mr. Ned Land hit me with his harpoon?"

I detected a controlled irritation in these words. But there was a perfectly natural reply to these charges, and I made it.

"Sir," I said, "you're surely unaware of the discussions that have taken place in Europe and America with yourself as the subject. You don't realize that various accidents, caused by collisions with your underwater machine, have aroused public passions on those two continents. I'll spare you the innumerable hypotheses with which we've tried to explain this inexplicable phenomenon, whose secret is yours alone. But please understand that the *Abraham Lincoln* chased you over the Pacific high seas in the belief it was hunting some powerful marine monster, which had to be purged from the ocean at all cost."

A half smile curled the commander's lips; then, in a calmer tone:

"Professor Aronnax," he replied, "do you dare claim that your frigate wouldn't have chased and cannonaded an underwater boat as readily as a monster?"

This question baffled me, since Commander Farragut would certainly have shown no such hesitation. He would have seen it as his sworn duty to destroy a contrivance of this kind just as promptly as a gigantic narwhale.

"So you understand, sir," the stranger went on, "that I have a right to treat you as my enemy."

I kept quiet, with good reason. What was the use of debating such a proposition, when superior force can wipe out the best arguments?

"It took me a good while to decide," the commander went on. "Nothing obliged me to grant you hospitality. If I were to part company with you, I'd have no personal interest in ever seeing you again. I could put you back on the platform of this ship that has served as your refuge. I could sink under the sea, and I could forget you ever existed. Wouldn't that be my right?"

"Perhaps it would be the right of a savage," I replied. "But not that of a civilized man."

"Professor," the commander replied swiftly, "I'm not what you term a civilized man! I've severed all ties with society, for reasons that I alone have the right to appreciate. Therefore I obey none of its regulations, and I insist that you never invoke them in front of me!"

This was plain speaking. A flash of anger and scorn lit up the stranger's eyes, and I glimpsed a fearsome past in this man's life. Not only had he placed himself beyond human laws, he had rendered himself independent, out of all reach, free in the strictest sense of the word! For who would dare chase him to the depths of the sea when he thwarted all attacks on the surface? What ship could withstand a collision with his underwater Monitor? What armor plate, no matter how heavy, could bear the thrusts of his spur? No man among men could call him to account for his actions. God, if he believed in Him, his conscience if he had one—these were the only judges to whom he was answerable.

These thoughts swiftly crossed my mind while this strange individual fell silent, like someone completely self-absorbed. I regarded him with a mixture of fear and fascination, in the same way, no doubt, that Œdipus regarded the Sphinx.

After a fairly long silence, the commander went on with our conversation.

"So I had difficulty deciding," he said. "But I concluded that my personal interests could be reconciled with that natural compassion to which every human being has a right. Since fate has brought you here, you'll stay aboard my vessel. You'll be free here, and in exchange for that freedom, moreover totally related to it, I'll lay on you just one condition. Your word that you'll submit to it will be sufficient."

"Go on, sir," I replied. "I assume this condition is one an honest man can accept?"

"Yes, sir. Just this. It's possible that certain unforeseen events may force me to confine you to your cabins for some hours, or even for some days as the case may be. Since I prefer never to use violence, I expect from you in such a case, even more than in any other, your unquestioning obedience. By acting in this way, I shield you from complicity, I absolve you of all responsibility, since I myself make it impossible for you to see what you aren't meant to see. Do you accept this condition?"

So things happened on board that were quite odd to say the least, things never to be seen by people not placing themselves beyond society's laws! Among all the surprises the future had in store for me, this would not be the mildest.

"We accept," I replied. "Only, I'll ask your permission, sir, to address a question to you, just one."

"Go ahead, sir."

"You said we'd be free aboard your vessel?"

"Completely."

"Then I would ask what you mean by this freedom."

"Why, the freedom to come, go, see, and even closely observe everything happening here—except under certain rare circumstances—in short, the freedom we ourselves enjoy, my companions and I."

It was obvious that we did not understand each other.

"Pardon me, sir," I went on, "but that's merely the freedom that every prisoner has, the freedom to pace his cell! That's not enough for us."

"Nevertheless, it will have to do!"

"What! We must give up seeing our homeland, friends, and relatives ever again?"

"Yes, sir. But giving up that intolerable earthly yoke that some men call freedom is perhaps less painful than you think!"

"By thunder!" Ned Land shouted. "I'll never promise I won't try getting out of here!"

"I didn't ask for such a promise, Mr. Land," the commander replied coldly.

"Sir," I replied, flaring up in spite of myself, "you're taking unfair advantage of us! This is sheer cruelty!"

"No, sir, it's an act of mercy! You're my prisoners of war! I've cared for you when, with a single word, I could plunge you back into the ocean depths! You attacked me! You've just stumbled on a secret no living man must probe, the secret of my entire existence! Do you think I'll send you back to a world that must know nothing more of me? Never! By keeping you on board, it isn't you whom I care for, it's me!"

These words indicated that the commander pursued a policy impervious to arguments.

"Then, sir," I went on, "you give us, quite simply, a choice between life and death?"

"Quite simply."

"My friends," I said, "to a question couched in these terms, our answer can be taken for granted. But no solemn promises bind us to the commander of this vessel."

"None, sir," the stranger replied.

Then, in a gentler voice, he went on:

"Now, allow me to finish what I have to tell you. I've heard of you, Professor Aronnax. You, if not your companions, won't perhaps complain too much about the stroke of fate that has brought us together. Among the books that make up my favorite reading, you'll find the work you've published on the great ocean depths. I've pored over it. You've taken your studies as far as terrestrial science can go. But you don't know everything because you haven't seen everything. Let me tell you, professor, you won't regret the time you spend aboard my vessel. You're going to voyage through a land of wonders. Stunned amazement will probably be your habitual state of mind. It will be a long while before you tire of the sights constantly before your eyes. I'm going to make another underwater tour of the world—perhaps my last, who knows?—and I'll review everything I've studied in the depths of these seas that I've crossed so often, and you can be my fellow student. Starting this very day, you'll enter a new element, you'll see what no human being has ever seen before—since my men and I no longer count—and thanks to me, you're going to learn the ultimate secrets of our planet."

I can't deny it; the commander's words had a tremendous effect on me. He had caught me on my weak side, and I momentarily forgot that not even this sublime experience was worth the loss of my freedom. Besides, I counted on the future to resolve this important question. So I was content to reply:

"Sir, even though you've cut yourself off from humanity,

I can see that you haven't disowned all human feeling. We're castaways whom you've charitably taken aboard, we'll never forget that. Speaking for myself, I don't rule out that the interests of science could override even the need for freedom, which promises me that, in exchange, our encounter will provide great rewards."

I thought the commander would offer me his hand, to seal our agreement. He did nothing of the sort. I regretted that.

"One last question," I said, just as this inexplicable being seemed ready to withdraw.

"Ask it, professor."

"By what name am I to call you?"

"Sir," the commander replied, "to you, I'm simply Captain Nemo; to me, you and your companions are simply passengers on the *Nautilus*."

Captain Nemo called out. A steward appeared. The captain gave him his orders in that strange language I couldn't even identify. Then, turning to the Canadian and Conseil:

"A meal is waiting for you in your cabin," he told them. "Kindly follow this man."

"That's an offer I can't refuse!" the harpooner replied.

After being confined for over thirty hours, he and Conseil were finally out of this cell.

"And now, Professor Aronnax, our own breakfast is ready. Allow me to lead the way."

"Yours to command, Captain."

I followed Captain Nemo, and as soon as I passed through the doorway, I went down a kind of electrically lit passageway that resembled a gangway on a ship. After a stretch of some ten meters, a second door opened before me.

I then entered a dining room, decorated and furnished in austere good taste. Inlaid with ebony trim, tall oaken sideboards stood at both ends of this room, and sparkling on their shelves were staggered rows of earthenware, porcelain, and glass of incalculable value. There silver-plated dinnerware gleamed under rays pouring from light fixtures in the ceiling, whose glare was softened and tempered by delicately painted designs.

In the center of this room stood a table, richly spread. Captain Nemo indicated the place I was to occupy.

"Be seated," he told me, "and eat like the famished man you must be."

Our breakfast consisted of several dishes whose contents were all supplied by the sea, and some foods whose nature and derivation were unknown to me. They were good, I admit, but with a peculiar flavor to which I would soon grow accustomed. These various food items seemed to be rich in phosphorous, and I thought that they, too, must have been of marine origin.

Captain Nemo stared at me. I had asked him nothing, but he read my thoughts, and on his own he answered the questions I was itching to address him.

"Most of these dishes are new to you," he told me. "But you can consume them without fear. They're healthy and nourishing. I renounced terrestrial foods long ago, and I'm none the worse for it. My crew are strong and full of energy, and they eat what I eat."

"So," I said, "all these foods are products of the sea?"

"Yes, professor, the sea supplies all my needs. Sometimes I cast my nets in our wake, and I pull them up ready to burst. Sometimes I go hunting right in the midst of this element that has long seemed so far out of man's reach, and I corner the game that dwells in my underwater forests. Like the flocks of old Proteus, King Neptune's shepherd, my herds graze without fear on the ocean's immense prairies. There I own vast properties that I harvest myself, and which are forever sown by the hand of the Creator of All Things."

I stared at Captain Nemo in definite astonishment, and I answered him:

"Sir, I understand perfectly how your nets can furnish excellent fish for your table; I understand less how you can chase aquatic game in your underwater forests; but how a piece of red meat, no matter how small, can figure in your menu, that I don't understand at all."

"Nor I, sir," Captain Nemo answered me. "I never touch the flesh of land animals."

"Nevertheless, this . . . ," I went on, pointing to a dish where some slices of loin were still left.

"What you believe to be red meat, professor, is nothing other than loin of sea turtle. Similarly, here are some dolphin livers you might mistake for stewed pork. My chef is a skillful food processor who excels at pickling and preserving these various exhibits from the ocean. Feel free to sample all of these foods. Here are some preserves of sea cucumber that a Malaysian would declare to be unrivaled in the entire world, here's cream from milk furnished by the udders of cetaceans, and sugar from the huge fucus plants in the North Sea; and finally, allow me to offer you some marmalade of sea anemone, equal to that from the tastiest fruits."

So I sampled away, more as a curiosity seeker than an epicure, while Captain Nemo delighted me with his incredible anecdotes.

"But this sea, Professor Aronnax," he told me, "this prodigious, inexhaustible wet nurse of a sea not only feeds me, she dresses me as well. That fabric covering you was woven from the masses of filaments that anchor certain seashells; as the ancients were wont to do, it was dyed with purple ink from the murex snail and shaded with violet tints that I extract from a marine slug, the Mediterranean sea hare. The perfumes you'll find on the washstand in your cabin were produced from the oozings of marine plants. Your mattress was made from the ocean's softest eelgrass. Your quill pen will be whalebone, your ink a juice secreted by cuttlefish or squid. Everything comes to me from the sea, just as someday everything will return to it!"

"You love the sea, Captain."

"Yes, I love it! The sea is the be all and end all! It covers seven-tenths of the planet earth. Its breath is clean and healthy. It's an immense wilderness where a man is never lonely, because he feels life astir on every side. The sea is simply the vehicle for a prodigious, unearthly mode of existence; it's simply movement and love; it's living infinity, as one of your poets put it. And in essence, professor, nature is here made manifest by all three of her kingdoms, mineral, vegetable, and animal. The last of these is amply represented by the four zoophyte groups, three classes of articulates, five classes of mollusks, and three vertebrate classes: mammals, reptiles, and those countless legions of fish, an infinite order of animals totaling more than 13,000 species, of which only one-tenth belong to fresh water. The sea is a vast pool of nature. Our globe began with the sea, so to speak, and who can say we won't end with it! Here lies supreme tranquility. The sea doesn't belong to tyrants. On its surface they can still exercise their iniquitous claims, battle each other, devour each other, haul every earthly horror. But thirty feet below sea level, their dominion ceases, their influence fades, their power vanishes! Ah, sir, live! Live in the heart of the seas! Here alone lies independence! Here I recognize no superiors! Here I'm free!"

Captain Nemo suddenly fell silent in the midst of this enthusiastic outpouring. Had he let himself get carried away, past the bounds of his habitual reserve? Had he said too much? For a few moments he strolled up and down, all aquiver. Then his nerves grew calmer, his facial features recovered their usual icy composure, and turning to me:

"Now, professor," he said, "if you'd like to inspect the *Nautilus*, I'm yours to command."

# CHAPTER 11

## The *Nautilus*

CAPTAIN NEMO stood up. I followed him. Contrived at the rear of the dining room, a double door opened, and I entered a room whose dimensions equaled the one I had just left.

It was a library. Tall, black–rosewood bookcases, inlaid with copperwork, held on their wide shelves a large number of uniformly bound books. These furnishings followed the contours of the room, their lower parts leading to huge couches upholstered in maroon leather and curved for maximum comfort. Light, movable reading stands, which could be pushed away or pulled near as desired, allowed books to be positioned on them for easy study. In the center stood a huge table covered with pamphlets, among which some newspapers, long out of date, were visible. Electric light flooded this whole harmonious totality, falling from four frosted half globes set in the scrollwork of the ceiling. I stared in genuine wonderment at this room so ingeniously laid out, and I couldn't believe my eyes.

"Captain Nemo," I told my host, who had just stretched out on a couch, "this is a library that would do credit to more than one continental palace, and I truly marvel to think it can go with you into the deepest seas."

"Where could one find greater silence or solitude, professor?" Captain Nemo replied. "Did your study at the museum afford you such a perfect retreat?"

"No, sir, and I might add that it's quite a humble one next to yours. You own 6,000 or 7,000 volumes here ..."

"12,000, Professor Aronnax. They're my sole remaining ties with dry land. But I was done with the shore the day my *Nautilus* submerged for the first time under the waters. That day I purchased my last volumes, my last pamphlets, my last newspapers, and ever since I've chosen to believe that humanity no longer thinks or writes. In any event, professor, these books are at your disposal, and you may use them freely."

I thanked Captain Nemo and approached the shelves of this library. Written in every language, books on science, ethics, and literature were there in abundance, but I didn't see a single work on economics—they seemed to be strictly banned on board. One odd detail: all these books were shelved indiscriminately without regard to the language in which they were written, and this jumble proved that the *Nautilus's* captain could read fluently whatever volumes he chanced to pick up.

Among these books I noted masterpieces by the greats of ancient and modern times, in other words, all of humanity's finest achievements in history, poetry, fiction, and science, from Homer to Victor Hugo, from Xenophon to Michelet, from Rabelais to Madame George Sand. But science, in particular, represented the major investment of this library: books on mechanics, ballistics, hydrography, meteorology, geography, geology, etc., held a place there no less important than works on natural history, and I realized that they made up the captain's chief reading. There I saw the complete works of Humboldt, the complete Arago, as well as works by Foucault, Henri Sainte-Claire Deville, Chasles, Milne-Edwards, Quatrefages, John Tyndall, Faraday, Berthelot, Father Secchi, Petermann, Commander Maury, Louis Agassiz, etc., plus the transactions of France's Academy of Sciences, bulletins from the various geographical societies, etc., and in a prime location, those two volumes on the great ocean depths that had perhaps earned me this comparatively charitable welcome from Captain Nemo. Among the works of Joseph Bertrand, his book entitled *The Founders of Astronomy* even gave me a definite date; and since I knew it had appeared in the course of 1865, I concluded that the fitting out of the *Nautilus* hadn't taken place before then. Accordingly, three years ago at the most, Captain Nemo had begun his underwater existence. Moreover, I hoped some books even more recent would permit me to pinpoint the date precisely; but I had plenty of time to look for them, and I didn't want to put off any longer our stroll through the wonders of the *Nautilus*.

"Sir," I told the captain, "thank you for placing this library at my disposal. There are scientific treasures here, and I'll take advantage of them."

"This room isn't only a library," Captain Nemo said, "it's also a smoking room."

"A smoking room?" I exclaimed. "Then one may smoke on board?"

"Surely."

"In that case, sir, I'm forced to believe that you've kept up relations with Havana."

"None whatever," the captain replied. "Try this cigar, Professor Aronnax, and even though it doesn't come from Havana, it will satisfy you if you're a connoisseur."

I took the cigar offered me, whose shape recalled those from Cuba; but it seemed to be made of gold leaf. I lit it at a small brazier supported by an elegant bronze stand, and I inhaled my first whiffs with the relish of a smoker who hasn't had a puff in days.

"It's excellent," I said, "but it's not from the tobacco plant."

"Right," the captain replied, "this tobacco comes from neither Havana nor the Orient. It's a kind of nicotine-rich seaweed that the ocean supplies me, albeit sparingly. Do you still miss your Cubans, sir?"

"Captain, I scorn them from this day forward."

"Then smoke these cigars whenever you like, without debating their origin. They bear no government seal of approval, but I imagine they're none the worse for it."

"On the contrary."

Just then Captain Nemo opened a door facing the one by which I had entered the library, and I passed into an immense, splendidly lit lounge.

It was a huge quadrilateral with canted corners, ten meters long, six wide, five high. A luminous ceiling, decorated with delicate arabesques, distributed a soft, clear daylight over all the wonders gathered in this museum. For a museum it truly was, in which clever hands had spared no expense to amass every natural and artistic treasure, displaying them with the helter–skelter picturesqueness that distinguishes a painter's studio.

Some thirty pictures by the masters, uniformly framed and separated by gleaming panoplies of arms, adorned walls on which were stretched tapestries of austere design. There I saw canvases of the highest value, the likes of which I had marveled at in private European collections and art exhibitions. The various schools of the old masters were represented by a Raphael Madonna, a Virgin by Leonardo da Vinci, a nymph by Correggio, a woman by Titian, an adoration of the Magi by Veronese, an assumption of the Virgin by Murillo, a Holbein portrait, a monk by Velazquez, a martyr by Ribera, a village fair by Rubens, two Flemish landscapes by Teniers, three little genre paintings by Gerard Dow, Metsu, and Paul Potter, two canvases by Gericault and Prud'hon, plus seascapes by Backhuysen and Vernet. Among the works of modern art were pictures signed by Delacroix, Ingres, Decamps, Troyon, Meissonier, Daubigny, etc., and some wonderful miniature statues in marble or bronze, modeled after antiquity's finest originals, stood on their pedestals in the corners of this magnificent museum. As the *Nautilus's* commander had predicted, my mind was already starting to fall into that promised state of stunned amazement.

"Professor," this strange man then said, "you must excuse the informality with which I receive you, and the disorder reigning in this lounge."

"Sir," I replied, "without prying into who you are, might I venture to identify you as an artist?"

"A collector, sir, nothing more. Formerly I loved acquiring these beautiful works created by the hand of man. I sought them greedily, ferreted them out tirelessly, and I've been able to gather some objects of great value. They're my last mementos of those shores that are now dead for me. In my eyes, your modern artists are already as old as the ancients. They've existed for 2,000 or 3,000 years, and I mix them up in my mind. The masters are ageless."

"What about these composers?" I said, pointing to sheet music by Weber, Rossini, Mozart, Beethoven, Haydn, Meyerbeer, Hérold, Wagner, Auber, Gounod, Victor Massé, and a number of others scattered over a full size piano–organ, which occupied one of the wall panels in this lounge.

"These composers," Captain Nemo answered me, "are the contemporaries of Orpheus, because in the annals of the dead, all chronological differences fade; and I'm dead, professor, quite as dead as those friends of yours sleeping six feet under!"

Captain Nemo fell silent and seemed lost in reverie. I regarded him with intense excitement, silently analyzing his strange facial expression. Leaning his elbow on the corner of a valuable mosaic table, he no longer saw me, he had forgotten my very presence.

I didn't disturb his meditations but continued to pass in review the curiosities that enriched this lounge.

After the works of art, natural rarities predominated. They consisted chiefly of plants, shells, and other exhibits from the ocean that must have been Captain Nemo's own personal finds. In the middle of the lounge, a jet of water, electrically lit, fell back into a basin made from a single giant clam. The delicately festooned rim of this shell, supplied by the biggest mollusk in the class Acephala, measured about six meters in circumference; so it was even bigger than those fine giant clams given to King François I by the Republic of Venice, and which the Church of Saint-Sulpice in Paris has made into two gigantic holy-water fonts.

Around this basin, inside elegant glass cases fastened with copper bands, there were classified and labeled the most valuable marine exhibits ever put before the eyes of a naturalist. My professorial glee may easily be imagined.

The zoophyte branch offered some very unusual specimens from its two groups, the polyps and the echinoderms. In the first group: organ-pipe coral, gorgonian coral arranged into fan shapes, soft sponges from Syria, isis coral from the Molucca Islands, sea-pen coral, wonderful coral of the genus Virgularia from the waters of Norway, various coral of the genus Umbellularia, alcyonarian coral, then a whole series of those madrepores that my mentor Professor Milne-Edwards has so shrewdly classified into divisions and among which I noted the wonderful genus Flabellina as well as the genus Oculina from Réunion Island, plus a Neptune's chariot from the Caribbean Sea—every superb variety of coral, and in short, every species of these unusual polyparies that congregate to form entire islands that will one day turn into continents. Among the echinoderms, notable for being covered with spines: starfish, feather stars, sea lilies, free-swimming crinoids, brittle stars, sea urchins, sea cucumbers, etc., represented a complete collection of the individuals in this group.

An excitable conchologist would surely have fainted dead away before other, more numerous glass cases in which were classified specimens from the mollusk branch. There I saw a collection of incalculable value that I haven't time to describe completely. Among these exhibits I'll mention, just for the record: an elegant royal hammer shell from the Indian Ocean, whose evenly spaced white spots stood out sharply against a base of red and brown; an imperial spiny oyster, brightly colored, bristling with thorns, a specimen rare to European museums, whose value I estimated at F20,000; a common hammer shell from the seas near Queensland, very hard to come by; exotic cockles from Senegal, fragile white bivalve shells that a single breath could pop like a soap bubble; several varieties of watering-pot shell from Java, a sort of limestone tube fringed with leafy folds and much fought over by collectors; a whole series of top-shell snails—greenish yellow ones fished up from American seas, others colored reddish brown that patronize the waters off Queensland, the former coming from the Gulf of Mexico and notable for their overlapping shells, the latter some sun-carrier shells found in the southernmost seas, finally and rarest of all, the magnificent spurred-star shell from New Zealand; then some wonderful peppery-furrow shells; several valuable species of cythera clams and venus clams; the trellis wentletrap snail from Tranquebar on India's eastern shore; a marbled turban snail gleaming with mother-of-pearl; green parrot shells from the seas of China; the virtually unknown cone snail from the genus Coenodullus; every variety of cowry used as money in India and Africa; a "glory-of-the-seas," the most valuable shell in the East Indies; finally, common periwinkles, delphinula snails, turret snails, violet snails, European cowries, volute snails, olive shells, miter shells, helmet shells, murex snails, whelks, harp shells, spiky periwinkles, triton snails, horn shells, spindle shells, conch shells, spider conchs, limpets, glass snails, sea butterflies—every kind of delicate, fragile seashell that science has baptized with its most delightful names.

Aside and in special compartments, strings of supremely beautiful pearls were spread out, the electric light flecking them with little fiery sparks: pink pearls pulled from saltwater fan shells in the Red Sea; green pearls from the rainbow abalone; yellow, blue, and black pearls, the unusual handiwork of various mollusks from every ocean and of certain mussels from rivers up north; in short, several specimens of incalculable worth that had been oozed by the rarest of shellfish. Some of these pearls were bigger than a pigeon egg; they more than equaled the one that the explorer Tavernier sold the Shah of Persia for F3,000,000, and they surpassed that other pearl owned by the Imam of Muscat, which I had believed to be unrivaled in the entire world.

Consequently, to calculate the value of this collection was, I should say, impossible. Captain Nemo must have spent millions in acquiring these different specimens, and I was wondering what financial resources he tapped to satisfy his collector's fancies, when these words interrupted me:

"You're examining my shells, professor? They're indeed able to fascinate a naturalist; but for me they have an added charm, since I've collected every one of them with my own two hands, and not a sea on the globe has escaped my investigations."

"I understand, Captain, I understand your delight at strolling in the midst of this wealth. You're a man who gathers his treasure in person. No museum in Europe owns such a collection of exhibits from the ocean. But if I exhaust all my wonderment on them, I'll have nothing left for the ship that carries them! I have absolutely no wish to probe those secrets of yours! But I confess that my curiosity is aroused to the limit by this *Nautilus*, the motor power it contains, the equipment enabling it to operate, the ultra powerful force that brings it to life. I see some instruments hanging on the walls of this lounge whose purposes are unknown to me. May I learn—"

"Professor Aronnax," Captain Nemo answered me, "I've said you'd be free aboard my vessel, so no part of the *Nautilus* is off–limits to you. You may inspect it in detail, and I'll be delighted to act as your guide."

"I don't know how to thank you, sir, but I won't abuse your good nature. I would only ask you about the uses intended for these instruments of physical measure—"

"Professor, these same instruments are found in my stateroom, where I'll have the pleasure of explaining their functions to you. But beforehand, come inspect the cabin set aside for you. You need to learn how you'll be lodged aboard the *Nautilus*."

I followed Captain Nemo, who, via one of the doors cut into the lounge's canted corners, led me back down the ship's gangways. He took me to the bow, and there I found not just a cabin but an elegant stateroom with a bed, a washstand, and various other furnishings.

I could only thank my host.

"Your stateroom adjoins mine," he told me, opening a door, "and mine leads into that lounge we've just left."

I entered the captain's stateroom. It had an austere, almost monastic appearance. An iron bedstead, a worktable, some washstand fixtures. Subdued lighting. No luxuries. Just the bare necessities.

Captain Nemo showed me to a bench.

"Kindly be seated," he told me.

I sat, and he began speaking as follows:

# CHAPTER 12

## Everything through Electricity

"SIR," CAPTAIN NEMO SAID, showing me the instruments hanging on the walls of his stateroom, "these are the devices needed to navigate the *Nautilus*. Here, as in the lounge, I always have them before my eyes, and they indicate my position and exact heading in the midst of the ocean. You're familiar with some of them, such as the thermometer, which gives the temperature inside the *Nautilus*; the barometer, which measures the heaviness of the outside air and forecasts changes in the weather; the humidistat, which indicates the degree of dryness in the atmosphere; the storm glass, whose mixture decomposes to foretell the arrival of tempests; the compass, which steers my course; the sextant, which takes the sun's altitude and tells me my latitude; chronometers, which allow me to calculate my longitude; and finally, spyglasses for both day and night, enabling me to scrutinize every point of the horizon once the *Nautilus* has risen to the surface of the waves."

"These are the normal navigational instruments," I replied, "and I'm familiar with their uses. But no doubt these others answer pressing needs unique to the *Nautilus*. That dial I see there, with the needle moving across it—isn't it a pressure gauge?"

"It is indeed a pressure gauge. It's placed in contact with the water, and it indicates the outside pressure on our hull, which in turn gives me the depth at which my submersible is sitting."

"And these are some new breed of sounding line?"

"They're thermometric sounding lines that report water temperatures in the different strata."

"And these other instruments, whose functions I can't even guess?"

"Here, professor, I need to give you some background information," Captain Nemo said. "So kindly hear me out."

He fell silent for some moments, then he said:

"There's a powerful, obedient, swift, and effortless force that can be bent to any use and which reigns supreme aboard my vessel. It does everything. It lights me, it warms me, it's the soul of my mechanical equipment. This force is electricity."

"Electricity!" I exclaimed in some surprise.

"Yes, sir."

"But, Captain, you have a tremendous speed of movement that doesn't square with the strength of electricity. Until now, its dynamic potential has remained quite limited, capable of producing only small amounts of power!"

"Professor," Captain Nemo replied, "my electricity isn't the run-of-the-mill variety, and with your permission, I'll leave it at that."

"I won't insist, sir, and I'll rest content with simply being flabbergasted at your results. I would ask one question, however, which you needn't answer if it's indiscreet. The electric cells you use to generate this marvelous force must be depleted very quickly. Their zinc component, for example: how do you replace it, since you no longer stay in contact with the shore?"

"That question deserves an answer," Captain Nemo replied. "First off, I'll mention that at the bottom of the sea there exist veins of zinc, iron, silver, and gold whose mining would quite certainly be feasible. But I've tapped none of these land-based metals, and I wanted to make demands only on the sea itself for the sources of my electricity."

"The sea itself?"

"Yes, professor, and there was no shortage of such sources. In fact, by establishing a circuit between two wires immersed to different depths, I'd be able to obtain electricity through the diverging temperatures they experience; but I preferred to use a more practical procedure."

"And that is?"

"You're familiar with the composition of salt water. In 1,000 grams one finds 96.5% water and about 2.66% sodium chloride; then small quantities of magnesium chloride, potassium chloride, magnesium bromide, sulfate of magnesia, calcium sulfate, and calcium carbonate. Hence you observe that sodium chloride is encountered there in significant proportions. Now then, it's this sodium that I extract from salt water and with which I compose my electric cells."

"Sodium?"

"Yes, sir. Mixed with mercury, it forms an amalgam that takes the place of zinc in Bunsen cells. The mercury is never depleted. Only the sodium is consumed, and the sea itself gives me that. Beyond this, I'll mention that sodium batteries have been found to generate the greater energy, and their electro-motor strength is twice that of zinc batteries."

"Captain, I fully understand the excellence of sodium under the conditions in which you're placed. The sea contains it. Fine. But it still has to be produced, in short, extracted. And how do you accomplish this? Obviously your batteries could do the extracting; but if I'm not mistaken, the consumption of sodium needed by your electric equipment would be greater than the quantity you'd extract. It would come about, then, that in the process of producing your sodium, you'd use up more than you'd make!"

"Accordingly, professor, I don't extract it with batteries; quite simply, I utilize the heat of coal from the earth."

"From the earth?" I said, my voice going up on the word.

"We'll say coal from the seafloor, if you prefer," Captain Nemo replied.

"And you can mine these veins of underwater coal?"

"You'll watch me work them, Professor Aronnax. I ask only a little patience of you, since you'll have ample time to be patient. Just remember one thing: I owe everything to the ocean; it generates electricity, and electricity gives the *Nautilus* heat, light, motion, and, in a word, life itself."

"But not the air you breathe?"

"Oh, I could produce the air needed on board, but it would be pointless, since I can rise to the surface of the sea whenever I like. However, even though electricity doesn't supply me with breathable air, it at least operates the powerful pumps that store it under pressure in special tanks; which, if need be, allows me to extend my stay in the lower strata for as long as I want."

"Captain," I replied, "I'll rest content with marveling. You've obviously found what all mankind will surely find one day, the true dynamic power of electricity."

"I'm not so certain they'll find it," Captain Nemo replied icily. "But be that as it may, you're already familiar with the first use I've found for this valuable force. It lights us, and with a uniformity and continuity not even possessed by sunlight. Now, look at that clock: it's electric, it runs with an accuracy rivaling the finest chronometers. I've had it divided into twenty-four hours like Italian clocks, since neither day nor night, sun nor moon, exist for me, but only this artificial light that I import into the depths of the seas! See, right now it's ten o'clock in the morning."

"That's perfect."

"Another use for electricity: that dial hanging before our eyes indicates how fast the *Nautilus* is going. An electric wire puts it in contact with the patent log; this needle shows me the actual speed of my submersible. And . . . hold on . . . just now we're proceeding at the moderate pace of fifteen miles per hour."

"It's marvelous," I replied, "and I truly see, Captain, how right you are to use this force; it's sure to take the place of wind, water, and steam."

"But that's not all, Professor Aronnax," Captain Nemo said, standing up. "And if you'd care to follow me, we'll inspect the *Nautilus's* stern."

In essence, I was already familiar with the whole forward part of this underwater boat, and here are its exact subdivisions going from amidships to its spur: the dining room, 5 meters long and separated from the library by a watertight bulkhead, in other words, it couldn't be penetrated by the sea; the library, 5 meters long; the main lounge, 10 meters long, separated from the captain's stateroom by a second watertight bulkhead; the aforesaid stateroom, 5 meters long; mine, 2.5 meters long; and finally, air tanks 7.5 meters long and extending to the stempost. Total: a length of 35 meters. Doors were cut into the watertight bulkheads and were shut hermetically by means of india–rubber seals, which insured complete safety aboard the *Nautilus* in the event of a leak in any one section.

I followed Captain Nemo down gangways located for easy transit, and I arrived amidships. There I found a sort of shaft heading upward between two watertight bulkheads. An iron ladder, clamped to the wall, led to the shaft's upper end. I asked the Captain what this ladder was for.

"It goes to the skiff," he replied.

"What! You have a skiff?" I replied in some astonishment.

"Surely. An excellent longboat, light and unsinkable, which is used for excursions and fishing trips."

"But when you want to set out, don't you have to return to the surface of the sea?"

"By no means. The skiff is attached to the topside of the *Nautilus's* hull and is set in a cavity expressly designed to receive it. It's completely decked over, absolutely watertight, and held solidly in place by bolts. This ladder leads to a manhole cut into the *Nautilus's* hull and corresponding to a comparable hole cut into the side of the skiff. I insert myself through this double opening into the longboat. My crew close up the hole belonging to the *Nautilus*; I close up the one belonging to the skiff, simply by screwing it into place. I undo the bolts holding the skiff to the submersible, and the longboat rises with prodigious speed to the surface of the sea. I then open the deck paneling, carefully closed until that point; I up mast and hoist sail—or I take out my oars—and I go for a spin."

"But how do you return to the ship?"

"I don't, Professor Aronnax; the *Nautilus* returns to me."

"At your command?"

"At my command. An electric wire connects me to the ship. I fire off a telegram, and that's that."

"Right," I said, tipsy from all these wonders, "nothing to it!"

After passing the well of the companionway that led to the platform, I saw a cabin 2 meters long in which Conseil and Ned Land, enraptured with their meal, were busy devouring it to the last crumb. Then a door opened into the galley, 3 meters long and located between the vessel's huge storage lockers.

There, even more powerful and obedient than gas, electricity did most of the cooking. Arriving under the stoves, wires transmitted to platinum griddles a heat that was distributed and sustained with perfect consistency. It also heated a distilling mechanism that, via evaporation, supplied excellent drinking water. Next to this galley was a bathroom, conveniently laid out, with faucets supplying hot or cold water at will.

After the galley came the crew's quarters, 5 meters long. But the door was closed and I couldn't see its accommodations, which might have told me the number of men it took to operate the *Nautilus*.

At the far end stood a fourth watertight bulkhead, separating the crew's quarters from the engine room. A door opened, and I stood in the compartment where Captain Nemo, indisputably a world–class engineer, had set up his locomotive equipment.

Brightly lit, the engine room measured at least 20 meters in length. It was divided, by function, into two parts: the first contained the cells for generating electricity, the second that mechanism transmitting movement to the propeller.

Right off, I detected an odor permeating the compartment that was *sui generis*. Captain Nemo noticed the negative impression it made on me.

"That," he told me, "is a gaseous discharge caused by our use of sodium, but it's only a mild inconvenience. In any event, every morning we sanitize the ship by ventilating it in the open air."

Meanwhile I examined the *Nautilus's* engine with a fascination easy to imagine.

"You observe," Captain Nemo told me, "that I use Bunsen cells, not Ruhmkorff cells. The latter would be ineffectual. One uses fewer Bunsen cells, but they're big and strong, and experience has proven their superiority. The electricity generated here makes its way to the stern, where electromagnets of huge size activate a special system of levers and gears that transmit movement to the propeller's shaft. The latter has a diameter of 6 meters, a pitch of 7.5 meters, and can do up to 120 revolutions per minute."

"And that gives you?"

"A speed of fifty miles per hour."

There lay a mystery, but I didn't insist on exploring it. How could electricity work with such power? Where did this nearly unlimited energy originate? Was it in the extraordinary voltage obtained from some new kind of induction coil? Could its transmission have been immeasurably increased by some unknown system of levers? This was the point I couldn't grasp.

"Captain Nemo," I said, "I'll vouch for the results and not

try to explain them. I've seen the *Nautilus* at work out in front of the *Abraham Lincoln*, and I know where I stand on its speed. But it isn't enough just to move, we have to see where we're going! We must be able to steer right or left, up or down! How do you reach the lower depths, where you meet an increasing resistance that's assessed in hundreds of atmospheres? How do you rise back to the surface of the ocean? Finally, how do you keep your ship at whatever level suits you? Am I indiscreet in asking you all these things?"

"Not at all, professor," the Captain answered me after a slight hesitation, "since you'll never leave this underwater boat. Come into the lounge. It's actually our work room, and there you'll learn the full story about the *Nautilus*!"

# CHAPTER 13

## Some Figures

A MOMENT LATER we were seated on a couch in the lounge, cigars between our lips. The Captain placed before my eyes a working drawing that gave the ground plan, cross section, and side view of the *Nautilus*. Then he began his description as follows:

"Here, Professor Aronnax, are the different dimensions of this boat now transporting you. It's a very long cylinder with conical ends. It noticeably takes the shape of a cigar, a shape already adopted in London for several projects of the same kind. The length of this cylinder from end to end is exactly seventy meters, and its maximum breadth of beam is eight meters. So it isn't quite built on the ten–to–one ratio of your high–speed steamers; but its lines are sufficiently long, and their tapering gradual enough, so that the displaced water easily slips past and poses no obstacle to the ship's movements.

"These two dimensions allow you to obtain, via a simple calculation, the surface area and volume of the *Nautilus*. Its surface area totals 1,011.45 square meters, its volume 1,507.2 cubic meters—which is tantamount to saying that when it's completely submerged, it displaces 1,500 cubic meters of water, or weighs 1,500 metric tons.

"In drawing up plans for a ship meant to navigate underwater, I wanted it, when floating on the waves, to lie nine–tenths below the surface and to emerge only one–tenth. Consequently, under these conditions it needed to displace only nine–tenths of its volume, hence 1,356.48 cubic meters; in other words, it was to weigh only that same number of metric tons. So I was obliged not to exceed this weight while building it to the aforesaid dimensions.

"The *Nautilus* is made up of two hulls, one inside the other; between them, joining them together, are iron T–bars that give this ship the utmost rigidity. In fact, thanks to this cellular arrangement, it has the resistance of a stone block, as if it were completely solid. Its plating can't give way; it's self–adhering and not dependent on the tightness of its rivets; and due to the perfect union of its materials, the solidarity of its construction allows it to defy the most violent seas.

"The two hulls are manufactured from boilerplate steel, whose relative density is 7.8 times that of water. The first hull has a thickness of no less than five centimeters and weighs 394.96 metric tons. My second hull, the outer cover, includes a keel fifty centimeters high by twenty–five wide, which by itself weighs 62 metric tons; this hull, the engine, the ballast, the various accessories and accommodations, plus the bulkheads and interior braces, have a combined weight of 961.52 metric tons, which when added to 394.96 metric tons, gives us the desired total of 1,356.48 metric tons. Clear?"

"Clear," I replied.

"So," the captain went on, "when the *Nautilus* lies on the waves under these conditions, one–tenth of it does emerge above water. Now then, if I provide some ballast tanks equal in capacity to that one–tenth, hence able to hold 150.72 metric tons, and if I fill them with water, the boat then displaces 1,507.2 metric tons—or it weighs that much—and it would be completely submerged. That's what comes about, professor. These ballast tanks exist within easy access in the lower reaches of the *Nautilus*. I open some stopcocks, the tanks fill, the boat sinks, and it's exactly flush with the surface of the water."

"Fine, captain, but now we come to a genuine difficulty.

You're able to lie flush with the surface of the ocean, that I understand. But lower down, while diving beneath that surface, isn't your submersible going to encounter a pressure, and consequently undergo an upward thrust, that must be assessed at one atmosphere per every thirty feet of water, hence at about one kilogram per each square centimeter?"

"Precisely, sir."

"Then unless you fill up the whole *Nautilus*, I don't see how you can force it down into the heart of these liquid masses."

"Professor," Captain Nemo replied, "static objects mustn't be confused with dynamic ones, or we'll be open to serious error. Comparatively little effort is spent in reaching the ocean's lower regions, because all objects have a tendency to become 'sinkers.' Follow my logic here."

"I'm all ears, captain."

"When I wanted to determine what increase in weight the *Nautilus* needed to be given in order to submerge, I had only to take note of the proportionate reduction in volume that salt water experiences in deeper and deeper strata."

"That's obvious," I replied.

"Now then, if water isn't absolutely incompressible, at least it compresses very little. In fact, according to the most recent calculations, this reduction is only .0000436 per atmosphere, or per every thirty feet of depth. For instance, to go 1,000 meters down, I must take into account the reduction in volume that occurs under a pressure equivalent to that from a 1,000–meter column of water, in other words, under a pressure of 100 atmospheres. In this instance the reduction would be .00436. Consequently, I'd have to increase my weight from 1,507.2 metric tons to 1,513.77. So the added weight would only be 6.57 metric tons."

"That's all?"

"That's all, Professor Aronnax, and the calculation is easy to check. Now then, I have supplementary ballast tanks capable of shipping 100 metric tons of water. So I can descend to considerable depths. When I want to rise again and lie flush with the surface, all I have to do is expel that water; and if I desire that the *Nautilus* emerge above the waves to one-tenth of its total capacity, I empty all the ballast tanks completely."

This logic, backed up by figures, left me without a single objection.

"I accept your calculations, Captain," I replied, "and I'd be ill-mannered to dispute them, since your daily experience bears them out. But at this juncture, I have a hunch that we're still left with one real difficulty."

"What's that, sir?"

"When you're at a depth of 1,000 meters, the *Nautilus's* plating bears a pressure of 100 atmospheres. If at this point you want to empty the supplementary ballast tanks in order to lighten your boat and rise to the surface, your pumps must overcome that pressure of 100 atmospheres, which is 100 kilograms per each square centimeter. This demands a strength—"

"That electricity alone can give me," Captain Nemo said swiftly. "Sir, I repeat: the dynamic power of my engines is nearly infinite. The *Nautilus's* pumps have prodigious strength, as you must have noticed when their waterspouts swept like a torrent over the *Abraham Lincoln*. Besides, I use my supplementary ballast tanks only to reach an average depth of 1,500 to 2,000 meters, and that with a view to conserving my machinery. Accordingly, when I have a mind to visit the ocean depths two or three vertical leagues beneath the surface, I use maneuvers that are more time-consuming but no less infallible."

"What are they, Captain?" I asked.

"Here I'm naturally led into telling you how the *Nautilus* is maneuvered."

"I can't wait to find out."

"In order to steer this boat to port or starboard, in short, to make turns on a horizontal plane, I use an ordinary, wide-bladed rudder that's fastened to the rear of the sternpost and worked by a wheel and tackle. But I can also move the *Nautilus* upward and downward on a vertical plane by the simple method of slanting its two fins, which are attached to its sides at its center of flotation; these fins are flexible, able to assume any position, and can be operated from inside by means of powerful levers. If these fins stay parallel with the boat, the latter moves horizontally. If they slant, the *Nautilus* follows the angle of that slant and, under its propeller's thrust, either sinks on a diagonal as steep as it suits me, or rises on that diagonal. And similarly, if I want to return more swiftly to the surface, I throw the propeller in gear, and the water's pressure makes the *Nautilus* rise vertically, as an air balloon inflated with hydrogen lifts swiftly into the skies."

"Bravo, Captain!" I exclaimed. "But in the midst of the waters, how can your helmsman follow the course you've given him?"

"My helmsman is stationed behind the windows of a pilothouse, which protrudes from the topside of the *Nautilus's* hull and is fitted with biconvex glass."

"Is glass capable of resisting such pressures?"

"Perfectly capable. Though fragile on impact, crystal can still offer considerable resistance. In 1864, during experiments on fishing by electric light in the middle of the North Sea, glass panes less than seven millimeters thick were seen to resist a pressure of sixteen atmospheres, all the while letting through strong, heat-generating rays whose warmth was unevenly distributed. Now then, I use glass windows measuring no less than twenty-one centimeters at their centers; in other words, they've thirty times the thickness."

"Fair enough, captain, but if we're going to see, we need light to drive away the dark, and in the midst of the murky waters, I wonder how your helmsman can—"

"Set astern of the pilothouse is a powerful electric reflector whose rays light up the sea for a distance of half a mile."

"Oh, bravo! Bravo three times over, Captain! That explains the phosphorescent glow from this so–called narwhale that so puzzled us scientists! Pertinent to this, I'll ask you if the *Nautilus's* running afoul of the *Scotia*, which caused such a great uproar, was the result of an accidental encounter?"

"Entirely accidental, sir. I was navigating two meters beneath the surface of the water when the collision occurred. However, I could see that it had no dire consequences."

"None, sir. But as for your encounter with the *Abraham Lincoln* . . . ?"

"Professor, that troubled me, because it's one of the best ships in the gallant American navy, but they attacked me and I had to defend myself! All the same, I was content simply to put the frigate in a condition where it could do me no harm; it won't have any difficulty getting repairs at the nearest port."

"Ah, Commander," I exclaimed with conviction, "your *Nautilus* is truly a marvelous boat!"

"Yes, professor," Captain Nemo replied with genuine excitement, "and I love it as if it were my own flesh and blood! Aboard a conventional ship, facing the ocean's perils, danger lurks everywhere; on the surface of the sea, your chief sensation is the constant feeling of an underlying chasm, as the Dutchman Jansen so aptly put it; but below the waves aboard the *Nautilus*, your heart never fails you! There are no structural deformities to worry about, because the double hull of this boat has the rigidity of iron; no rigging to be worn out by rolling and pitching on the waves; no sails for the wind to carry off; no boilers for steam to burst open; no fires to fear, because this submersible is made of sheet iron not wood; no coal to run out of, since electricity is its mechanical force; no collisions to fear, because it navigates the watery deep all by itself; no storms to brave, because just a few meters beneath the waves, it finds absolute tranquility! There, sir. There's the ideal ship! And if it's true that the engineer has more confidence in a craft than the builder, and the builder more than the captain himself, you can understand the utter abandon with which I place my trust in this *Nautilus*, since I'm its captain, builder, and engineer all in one!"

Captain Nemo spoke with winning eloquence. The fire in his eyes and the passion in his gestures transfigured him. Yes, he loved his ship the same way a father loves his child!

But one question, perhaps indiscreet, naturally popped up, and I couldn't resist asking it.

"You're an engineer, then, Captain Nemo?"

"Yes, professor," he answered me. "I studied in London, Paris, and New York back in the days when I was a resident of the Earth's continents."

"But how were you able to build this wonderful *Nautilus* in secret?"

"Each part of it, Professor Aronnax, came from a different spot on the globe and reached me at a cover address. Its keel was forged by Creusot in France, its propeller shaft by Pen & Co. in London, the sheet–iron plates for its hull by Laird's in Liverpool, its propeller by Scott's in Glasgow. Its tanks were manufactured by Cail & Co. in Paris, its engine by Krupp in Prussia, its spur by the Motala workshops in Sweden, its precision instruments by Hart Bros. in New York, etc.; and each of these suppliers received my specifications under a different name."

"But," I went on, "once these parts were manufactured, didn't they have to be mounted and adjusted?"

"Professor, I set up my workshops on a deserted islet in midocean. There our *Nautilus* was completed by me and my workmen, in other words, by my gallant companions whom I've molded and educated. Then, when the operation was over, we burned every trace of our stay on that islet, which if I could have, I'd have blown up."

"From all this, may I assume that such a boat costs a fortune?"

"An iron ship, Professor Aronnax, runs F1,125 per metric ton. Now then, the *Nautilus* has a burden of 1,500 metric tons. Consequently, it cost F1,687,000, hence F2,000,000 including its accommodations, and F4,000,000 or F5,000,000 with all the collections and works of art it contains."

"One last question, Captain Nemo."

"Ask, professor."

"You're rich, then?"

"Infinitely rich, sir, and without any trouble, I could pay off the ten–billion–franc French national debt!"

I gaped at the bizarre individual who had just spoken these words. Was he playing on my credulity? Time would tell.

# CHAPTER 14

## The Black Current

THE PART OF THE planet earth that the seas occupy has been assessed at 3,832,558 square myriameters, hence more than 38,000,000,000 hectares. This liquid mass totals 2,250,000,000 cubic miles and could form a sphere with a diameter of sixty leagues, whose weight would be three quintillion metric tons. To appreciate such a number, we should remember that a quintillion is to a billion what a billion is to one, in other words, there are as many billions in a quintillion as ones in a billion! Now then, this liquid mass nearly equals the total amount of water that has poured through all the earth's rivers for the past 40,000 years!

During prehistoric times, an era of fire was followed by an era of water. At first there was ocean everywhere. Then, during the Silurian period, the tops of mountains gradually appeared above the waves, islands emerged, disappeared beneath temporary floods, rose again, were fused to form continents, and finally the earth's geography settled into what we have today. Solid matter had wrested from liquid matter some 37,657,000 square miles, hence 12,916,000,000 hectares.

The outlines of the continents allow the seas to be divided into five major parts: the frozen Arctic and Antarctic oceans, the Indian Ocean, the Atlantic Ocean, and the Pacific Ocean.

The Pacific Ocean extends north to south between the two polar circles and east to west between America and Asia over an expanse of 145° of longitude. It's the most tranquil of the seas; its currents are wide and slow–moving, its tides moderate, its rainfall abundant. And this was the ocean that I was first destined to cross under these strangest of auspices.

"If you don't mind, professor," Captain Nemo told me, "we'll determine our exact position and fix the starting point of our voyage. It's fifteen minutes before noon. I'm going to rise to the surface of the water."

The captain pressed an electric bell three times. The pumps began to expel water from the ballast tanks; on the pressure gauge, a needle marked the decreasing pressures that indicated the Nautilus's upward progress; then the needle stopped.

"Here we are," the Captain said.

I made my way to the central companionway, which led to the platform. I climbed its metal steps, passed through the open hatches, and arrived topside on the Nautilus.

The platform emerged only eighty centimeters above the waves. The Nautilus's bow and stern boasted that spindle–shaped outline that had caused the ship to be compared appropriately to a long cigar. I noted the slight overlap of its sheet–iron plates, which resembled the scales covering the bodies of our big land reptiles. So I had a perfectly natural explanation for why, despite the best spyglasses, this boat had always been mistaken for a marine animal.

Near the middle of the platform, the skiff was half set in the ship's hull, making a slight bulge. Fore and aft stood two cupolas of moderate height, their sides slanting and partly inset with heavy biconvex glass, one reserved for the helmsman steering the Nautilus, the other for the brilliance of the powerful electric beacon lighting his way.

The sea was magnificent, the skies clear. This long aquatic vehicle could barely feel the broad undulations of the ocean. A mild breeze out of the east rippled the surface of the water. Free of all mist, the horizon was ideal for taking sights.

There was nothing to be seen. Not a reef, not an islet. No

more *Abraham Lincoln*. A deserted immenseness.

Raising his sextant, Captain Nemo took the altitude of the sun, which would give him his latitude. He waited for a few minutes until the orb touched the rim of the horizon. While he was taking his sights, he didn't move a muscle, and the instrument couldn't have been steadier in hands made out of marble.

"Noon," he said. "Professor, whenever you're ready. . . ."

I took one last look at the sea, a little yellowish near the landing places of Japan, and I went below again to the main lounge.

There the captain fixed his position and used a chronometer to calculate his longitude, which he double-checked against his previous observations of hour angles. Then he told me:

"Professor Aronnax, we're in longitude 137° 15' west—"

"West of which meridian?" I asked quickly, hoping the captain's reply might give me a clue to his nationality.

"Sir," he answered me, "I have chronometers variously set to the meridians of Paris, Greenwich, and Washington, D.C. But in your honor, I'll use the one for Paris."

This reply told me nothing. I bowed, and the commander went on:

"We're in longitude 137° 15' west of the meridian of Paris, and latitude 30° 7' north, in other words, about 300 miles from the shores of Japan. At noon on this day of November 8, we hereby begin our voyage of exploration under the waters."

"May God be with us!" I replied.

"And now, professor," the captain added, "I'll leave you to your intellectual pursuits. I've set our course east–northeast at a depth of fifty meters. Here are some large–scale charts on which you'll be able to follow that course. The lounge is at your disposal, and with your permission, I'll take my leave."

Captain Nemo bowed. I was left to myself, lost in my thoughts. They all centered on the *Nautilus's* commander.

Would I ever learn the nationality of this eccentric man who had boasted of having none? His sworn hate for humanity, a hate that perhaps was bent on some dreadful revenge—what had provoked it? Was he one of those unappreciated scholars, one of those geniuses "embittered by the world," as Conseil expressed it, a latter–day Galileo, or maybe one of those men of science, like America's Commander Maury, whose careers were ruined by political revolutions? I couldn't say yet. As for me, whom fate had just brought aboard his vessel, whose life he had held in the balance: he had received me coolly but hospitably. Only, he never took the hand I extended to him. He never extended his own.

For an entire hour I was deep in these musings, trying to probe this mystery that fascinated me so. Then my eyes focused on a huge world map displayed on the table, and I put my finger on the very spot where our just–determined longitude and latitude intersected.

Like the continents, the sea has its rivers. These are exclusive currents that can be identified by their temperature and color, the most remarkable being the one called the Gulf Stream. Science has defined the global paths of five chief currents: one in the north Atlantic, a second in the south Atlantic, a third in the north Pacific, a fourth in the south Pacific, and a fifth in the southern Indian Ocean. Also it's likely that a sixth current used to exist in the northern Indian Ocean, when the Caspian and Aral Seas joined up with certain large Asian lakes to form a single uniform expanse of water.

Now then, at the spot indicated on the world map, one of these seagoing rivers was rolling by, the Kuroshio of the Japanese, the Black Current: heated by perpendicular rays from the tropical sun, it leaves the Bay of Bengal, crosses the Strait of Malacca, goes up the shores of Asia, and curves into the north Pacific as far as the Aleutian Islands, carrying along trunks of camphor trees and other local items, the pure indigo of its warm waters sharply contrasting with the ocean's waves. It was this current the *Nautilus* was about to cross. I watched it on the map with my eyes, I saw it lose itself in the immenseness of the Pacific, and I felt myself swept along with it, when Ned Land and Conseil appeared in the lounge doorway.

My two gallant companions stood petrified at the sight of the wonders on display.

"Where are we?" the Canadian exclaimed. "In the Quebec Museum?"

"Begging master's pardon," Conseil answered, "but this seems more like the Sommerard artifacts exhibition!"

"My friends," I replied, signaling them to enter, "you're in neither Canada nor France, but securely aboard the *Nautilus*, fifty meters below sea level."

"If master says so, then so be it," Conseil answered. "But in all honesty, this lounge is enough to astonish even someone Flemish like myself."

"Indulge your astonishment, my friend, and have a look, because there's plenty of work here for a classifier of your talents."

Conseil needed no encouraging. Bending over the glass cases, the gallant lad was already muttering choice words from the naturalist's vocabulary: class Gastropoda, family Buccinoidea, genus Cowry, species Cypraea madagascariensis, etc.

Meanwhile Ned Land, less dedicated to conchology, questioned me about my interview with Captain Nemo. Had I discovered who he was, where he came from, where he was heading, how deep he was taking us? In short, a thousand questions I had no time to answer.

I told him everything I knew—or, rather, everything I didn't know—and I asked him what he had seen or heard on his part.

"Haven't seen or heard a thing!" the Canadian replied.

"I haven't even spotted the crew of this boat. By any chance, could they be electric too?"

"Electric?"

"Oh ye gods, I'm half tempted to believe it! But back to you, Professor Aronnax," Ned Land said, still hanging on to his ideas. "Can't you tell me how many men are on board? Ten, twenty, fifty, a hundred?"

"I'm unable to answer you, Mr. Land. And trust me on this: for the time being, get rid of these notions of taking over the *Nautilus* or escaping from it. This boat is a masterpiece of modern technology, and I'd be sorry to have missed it! Many people would welcome the circumstances that have been handed us, just to walk in the midst of these wonders. So keep calm, and let's see what's happening around us."

"See!" the harpooner exclaimed. "There's nothing to see, nothing we'll ever see from this sheet-iron prison! We're simply running around blindfolded—"

Ned Land was just pronouncing these last words when we were suddenly plunged into darkness, utter darkness. The ceiling lights went out so quickly, my eyes literally ached, just as if we had experienced the opposite sensation of going from the deepest gloom to the brightest sunlight.

We stood stock-still, not knowing what surprise was waiting for us, whether pleasant or unpleasant. But a sliding sound became audible. You could tell that some panels were shifting over the *Nautilus's* sides.

"It's the beginning of the end!" Ned Land said.

". . . order Hydromedusa," Conseil muttered.

Suddenly, through two oblong openings, daylight appeared on both sides of the lounge. The liquid masses came into view, brightly lit by the ship's electric outpourings. We were separated from the sea by two panes of glass. Initially I shuddered at the thought that these fragile partitions could break; but strong copper bands secured them, giving them nearly infinite resistance.

The sea was clearly visible for a one–mile radius around the *Nautilus*. What a sight! What pen could describe it? Who could portray the effects of this light through these translucent sheets of water, the subtlety of its progressive shadings into the ocean's upper and lower strata?

The transparency of salt water has long been recognized. Its clarity is believed to exceed that of spring water. The mineral and organic substances it holds in suspension actually increase its translucency. In certain parts of the Caribbean Sea, you can see the sandy bottom with startling distinctness as deep as 145 meters down, and the penetrating power of the sun's rays seems to give out only at a depth of 300 meters. But in this fluid setting traveled by the *Nautilus*, our electric glow was being generated in the very heart of the waves. It was no longer illuminated water, it was liquid light.

If we accept the hypotheses of the microbiologist Ehrenberg—who believes that these underwater depths are lit up by phosphorescent organisms—nature has certainly saved one of her most prodigious sights for residents of the sea, and I could judge for myself from the thousandfold play of the light. On both sides I had windows opening over these unexplored depths. The darkness in the lounge enhanced the brightness outside, and we stared as if this clear glass were the window of an immense aquarium.

The *Nautilus* seemed to be standing still. This was due to the lack of landmarks. But streaks of water, parted by the ship's spur, sometimes threaded before our eyes with extraordinary speed.

In wonderment, we leaned on our elbows before these show windows, and our stunned silence remained unbroken until Conseil said:

"You wanted to see something, Ned my friend; well, now you have something to see!"

"How unusual!" the Canadian put in, setting aside his

tantrums and getaway schemes while submitting to this irresistible allure. "A man would go an even greater distance just to stare at such a sight!"

"Ah!" I exclaimed. "I see our captain's way of life! He's found himself a separate world that saves its most astonishing wonders just for him!"

"But where are the fish?" the Canadian ventured to observe. "I don't see any fish!"

"Why would you care, Ned my friend?" Conseil replied. "Since you have no knowledge of them."

"Me? A fisherman!" Ned Land exclaimed.

And on this subject a dispute arose between the two friends, since both were knowledgeable about fish, but from totally different standpoints.

Everyone knows that fish make up the fourth and last class in the vertebrate branch. They have been quite aptly defined as:

"cold-blooded vertebrates with a double circulatory system, breathing through gills, and designed to live in water."

They consist of two distinct series: the series of bony fish, in other words, those whose spines have vertebrae made of bone; and cartilaginous fish, in other words, those whose spines have vertebrae made of cartilage.

Possibly the Canadian was familiar with this distinction, but Conseil knew far more about it; and since he and Ned were now fast friends, he just had to show off. So he told the harpooner:

"Ned my friend, you're a slayer of fish, a highly skilled fisherman. You've caught a large number of these fascinating animals. But I'll bet you don't know how they're classified."

"Sure I do," the harpooner replied in all seriousness. "They're classified into fish we eat and fish we don't eat!"

"Spoken like a true glutton," Conseil replied. "But tell me, are you familiar with the differences between bony fish and cartilaginous fish?"

"Just maybe, Conseil."

"And how about the subdivisions of these two large classes?"

"I haven't the foggiest notion," the Canadian replied.

"All right, listen and learn, Ned my friend! Bony fish are subdivided into six orders. Primo, the acanthopterygians, whose upper jaw is fully formed and free-moving, and whose gills take the shape of a comb. This order consists of fifteen families, in other words, three-quarters of all known fish. Example: the common perch."

"Pretty fair eating," Ned Land replied.

"Secundo," Conseil went on, "the abdominals, whose pelvic fins hang under the abdomen to the rear of the pectorals but aren't attached to the shoulder bone, an order that's divided into five families and makes up the great majority of freshwater fish. Examples: carp, pike."

"Ugh!" the Canadian put in with distinct scorn. "You can keep the freshwater fish!"

"Tertio," Conseil said, "the subbrachians, whose pelvic fins are attached under the pectorals and hang directly from the shoulder bone. This order contains four families. Examples: flatfish such as sole, turbot, dab, plaice, brill, etc."

"Excellent, really excellent!" the harpooner exclaimed, interested in fish only from an edible viewpoint.

"Quarto," Conseil went on, unabashed, "the apods, with long bodies that lack pelvic fins and are covered by a heavy, often glutinous skin, an order consisting of only one family. Examples: common eels and electric eels."

"So-so, just so-so!" Ned Land replied.

"Quinto," Conseil said, "the lophobranchians, which have fully formed, free-moving jaws but whose gills consist of little tufts arranged in pairs along their gill arches. This order includes only one family. Examples: seahorses and dragonfish."

"Bad, very bad!" the harpooner replied.

"Sexto and last," Conseil said, "the plectognaths, whose maxillary bone is firmly attached to the side of the intermaxillary that forms the jaw, and whose palate arch is locked to the skull by sutures that render the jaw immovable, an order lacking true pelvic fins and which consists of two families. Examples: puffers and moonfish."

"They're an insult to a frying pan!" the Canadian exclaimed.

"Are you grasping all this, Ned my friend?" asked the scholarly Conseil.

"Not a lick of it, Conseil my friend," the harpooner replied. "But keep going, because you fill me with fascination."

"As for cartilaginous fish," Conseil went on unflappably, "they consist of only three orders."

"Good news," Ned put in.

"Primo, the cyclostomes, whose jaws are fused into a flexible ring and whose gill openings are simply a large number of holes, an order consisting of only one family. Example: the lamprey."

"An acquired taste," Ned Land replied.

"Secundo, the selacians, with gills resembling those of the cyclostomes but whose lower jaw is free-moving. This order, which is the most important in the class, consists of two families. Examples: the ray and the shark."

"What!" Ned Land exclaimed. "Rays and man-eaters in the same order? Well, Conseil my friend, on behalf of the rays, I wouldn't advise you to put them in the same fish tank!"

"Tertio," Conseil replied, "The sturionians, whose gill opening is the usual single slit adorned with a gill cover, an order consisting of four genera. Example: the sturgeon."

"Ah, Conseil my friend, you saved the best for last, in my opinion anyhow! And that's all of 'em?"

"Yes, my gallant Ned," Conseil replied. "And note well, even when one has grasped all this, one still knows next to nothing, because these families are subdivided into genera, subgenera, species, varieties—"

"All right, Conseil my friend," the harpooner said, leaning toward the glass panel, "here come a couple of your varieties now!"

"Yes! Fish!" Conseil exclaimed. "One would think he was in front of an aquarium!"

"No," I replied, "because an aquarium is nothing more than a cage, and these fish are as free as birds in the air!"

"Well, Conseil my friend, identify them! Start naming them!" Ned Land exclaimed.

"Me?" Conseil replied. "I'm unable to! That's my employer's bailiwick!"

And in truth, although the fine lad was a classifying maniac, he was no naturalist, and I doubt that he could tell a bonito from a tuna. In short, he was the exact opposite of the Canadian, who knew nothing about classification but could instantly put a name to any fish.

"A triggerfish," I said.

"It's a Chinese triggerfish," Ned Land replied.

"Genus Balistes, family Scleroderma, order Plectognatha," Conseil muttered.

Assuredly, Ned and Conseil in combination added up to one outstanding naturalist.

The Canadian was not mistaken. Cavorting around the *Nautilus* was a school of triggerfish with flat bodies, grainy skins, armed with stings on their dorsal fins, and with four prickly rows of quills quivering on both sides of their tails. Nothing could have been more wonderful than the skin covering them: white underneath, gray above, with spots of gold sparkling in the dark eddies of the waves. Around them, rays were undulating like sheets flapping in the wind, and among these I spotted, much to my glee, a Chinese ray, yellowish on its topside, a dainty pink on its belly, and armed with three stings behind its eyes; a rare species whose very existence was still doubted in Lacépède's day, since that pioneering classifier of fish had seen one only in a portfolio of Japanese drawings.

For two hours a whole aquatic army escorted the *Nautilus*. In the midst of their leaping and cavorting, while they competed with each other in beauty, radiance, and speed, I could distinguish some green wrasse, bewhiskered mullet marked with pairs of black lines, white gobies from the genus Eleotris with curved caudal fins and violet spots on the back, wonderful Japanese mackerel from the genus Scomber with blue bodies and silver heads, glittering azure goldfish whose name by itself gives their full description, several varieties of porgy or gilthead (some banded gilthead with fins variously blue and yellow, some with horizontal heraldic bars and enhanced by a black strip around their caudal area, some with color zones and elegantly corseted in their six waistbands), trumpetfish with flutelike beaks that looked like genuine seafaring woodcocks and were sometimes a meter long, Japanese salamanders, serpentine moray eels from the genus Echidna that were six feet long with sharp little eyes and a huge mouth bristling with teeth; etc.

Our wonderment stayed at an all-time fever pitch. Our exclamations were endless. Ned identified the fish, Conseil classified them, and as for me, I was in ecstasy over the verve of their movements and the beauty of their forms. Never before had I been given the chance to glimpse these animals alive and at large in their native element.

Given such a complete collection from the seas of Japan and China, I won't mention every variety that passed before our dazzled eyes. More numerous than birds in the air, these fish raced right up to us, no doubt attracted by the brilliant glow of our electric beacon.

Suddenly daylight appeared in the lounge. The sheet-iron panels slid shut. The magical vision disappeared. But for a good while I kept dreaming away, until the moment my eyes focused on the instruments hanging on the wall. The compass still showed our heading as east–northeast, the pressure gauge indicated a pressure of five atmospheres (corresponding to a depth of fifty meters), and the electric log gave our speed as fifteen miles per hour.

I waited for Captain Nemo. But he didn't appear. The clock marked the hour of five.

Ned Land and Conseil returned to their cabin. As for me, I repaired to my stateroom. There I found dinner ready for me. It consisted of turtle soup made from the daintiest hawksbill, a red mullet with white, slightly flaky flesh, whose liver, when separately prepared, makes delicious eating, plus loin of imperial angelfish, whose flavor struck me as even better than salmon.

I spent the evening in reading, writing, and thinking. Then drowsiness overtook me, I stretched out on my eelgrass mattress, and I fell into a deep slumber, while the *Nautilus* glided through the swiftly flowing Black Current.

# CHAPTER 15

### An Invitation in Writing

THE NEXT DAY, November 9, I woke up only after a long, twelve-hour slumber. Conseil, a creature of habit, came to ask "how master's night went," and to offer his services. He had left his Canadian friend sleeping like a man who had never done anything else.

I let the gallant lad babble as he pleased, without giving him much in the way of a reply. I was concerned about Captain Nemo's absence during our session the previous afternoon, and I hoped to see him again today.

Soon I had put on my clothes, which were woven from strands of seashell tissue. More than once their composition provoked comments from Conseil. I informed him that they were made from the smooth, silken filaments with which the fan mussel, a type of seashell quite abundant along Mediterranean beaches, attaches itself to rocks. In olden times, fine fabrics, stockings, and gloves were made from such filaments, because they were both very soft and very warm. So the *Nautilus's* crew could dress themselves at little cost, without needing a thing from cotton growers, sheep, or silkworms on shore.

As soon as I was dressed, I made my way to the main lounge. It was deserted.

I dove into studying the conchological treasures amassed inside the glass cases. I also investigated the huge plant albums that were filled with the rarest marine herbs, which, although they were pressed and dried, still kept their wonderful colors.

Among these valuable water plants, I noted various seaweed: some Cladostephus verticillatus, peacock's tails, fig–leafed caulerpa, grain–bearing beauty bushes, delicate rosetangle tinted scarlet, sea colander arranged into fan shapes, mermaid's cups that looked like the caps of squat mushrooms and for years had been classified among the zoophytes; in short, a complete series of algae.

The entire day passed without my being honored by a visit from Captain Nemo. The panels in the lounge didn't open. Perhaps they didn't want us to get tired of these beautiful things.

The *Nautilus* kept to an east–northeasterly heading, a speed of twelve miles per hour, and a depth between fifty and sixty meters.

Next day, November 10: the same neglect, the same solitude. I didn't see a soul from the crew. Ned and Conseil spent the better part of the day with me. They were astonished at the captain's inexplicable absence. Was this eccentric man ill? Did he want to change his plans concerning us?

But after all, as Conseil noted, we enjoyed complete freedom, we were daintily and abundantly fed. Our host had kept to the terms of his agreement. We couldn't complain, and moreover the very uniqueness of our situation had such generous rewards in store for us, we had no grounds for criticism.

That day I started my diary of these adventures, which has enabled me to narrate them with the most scrupulous accuracy; and one odd detail: I wrote it on paper manufactured from marine eelgrass.

Early in the morning on November 11, fresh air poured through the *Nautilus's* interior, informing me that we had returned to the surface of the ocean to renew our oxygen supply. I headed for the central companionway and climbed onto the platform.

It was six o'clock. I found the weather overcast, the sea gray but calm. Hardly a billow. I hoped to encounter Captain Nemo there—would he come? I saw only the helmsman imprisoned in his glass–windowed pilothouse. Seated on the ledge furnished by the hull of the skiff, I inhaled the sea's salty aroma with great pleasure.

Little by little, the mists were dispersed under the action of the sun's rays. The radiant orb cleared the eastern horizon. Under its gaze, the sea caught on fire like a trail of gunpowder. Scattered on high, the clouds were colored in bright, wonderfully shaded hues, and numerous "ladyfingers" warned of daylong winds.

But what were mere winds to this *Nautilus*, which no storms could intimidate!

So I was marveling at this delightful sunrise, so life–giving and cheerful, when I heard someone climbing onto the platform.

I was prepared to greet Captain Nemo, but it was his chief officer who appeared—whom I had already met during our first visit with the captain. He advanced over the platform, not seeming to notice my presence. A powerful spyglass to his eye, he scrutinized every point of the horizon with the utmost care. Then, his examination over, he approached the hatch and pronounced a phrase whose exact wording follows below. I remember it because, every morning, it was repeated under the same circumstances. It ran like this:

"Nautron respoc lorni virch."

What it meant I was unable to say.

These words pronounced, the chief officer went below again. I thought the *Nautilus* was about to resume its underwater navigating. So I went down the hatch and back through the gangways to my stateroom.

Five days passed in this way with no change in our situation. Every morning I climbed onto the platform. The same phrase was pronounced by the same individual. Captain Nemo did not appear.

I was pursuing the policy that we had seen the last of him, when on November 16, while re-entering my stateroom with Ned and Conseil, I found a note addressed to me on the table.

I opened it impatiently. It was written in a script that was clear and neat but a bit "Old English" in style, its characters reminding me of German calligraphy.

The note was worded as follows:

> Professor Aronnax
> Aboard the *Nautilus*
> November 16, 1867
>
> Captain Nemo invites Professor Aronnax on a hunting trip that will take place tomorrow morning in his Crespo Island forests. He hopes nothing will prevent the professor from attending, and he looks forward with pleasure to the professor's companions joining him.
>
> CAPTAIN NEMO,
> Commander of the *Nautilus*.

"A hunting trip!" Ned exclaimed.

"And in his forests on Crespo Island!" Conseil added.

"But does this mean the old boy goes ashore?" Ned Land went on.

"That seems to be the gist of it," I said, rereading the letter.

"Well, we've got to accept!" the Canadian answered. "Once we're on solid ground, we'll figure out a course of action. Besides, it wouldn't pain me to eat a couple slices of fresh venison!"

Without trying to reconcile the contradictions between Captain Nemo's professed horror of continents or islands and his invitation to go hunting in a forest, I was content to reply:

"First let's look into this Crespo Island."

I consulted the world map; and in latitude 32° 40' north and longitude 167° 50' west, I found an islet that had been discovered in 1801 by Captain Crespo, which old Spanish charts called Rocca de la Plata, in other words, "Silver Rock." So we were about 1,800 miles from our starting point, and by a slight change of heading, the Nautilus was bringing us back toward the southeast.

I showed my companions this small, stray rock in the middle of the north Pacific.

"If Captain Nemo does sometimes go ashore," I told them, "at least he only picks desert islands!"

Ned Land shook his head without replying; then he and Conseil left me. After supper was served me by the mute and emotionless steward, I fell asleep; but not without some anxieties.

When I woke up the next day, November 17, I sensed that the Nautilus was completely motionless. I dressed hurriedly and entered the main lounge.

Captain Nemo was there waiting for me. He stood up, bowed, and asked if it suited me to come along.

Since he made no allusion to his absence the past eight days, I also refrained from mentioning it, and I simply answered that my companions and I were ready to go with him.

"Only, sir," I added, "I'll take the liberty of addressing a question to you."

"Address away, Professor Aronnax, and if I'm able to answer, I will."

"Well then, Captain, how is it that you've severed all ties with the shore, yet you own forests on Crespo Island?"

"Professor," the captain answered me, "these forests of mine don't bask in the heat and light of the sun. They aren't frequented by lions, tigers, panthers, or other quadrupeds. They're known only to me. They grow only for me. These forests aren't on land, they're actual underwater forests."

"Underwater forests!" I exclaimed.

"Yes, professor."

"And you're offering to take me to them?"

"Precisely."

"On foot?"

"Without getting your feet wet."

"While hunting?"

"While hunting."

"Rifles in hand?"

"Rifles in hand."

I stared at the *Nautilus's* commander with an air anything but flattering to the man.

"Assuredly," I said to myself, "he's contracted some mental illness. He's had a fit that's lasted eight days and isn't over even yet. What a shame! I liked him better eccentric than insane!"

These thoughts were clearly readable on my face; but Captain Nemo remained content with inviting me to follow him, and I did so like a man resigned to the worst.

We arrived at the dining room, where we found breakfast served.

"Professor Aronnax," the captain told me, "I beg you to share my breakfast without formality. We can chat while we eat. Because, although I promised you a stroll in my forests, I made no pledge to arrange for your encountering a restaurant there. Accordingly, eat your breakfast like a man who'll probably eat dinner only when it's extremely late."

I did justice to this meal. It was made up of various fish and some slices of sea cucumber, that praiseworthy zoophyte, all garnished with such highly appetizing seaweed as the Porphyra laciniata and the Laurencia primafetida. Our beverage consisted of clear water to which, following the captain's example, I added some drops of a fermented liquor extracted by the Kamchatka process from the seaweed known by name as Rhodymenia palmata.

At first Captain Nemo ate without pronouncing a single word. Then he told me:

"Professor, when I proposed that you go hunting in my Crespo forests, you thought I was contradicting myself. When I informed you that it was an issue of underwater forests, you thought I'd gone insane. Professor, you must never make snap judgments about your fellow man."

"But, Captain, believe me—"

"Kindly listen to me, and you'll see if you have grounds for accusing me of insanity or self-contradiction."

"I'm all attention."

"Professor, you know as well as I do that a man can live underwater so long as he carries with him his own supply of breathable air. For underwater work projects, the workman wears a waterproof suit with his head imprisoned in a metal capsule, while he receives air from above by means of force pumps and flow regulators."

"That's the standard equipment for a diving suit," I said.

"Correct, but under such conditions the man has no freedom. He's attached to a pump that sends him air through an india–rubber hose; it's an actual chain that fetters him to the shore, and if we were to be bound in this way to the *Nautilus*, we couldn't go far either."

"Then how do you break free?" I asked.

"We use the Rouquayrol–Denayrouze device, invented by two of your fellow countrymen but refined by me for my own special uses, thereby enabling you to risk these new physiological conditions without suffering any organic disorders. It consists of a tank built from heavy sheet iron in which I store air under a pressure of fifty atmospheres. This tank is fastened to the back by means of straps, like a soldier's knapsack. Its top part forms a box where the air is regulated by a bellows mechanism and can be released only at its proper tension. In the Rouquayrol device that has been in general use, two india–rubber hoses leave this box and feed to a kind of tent that imprisons the operator's nose and mouth; one hose is for the entrance of air to be inhaled, the other for the exit of air to be exhaled, and the tongue closes off the former or the latter depending on the breather's needs. But in my case, since I face considerable pressures at the bottom of the sea, I needed to enclose my head in a copper sphere, like those found on standard diving suits, and the two hoses for inhalation and exhalation now feed to that sphere."

"That's perfect, Captain Nemo, but the air you carry must be quickly depleted; and once it contains no more than 15% oxygen, it becomes unfit for breathing."

"Surely, but as I told you, Professor Aronnax, the Nautilus's pumps enable me to store air under considerable pressure, and given this circumstance, the tank on my diving equipment can supply breathable air for nine or ten hours."

"I've no more objections to raise," I replied. "I'll only ask you, Captain: how can you light your way at the bottom of the ocean?"

"With the Ruhmkorff device, Professor Aronnax. If the first is carried on the back, the second is fastened to the belt. It consists of a Bunsen battery that I activate not with potassium dichromate but with sodium. An induction coil gathers the electricity generated and directs it to a specially designed lantern. In this lantern one finds a glass spiral that contains only a residue of carbon dioxide gas. When the device is operating, this gas becomes luminous and gives off a continuous whitish light. Thus provided for, I breathe and I see."

"Captain Nemo, to my every objection you give such crushing answers, I'm afraid to entertain a single doubt. However, though I have no choice but to accept both the Rouquayrol and Ruhmkorff devices, I'd like to register some reservations about the rifle with which you'll equip me."

"But it isn't a rifle that uses gunpowder," the captain replied.

"Then it's an air gun?"

"Surely. How can I make gunpowder on my ship when I have no saltpeter, sulfur, or charcoal?"

"Even so," I replied, "to fire underwater in a medium that's 855 times denser than air, you'd have to overcome considerable resistance."

"That doesn't necessarily follow. There are certain Fulton-style guns perfected by the Englishmen Philippe–Coles and Burley, the Frenchman Furcy, and the Italian Landi; they're equipped with a special system of airtight fastenings and can fire in underwater conditions. But I repeat: having no gunpowder, I've replaced it with air at high pressure, which is abundantly supplied me by the *Nautilus's* pumps."

"But this air must be swiftly depleted."

"Well, in a pinch can't my Rouquayrol tank supply me with more? All I have to do is draw it from an ad hoc spigot. Besides, Professor Aronnax, you'll see for yourself that during these underwater hunting trips, we make no great expenditure of either air or bullets."

"But it seems to me that in this semidarkness, amid this liquid that's so dense in comparison to the atmosphere, a gunshot couldn't carry far and would prove fatal only with difficulty!"

"On the contrary, sir, with this rifle every shot is fatal; and as soon as the animal is hit, no matter how lightly, it falls as if struck by lightning."

"Why?"

"Because this rifle doesn't shoot ordinary bullets but little glass capsules invented by the Austrian chemist Leniebroek, and I have a considerable supply of them. These glass capsules are covered with a strip of steel and weighted with a lead base; they're genuine little Leyden jars charged with high–voltage electricity. They go off at the slightest impact, and the animal, no matter how strong, drops dead. I might add that these capsules are no bigger than number 4 shot, and the chamber of any ordinary rifle could hold ten of them."

"I'll quit debating," I replied, getting up from the table. "And all that's left is for me to shoulder my rifle. So where you go, I'll go."

Captain Nemo led me to the *Nautilus*'s stern, and passing by Ned and Conseil's cabin, I summoned my two companions, who instantly followed us.

Then we arrived at a cell located within easy access of the engine room; in this cell we were to get dressed for our stroll.

# CHAPTER 16

### Strolling the Plains

THIS CELL, properly speaking, was the *Nautilus's* arsenal and wardrobe. Hanging from its walls, a dozen diving outfits were waiting for anybody who wanted to take a stroll.

After seeing these, Ned Land exhibited an obvious distaste for the idea of putting one on.

"But my gallant Ned," I told him, "the forests of Crespo Island are simply underwater forests!"

"Oh great!" put in the disappointed harpooner, watching his dreams of fresh meat fade away. "And you, Professor Aronnax, are you going to stick yourself inside these clothes?"

"It has to be, Mr. Ned."

"Have it your way, sir," the harpooner replied, shrugging his shoulders. "But speaking for myself, I'll never get into those things unless they force me!"

"No one will force you, Mr. Land," Captain Nemo said.

"And is Conseil going to risk it?" Ned asked.

"Where master goes, I go," Conseil replied.

At the captain's summons, two crewmen came to help us put on these heavy, waterproof clothes, made from seamless india rubber and expressly designed to bear considerable pressures. They were like suits of armor that were both yielding and resistant, you might say. These clothes consisted of jacket and pants. The pants ended in bulky footwear adorned with heavy lead soles. The fabric of the jacket was reinforced with copper mail that shielded the chest, protected it from the water's pressure, and allowed the lungs to function freely; the sleeves ended in supple gloves that didn't impede hand movements.

These perfected diving suits, it was easy to see, were a far cry from such misshapen costumes as the cork breastplates, leather jumpers, seagoing tunics, barrel helmets, etc., invented and acclaimed in the 18th century.

Conseil and I were soon dressed in these diving suits, as were Captain Nemo and one of his companions—a herculean type who must have been prodigiously strong. All that remained was to encase one's head in its metal sphere. But before proceeding with this operation, I asked the captain for permission to examine the rifles set aside for us.

One of the Nautilus's men presented me with a streamlined rifle whose butt was boilerplate steel, hollow inside, and of fairly large dimensions. This served as a tank for the compressed air, which a trigger–operated valve could release into the metal chamber. In a groove where the butt was heaviest, a cartridge clip held some twenty electric bullets that, by means of a spring, automatically took their places in the barrel of the rifle. As soon as one shot had been fired, another was ready to go off.

"Captain Nemo," I said, "this is an ideal, easy–to–use weapon. I ask only to put it to the test. But how will we reach the bottom of the sea?"

"Right now, professor, the Nautilus is aground in ten meters of water, and we've only to depart."

"But how will we set out?"

"You'll see."

Captain Nemo inserted his cranium into its spherical headgear. Conseil and I did the same, but not without hearing the Canadian toss us a sarcastic "happy hunting." On top, the suit ended in a collar of threaded copper onto which the metal helmet was screwed. Three holes, protected by heavy glass, allowed us to see in any direction with simply a turn of the head inside the sphere. Placed on our backs, the Rouquayrol device went into operation as soon as it was in position, and for my part, I could breathe with ease.

The Ruhmkorff lamp hanging from my belt, my rifle in hand, I was ready to go forth. But in all honesty, while imprisoned in these heavy clothes and nailed to the deck by my lead soles, it was impossible for me to take a single step.

But this circumstance had been foreseen, because I felt myself propelled into a little room adjoining the wardrobe. Towed in the same way, my companions went with me. I heard a door with watertight seals close after us, and we were surrounded by profound darkness.

After some minutes a sharp hissing reached my ears. I felt a distinct sensation of cold rising from my feet to my chest. Apparently a stopcock inside the boat was letting in water from outside, which overran us and soon filled up the room. Contrived in the *Nautilus's* side, a second door then opened. We were lit by a subdued light. An instant later our feet were treading the bottom of the sea.

And now, how can I convey the impressions left on me by this stroll under the waters. Words are powerless to describe such wonders! When even the painter's brush can't depict the effects unique to the liquid element, how can the writer's pen hope to reproduce them?

Captain Nemo walked in front, and his companion followed us a few steps to the rear. Conseil and I stayed next to each other, as if daydreaming that through our metal carapaces, a little polite conversation might still be possible! Already I no longer felt the bulkiness of my clothes, footwear, and air tank, nor the weight of the heavy sphere inside which my head was rattling like an almond in its shell. Once immersed in water, all these objects lost a part of their weight equal to the weight of the liquid they displaced, and thanks to this law of physics discovered by Archimedes, I did just fine. I was no longer an inert mass, and I had, comparatively speaking, great freedom of movement.

Lighting up the seafloor even thirty feet beneath the surface of the ocean, the sun astonished me with its power. The solar rays easily crossed this aqueous mass and dispersed its dark colors. I could easily distinguish objects 100 meters away. Farther on, the bottom was tinted with fine shades of ultramarine; then, off in the distance, it turned blue and faded in the midst of a hazy darkness. Truly, this water surrounding me was just a kind of air, denser than the atmosphere on land but almost as transparent. Above me I could see the calm surface of the ocean.

We were walking on sand that was fine-grained and smooth, not wrinkled like beach sand, which preserves the impressions left by the waves. This dazzling carpet was a real mirror, throwing back the sun's rays with startling intensity. The outcome: an immense vista of reflections that penetrated every liquid molecule. Will anyone believe me if I assert that at this thirty-foot depth, I could see as if it was broad daylight?

For a quarter of an hour, I trod this blazing sand, which was strewn with tiny crumbs of seashell. Looming like a long reef, the *Nautilus's* hull disappeared little by little, but when night fell in the midst of the waters, the ship's beacon would surely facilitate our return on board, since its rays carried with perfect distinctness. This effect is difficult to understand for anyone who has never seen light beams so sharply defined on shore. There the dust that saturates the air gives such rays the appearance of a luminous fog; but above water as well as underwater, shafts of electric light are transmitted with incomparable clarity.

Meanwhile we went ever onward, and these vast plains of sand seemed endless. My hands parted liquid curtains that closed again behind me, and my footprints faded swiftly under the water's pressure.

Soon, scarcely blurred by their distance from us, the forms of some objects took shape before my eyes. I recognized the lower slopes of some magnificent rocks carpeted by the finest zoophyte specimens, and right off, I was struck by an effect unique to this medium.

By then it was ten o'clock in the morning. The sun's rays hit the surface of the waves at a fairly oblique angle, decomposing by refraction as though passing through a prism; and when this light came in contact with flowers, rocks, buds, seashells, and polyps, the edges of these objects were shaded with all seven hues of the solar spectrum. This riot of rainbow tints was a wonder, a feast for the eyes: a genuine kaleidoscope of red, green, yellow, orange, violet, indigo, and blue; in short, the whole palette of a color–happy painter! If only I had been able to share with Conseil the intense sensations rising in my brain, competing with him in exclamations of wonderment! If only I had known, like Captain Nemo and his companion, how to exchange thoughts by means of prearranged signals! So, for lack of anything better, I talked to myself: I declaimed inside this copper box that topped my head, spending more air on empty words than was perhaps advisable.

Conseil, like me, had stopped before this splendid sight. Obviously, in the presence of these zoophyte and mollusk specimens, the fine lad was classifying his head off. Polyps and echinoderms abounded on the seafloor: various isis coral, cornularian coral living in isolation, tufts of virginal genus Oculina formerly known by the name "white coral," prickly fungus coral in the shape of mushrooms, sea anemone holding on by their muscular disks, providing a literal flowerbed adorned by jellyfish from the genus Porpita wearing collars of azure tentacles, and starfish that spangled the sand, including veinlike feather stars from the genus Asterophyton that were like fine lace embroidered by the hands of water nymphs, their festoons swaying to the faint undulations caused by our walking. It filled me with real chagrin to crush underfoot the gleaming mollusk samples that littered the seafloor by the thousands: concentric comb shells, hammer shells, coquina (seashells that actually hop around), top-shell snails, red helmet shells, angel-wing conchs, sea hares, and so many other exhibits from this inexhaustible ocean. But we had to keep walking, and we went forward while overhead there scudded schools of Portuguese men-of-war that let their ultramarine tentacles drift in their wakes, medusas whose milky white or dainty pink parasols were festooned with azure tassels and shaded us from the sun's rays, plus jellyfish of the species Pelagia panopyra that, in the dark, would have strewn our path with phosphorescent glimmers!

All these wonders I glimpsed in the space of a quarter of a mile, barely pausing, following Captain Nemo whose gestures kept beckoning me onward. Soon the nature of the seafloor changed. The plains of sand were followed by a bed of that viscous slime Americans call "ooze," which is composed exclusively of seashells rich in limestone or silica. Then we crossed a prairie of algae, open-sea plants that the waters hadn't yet torn loose, whose vegetation grew in wild profusion. Soft to the foot, these densely textured lawns would have rivaled the most luxuriant carpets woven by the hand of man. But while this greenery was sprawling under our steps, it didn't neglect us overhead. The surface of the water was crisscrossed by a floating arbor of marine plants belonging to that superabundant algae family that numbers more than 2,000 known species. I saw long ribbons of fucus drifting above me, some globular, others tubular: Laurencia, Cladostephus with the slenderest foliage, Rhodymenia palmata resembling the fan shapes of cactus. I observed that green-colored plants kept closer to the surface of the sea, while reds occupied a medium depth, which left blacks and browns in charge of designing gardens and flowerbeds in the ocean's lower strata.

These algae are a genuine prodigy of creation, one of the wonders of world flora. This family produces both the biggest and smallest vegetables in the world. Because, just as 40,000 near-invisible buds have been counted in one five-square-millimeter space, so also have fucus plants been gathered that were over 500 meters long!

We had been gone from the *Nautilus* for about an hour and a half. It was almost noon. I spotted this fact in the perpendicularity of the sun's rays, which were no longer refracted. The magic of these solar colors disappeared little by little, with emerald and sapphire shades vanishing from our surroundings altogether. We walked with steady steps that rang on the seafloor with astonishing intensity. The tiniest sounds were transmitted with a speed to which the ear is unaccustomed on shore. In fact, water is a better conductor of sound than air, and under the waves noises carry four times as fast.

Just then the seafloor began to slope sharply downward. The light took on a uniform hue. We reached a depth of 100 meters, by which point we were undergoing a pressure of ten atmospheres. But my diving clothes were built along such lines that I never suffered from this pressure. I felt only a certain tightness in the joints of my fingers, and even this discomfort soon disappeared. As for the exhaustion bound to accompany a two-hour stroll in such unfamiliar trappings—it was nil. Helped by the water, my movements were executed with startling ease.

Arriving at this 300-foot depth, I still detected the sun's rays, but just barely. Their intense brilliance had been followed by a reddish twilight, a midpoint between day and night. But we could see well enough to find our way, and it still wasn't necessary to activate the Ruhmkorff device.

Just then Captain Nemo stopped. He waited until I joined

him, then he pointed a finger at some dark masses outlined in the shadows a short distance away.

"It's the forest of Crespo Island," I thought; and I was not mistaken.

# CHAPTER 17

An Underwater Forest

WE HAD FINALLY arrived on the outskirts of this forest, surely one of the finest in Captain Nemo's immense domains. He regarded it as his own and had laid the same claim to it that, in the first days of the world, the first men had to their forests on land. Besides, who else could dispute his ownership of this underwater property? What other, bolder pioneer would come, ax in hand, to clear away its dark underbrush?

This forest was made up of big treelike plants, and when we entered beneath their huge arches, my eyes were instantly struck by the unique arrangement of their branches—an arrangement that I had never before encountered.

None of the weeds carpeting the seafloor, none of the branches bristling from the shrubbery, crept, or leaned, or stretched on a horizontal plane. They all rose right up toward the surface of the ocean. Every filament or ribbon, no matter how thin, stood ramrod straight. Fucus plants and creepers were growing in stiff perpendicular lines, governed by the density of the element that generated them. After I parted them with my hands, these otherwise motionless plants would shoot right back to their original positions. It was the regime of verticality.

I soon grew accustomed to this bizarre arrangement, likewise to the comparative darkness surrounding us. The seafloor in this forest was strewn with sharp chunks of stone that were hard to avoid. Here the range of underwater flora seemed pretty comprehensive to me, as well as more abundant than it might have been in the arctic or tropical zones, where such exhibits are less common. But for a few minutes I kept accidentally confusing the two kingdoms, mistaking zoophytes for water plants, animals for vegetables. And who hasn't made the same blunder? Flora and fauna are so closely associated in the underwater world!

I observed that all these exhibits from the vegetable kingdom were attached to the seafloor by only the most makeshift methods. They had no roots and didn't care which solid objects secured them, sand, shells, husks, or pebbles; they didn't ask their hosts for sustenance, just a point of purchase. These plants are entirely self-propagating, and the principle of their existence lies in the water that sustains and nourishes them. In place of leaves, most of them sprouted blades of unpredictable shape, which were confined to a narrow gamut of colors consisting only of pink, crimson, green, olive, tan, and brown. There I saw again, but not yet pressed and dried like the *Nautilus's* specimens, some peacock's tails spread open like fans to stir up a cooling breeze, scarlet rosetangle, sea tangle stretching out their young and edible shoots, twisting strings of kelp from the genus Nereocystis that bloomed to a height of fifteen meters, bouquets of mermaid's cups whose stems grew wider at the top, and a number of other open-sea plants, all without flowers. "It's an odd anomaly in this bizarre element!" as one witty naturalist puts it. "The animal kingdom blossoms, and the vegetable kingdom doesn't!"

These various types of shrubbery were as big as trees in the temperate zones; in the damp shade between them, there were clustered actual bushes of moving flowers, hedges of zoophytes in which there grew stony coral striped with twisting furrows, yellowish sea anemone from the genus Caryophylia with translucent tentacles, plus anemone with grassy tufts from the genus Zoantharia; and to complete the illusion, minnows flitted from branch to branch like a swarm of hummingbirds, while there rose underfoot, like a covey of snipe, yellow fish from the genus Lepisocanthus with bristling jaws and sharp scales, flying gurnards, and pinecone fish.

Near one o'clock, Captain Nemo gave the signal to halt. Speaking for myself, I was glad to oblige, and we stretched out beneath an arbor of winged kelp, whose long thin tendrils stood up like arrows.

This short break was a delight. It lacked only the charm of conversation. But it was impossible to speak, impossible to reply. I simply nudged my big copper headpiece against Conseil's headpiece. I saw a happy gleam in the gallant lad's eyes, and to communicate his pleasure, he jiggled around inside his carapace in the world's silliest way.

After four hours of strolling, I was quite astonished not to feel any intense hunger. What kept my stomach in such a good mood I'm unable to say. But, in exchange, I experienced that irresistible desire for sleep that comes over every diver. Accordingly, my eyes soon closed behind their heavy glass windows and I fell into an uncontrollable doze, which until then I had been able to fight off only through the movements of our walking. Captain Nemo and his muscular companion were already stretched out in this clear crystal, setting us a fine naptime example.

How long I was sunk in this torpor I cannot estimate; but when I awoke, it seemed as if the sun were settling toward the horizon. Captain Nemo was already up, and I had started to stretch my limbs, when an unexpected apparition brought me sharply to my feet.

A few paces away, a monstrous, meter-high sea spider was staring at me with beady eyes, poised to spring at me. Although my diving suit was heavy enough to protect me from this animal's bites, I couldn't keep back a shudder of horror. Just then Conseil woke up, together with the *Nautilus's* sailor. Captain Nemo alerted his companion to this hideous crustacean, which a swing of the rifle butt quickly brought down, and I watched the monster's horrible legs writhing in dreadful convulsions.

This encounter reminded me that other, more daunting animals must be lurking in these dark reaches, and my diving suit might not be adequate protection against their attacks. Such thoughts hadn't previously crossed my mind, and I was determined to keep on my guard. Meanwhile I had assumed this rest period would be the turning point in our stroll, but I was mistaken; and instead of heading back to the *Nautilus*, Captain Nemo continued his daring excursion.

The seafloor kept sinking, and its significantly steeper slope took us to greater depths. It must have been nearly three o'clock when we reached a narrow valley gouged between high, vertical walls and located 150 meters down. Thanks to the perfection of our equipment, we had thus gone ninety meters below the limit that nature had, until then, set on man's underwater excursions.

I say 150 meters, although I had no instruments for estimating this distance. But I knew that the sun's rays, even in the clearest seas, could reach no deeper. So at precisely this point the darkness became profound. Not a single object was visible past ten paces. Consequently, I had begun to grope my way when suddenly I saw the glow of an intense white light. Captain Nemo had just activated his electric device. His companion did likewise. Conseil and I followed suit. By turning a switch, I established contact between the induction coil and the glass spiral, and the sea, lit up by our four lanterns, was illuminated for a radius of twenty-five meters.

Captain Nemo continued to plummet into the dark depths of this forest, whose shrubbery grew ever more sparse. I observed that vegetable life was disappearing more quickly than animal life. The open-sea plants had already left behind the increasingly arid seafloor, where a prodigious number of animals were still swarming: zoophytes, articulates, mollusks, and fish.

While we were walking, I thought the lights of our Ruhmkorff devices would automatically attract some inhabitants of these dark strata. But if they did approach us, at least they kept at a distance regrettable from the hunter's standpoint. Several times I saw Captain Nemo stop and take aim with his rifle; then, after sighting down its barrel for a few seconds, he would straighten up and resume his walk.

Finally, at around four o'clock, this marvelous excursion came to an end. A wall of superb rocks stood before us, imposing in its sheer mass: a pile of gigantic stone blocks, an enormous granite cliffside pitted with dark caves but not offering a single gradient we could climb up. This was the underpinning of Crespo Island. This was land.

The captain stopped suddenly. A gesture from him brought us to a halt, and however much I wanted to clear this wall, I had to stop. Here ended the domains of Captain Nemo. He had no desire to pass beyond them. Farther on lay a part of the globe he would no longer tread underfoot.

Our return journey began. Captain Nemo resumed the lead in our little band, always heading forward without hesitation. I noted that we didn't follow the same path in returning to the *Nautilus*. This new route, very steep and hence very arduous, quickly took us close to the surface of the sea. But this return to the upper strata wasn't so sudden that decompression took place too quickly, which could have led to serious organic disorders and given us those internal injuries so fatal to divers. With great promptness, the light reappeared and grew stronger; and the refraction of the sun, already low on the horizon, again ringed the edges of various objects with the entire color spectrum.

At a depth of ten meters, we walked amid a swarm of small fish from every species, more numerous than birds in the air, more agile too; but no aquatic game worthy of a gunshot had yet been offered to our eyes.

Just then I saw the captain's weapon spring to his shoulder and track a moving object through the bushes. A shot went off, I heard a faint hissing, and an animal dropped a few paces away, literally struck by lightning.

It was a magnificent sea otter from the genus Enhydra, the only exclusively marine quadruped. One and a half meters long, this otter had to be worth a good high price. Its coat, chestnut brown above and silver below, would have made one of those wonderful fur pieces so much in demand in the Russian and Chinese markets; the fineness and luster of its pelt guaranteed that it would go for at least F2,000. I was full of wonderment at this unusual mammal, with its circular head adorned by short ears, its round eyes, its white whiskers like those on a cat, its webbed and clawed feet, its bushy tail. Hunted and trapped by fishermen, this valuable carnivore has become extremely rare, and it takes refuge chiefly in the northernmost parts of the Pacific, where in all likelihood its species will soon be facing extinction.

Captain Nemo's companion picked up the animal, loaded it on his shoulder, and we took to the trail again.

For an hour plains of sand unrolled before our steps. Often the seafloor rose to within two meters of the surface of the water. I could then see our images clearly mirrored on the underside of the waves, but reflected upside down: above us there appeared an identical band that duplicated our every movement and gesture; in short, a perfect likeness of the quartet near which it walked, but with heads down and feet in the air.

Another unusual effect. Heavy clouds passed above us, forming and fading swiftly. But after thinking it over, I realized that these so-called clouds were caused simply by the changing densities of the long ground swells, and I even spotted the foaming "white caps" that their breaking crests were proliferating over the surface of the water. Lastly, I couldn't help seeing the actual shadows of large birds passing over our heads, swiftly skimming the surface of the sea.

On this occasion I witnessed one of the finest gunshots ever to thrill the marrow of a hunter. A large bird with a wide wingspan, quite clearly visible, approached and hovered over us. When it was just a few meters above the waves, Captain Nemo's companion took aim and fired. The animal dropped, electrocuted, and its descent brought it within reach of our adroit hunter, who promptly took possession of it. It was an albatross of the finest species, a wonderful specimen of these open-sea fowl.

This incident did not interrupt our walk. For two hours we were sometimes led over plains of sand, sometimes over prairies of seaweed that were quite arduous to cross. In all honesty, I was dead tired by the time I spotted a hazy glow half a mile away, cutting through the darkness of the waters. It was the *Nautilus's* beacon. Within twenty minutes we would be on board, and there I could breathe easy again—because my tank's current air supply seemed to be quite low in oxygen. But I was reckoning without an encounter that slightly delayed our arrival.

I was lagging behind some twenty paces when I saw Captain Nemo suddenly come back toward me. With his powerful hands he sent me buckling to the ground, while his companion did the same to Conseil. At first I didn't know what to make of this sudden assault, but I was reassured to observe the captain lying motionless beside me.

I was stretched out on the seafloor directly beneath some bushes of algae, when I raised my head and spied two enormous masses hurtling by, throwing off phosphorescent glimmers.

My blood turned cold in my veins! I saw that we were under threat from a fearsome pair of sharks. They were blue sharks, dreadful man–eaters with enormous tails, dull, glassy stares, and phosphorescent matter oozing from holes around their snouts. They were like monstrous fireflies that could thoroughly pulverize a man in their iron jaws! I don't know if Conseil was busy with their classification, but as for me, I looked at their silver bellies, their fearsome mouths bristling with teeth, from a viewpoint less than scientific—more as a victim than as a professor of natural history.

Luckily these voracious animals have poor eyesight. They went by without noticing us, grazing us with their brownish fins; and miraculously, we escaped a danger greater than encountering a tiger deep in the jungle.

Half an hour later, guided by its electric trail, we reached the *Nautilus*. The outside door had been left open, and Captain Nemo closed it after we re-entered the first cell. Then he pressed a button. I heard pumps operating within the ship, I felt the water lowering around me, and in a few moments the cell was completely empty. The inside door opened, and we passed into the wardrobe.

There our diving suits were removed, not without difficulty; and utterly exhausted, faint from lack of food and rest, I repaired to my stateroom, full of wonder at this startling excursion on the bottom of the sea.

# CHAPTER 18

Four Thousand Leagues Under the Pacific

BY THE NEXT MORNING, November 18, I was fully recovered from my exhaustion of the day before, and I climbed onto the platform just as the *Nautilus's* chief officer was pronouncing his daily phrase. It then occurred to me that these words either referred to the state of the sea, or that they meant: "There's nothing in sight."

And in truth, the ocean was deserted. Not a sail on the horizon. The tips of Crespo Island had disappeared during the night. The sea, absorbing every color of the prism except its blue rays, reflected the latter in every direction and sported a wonderful indigo tint. The undulating waves regularly took on the appearance of watered silk with wide stripes.

I was marveling at this magnificent ocean view when Captain Nemo appeared. He didn't seem to notice my presence and began a series of astronomical observations. Then, his operations finished, he went and leaned his elbows on the beacon housing, his eyes straying over the surface of the ocean.

Meanwhile some twenty of the *Nautilus's* sailors—all energetic, well–built fellows—climbed onto the platform. They had come to pull up the nets left in our wake during the night. These seamen obviously belonged to different nationalities, although indications of European physical traits could be seen in them all. If I'm not mistaken, I recognized some Irishmen, some Frenchmen, a few Slavs, and a native of either Greece or Crete. Even so, these men were frugal of speech and used among themselves only that bizarre dialect whose origin I couldn't even guess. So I had to give up any notions of questioning them.

The nets were hauled on board. They were a breed of trawl resembling those used off the Normandy coast, huge pouches held half open by a floating pole and a chain laced through the lower meshes. Trailing in this way from these iron glove makers, the resulting receptacles scoured the ocean floor and collected every marine exhibit in their path. That day they gathered up some unusual specimens from these fish–filled waterways: anglerfish whose comical movements qualify them for the epithet "clowns," black Commerson anglers equipped with their antennas, undulating triggerfish encircled by little red bands, bloated puffers whose venom is extremely insidious, some olive–hued lampreys, snipefish covered with silver scales, cutlass fish whose electrocuting power equals that of the electric eel and the electric ray, scaly featherbacks with brown crosswise bands, greenish codfish, several varieties of goby, etc.; finally, some fish of larger proportions: a one–meter jack with a prominent head, several fine bonito from the genus Scomber decked out in the colors blue and silver, and three magnificent tuna whose high speeds couldn't save them from our trawl.

I estimate that this cast of the net brought in more than 1,000 pounds of fish. It was a fine catch but not surprising. In essence, these nets stayed in our wake for several hours, incarcerating an entire aquatic world in prisons made of thread. So we were never lacking in provisions of the highest quality, which the Nautilus's speed and the allure of its electric light could continually replenish.

These various exhibits from the sea were immediately lowered down the hatch in the direction of the storage lockers, some to be eaten fresh, others to be preserved.

After its fishing was finished and its air supply renewed, I thought the *Nautilus* would resume its underwater excursion, and I was getting ready to return to my stateroom, when Captain Nemo turned to me and said without further preamble:

"Look at this ocean, professor! Doesn't it have the actual gift of life? Doesn't it experience both anger and affection? Last evening it went to sleep just as we did, and there it is, waking up after a peaceful night!"

No hellos or good mornings for this gent! You would have thought this eccentric individual was simply continuing a conversation we'd already started!

"See!" he went on. "It's waking up under the sun's caresses! It's going to relive its daily existence! What a fascinating field of study lies in watching the play of its organism. It owns a pulse and arteries, it has spasms, and I side with the scholarly Commander Maury, who discovered that it has a circulation as real as the circulation of blood in animals."

I'm sure that Captain Nemo expected no replies from me, and it seemed pointless to pitch in with "Ah yes," "Exactly," or "How right you are!" Rather, he was simply talking to himself, with long pauses between sentences. He was meditating out loud.

"Yes," he said, "the ocean owns a genuine circulation, and to start it going, the Creator of All Things has only to increase its heat, salt, and microscopic animal life. In essence, heat creates the different densities that lead to currents and countercurrents. Evaporation, which is nil in the High Arctic regions and very active in equatorial zones, brings about a constant interchange of tropical and polar waters. What's more, I've detected those falling and rising currents that make up the ocean's true breathing. I've seen a molecule of salt water heat up at the surface, sink into the depths, reach maximum density at −2° centigrade, then cool off, grow lighter, and rise again. At the poles you'll see the consequences of this phenomenon, and through this law of farseeing nature, you'll understand why water can freeze only at the surface!"

As the captain was finishing his sentence, I said to myself: "The pole! Is this brazen individual claiming he'll take us even to that location?"

Meanwhile the captain fell silent and stared at the element he had studied so thoroughly and unceasingly. Then, going on:

"Salts," he said, "fill the sea in considerable quantities, professor, and if you removed all its dissolved saline content, you'd create a mass measuring 4,500,000 cubic leagues, which if it were spread all over the globe, would form a layer more than ten meters high. And don't think that the presence of these salts is due merely to some whim of nature. No. They make ocean water less open to evaporation and prevent winds from carrying off excessive amounts of steam, which, when condensing, would submerge the temperate zones. Salts play a leading role, the role of stabilizer for the general ecology of the globe!"

Captain Nemo stopped, straightened up, took a few steps along the platform, and returned to me:

"As for those billions of tiny animals," he went on, "those infusoria that live by the millions in one droplet of water, 800,000 of which are needed to weigh one milligram, their role is no less important. They absorb the marine salts, they assimilate the solid elements in the water, and since they create coral and madrepores, they're the true builders of limestone continents! And so, after they've finished depriving our water drop of its mineral nutrients, the droplet gets lighter, rises to the surface, there absorbs more salts left behind through evaporation, gets heavier, sinks again, and brings those tiny animals new elements to absorb. The outcome: a double current, rising and falling, constant movement, constant life! More intense than on land, more abundant, more infinite, such life blooms in every part of this ocean, an element fatal to man, they say, but vital to myriads of animals—and to me!"

When Captain Nemo spoke in this way, he was transfigured, and he filled me with extraordinary excitement.

"There," he added, "out there lies true existence! And I can imagine the founding of nautical towns, clusters of underwater households that, like the *Nautilus*, would return to the surface of the sea to breathe each morning, free towns if ever there were, independent cities! Then again, who knows whether some tyrant . . ."

Captain Nemo finished his sentence with a vehement gesture. Then, addressing me directly, as if to drive away an ugly thought:

"Professor Aronnax," he asked me, "do you know the depth of the ocean floor?"

"At least, Captain, I know what the major soundings tell us."

"Could you quote them to me, so I can double-check them as the need arises?"

"Here," I replied, "are a few of them that stick in my memory. If I'm not mistaken, an average depth of 8,200 meters was found in the north Atlantic, and 2,500 meters in the Mediterranean. The most remarkable soundings were taken in the south Atlantic near the 35th parallel, and they gave 12,000 meters, 14,091 meters, and 15,149 meters. All in all, it's estimated that if the sea bottom were made level, its average depth would be about seven kilometers."

"Well, professor," Captain Nemo replied, "we'll show you better than that, I hope. As for the average depth of this part of the Pacific, I'll inform you that it's a mere 4,000 meters."

This said, Captain Nemo headed to the hatch and disappeared down the ladder. I followed him and went back to the main lounge. The propeller was instantly set in motion, and the log gave our speed as twenty miles per hour.

Over the ensuing days and weeks, Captain Nemo was very frugal with his visits. I saw him only at rare intervals. His chief officer regularly fixed the positions I found reported on the chart, and in such a way that I could exactly plot the *Nautilus's* course.

Conseil and Land spent the long hours with me. Conseil had told his friend about the wonders of our undersea stroll, and the Canadian was sorry he hadn't gone along. But I hoped an opportunity would arise for a visit to the forests of Oceania.

Almost every day the panels in the lounge were open for some hours, and our eyes never tired of probing the mysteries of the underwater world.

The *Nautilus's* general heading was southeast, and it stayed at a depth between 100 and 150 meters. However, from Lord-knows-what whim, one day it did a diagonal dive by means of its slanting fins, reaching strata located 2,000 meters underwater. The thermometer indicated a temperature of 4.25° centigrade, which at this depth seemed to be a temperature common to all latitudes.

On November 26, at three o'clock in the morning, the *Nautilus* cleared the Tropic of Cancer at longitude 172°. On the 27th it passed in sight of the Hawaiian Islands, where the famous Captain Cook met his death on February 14, 1779. By then we had fared 4,860 leagues from our starting point. When I arrived on the platform that morning, I saw the Island of Hawaii two miles to leeward, the largest of the seven islands making up this group. I could clearly distinguish the tilled soil on its outskirts, the various mountain chains running parallel with its coastline, and its volcanoes, crowned by Mauna Kea, whose elevation is 5,000 meters above sea level. Among other specimens from these waterways, our nets brought up some peacock-tailed flabellarian coral, polyps flattened into stylish shapes and unique to this part of the ocean.

The *Nautilus* kept to its southeasterly heading. On December 1 it cut the equator at longitude 142°, and on the 4th of the same month, after a quick crossing marked by no incident, we raised the Marquesas Islands. Three miles off, in latitude 8° 57' south and longitude 139° 32' west, I spotted Martin Point on Nuku Hiva, chief member of this island group that belongs to France. I could make out only its wooded mountains on the horizon, because Captain Nemo hated to hug shore. There our nets brought up some fine fish samples: dolphinfish with azure fins, gold tails, and flesh that's unrivaled in the entire world, wrasse from the genus Hologymnosus that were nearly denuded of scales but exquisite in flavor, knifejaws with bony beaks, yellowish albacore that were as tasty as bonito, all fish worth classifying in the ship's pantry.

After leaving these delightful islands to the protection of the French flag, the *Nautilus* covered about 2,000 miles from December 4 to the 11th. Its navigating was marked by an encounter with an immense school of squid, unusual mollusks that are near neighbors of the cuttlefish. French fishermen give them the name "cuckoldfish," and they belong to the class Cephalopoda, family Dibranchiata, consisting of themselves together with cuttlefish and argonauts. The naturalists of antiquity made a special study of them, and these animals furnished many ribald figures of speech for soapbox orators in the Greek marketplace, as well as excellent dishes for the tables of rich citizens, if we're to believe Athenæus, a Greek physician predating Galen.

It was during the night of December 9–10 that the *Nautilus* encountered this army of distinctly nocturnal mollusks. They numbered in the millions. They were migrating from the temperate zones toward zones still warmer, following the itineraries of herring and sardines. We stared at them through our thick glass windows: they swam backward with tremendous speed, moving by means of their locomotive tubes, chasing fish and mollusks, eating the little ones, eaten by the big ones, and tossing in indescribable confusion the ten feet that nature has rooted in their heads like a hairpiece of pneumatic snakes.

Despite its speed, the *Nautilus* navigated for several hours in the midst of this school of animals, and its nets brought up an incalculable number, among which I recognized all nine species that Professor Orbigny has classified as native to the Pacific Ocean.

During this crossing, the sea continually lavished us with the most marvelous sights. Its variety was infinite. It changed its setting and decor for the mere pleasure of our eyes, and we were called upon not simply to contemplate the works of our Creator in the midst of the liquid element, but also to probe the ocean's most daunting mysteries.

During the day of December 11, I was busy reading in the main lounge. Ned Land and Conseil were observing the luminous waters through the gaping panels. The *Nautilus* was motionless. Its ballast tanks full, it was sitting at a depth of 1,000 meters in a comparatively unpopulated region of the ocean where only larger fish put in occasional appearances.

Just then I was studying a delightful book by Jean Macé, *The Servants of the Stomach*, and savoring its ingenious teachings, when Conseil interrupted my reading.

"Would master kindly come here for an instant?" he said to me in an odd voice.

"What is it, Conseil?"

"It's something that master should see."

I stood up, went, leaned on my elbows before the window, and I saw it.

In the broad electric daylight, an enormous black mass, quite motionless, hung suspended in the midst of the waters. I observed it carefully, trying to find out the nature of this gigantic cetacean. Then a sudden thought crossed my mind.

"A ship!" I exclaimed.

"Yes," the Canadian replied, "a disabled craft that's sinking straight down!"

Ned Land was not mistaken. We were in the presence of

a ship whose severed shrouds still hung from their clasps. Its hull looked in good condition, and it must have gone under only a few hours before. The stumps of three masts, chopped off two feet above the deck, indicated a flooding ship that had been forced to sacrifice its masting. But it had heeled sideways, filling completely, and it was listing to port even yet. A sorry sight, this carcass lost under the waves, but sorrier still was the sight on its deck, where, lashed with ropes to prevent their being washed overboard, some human corpses still lay! I counted four of them—four men, one still standing at the helm—then a woman, halfway out of a skylight on the afterdeck, holding a child in her arms. This woman was young. Under the brilliant lighting of the *Nautilus's* rays, I could make out her features, which the water hadn't yet decomposed. With a supreme effort, she had lifted her child above her head, and the poor little creature's arms were still twined around its mother's neck! The postures of the four seamen seemed ghastly to me, twisted from convulsive movements, as if making a last effort to break loose from the ropes that bound them to their ship. And the helmsman, standing alone, calmer, his face smooth and serious, his grizzled hair plastered to his brow, his hands clutching the wheel, seemed even yet to be guiding his wrecked three-master through the ocean depths!

What a scene! We stood dumbstruck, hearts pounding, before this shipwreck caught in the act, as if it had been photographed in its final moments, so to speak! And already I could see enormous sharks moving in, eyes ablaze, drawn by the lure of human flesh!

Meanwhile, turning, the *Nautilus* made a circle around the sinking ship, and for an instant I could read the board on its stern:

The Florida
Sunderland, England

# CHAPTER 19

## Vanikoro

THIS DREADFUL SIGHT was the first of a whole series of maritime catastrophes that the *Nautilus* would encounter on its run. When it plied more heavily traveled seas, we often saw wrecked hulls rotting in midwater, and farther down, cannons, shells, anchors, chains, and a thousand other iron objects rusting away.

Meanwhile, continuously swept along by the *Nautilus*, where we lived in near isolation, we raised the Tuamotu Islands on December 11, that old "dangerous group" associated with the French global navigator Commander Bougainville; it stretches from Ducie Island to Lazareff Island over an area of 500 leagues from the east–southeast to the west–northwest, between latitude 13° 30' and 23° 50' south, and between longitude 125° 30' and 151° 30' west. This island group covers a surface area of 370 square leagues, and it's made up of some sixty subgroups, among which we noted the Gambier group, which is a French protectorate. These islands are coral formations. Thanks to the work of polyps, a slow but steady upheaval will someday connect these islands to each other. Later on, this new island will be fused to its neighboring island groups, and a fifth continent will stretch from New Zealand and New Caledonia as far as the Marquesas Islands.

The day I expounded this theory to Captain Nemo, he answered me coldly:

"The earth doesn't need new continents, but new men!"

Sailors' luck led the *Nautilus* straight to Reao Island, one of the most unusual in this group, which was discovered in 1822 by Captain Bell aboard the Minerva. So I was able to study the madreporic process that has created the islands in this ocean.

Madrepores, which one must guard against confusing with precious coral, clothe their tissue in a limestone crust, and their variations in structure have led my famous mentor Professor Milne–Edwards to classify them into five divisions. The tiny microscopic animals that secrete this polypary live by the billions in the depths of their cells. Their limestone deposits build up into rocks, reefs, islets, islands. In some places, they form atolls, a circular ring surrounding a lagoon or small inner lake that gaps place in contact with the sea. Elsewhere, they take the shape of barrier reefs, such as those that exist along the coasts of New Caledonia and several of the Tuamotu Islands. In still other localities, such as Réunion Island and the island of Mauritius, they build fringing reefs, high, straight walls next to which the ocean's depth is considerable.

While cruising along only a few cable lengths from the underpinning of Reao Island, I marveled at the gigantic piece of work accomplished by these microscopic laborers. These walls were the express achievements of madrepores known by the names fire coral, finger coral, star coral, and stony coral. These polyps grow exclusively in the agitated strata at the surface of the sea, and so it's in the upper reaches that they begin these substructures, which sink little by little together with the secreted rubble binding them. This, at least, is the theory of Mr. Charles Darwin, who thus explains the formation of atolls—a theory superior, in my view, to the one that says these madreporic edifices sit on the summits of mountains or volcanoes submerged a few feet below sea level.

I could observe these strange walls quite closely: our sounding lines indicated that they dropped perpendicularly for more than 300 meters, and our electric beams made the bright limestone positively sparkle.

In reply to a question Conseil asked me about the growth rate of these colossal barriers, I thoroughly amazed him by saying that scientists put it at an eighth of an inch per biennium.

"Therefore," he said to me, "to build these walls, it took . . . ?"

"192,000 years, my gallant Conseil, which significantly extends the biblical Days of Creation. What's more, the formation of coal—in other words, the petrification of forests swallowed by floods—and the cooling of basaltic rocks likewise call for a much longer period of time. I might add that those 'days' in the Bible must represent whole epochs and not literally the lapse of time between two sunrises, because according to the Bible itself, the sun doesn't date from the first day of Creation."

When the *Nautilus* returned to the surface of the ocean, I could take in Reao Island over its whole flat, wooded expanse. Obviously its madreporic rocks had been made fertile by tornadoes and thunderstorms. One day, carried off by a hurricane from neighboring shores, some seed fell onto these limestone beds, mixing with decomposed particles of fish and marine plants to form vegetable humus. Propelled by the waves, a coconut arrived on this new coast. Its germ took root. Its tree grew tall, catching steam off the water. A brook was born. Little by little, vegetation spread. Tiny animals—worms, insects—rode ashore on tree trunks snatched from islands to windward. Turtles came to lay their eggs. Birds nested in the young trees. In this way animal life developed, and drawn by the greenery and fertile soil, man appeared. And that's how these islands were formed, the immense achievement of microscopic animals.

Near evening Reao Island melted into the distance, and the *Nautilus* noticeably changed course. After touching the Tropic of Capricorn at longitude 135°, it headed west–northwest, going back up the whole intertropical zone. Although the summer sun lavished its rays on us, we never suffered from the heat, because thirty or forty meters underwater, the temperature didn't go over 10° to 12° centigrade.

By December 15 we had left the alluring Society Islands in the west, likewise elegant Tahiti, queen of the Pacific. In the morning I spotted this island's lofty summits a few miles to leeward. Its waters supplied excellent fish for the tables on board: mackerel, bonito, albacore, and a few varieties of that sea serpent named the moray eel.

The *Nautilus* had cleared 8,100 miles. We logged 9,720 miles when we passed between the Tonga Islands, where crews from the Argo, Port–au–Prince, and Duke of Portland had perished, and the island group of Samoa, scene of the slaying of Captain de Langle, friend of that long–lost navigator, the Count de La Pérouse. Then we raised the Fiji Islands, where savages slaughtered sailors from the *Union*, as well as Captain Bureau, commander of the *Darling Josephine* out of Nantes, France.

Extending over an expanse of 100 leagues north to south, and over 90 leagues east to west, this island group lies between latitude 2° and 6° south, and between longitude 174° and 179° west. It consists of a number of islands, islets, and reefs, among which we noted the islands of Viti Levu, Vanua Levu, and Kadavu.

It was the Dutch navigator Tasman who discovered this group in 1643, the same year the Italian physicist Torricelli invented the barometer and King Louis XIV ascended the French throne. I'll let the reader decide which of these deeds was more beneficial to humanity. Coming later, Captain Cook in 1774, Rear Admiral d'Entrecasteaux in 1793, and finally Captain Dumont d'Urville in 1827, untangled the whole chaotic geography of this island group. The *Nautilus* drew near Wailea Bay, an unlucky place for England's Captain Dillon, who was the first to shed light on the longstanding mystery

surrounding the disappearance of ships under the Count de
La Pérouse.

This bay, repeatedly dredged, furnished a huge supply
of excellent oysters. As the Roman playwright Seneca
recommended, we opened them right at our table, then stuffed
ourselves. These mollusks belonged to the species known by
name as Ostrea lamellosa, whose members are quite common
off Corsica. This Wailea oysterbank must have been extensive,
and for certain, if they hadn't been controlled by numerous
natural checks, these clusters of shellfish would have ended
up jam–packing the bay, since as many as 2,000,000 eggs have
been counted in a single individual.

And if Mr. Ned Land did not repent of his gluttony at our
oyster fest, it's because oysters are the only dish that never
causes indigestion. In fact, it takes no less than sixteen dozen
of these headless mollusks to supply the 315 grams that satisfy
one man's minimum daily requirement for nitrogen.

On December 25 the Nautilus navigated amid the island
group of the New Hebrides, which the Portuguese seafarer
Queirós discovered in 1606, which Commander Bougainville
explored in 1768, and to which Captain Cook gave its current
name in 1773. This group is chiefly made up of nine large islands
and forms a 120–league strip from the north–northwest to the
south–southeast, lying between latitude 2° and 15° south, and
between longitude 164° and 168°. At the moment of our noon
sights, we passed fairly close to the island of Aurou, which
looked to me like a mass of green woods crowned by a peak
of great height.

That day it was yuletide, and it struck me that Ned Land
badly missed celebrating "Christmas," that genuine family
holiday where Protestants are such zealots.

I hadn't seen Captain Nemo for over a week, when, on the
morning of the 27th, he entered the main lounge, as usual
acting as if he'd been gone for just five minutes. I was busy

tracing the *Nautilus's* course on the world map. The captain approached, placed a finger over a position on the chart, and pronounced just one word:

"Vanikoro."

This name was magic! It was the name of those islets where vessels under the Count de La Pérouse had miscarried. I straightened suddenly.

"The *Nautilus* is bringing us to Vanikoro?" I asked.

"Yes, professor," the captain replied.

"And I'll be able to visit those famous islands where the *Compass* and the *Astrolabe* came to grief?"

"If you like, professor."

"When will we reach Vanikoro?"

"We already have, professor."

Followed by Captain Nemo, I climbed onto the platform, and from there my eyes eagerly scanned the horizon.

In the northeast there emerged two volcanic islands of unequal size, surrounded by a coral reef whose circuit measured forty miles. We were facing the island of Vanikoro proper, to which Captain Dumont d'Urville had given the name "Island of the Search"; we lay right in front of the little harbor of Vana, located in latitude 16° 4' south and longitude 164° 32' east. Its shores seemed covered with greenery from its beaches to its summits inland, crowned by Mt. Kapogo, which is 476 fathoms high.

After clearing the outer belt of rocks via a narrow passageway, the *Nautilus* lay inside the breakers where the sea had a depth of thirty to forty fathoms. Under the green shade of some tropical evergreens, I spotted a few savages who looked extremely startled at our approach. In this long, blackish object advancing flush with the water, didn't they see some fearsome cetacean that they were obliged to view with distrust?

Just then Captain Nemo asked me what I knew about the

shipwreck of the Count de La Pérouse.

"What everybody knows, captain," I answered him.

"And could you kindly tell me what everybody knows?" he asked me in a gently ironic tone.

"Very easily."

I related to him what the final deeds of Captain Dumont d'Urville had brought to light, deeds described here in this heavily condensed summary of the whole matter.

In 1785 the Count de La Pérouse and his subordinate, Captain de Langle, were sent by King Louis XVI of France on a voyage to circumnavigate the globe. They boarded two sloops of war, the *Compass* and the *Astrolabe*, which were never seen again.

In 1791, justly concerned about the fate of these two sloops of war, the French government fitted out two large cargo boats, the *Search* and the *Hope*, which left Brest on September 28 under orders from Rear Admiral Bruni d'Entrecasteaux. Two months later, testimony from a certain Commander Bowen, aboard the *Albemarle*, alleged that rubble from shipwrecked vessels had been seen on the coast of New Georgia. But d'Entrecasteaux was unaware of this news—which seemed a bit dubious anyhow—and headed toward the Admiralty Islands, which had been named in a report by one Captain Hunter as the site of the Count de La Pérouse's shipwreck.

They looked in vain. The *Hope* and the *Search* passed right by Vanikoro without stopping there; and overall, this voyage was plagued by misfortune, ultimately costing the lives of Rear Admiral d'Entrecasteaux, two of his subordinate officers, and several seamen from his crew.

It was an old hand at the Pacific, the English adventurer Captain Peter Dillon, who was the first to pick up the trail left by castaways from the wrecked vessels. On May 15, 1824, his ship, the *St. Patrick*, passed by Tikopia Island, one of the New Hebrides. There a native boatman pulled alongside in a dugout canoe and sold Dillon a silver sword hilt bearing the imprint of characters engraved with a cutting tool known as a burin. Furthermore, this native boatman claimed that during a stay in Vanikoro six years earlier, he had seen two Europeans belonging to ships that had run aground on the island's reefs many years before.

Dillon guessed that the ships at issue were those under the Count de La Pérouse, ships whose disappearance had shaken the entire world. He tried to reach Vanikoro, where, according to the native boatman, a good deal of rubble from the shipwreck could still be found, but winds and currents prevented his doing so.

Dillon returned to Calcutta. There he was able to interest the Asiatic Society and the East India Company in his discovery. A ship named after the *Search* was placed at his disposal, and he departed on January 23, 1827, accompanied by a French deputy.

This new *Search*, after putting in at several stops over the Pacific, dropped anchor before Vanikoro on July 7, 1827, in the same harbor of Vana where the *Nautilus* was currently floating.

There Dillon collected many relics of the shipwreck: iron utensils, anchors, eyelets from pulleys, swivel guns, an eighteen–pound shell, the remains of some astronomical instruments, a piece of sternrail, and a bronze bell bearing the inscription "Made by Bazin," the foundry mark at Brest Arsenal around 1785. There could no longer be any doubt.

Finishing his investigations, Dillon stayed at the site of the casualty until the month of October. Then he left Vanikoro, headed toward New Zealand, dropped anchor at Calcutta on April 7, 1828, and returned to France, where he received a very cordial welcome from King Charles X.

But just then the renowned French explorer Captain Dumont d'Urville, unaware of Dillon's activities, had already set sail to search elsewhere for the site of the shipwreck. In essence, a whaling vessel had reported that some medals and a Cross of St. Louis had been found in the hands of savages in the Louisiade Islands and New Caledonia.

So Captain Dumont d'Urville had put to sea in command of a vessel named after the *Astrolabe*, and just two months after Dillon had left Vanikoro, Dumont d'Urville dropped anchor before Hobart. There he heard about Dillon's findings, and he further learned that a certain James Hobbs, chief officer on the *Union* out of Calcutta, had put to shore on an island located in latitude 8° 18' south and longitude 156° 30' east, and had noted the natives of those waterways making use of iron bars and red fabrics.

Pretty perplexed, Dumont d'Urville didn't know if he should give credence to these reports, which had been carried in some of the less reliable newspapers; nevertheless, he decided to start on Dillon's trail.

On February 10, 1828, the new *Astrolabe* hove before Tikopia Island, took on a guide and interpreter in the person of a deserter who had settled there, plied a course toward Vanikoro, raised it on February 12, sailed along its reefs until the 14th, and only on the 20th dropped anchor inside its barrier in the harbor of Vana.

On the 23rd, several officers circled the island and brought back some rubble of little importance. The natives, adopting a system of denial and evasion, refused to guide them to the site of the casualty. This rather shady conduct aroused the suspicion that the natives had mistreated the castaways; and in truth, the natives seemed afraid that Dumont d'Urville had come to avenge the Count de La Pérouse and his unfortunate companions.

But on the 26th, appeased with gifts and seeing that they didn't need to fear any reprisals, the natives led the chief officer, Mr. Jacquinot, to the site of the shipwreck.

At this location, in three or four fathoms of water between

the Paeu and Vana reefs, there lay some anchors, cannons, and ingots of iron and lead, all caked with limestone concretions. A launch and whaleboat from the new *Astrolabe* were steered to this locality, and after going to exhausting lengths, their crews managed to dredge up an anchor weighing 1,800 pounds, a cast–iron eight–pounder cannon, a lead ingot, and two copper swivel guns.

Questioning the natives, Captain Dumont d'Urville also learned that after La Pérouse's two ships had miscarried on the island's reefs, the count had built a smaller craft, only to go off and miscarry a second time. Where? Nobody knew.

The commander of the new *Astrolabe* then had a monument erected under a tuft of mangrove, in memory of the famous navigator and his companions. It was a simple quadrangular pyramid, set on a coral base, with no ironwork to tempt the natives' avarice.

Then Dumont d'Urville tried to depart; but his crews were run down from the fevers raging on these unsanitary shores, and quite ill himself, he was unable to weigh anchor until March 17.

Meanwhile, fearing that Dumont d'Urville wasn't abreast of Dillon's activities, the French government sent a sloop of war to Vanikoro, the Bayonnaise under Commander Legoarant de Tromelin, who had been stationed on the American west coast. Dropping anchor before Vanikoro a few months after the new *Astrolabe*'s departure, the Bayonnaise didn't find any additional evidence but verified that the savages hadn't disturbed the memorial honoring the Count de La Pérouse.

This is the substance of the account I gave Captain Nemo.

"So," he said to me, "the castaways built a third ship on Vanikoro Island, and to this day, nobody knows where it went and perished?"

"Nobody knows."

Captain Nemo didn't reply but signaled me to follow him

180 TWENTY THOUSAND LEAGUES UNDER THE SEA

to the main lounge. The *Nautilus* sank a few meters beneath the waves, and the panels opened.

I rushed to the window and saw crusts of coral: fungus coral, siphonula coral, alcyon coral, sea anemone from the genus Caryophylia, plus myriads of charming fish including greenfish, damselfish, sweepers, snappers, and squirrelfish; underneath this coral covering I detected some rubble the old dredges hadn't been able to tear free—iron stirrups, anchors, cannons, shells, tackle from a capstan, a stempost, all objects hailing from the wrecked ships and now carpeted in moving flowers.

And as I stared at this desolate wreckage, Captain Nemo told me in a solemn voice:

"Commander La Pérouse set out on December 7, 1785, with his ships, the *Compass* and the *Astrolabe*. He dropped anchor first at Botany Bay, visited the Tonga Islands and New Caledonia, headed toward the Santa Cruz Islands, and put in at Nomuka, one of the islands in the Ha'apai group. Then his ships arrived at the unknown reefs of Vanikoro. Traveling in the lead, the *Compass* ran afoul of breakers on the southerly coast. The *Astrolabe* went to its rescue and also ran aground. The first ship was destroyed almost immediately. The second, stranded to leeward, held up for some days. The natives gave the castaways a fair enough welcome. The latter took up residence on the island and built a smaller craft with rubble from the two large ones. A few seamen stayed voluntarily in Vanikoro. The others, weak and ailing, set sail with the Count de La Pérouse. They headed to the Solomon Islands, and they perished with all hands on the westerly coast of the chief island in that group, between Cape Deception and Cape Satisfaction!"

"And how do you know all this?" I exclaimed.

"Here's what I found at the very site of that final shipwreck!"

Captain Nemo showed me a tin box, stamped with the coat of arms of France and all corroded by salt water. He opened it and I saw a bundle of papers, yellowed but still legible.

They were the actual military orders given by France's Minister of the Navy to Commander La Pérouse, with notes along the margin in the handwriting of King Louis XVI!

"Ah, what a splendid death for a seaman!" Captain Nemo then said. "A coral grave is a tranquil grave, and may Heaven grant that my companions and I rest in no other!"

# CHAPTER 20

## The Torres Strait

DURING THE NIGHT of December 27–28, the *Nautilus* left the waterways of Vanikoro behind with extraordinary speed. Its heading was southwesterly, and in three days it had cleared the 750 leagues that separated La Pérouse's islands from the southeastern tip of Papua.

On January 1, 1868, bright and early, Conseil joined me on the platform.

"Will master," the gallant lad said to me, "allow me to wish him a happy new year?"

"Good heavens, Conseil, it's just like old times in my office at the Botanical Gardens in Paris! I accept your kind wishes and I thank you for them. Only, I'd like to know what you mean by a 'happy year' under the circumstances in which we're placed. Is it a year that will bring our imprisonment to an end, or a year that will see this strange voyage continue?"

"Ye gods," Conseil replied, "I hardly know what to tell master. We're certainly seeing some unusual things, and for two months we've had no time for boredom. The latest wonder is always the most astonishing, and if this progression keeps up, I can't imagine what its climax will be. In my opinion, we'll never again have such an opportunity."

"Never, Conseil."

"Besides, Mr. Nemo really lives up to his Latin name, since he couldn't be less in the way if he didn't exist."

"True enough, Conseil."

"Therefore, with all due respect to master, I think a 'happy year' would be a year that lets us see everything—"

"Everything, Conseil? No year could be that long. But what does Ned Land think about all this?"

"Ned Land's thoughts are exactly the opposite of mine," Conseil replied. "He has a practical mind and a demanding stomach. He's tired of staring at fish and eating them day in and day out. This shortage of wine, bread, and meat isn't suitable for an upstanding Anglo–Saxon, a man accustomed to beefsteak and unfazed by regular doses of brandy or gin!"

"For my part, Conseil, that doesn't bother me in the least, and I've adjusted very nicely to the diet on board."

"So have I," Conseil replied. "Accordingly, I think as much about staying as Mr. Land about making his escape. Thus, if this new year isn't a happy one for me, it will be for him, and vice versa. No matter what happens, one of us will be pleased. So, in conclusion, I wish master to have whatever his heart desires."

"Thank you, Conseil. Only I must ask you to postpone the question of new year's gifts, and temporarily accept a hearty handshake in their place. That's all I have on me."

"Master has never been more generous," Conseil replied.

And with that, the gallant lad went away.

By January 2 we had fared 11,340 miles, hence 5,250 leagues, from our starting point in the seas of Japan. Before the Nautilus's spur there stretched the dangerous waterways of the Coral Sea, off the northeast coast of Australia. Our boat cruised along a few miles away from that daunting shoal where Captain Cook's ships wellnigh miscarried on June 10, 1770. The craft that Cook was aboard charged into some coral rock, and if his vessel didn't go down, it was thanks to the circumstance that a piece of coral broke off in the collision and plugged the very hole it had made in the hull.

I would have been deeply interested in visiting this long,

360–league reef, against which the ever–surging sea broke with the fearsome intensity of thunderclaps. But just then the *Nautilus's* slanting fins took us to great depths, and I could see nothing of those high coral walls. I had to rest content with the various specimens of fish brought up by our nets. Among others I noted some long–finned albacore, a species in the genus Scomber, as big as tuna, bluish on the flanks, and streaked with crosswise stripes that disappear when the animal dies. These fish followed us in schools and supplied our table with very dainty flesh. We also caught a large number of yellow–green gilthead, half a decimeter long and tasting like dorado, plus some flying gurnards, authentic underwater swallows that, on dark nights, alternately streak air and water with their phosphorescent glimmers. Among mollusks and zoophytes, I found in our trawl's meshes various species of alcyonarian coral, sea urchins, hammer shells, spurred–star shells, wentletrap snails, horn shells, glass snails. The local flora was represented by fine floating algae: sea tangle, and kelp from the genus Macrocystis, saturated with the mucilage their pores perspire, from which I selected a wonderful Nemastoma geliniaroidea, classifying it with the natural curiosities in the museum.

On January 4, two days after crossing the Coral Sea, we raised the coast of Papua. On this occasion Captain Nemo told me that he intended to reach the Indian Ocean via the Torres Strait. This was the extent of his remarks. Ned saw with pleasure that this course would bring us, once again, closer to European seas.

The Torres Strait is regarded as no less dangerous for its bristling reefs than for the savage inhabitants of its coasts. It separates Queensland from the huge island of Papua, also called New Guinea.

Papua is 400 leagues long by 130 leagues wide, with a surface area of 40,000 geographic leagues. It's located between latitude 0° 19' and 10° 2' south, and between longitude 128° 23' and 146° 15'. At noon, while the chief officer was taking the sun's altitude, I spotted the summits of the Arfak Mountains, rising in terraces and ending in sharp peaks.

Discovered in 1511 by the Portuguese Francisco Serrano, these shores were successively visited by Don Jorge de Meneses in 1526, by Juan de Grijalva in 1527, by the Spanish general Alvaro de Saavedra in 1528, by Inigo Ortiz in 1545, by the Dutchman Schouten in 1616, by Nicolas Sruick in 1753, by Tasman, Dampier, Fumel, Carteret, Edwards, Bougainville, Cook, McClure, and Thomas Forrest, by Rear Admiral d'Entrecasteaux in 1792, by Louis–Isidore Duperrey in 1823, and by Captain Dumont d'Urville in 1827. "It's the heartland of the blacks who occupy all Malaysia," Mr. de Rienzi has said; and I hadn't the foggiest inkling that sailors' luck was about to bring me face to face with these daunting Andaman aborigines.

So the *Nautilus* hove before the entrance to the world's most dangerous strait, a passageway that even the boldest navigators hesitated to clear: the strait that Luis Vaez de Torres faced on returning from the South Seas in Melanesia, the strait in which sloops of war under Captain Dumont d'Urville ran aground in 1840 and nearly miscarried with all hands. And even the *Nautilus*, rising superior to every danger in the sea, was about to become intimate with its coral reefs.

The Torres Strait is about thirty–four leagues wide, but it's obstructed by an incalculable number of islands, islets, breakers, and rocks that make it nearly impossible to navigate. Consequently, Captain Nemo took every desired precaution in crossing it. Floating flush with the water, the *Nautilus* moved ahead at a moderate pace. Like a cetacean's tail, its propeller churned the waves slowly.

Taking advantage of this situation, my two companions and I found seats on the ever–deserted platform. In front of us stood the pilothouse, and unless I'm extremely mistaken,

Captain Nemo must have been inside, steering his *Nautilus* himself.

Under my eyes I had the excellent charts of the Torres Strait that had been surveyed and drawn up by the hydrographic engineer Vincendon Dumoulin and Sublieutenant (now Admiral) Coupvent-Desbois, who were part of Dumont d'Urville's general staff during his final voyage to circumnavigate the globe. These, along with the efforts of Captain King, are the best charts for untangling the snarl of this narrow passageway, and I consulted them with scrupulous care.

Around the *Nautilus* the sea was boiling furiously. A stream of waves, bearing from southeast to northwest at a speed of two and a half miles per hour, broke over heads of coral emerging here and there.

"That's one rough sea!" Ned Land told me.

"Abominable indeed," I replied, "and hardly suitable for a craft like the *Nautilus*."

"That damned captain," the Canadian went on, "must really be sure of his course, because if these clumps of coral so much as brush us, they'll rip our hull into a thousand pieces!"

The situation was indeed dangerous, but as if by magic, the *Nautilus* seemed to glide right down the middle of these rampaging reefs. It didn't follow the exact course of the *Zealous* and the new *Astrolabe*, which had proved so ill-fated for Captain Dumont d'Urville. It went more to the north, hugged the Murray Islands, and returned to the southwest near Cumberland Passage. I thought it was about to charge wholeheartedly into this opening, but it went up to the northwest, through a large number of little-known islands and islets, and steered toward Tound Island and the Bad Channel.

I was already wondering if Captain Nemo, rash to the point of sheer insanity, wanted his ship to tackle the narrows where Dumont d'Urville's two sloops of war had gone aground, when he changed direction a second time and cut straight to the west, heading toward Gueboroa Island.

By then it was three o'clock in the afternoon. The current was slacking off, it was almost full tide. The *Nautilus* drew near this island, which I can see to this day with its remarkable fringe of screw pines. We hugged it from less than two miles out.

A sudden jolt threw me down. The *Nautilus* had just struck a reef, and it remained motionless, listing slightly to port.

When I stood up, I saw Captain Nemo and his chief officer on the platform. They were examining the ship's circumstances, exchanging a few words in their incomprehensible dialect.

Here is what those circumstances entailed. Two miles to starboard lay Gueboroa Island, its coastline curving north to west like an immense arm. To the south and east, heads of coral were already on display, left uncovered by the ebbing waters. We had run aground at full tide and in one of those seas whose tides are moderate, an inconvenient state of affairs for floating the *Nautilus* off. However, the ship hadn't suffered in any way, so solidly joined was its hull. But although it could neither sink nor split open, it was in serious danger of being permanently attached to these reefs, and that would have been the finish of Captain Nemo's submersible.

I was mulling this over when the captain approached, cool and calm, forever in control of himself, looking neither alarmed nor annoyed.

"An accident?" I said to him.

"No, an incident," he answered me.

"But an incident," I replied, "that may oblige you to become a resident again of these shores you avoid!"

Captain Nemo gave me an odd look and gestured no. Which told me pretty clearly that nothing would ever force him to set foot on a land mass again. Then he said:

"No, Professor Aronnax, the *Nautilus* isn't consigned to perdition. It will still carry you through the midst of the ocean's wonders. Our voyage is just beginning, and I've no desire to deprive myself so soon of the pleasure of your company."

"Even so, Captain Nemo," I went on, ignoring his ironic turn of phrase, "the *Nautilus* has run aground at a moment when the sea is full. Now then, the tides aren't strong in the Pacific, and if you can't unballast the *Nautilus*, which seems impossible to me, I don't see how it will float off."

"You're right, professor, the Pacific tides aren't strong," Captain Nemo replied. "But in the Torres Strait, one still finds a meter-and-a-half difference in level between high and low seas. Today is January 4, and in five days the moon will be full. Now then, I'll be quite astonished if that good-natured satellite doesn't sufficiently raise these masses of water and do me a favor for which I'll be forever grateful."

This said, Captain Nemo went below again to the *Nautilus's* interior, followed by his chief officer. As for our craft, it no longer stirred, staying as motionless as if these coral polyps had already walled it in with their indestructible cement.

"Well, sir?" Ned Land said to me, coming up after the captain's departure.

"Well, Ned my friend, we'll serenely wait for the tide on the 9th, because it seems the moon will have the good nature to float us away!"

"As simple as that?"

"As simple as that."

"So our captain isn't going to drop his anchors, put his engines on the chains, and do anything to haul us off?"

"Since the tide will be sufficient," Conseil replied simply.

The Canadian stared at Conseil, then he shrugged his shoulders. The seaman in him was talking now.

"Sir," he answered, "you can trust me when I say this hunk of iron will never navigate again, on the seas or under them. It's only fit to be sold for its weight. So I think it's time we gave Captain Nemo the slip."

"Ned my friend," I replied, "unlike you, I haven't given up on our valiant *Nautilus*, and in four days we'll know where we stand on these Pacific tides. Besides, an escape attempt might be timely if we were in sight of the coasts of England or Provence, but in the waterways of Papua it's another story. And we'll always have that as a last resort if the *Nautilus* doesn't right itself, which I'd regard as a real calamity."

"But couldn't we at least get the lay of the land?" Ned went on. "Here's an island. On this island there are trees. Under those trees land animals loaded with cutlets and roast beef, which I'd be happy to sink my teeth into."

"In this instance our friend Ned is right," Conseil said, "and I side with his views. Couldn't master persuade his friend Captain Nemo to send the three of us ashore, if only so our feet don't lose the knack of treading on the solid parts of our planet?"

"I can ask him," I replied, "but he'll refuse."

"Let master take the risk," Conseil said, "and we'll know where we stand on the captain's affability."

Much to my surprise, Captain Nemo gave me the permission I asked for, and he did so with grace and alacrity, not even exacting my promise to return on board. But fleeing across the New Guinea territories would be extremely dangerous, and I wouldn't have advised Ned Land to try it. Better to be prisoners aboard the *Nautilus* than to fall into the hands of Papuan natives.

The skiff was put at our disposal for the next morning. I hardly needed to ask whether Captain Nemo would be coming along. I likewise assumed that no crewmen would be assigned to us, that Ned Land would be in sole charge of piloting the longboat. Besides, the shore lay no more than two miles off, and it would be child's play for the Canadian to guide that nimble skiff through those rows of reefs so ill-fated for big ships.

The next day, January 5, after its deck paneling was opened, the skiff was wrenched from its socket and launched to sea from the top of the platform. Two men were sufficient for this operation. The oars were inside the longboat and we had only to take our seats.

At eight o'clock, armed with rifles and axes, we pulled clear of the *Nautilus*. The sea was fairly calm. A mild breeze blew from shore. In place by the oars, Conseil and I rowed vigorously, and Ned steered us into the narrow lanes between the breakers. The skiff handled easily and sped swiftly.

Ned Land couldn't conceal his glee. He was a prisoner escaping from prison and never dreaming he would need to re-enter it.

"Meat!" he kept repeating. "Now we'll eat red meat! Actual game! A real mess call, by thunder! I'm not saying fish aren't good for you, but we mustn't overdo 'em, and a slice of fresh venison grilled over live coals will be a nice change from our standard fare."

"You glutton," Conseil replied, "you're making my mouth water!"

"It remains to be seen," I said, "whether these forests do contain game, and if the types of game aren't of such size that they can hunt the hunter."

"Fine, Professor Aronnax!" replied the Canadian, whose teeth seemed to be as honed as the edge of an ax. "But if there's no other quadruped on this island, I'll eat tiger—tiger sirloin."

"Our friend Ned grows disturbing," Conseil replied.

"Whatever it is," Ned Land went on, "any animal having four feet without feathers, or two feet with feathers, will be greeted by my very own one-gun salute."

"Oh good!" I replied. "The reckless Mr. Land is at it again!"

"Don't worry, Professor Aronnax, just keep rowing!" the Canadian replied. "I only need twenty-five minutes to serve you one of my own special creations."

By 8:30 the *Nautilus's* skiff had just run gently aground on a sandy strand, after successfully clearing the ring of coral that surrounds Gueboroa Island.

# CHAPTER 21

## Some Days Ashore

STEPPING ASHORE had an exhilarating effect on me. Ned Land tested the soil with his foot, as if he were laying claim to it. Yet it had been only two months since we had become, as Captain Nemo expressed it, "passengers on the *Nautilus*," in other words, the literal prisoners of its commander.

In a few minutes we were a gunshot away from the coast. The soil was almost entirely madreporic, but certain dry stream beds were strewn with granite rubble, proving that this island was of primordial origin. The entire horizon was hidden behind a curtain of wonderful forests. Enormous trees, sometimes as high as 200 feet, were linked to each other by garlands of tropical creepers, genuine natural hammocks that swayed in a mild breeze. There were mimosas, banyan trees, beefwood, teakwood, hibiscus, screw pines, palm trees, all mingling in wild profusion; and beneath the shade of their green canopies, at the feet of their gigantic trunks, there grew orchids, leguminous plants, and ferns.

Meanwhile, ignoring all these fine specimens of Papuan flora, the Canadian passed up the decorative in favor of the functional. He spotted a coconut palm, beat down some of its fruit, broke them open, and we drank their milk and ate their meat with a pleasure that was a protest against our standard fare on the *Nautilus*.

"Excellent!" Ned Land said.

"Exquisite!" Conseil replied.

"And I don't think," the Canadian said, "that your Nemo would object to us stashing a cargo of coconuts aboard his vessel?"

"I imagine not," I replied, "but he won't want to sample them."

"Too bad for him!" Conseil said.

"And plenty good for us!" Ned Land shot back. "There'll be more left over!"

"A word of caution, Mr. Land," I told the harpooner, who was about to ravage another coconut palm. "Coconuts are admirable things, but before we stuff the skiff with them, it would be wise to find out whether this island offers other substances just as useful. Some fresh vegetables would be well received in the *Nautilus's* pantry."

"Master is right," Conseil replied, "and I propose that we set aside three places in our longboat: one for fruit, another for vegetables, and a third for venison, of which I still haven't glimpsed the tiniest specimen."

"Don't give up so easily, Conseil," the Canadian replied.

"So let's continue our excursion," I went on, "but keep a sharp lookout. This island seems uninhabited, but it still might harbor certain individuals who aren't so finicky about the sort of game they eat!"

"Hee hee!" Ned put in, with a meaningful movement of his jaws.

"Ned! Oh horrors!" Conseil exclaimed.

"Ye gods," the Canadian shot back, "I'm starting to appreciate the charms of cannibalism!"

"Ned, Ned! Don't say that!" Conseil answered. "You a cannibal? Why, I'll no longer be safe next to you, I who share your cabin! Does this mean I'll wake up half devoured one fine day?"

"I'm awfully fond of you, Conseil my friend, but not enough to eat you when there's better food around."

"Then I daren't delay," Conseil replied. "The hunt is on! We absolutely must bag some game to placate this man–eater, or one of these mornings master won't find enough pieces of his manservant to serve him."

While exchanging this chitchat, we entered beneath the dark canopies of the forest, and for two hours we explored it in every direction.

We couldn't have been luckier in our search for edible vegetation, and some of the most useful produce in the tropical zones supplied us with a valuable foodstuff missing on board.

I mean the breadfruit tree, which is quite abundant on Gueboroa Island, and there I chiefly noted the seedless variety that in Malaysia is called "rima."

This tree is distinguished from other trees by a straight trunk forty feet high. To the naturalist's eye, its gracefully rounded crown, formed of big multilobed leaves, was enough to denote the artocarpus that has been so successfully transplanted to the Mascarene Islands east of

Madagascar. From its mass of greenery, huge globular fruit stood out, a decimeter wide and furnished on the outside with creases that assumed a hexangular pattern. It's a handy plant that nature gives to regions lacking in wheat; without needing to be cultivated, it bears fruit eight months out of the year.

Ned Land was on familiar terms with this fruit. He had already eaten it on his many voyages and knew how to cook its edible substance. So the very sight of it aroused his appetite, and he couldn't control himself.

"Sir," he told me, "I'll die if I don't sample a little breadfruit pasta!"

"Sample some, Ned my friend, sample all you like. We're here to conduct experiments, let's conduct them."

"It won't take a minute," the Canadian replied.

Equipped with a magnifying glass, he lit a fire of deadwood that was soon crackling merrily. Meanwhile Conseil and I selected the finest artocarpus fruit. Some still weren't ripe enough, and their thick skins covered white, slightly fibrous pulps. But a great many others were yellowish and gelatinous, just begging to be picked.

This fruit contained no pits. Conseil brought a dozen of them to Ned Land, who cut them into thick slices and placed them over a fire of live coals, all the while repeating:

"You'll see, sir, how tasty this bread is!"

"Especially since we've gone without baked goods for so long," Conseil said.

"It's more than just bread," the Canadian added. "It's a dainty pastry. You've never eaten any, sir?"

"No, Ned."

"All right, get ready for something downright delectable! If you don't come back for seconds, I'm no longer the King of Harpooners!"

After a few minutes, the parts of the fruit exposed to the fire were completely toasted. On the inside there appeared some white pasta, a sort of soft bread center whose flavor reminded me of artichoke.

This bread was excellent, I must admit, and I ate it with great pleasure.

"Unfortunately," I said, "this pasta won't stay fresh, so it seems pointless to make a supply for on board."

"By thunder, sir!" Ned Land exclaimed. "There you go, talking like a naturalist, but meantime I'll be acting like a baker! Conseil, harvest some of this fruit to take with us when we go back."

"And how will you prepare it?" I asked the Canadian.

"I'll make a fermented batter from its pulp that'll keep indefinitely without spoiling. When I want some, I'll just cook it in the galley on board—it'll have a slightly tart flavor, but you'll find it excellent."

"So, Mr. Ned, I see that this bread is all we need—"

"Not quite, professor," the Canadian replied. "We need some fruit to go with it, or at least some vegetables."

"Then let's look for fruit and vegetables."

When our breadfruit harvesting was done, we took to the trail to complete this "dry–land dinner."

We didn't search in vain, and near noontime we had an ample supply of bananas. This delicious produce from the Torrid Zones ripens all year round, and Malaysians, who give them the name "pisang," eat them without bothering to cook them. In addition to bananas, we gathered some enormous jackfruit with a very tangy flavor, some tasty mangoes, and some pineapples of unbelievable size. But this foraging took up a good deal of our time, which, even so, we had no cause to regret.

Conseil kept Ned under observation. The harpooner walked in the lead, and during his stroll through this forest, he gathered with sure hands some excellent fruit that should have completed his provisions.

"So," Conseil asked, "you have everything you need, Ned my friend?"

"Humph!" the Canadian put in.

"What! You're complaining?"

"All this vegetation doesn't make a meal," Ned replied. "Just side dishes, dessert. But where's the soup course? Where's the roast?"

"Right," I said. "Ned promised us cutlets, which seems highly questionable to me."

"Sir," the Canadian replied, "our hunting not only isn't over, it hasn't even started. Patience! We're sure to end up bumping into some animal with either feathers or fur, if not in this locality, then in another."

"And if not today, then tomorrow, because we mustn't wander too far off," Conseil added. "That's why I propose that we return to the skiff."

"What! Already!" Ned exclaimed.

"We ought to be back before nightfall," I said.

"But what hour is it, then?" the Canadian asked.

"Two o'clock at least," Conseil replied.

"How time flies on solid ground!" exclaimed Mr. Ned Land with a sigh of regret.

"Off we go!" Conseil replied.

So we returned through the forest, and we completed our harvest by making a clean sweep of some palm cabbages that had to be picked from the crowns of their trees, some small beans that I recognized as the "abrou" of the Malaysians, and some high-quality yams.

We were overloaded when we arrived at the skiff. However, Ned Land still found these provisions inadequate. But fortune smiled on him. Just as we were boarding, he spotted several trees twenty-five to thirty feet high, belonging to the palm species. As valuable as the actocarpus, these trees are justly ranked among the most useful produce in Malaysia.

They were sago palms, vegetation that grows without being cultivated; like mulberry trees, they reproduce by means of shoots and seeds.

Ned Land knew how to handle these trees. Taking his ax and wielding it with great vigor, he soon stretched out on the ground two or three sago palms, whose maturity was revealed by the white dust sprinkled over their palm fronds.

I watched him more as a naturalist than as a man in hunger. He began by removing from each trunk an inch-thick strip of bark that covered a network of long, hopelessly tangled fibers that were puttied with a sort of gummy flour. This flour was the starch-like sago, an edible substance chiefly consumed by the Melanesian peoples.

For the time being, Ned Land was content to chop these trunks into pieces, as if he were making firewood; later he would extract the flour by sifting it through cloth to separate it from its fibrous ligaments, let it dry out in the sun, and leave it to harden inside molds.

Finally, at five o'clock in the afternoon, laden with all our treasures, we left the island beach and half an hour later pulled alongside the *Nautilus*. Nobody appeared on our arrival. The enormous sheet–iron cylinder seemed deserted. Our provisions loaded on board, I went below to my stateroom. There I found my supper ready. I ate and then fell asleep.

The next day, January 6: nothing new on board. Not a sound inside, not a sign of life. The skiff stayed alongside in the same place we had left it. We decided to return to Gueboroa Island. Ned Land hoped for better luck in his hunting than on the day before, and he wanted to visit a different part of the forest.

By sunrise we were off. Carried by an inbound current, the longboat reached the island in a matter of moments.

We disembarked, and thinking it best to abide by the Canadian's instincts, we followed Ned Land, whose long legs threatened to outpace us.

Ned Land went westward up the coast; then, fording some stream beds, he reached open plains that were bordered by wonderful forests. Some kingfishers lurked along the watercourses, but they didn't let us approach. Their cautious behavior proved to me that these winged creatures knew where they stood on bipeds of our species, and I concluded that if this island wasn't inhabited, at least human beings paid it frequent visits.

After crossing a pretty lush prairie, we arrived on the outskirts of a small wood, enlivened by the singing and soaring of a large number of birds.

"Still, they're merely birds," Conseil said.

"But some are edible," the harpooner replied.

"Wrong, Ned my friend," Conseil answered, "because I see only ordinary parrots here."

"Conseil my friend," Ned replied in all seriousness, "parrots are like pheasant to people with nothing else on their plates."

"And I might add," I said, "that when these birds are properly cooked, they're at least worth a stab of the fork."

Indeed, under the dense foliage of this wood, a whole host of parrots fluttered from branch to branch, needing only the proper upbringing to speak human dialects. At present they were cackling in chorus with parakeets of every color, with solemn cockatoos that seemed to be pondering some philosophical problem, while bright red lories passed by like pieces of bunting borne on the breeze, in the midst of kalao parrots raucously on the wing, Papuan lories painted the subtlest shades of azure, and a whole variety of delightful winged creatures, none terribly edible.

However, one bird unique to these shores, which never passes beyond the boundaries of the Aru and Papuan Islands, was missing from this collection. But I was given a chance to marvel at it soon enough.

After crossing through a moderately dense thicket, we again found some plains obstructed by bushes. There I saw some magnificent birds soaring aloft, the arrangement of their long feathers causing them to head into the wind. Their undulating flight, the grace of their aerial curves, and the play of their colors allured and delighted the eye. I had no trouble identifying them.

"Birds of paradise!" I exclaimed.

"Order Passeriforma, division Clystomora," Conseil replied.

"Partridge family?" Ned Land asked.

"I doubt it, Mr. Land. Nevertheless, I'm counting on your dexterity to catch me one of these delightful representatives of tropical nature!"

"I'll give it a try, professor, though I'm handier with a harpoon than a rifle."

Malaysians, who do a booming business in these birds with the Chinese, have various methods for catching them that we couldn't use. Sometimes they set snares on the tops of the tall trees that the bird of paradise prefers to inhabit. At other times they capture it with a tenacious glue that paralyzes its movements. They will even go so far as to poison the springs where these fowl habitually drink. But in our case, all we could do was fire at them on the wing, which left us little chance of getting one. And in truth, we used up a good part of our ammunition in vain.

Near eleven o'clock in the morning, we cleared the lower slopes of the mountains that form the island's center, and we still hadn't bagged a thing. Hunger spurred us on. The hunters had counted on consuming the proceeds of their hunting, and they had miscalculated. Luckily, and much to his surprise, Conseil pulled off a right-and-left shot and insured our breakfast. He brought down a white pigeon and a ringdove, which were briskly plucked, hung from a spit, and roasted over a blazing fire of deadwood. While these fascinating animals were cooking, Ned prepared some bread from the artocarpus. Then the pigeon and ringdove were devoured to the bones and declared excellent. Nutmeg, on which these birds habitually gorge themselves, sweetens their flesh and makes it delicious eating.

"They taste like chicken stuffed with truffles," Conseil said.

"All right, Ned," I asked the Canadian, "now what do you need?"

"Game with four paws, Professor Aronnax," Ned Land replied. "All these pigeons are only appetizers, snacks. So till I've bagged an animal with cutlets, I won't be happy!"

"Nor I, Ned, until I've caught a bird of paradise."

"Then let's keep hunting," Conseil replied, "but while heading back to the sea. We've arrived at the foothills of these mountains, and I think we'll do better if we return to the forest regions."

It was good advice and we took it. After an hour's walk we reached a genuine sago palm forest. A few harmless snakes fled underfoot. Birds of paradise stole off at our approach, and I was in real despair of catching one when Conseil, walking in the lead, stooped suddenly, gave a triumphant shout, and came back to me, carrying a magnificent bird of paradise.

"Oh bravo, Conseil!" I exclaimed.

"Master is too kind," Conseil replied.

"Not at all, my boy. That was a stroke of genius, catching one of these live birds with your bare hands!"

"If master will examine it closely, he'll see that I deserve no great praise."

"And why not, Conseil?"

"Because this bird is as drunk as a lord."

"Drunk?"

"Yes, master, drunk from the nutmegs it was devouring under that nutmeg tree where I caught it. See, Ned my friend, see the monstrous results of intemperance!"

"Damnation!" the Canadian shot back. "Considering the amount of gin I've had these past two months, you've got nothing to complain about!"

Meanwhile I was examining this unusual bird. Conseil was not mistaken. Tipsy from that potent juice, our bird of paradise had been reduced to helplessness. It was unable to fly. It was barely able to walk. But this didn't alarm me, and I just let it sleep off its nutmeg.

This bird belonged to the finest of the eight species credited to Papua and its neighboring islands. It was a "great emerald," one of the rarest birds of paradise. It measured three decimeters long. Its head was comparatively small, and its eyes, placed near the opening of its beak, were also small. But it offered a wonderful mixture of hues: a yellow beak, brown feet and claws, hazel wings with purple tips, pale yellow head and scruff of the neck, emerald throat, the belly and chest maroon to brown. Two strands, made of a horn substance covered with down, rose over its tail, which was lengthened by long, very light feathers of wonderful fineness, and they completed the costume of this marvelous bird that the islanders have poetically named "the sun bird."

How I wished I could take this superb bird of paradise back to Paris, to make a gift of it to the zoo at the Botanical Gardens, which doesn't own a single live specimen.

"So it must be a rarity or something?" the Canadian asked, in the tone of a hunter who, from the viewpoint of his art, gives the game a pretty low rating.

"A great rarity, my gallant comrade, and above all very hard to capture alive. And even after they're dead, there's still a major market for these birds. So the natives have figured out how to create fake ones, like people create fake pearls or diamonds."

"What!" Conseil exclaimed. "They make counterfeit birds of paradise?"

"Yes, Conseil."

"And is master familiar with how the islanders go about it?"

"Perfectly familiar. During the easterly monsoon season, birds of paradise lose the magnificent feathers around their tails that naturalists call 'below-the-wing' feathers. These feathers are gathered by the fowl forgers and skillfully fitted onto some poor previously mutilated parakeet. Then they paint over the suture, varnish the bird, and ship the fruits of their unique labors to museums and collectors in Europe."

"Good enough!" Ned Land put in. "If it isn't the right bird, it's still the right feathers, and so long as the merchandise isn't meant to be eaten, I see no great harm!"

But if my desires were fulfilled by the capture of this bird of paradise, those of our Canadian huntsman remained unsatisfied. Luckily, near two o'clock Ned Land brought down a magnificent wild pig of the type the natives call "bari-outang." This animal came in the nick of time for us to bag some real quadruped meat, and it was warmly welcomed. Ned Land proved himself quite gloriously with his gunshot. Hit by an electric bullet, the pig dropped dead on the spot.

The Canadian properly skinned and cleaned it, after removing half a dozen cutlets destined to serve as the grilled meat course of our evening meal. Then the hunt was on again, and once more would be marked by the exploits of Ned and Conseil.

In essence, beating the bushes, the two friends flushed a herd of kangaroos that fled by bounding away on their elastic paws. But these animals didn't flee so swiftly that our electric capsules couldn't catch up with them.

"Oh, professor!" shouted Ned Land, whose hunting fever had gone to his brain. "What excellent game, especially in a stew! What a supply for the *Nautilus*! Two, three, five down! And just think how we'll devour all this meat ourselves, while those numbskulls on board won't get a shred!"

In his uncontrollable glee, I think the Canadian might have slaughtered the whole horde, if he hadn't been so busy talking! But he was content with a dozen of these fascinating marsupials, which make up the first order of aplacental mammals, as Conseil just had to tell us.

These animals were small in stature. They were a species of those "rabbit kangaroos" that usually dwell in the hollows of trees and are tremendously fast; but although of moderate dimensions, they at least furnish a meat that's highly prized.

We were thoroughly satisfied with the results of our hunting. A gleeful Ned proposed that we return the next day to this magic island, which he planned to depopulate of its every edible quadruped. But he was reckoning without events.

By six o'clock in the evening, we were back on the beach. The skiff was aground in its usual place. The *Nautilus*, looking like a long reef, emerged from the waves two miles offshore.

Without further ado, Ned Land got down to the important

business of dinner. He came wonderfully to terms with its entire cooking. Grilling over the coals, those cutlets from the "bari–outang" soon gave off a succulent aroma that perfumed the air.

But I catch myself following in the Canadian's footsteps. Look at me—in ecstasy over freshly grilled pork! Please grant me a pardon as I've already granted one to Mr. Land, and on the same grounds!

In short, dinner was excellent. Two ringdoves rounded out this extraordinary menu. Sago pasta, bread from the artocarpus, mangoes, half a dozen pineapples, and the fermented liquor from certain coconuts heightened our glee. I suspect that my two fine companions weren't quite as clearheaded as one could wish.

"What if we don't return to the *Nautilus* this evening?" Conseil said.

"What if we never return to it?" Ned Land added.

Just then a stone whizzed toward us, landed at our feet, and cut short the harpooner's proposition.

# CHAPTER 22

The Lightning Bolts of Captain Nemo

WITHOUT STANDING UP, we stared in the direction of the forest, my hand stopping halfway to my mouth, Ned Land's completing its assignment.

"Stones don't fall from the sky," Conseil said, "or else they deserve to be called meteorites."

A second well–polished stone removed a tasty ringdove leg from Conseil's hand, giving still greater relevance to his observation.

We all three stood up, rifles to our shoulders, ready to answer any attack.

"Apes maybe?" Ned Land exclaimed.

"Nearly," Conseil replied. "Savages."

"Head for the skiff!" I said, moving toward the sea.

Indeed, it was essential to beat a retreat because some twenty natives, armed with bows and slings, appeared barely a hundred paces off, on the outskirts of a thicket that masked the horizon to our right.

The skiff was aground ten fathoms away from us.

The savages approached without running, but they favored us with a show of the greatest hostility. It was raining stones and arrows.

Ned Land was unwilling to leave his provisions behind, and despite the impending danger, he clutched his pig on one side, his kangaroos on the other, and scampered off with respectable speed.

In two minutes we were on the strand. Loading provisions and weapons into the skiff, pushing it to sea, and positioning its two oars were the work of an instant. We hadn't gone two cable lengths when a hundred savages, howling and gesticulating, entered the water up to their waists. I looked to see if their appearance might draw some of the *Nautilus's* men onto the platform. But no. Lying well out, that enormous machine still seemed completely deserted.

Twenty minutes later we boarded ship. The hatches were open. After mooring the skiff, we re-entered the *Nautilus's* interior.

I went below to the lounge, from which some chords were wafting. Captain Nemo was there, leaning over the organ, deep in a musical trance.

"Captain!" I said to him.

He didn't hear me.

"Captain!" I went on, touching him with my hand.

He trembled, and turning around:

"Ah, it's you, professor!" he said to me. "Well, did you have a happy hunt? Was your herb gathering a success?"

"Yes, captain," I replied, "but unfortunately we've brought back a horde of bipeds whose proximity worries me."

"What sort of bipeds?"

"Savages."

"Savages!" Captain Nemo replied in an ironic tone. "You set foot on one of the shores of this globe, professor, and you're surprised to find savages there? Where aren't there savages? And besides, are they any worse than men elsewhere, these people you call savages?"

"But Captain—"

"Speaking for myself, sir, I've encountered them everywhere."

"Well then," I replied, "if you don't want to welcome them aboard the *Nautilus*, you'd better take some precautions!"

"Easy, professor, no cause for alarm."

"But there are a large number of these natives."

"What's your count?"

"At least a hundred."

"Professor Aronnax," replied Captain Nemo, whose fingers took their places again on the organ keys, "if every islander in Papua were to gather on that beach, the *Nautilus* would still have nothing to fear from their attacks!"

The captain's fingers then ran over the instrument's keyboard, and I noticed that he touched only its black keys, which gave his melodies a basically Scottish color. Soon he had forgotten my presence and was lost in a reverie that I no longer tried to dispel.

I climbed onto the platform. Night had already fallen, because in this low latitude the sun sets quickly, without any twilight. I could see Gueboroa Island only dimly. But numerous fires had been kindled on the beach, attesting that the natives had no thoughts of leaving it.

For several hours I was left to myself, sometimes musing on the islanders—but no longer fearing them because the captain's unflappable confidence had won me over—and sometimes forgetting them to marvel at the splendors of this tropical night. My memories took wing toward France, in the wake of those zodiacal stars due to twinkle over it in a few hours. The moon shone in the midst of the constellations at their zenith. I then remembered that this loyal, good-natured satellite would return to this same place the day after tomorrow, to raise the tide and tear the *Nautilus* from its coral bed. Near midnight, seeing that all was quiet over the darkened waves as well as under the waterside trees, I repaired to my cabin and fell into a peaceful sleep.

The night passed without mishap. No doubt the Papuans had been frightened off by the mere sight of this monster aground in the bay, because our hatches stayed open, offering easy access to the *Nautilus's* interior.

At six o'clock in the morning, January 8, I climbed onto the platform. The morning shadows were lifting. The island was soon on view through the dissolving mists, first its beaches, then its summits.

The islanders were still there, in greater numbers than on the day before, perhaps 500 or 600 of them. Taking advantage of the low tide, some of them had moved forward over the heads of coral to within two cable lengths of the *Nautilus*. I could easily distinguish them. They obviously were true Papuans, men of fine stock, athletic in build, forehead high and broad, nose large but not flat, teeth white. Their woolly, red–tinted hair was in sharp contrast to their bodies, which were black and glistening like those of Nubians. Beneath their pierced, distended earlobes there dangled strings of beads made from bone. Generally these savages were naked. I noted some women among them, dressed from hip to knee in grass skirts held up by belts made of vegetation. Some of the chieftains adorned their necks with crescents and with necklaces made from beads of red and white glass. Armed with bows, arrows, and shields, nearly all of them carried from their shoulders a sort of net, which held those polished stones their slings hurl with such dexterity.

One of these chieftains came fairly close to the *Nautilus*, examining it with care. He must have been a "mado" of high rank, because he paraded in a mat of banana leaves that had ragged edges and was accented with bright colors.

I could easily have picked off this islander, he stood at such close range; but I thought it best to wait for an actual show of hostility. Between Europeans and savages, it's acceptable for Europeans to shoot back but not to attack first.

During this whole time of low tide, the islanders lurked near the *Nautilus*, but they weren't boisterous. I often heard them repeat the word "assai," and from their gestures I understood they were inviting me to go ashore, an invitation I felt obliged to decline.

So the skiff didn't leave shipside that day, much to the displeasure of Mr. Land who couldn't complete his provisions. The adroit Canadian spent his time preparing the meat and flour products he had brought from Gueboroa Island. As for the savages, they went back to shore near eleven o'clock in the morning, when the heads of coral began to disappear under the waves of the rising tide. But I saw their numbers swell considerably on the beach. It was likely that they had come from neighboring islands or from the mainland of Papua proper. However, I didn't see one local dugout canoe.

Having nothing better to do, I decided to dredge these beautiful, clear waters, which exhibited a profusion of shells, zoophytes, and open-sea plants. Besides, it was the last day the *Nautilus* would spend in these waterways, if, tomorrow, it still floated off to the open sea as Captain Nemo had promised.

So I summoned Conseil, who brought me a small, light dragnet similar to those used in oyster fishing.

"What about these savages?" Conseil asked me. "With all due respect to master, they don't strike me as very wicked!"

"They're cannibals even so, my boy."

"A person can be both a cannibal and a decent man," Conseil replied, "just as a person can be both gluttonous and honorable. The one doesn't exclude the other."

"Fine, Conseil! And I agree that there are honorable cannibals who decently devour their prisoners. However, I'm opposed to being devoured, even in all decency, so I'll keep on my guard, especially since the *Nautilus's* commander seems to be taking no precautions. And now let's get to work!"

For two hours our fishing proceeded energetically but without bringing up any rarities. Our dragnet was filled with Midas abalone, harp shells, obelisk snails, and especially the finest hammer shells I had seen to that day. We also gathered in a few sea cucumbers, some pearl oysters, and a dozen small turtles that we saved for the ship's pantry.

But just when I least expected it, I laid my hands on a wonder, a natural deformity I'd have to call it, something very seldom encountered. Conseil had just made a cast of the dragnet, and his gear had come back up loaded with a variety of fairly ordinary seashells, when suddenly he saw me plunge my arms swiftly into the net, pull out a shelled animal, and give a conchological yell, in other words, the most piercing yell a human throat can produce.

"Eh? What happened to master?" Conseil asked, very startled. "Did master get bitten?"

"No, my boy, but I'd gladly have sacrificed a finger for such a find!"

"What find?"

"This shell," I said, displaying the subject of my triumph.

"But that's simply an olive shell of the 'tent olive' species, genus Oliva, order Pectinibranchia, class Gastropoda, branch Mollusca—"

"Yes, yes, Conseil! But instead of coiling from right to left, this olive shell rolls from left to right!"

"It can't be!" Conseil exclaimed.

"Yes, my boy, it's a left–handed shell!"

"A left–handed shell!" Conseil repeated, his heart pounding.

"Look at its spiral!"

"Oh, master can trust me on this," Conseil said, taking the valuable shell in trembling hands, "but never have I felt such excitement!"

And there was good reason to be excited! In fact, as naturalists have ventured to observe, "dextrality" is a well-known law of nature. In their rotational and orbital movements, stars and their satellites go from right to left. Man uses his right hand more often than his left, and consequently his various instruments and equipment (staircases, locks, watch springs, etc.) are designed to be used in a right–to–left manner. Now then, nature has generally obeyed this law in coiling her shells. They're right–handed with only rare exceptions, and when by chance a shell's spiral is left–handed, collectors will pay its weight in gold for it.

So Conseil and I were deep in the contemplation of our treasure, and I was solemnly promising myself to enrich the Paris Museum with it, when an ill–timed stone, hurled by one of the islanders, whizzed over and shattered the valuable object in Conseil's hands.

I gave a yell of despair! Conseil pounced on his rifle and aimed at a savage swinging a sling just ten meters away from him. I tried to stop him, but his shot went off and shattered a bracelet of amulets dangling from the islander's arm.

"Conseil!" I shouted. "Conseil!"

"Eh? What? Didn't master see that this man–eater initiated the attack?"

"A shell isn't worth a human life!" I told him.

"Oh, the rascal!" Conseil exclaimed. "I'd rather he cracked my shoulder!"

Conseil was in dead earnest, but I didn't subscribe to his views. However, the situation had changed in only a short time and we hadn't noticed. Now some twenty dugout canoes were surrounding the *Nautilus*. Hollowed from tree trunks, these dugouts were long, narrow, and well designed for speed, keeping their balance by means of two bamboo poles that floated on the surface of the water. They were maneuvered by skillful, half–naked paddlers, and I viewed their advance with definite alarm.

It was obvious these Papuans had already entered into relations with Europeans and knew their ships. But this long, iron cylinder lying in the bay, with no masts or funnels—what were they to make of it? Nothing good, because at first they kept it at a respectful distance. However, seeing that it stayed motionless, they regained confidence little by little and tried to become more familiar with it. Now then, it was precisely this familiarity that we needed to prevent. Since our weapons made no sound when they went off, they would have only a moderate effect on these islanders, who reputedly respect nothing but noisy mechanisms. Without thunderclaps, lightning bolts would be much less frightening, although the danger lies in the flash, not the noise.

Just then the dugout canoes drew nearer to the *Nautilus*, and a cloud of arrows burst over us.

"Fire and brimstone, it's hailing!" Conseil said. "And poisoned hail perhaps!"

"We've got to alert Captain Nemo," I said, re-entering the hatch.

I went below to the lounge. I found no one there. I ventured a knock at the door opening into the captain's stateroom.

The word "Enter!" answered me. I did so and found Captain Nemo busy with calculations in which there was no shortage of X and other algebraic signs.

"Am I disturbing you?" I said out of politeness.

"Correct, Professor Aronnax," the captain answered me. "But I imagine you have pressing reasons for looking me up?"

"Very pressing. Native dugout canoes are surrounding us, and in a few minutes we're sure to be assaulted by several hundred savages."

"Ah!" Captain Nemo put in serenely. "They've come in their dugouts?"

"Yes, sir."

"Well, sir, closing the hatches should do the trick."

"Precisely, and that's what I came to tell you—"

"Nothing easier," Captain Nemo said.

And he pressed an electric button, transmitting an order to the crew's quarters.

"There, sir, all under control!" he told me after a few

moments. "The skiff is in place and the hatches are closed. I don't imagine you're worried that these gentlemen will stave in walls that shells from your frigate couldn't breach?"

"No, Captain, but one danger still remains."

"What's that, sir?"

"Tomorrow at about this time, we'll need to reopen the hatches to renew the *Nautilus's* air."

"No argument, sir, since our craft breathes in the manner favored by cetaceans."

"But if these Papuans are occupying the platform at that moment, I don't see how you can prevent them from entering."

"Then, sir, you assume they'll board the ship?"

"I'm certain of it."

"Well, sir, let them come aboard. I see no reason to prevent them. Deep down they're just poor devils, these Papuans, and I don't want my visit to Gueboroa Island to cost the life of a single one of these unfortunate people!"

On this note I was about to withdraw; but Captain Nemo detained me and invited me to take a seat next to him. He questioned me with interest on our excursions ashore and on our hunting, but seemed not to understand the Canadian's passionate craving for red meat. Then our conversation skimmed various subjects, and without being more forthcoming, Captain Nemo proved more affable.

Among other things, we came to talk of the *Nautilus's* circumstances, aground in the same strait where Captain Dumont d'Urville had nearly miscarried. Then, pertinent to this:

"He was one of your great seamen," the captain told me, "one of your shrewdest navigators, that d'Urville! He was the Frenchman's Captain Cook. A man wise but unlucky! Braving the ice banks of the South Pole, the coral of Oceania, the cannibals of the Pacific, only to perish wretchedly in a train wreck! If that energetic man was able to think about his life in its last seconds, imagine what his final thoughts must have been!"

As he spoke, Captain Nemo seemed deeply moved, an emotion I felt was to his credit.

Then, chart in hand, we returned to the deeds of the French navigator: his voyages to circumnavigate the globe, his double attempt at the South Pole, which led to his discovery of the Adélie Coast and the Louis–Philippe Peninsula, finally his hydrographic surveys of the chief islands in Oceania.

"What your d'Urville did on the surface of the sea," Captain Nemo told me, "I've done in the ocean's interior, but more easily, more completely than he. Constantly tossed about by hurricanes, the *Zealous* and the new *Astrolabe* couldn't compare with the *Nautilus*, a quiet work room truly at rest in the midst of the waters!"

"Even so, Captain," I said, "there is one major similarity between Dumont d'Urville's sloops of war and the *Nautilus*."

"What's that, sir?"

"Like them, the *Nautilus* has run aground!"

"The *Nautilus* is not aground, sir," Captain Nemo replied icily. "The *Nautilus* was built to rest on the ocean floor, and I don't need to undertake the arduous labors, the maneuvers d'Urville had to attempt in order to float off his sloops of war. The *Zealous* and the new *Astrolabe* wellnigh perished, but my *Nautilus* is in no danger. Tomorrow, on the day stated and at the hour stated, the tide will peacefully lift it off, and it will resume its navigating through the seas."

"Captain," I said, "I don't doubt—"

"Tomorrow," Captain Nemo added, standing up, "tomorrow at 2:40 in the afternoon, the *Nautilus* will float off and exit the Torres Strait undamaged."

Pronouncing these words in an extremely sharp tone, Captain Nemo gave me a curt bow. This was my dismissal, and I re-entered my stateroom.

There I found Conseil, who wanted to know the upshot of my interview with the captain.

"My boy," I replied, "when I expressed the belief that these Papuan natives were a threat to his *Nautilus*, the captain answered me with great irony. So I've just one thing to say to you: have faith in him and sleep in peace."

"Master has no need for my services?"

"No, my friend. What's Ned Land up to?"

"Begging master's indulgence," Conseil replied, "but our friend Ned is concocting a kangaroo pie that will be the eighth wonder!"

I was left to myself; I went to bed but slept pretty poorly. I kept hearing noises from the savages, who were stamping on the platform and letting out deafening yells. The night passed in this way, without the crew ever emerging from their usual inertia. They were no more disturbed by the presence of these man–eaters than soldiers in an armored fortress are troubled by ants running over the armor plate.

I got up at six o'clock in the morning. The hatches weren't open. So the air inside hadn't been renewed; but the air tanks were kept full for any eventuality and would function appropriately to shoot a few cubic meters of oxygen into the *Nautilus's* thin atmosphere.

I worked in my stateroom until noon without seeing Captain Nemo even for an instant. Nobody on board seemed to be making any preparations for departure.

I still waited for a while, then I made my way to the main lounge. Its timepiece marked 2:30. In ten minutes the tide would reach its maximum elevation, and if Captain Nemo hadn't made a rash promise, the *Nautilus* would immediately break free. If not, many months might pass before it could leave its coral bed.

But some preliminary vibrations could soon be felt over the boat's hull. I heard its plating grind against the limestone roughness of that coral base.

At 2:35 Captain Nemo appeared in the lounge.

"We're about to depart," he said.

"Ah!" I put in.

"I've given orders to open the hatches."

"What about the Papuans?"

"What about them?" Captain Nemo replied, with a light shrug of his shoulders.

"Won't they come inside the *Nautilus*?"

"How will they manage that?"

"By jumping down the hatches you're about to open."

"Professor Aronnax," Captain Nemo replied serenely, "the *Nautilus's* hatches aren't to be entered in that fashion even when they're open."

I gaped at the captain.

"You don't understand?" he said to me.

"Not in the least."

"Well, come along and you'll see!"

I headed to the central companionway. There, very puzzled, Ned Land and Conseil watched the crewmen opening the hatches, while a frightful clamor and furious shouts resounded outside.

The hatch lids fell back onto the outer plating. Twenty horrible faces appeared. But when the first islander laid hands on the companionway railing, he was flung backward by some invisible power, lord knows what! He ran off, howling in terror and wildly prancing around.

Ten of his companions followed him. All ten met the same fate.

Conseil was in ecstasy. Carried away by his violent instincts, Ned Land leaped up the companionway. But as soon as his hands seized the railing, he was thrown backward in his turn.

"Damnation!" he exclaimed. "I've been struck by a lightning bolt!"

These words explained everything to me. It wasn't just a railing that led to the platform, it was a metal cable fully charged with the ship's electricity. Anyone who touched it got a fearsome shock—and such a shock would have been fatal if Captain Nemo had thrown the full current from his equipment into this conducting cable! It could honestly be said that he had stretched between himself and his assailants a network of electricity no one could clear with impunity.

Meanwhile, crazed with terror, the unhinged Papuans beat a retreat. As for us, half laughing, we massaged and comforted poor Ned Land, who was swearing like one possessed.

But just then, lifted off by the tide's final undulations, the *Nautilus* left its coral bed at exactly that fortieth minute pinpointed by the captain. Its propeller churned the waves with lazy majesty. Gathering speed little by little, the ship navigated on the surface of the ocean, and safe and sound, it left behind the dangerous narrows of the Torres Strait.

# CHAPTER 23

"Aegri Somnia"

THE FOLLOWING DAY, January 10, the *Nautilus* resumed its travels in midwater but at a remarkable speed that I estimated to be at least thirty–five miles per hour. The propeller was going so fast I could neither follow nor count its revolutions.

I thought about how this marvelous electric force not only gave motion, heat, and light to the *Nautilus* but even protected it against outside attack, transforming it into a sacred ark no profane hand could touch without being blasted; my wonderment was boundless, and it went from the submersible itself to the engineer who had created it.

We were traveling due west and on January 11 we doubled Cape Wessel, located in longitude 135° and latitude 10° north, the western tip of the Gulf of Carpentaria. Reefs were still numerous but more widely scattered and were fixed on the chart with the greatest accuracy. The *Nautilus* easily avoided the Money breakers to port and the Victoria reefs to starboard, positioned at longitude 130° on the tenth parallel, which we went along rigorously.

On January 13, arriving in the Timor Sea, Captain Nemo raised the island of that name at longitude 122°. This island, whose surface area measures 1,625 square leagues, is governed by rajahs. These aristocrats deem themselves the sons of crocodiles, in other words, descendants with the most exalted origins to which a human being can lay claim. Accordingly, their scaly ancestors infest the island's rivers and are the subjects of special veneration. They are sheltered, nurtured, flattered, pampered, and offered a ritual diet of nubile maidens; and woe to the foreigner who lifts a finger against these sacred saurians.

But the *Nautilus* wanted nothing to do with these nasty animals. Timor Island was visible for barely an instant at noon while the chief officer determined his position. I also caught only a glimpse of little Roti Island, part of this same group, whose women have a well–established reputation for beauty in the Malaysian marketplace.

After our position fix, the *Nautilus's* latitude bearings were modulated to the southwest. Our prow pointed to the Indian Ocean. Where would Captain Nemo's fancies take us? Would he head up to the shores of Asia? Would he pull nearer to the beaches of Europe? Unlikely choices for a man who avoided populated areas! So would he go down south? Would he double the Cape of Good Hope, then Cape Horn, and push on to the Antarctic pole? Finally, would he return to the seas of the Pacific, where his *Nautilus* could navigate freely and easily? Time would tell.

After cruising along the Cartier, Hibernia, Seringapatam, and Scott reefs, the solid element's last exertions against the liquid element, we were beyond all sight of shore by January 14. The *Nautilus* slowed down in an odd manner, and very unpredictable in its ways, it sometimes swam in the midst of the waters, sometimes drifted on their surface.

During this phase of our voyage, Captain Nemo conducted interesting experiments on the different temperatures in various strata of the sea. Under ordinary conditions, such readings are obtained using some pretty complicated instruments whose findings are dubious to say the least, whether they're thermometric sounding lines, whose glass often shatters under the water's pressure, or those devices based on the varying resistance of metals to electric currents. The results so obtained can't be adequately double-checked. By contrast, Captain Nemo would seek the sea's temperature by going himself into its depths, and when he placed his thermometer in contact with the various layers of liquid, he found the sought-for degree immediately and with certainty.

And so, by loading up its ballast tanks, or by sinking obliquely with its slanting fins, the *Nautilus* successively reached depths of 3,000, 4,000, 5,000, 7,000, 9,000, and 10,000 meters, and the ultimate conclusion from these experiments was that, in all latitudes, the sea had a permanent temperature of 4.5° centigrade at a depth of 1,000 meters.

I watched these experiments with the most intense fascination. Captain Nemo brought a real passion to them. I often wondered why he took these observations. Were they for the benefit of his fellow man? It was unlikely, because sooner or later his work would perish with him in some unknown sea! Unless he intended the results of his experiments for me. But that meant this strange voyage of mine would come to an end, and no such end was in sight.

Be that as it may, Captain Nemo also introduced me to the different data he had obtained on the relative densities of the water in our globe's chief seas. From this news I derived some personal enlightenment having nothing to do with science.

It happened the morning of January 15. The captain, with whom I was strolling on the platform, asked me if I knew how salt water differs in density from sea to sea. I said no, adding that there was a lack of rigorous scientific observations on this subject.

"I've taken such observations," he told me, "and I can vouch for their reliability."

"Fine," I replied, "but the *Nautilus* lives in a separate world, and the secrets of its scientists don't make their way ashore."

"You're right, professor," he told me after a few moments

of silence. "This is a separate world. It's as alien to the earth as the planets accompanying our globe around the sun, and we'll never become familiar with the work of scientists on Saturn or Jupiter. But since fate has linked our two lives, I can reveal the results of my observations to you."

"I'm all attention, Captain."

"You're aware, Professor, that salt water is denser than fresh water, but this density isn't uniform. In essence, if I represent the density of fresh water by 1.000, then I find 1.028 for the waters of the Atlantic, 1.026 for the waters of the Pacific, 1.030 for the waters of the Mediterranean—"

Aha, I thought, so he ventures into the Mediterranean?

"—1.018 for the waters of the Ionian Sea, and 1.029 for the waters of the Adriatic."

Assuredly, the *Nautilus* didn't avoid the heavily traveled seas of Europe, and from this insight I concluded that the ship would take us back—perhaps very soon—to more civilized shores. I expected Ned Land to greet this news with unfeigned satisfaction.

For several days our work hours were spent in all sorts of experiments, on the degree of salinity in waters of different depths, or on their electric properties, coloration, and transparency, and in every instance Captain Nemo displayed an ingenuity equaled only by his graciousness toward me. Then I saw no more of him for some days and again lived on board in seclusion.

On January 16 the *Nautilus* seemed to have fallen asleep just a few meters beneath the surface of the water. Its electric equipment had been turned off, and the motionless propeller let it ride with the waves. I assumed that the crew were busy with interior repairs, required by the engine's strenuous mechanical action.

My companions and I then witnessed an unusual sight. The panels in the lounge were open, and since the *Nautilus's* beacon was off, a hazy darkness reigned in the midst of the waters. Covered with heavy clouds, the stormy sky gave only the faintest light to the ocean's upper strata.

I was observing the state of the sea under these conditions, and even the largest fish were nothing more than ill-defined shadows, when the *Nautilus* was suddenly transferred into broad daylight. At first I thought the beacon had gone back on and was casting its electric light into the liquid mass. I was mistaken, and after a hasty examination I discovered my error.

The *Nautilus* had drifted into the midst of some phosphorescent strata, which, in this darkness, came off as positively dazzling. This effect was caused by myriads of tiny, luminous animals whose brightness increased when they glided over the metal hull of our submersible. In the midst of these luminous sheets of water, I then glimpsed flashes of light, like those seen inside a blazing furnace from streams of molten lead or from masses of metal brought to a white heat—flashes so intense that certain areas of the light became shadows by comparison, in a fiery setting from which every shadow should seemingly have been banished. No, this was no longer the calm emission of our usual lighting! This light throbbed with unprecedented vigor and activity! You sensed that it was alive!

In essence, it was a cluster of countless open-sea infusoria, of noctiluca an eighth of an inch wide, actual globules of transparent jelly equipped with a threadlike tentacle, up to 25,000 of which have been counted in thirty cubic centimeters of water. And the power of their light was increased by those glimmers unique to medusas, starfish, common jellyfish, angel-wing clams, and other phosphorescent zoophytes, which were saturated with grease from organic matter decomposed by the sea, and perhaps with mucus secreted by fish.

For several hours the *Nautilus* drifted in this brilliant tide, and our wonderment grew when we saw huge marine animals cavorting in it, like the fire–dwelling salamanders of myth. In the midst of these flames that didn't burn, I could see swift, elegant porpoises, the tireless pranksters of the seas, and sailfish three meters long, those shrewd heralds of hurricanes, whose fearsome broadswords sometimes banged against the lounge window. Then smaller fish appeared: miscellaneous triggerfish, leather jacks, unicornfish, and a hundred others that left stripes on this luminous atmosphere in their course.

Some magic lay behind this dazzling sight! Perhaps some atmospheric condition had intensified this phenomenon? Perhaps a storm had been unleashed on the surface of the waves? But only a few meters down, the *Nautilus* felt no tempest's fury, and the ship rocked peacefully in the midst of the calm waters.

And so it went, some new wonder constantly delighting us. Conseil observed and classified his zoophytes, articulates, mollusks, and fish. The days passed quickly, and I no longer kept track of them. Ned, as usual, kept looking for changes of pace from our standard fare. Like actual snails, we were at home in our shell, and I can vouch that it's easy to turn into a full–fledged snail.

So this way of living began to seem simple and natural to us, and we no longer envisioned a different lifestyle on the surface of the planet earth, when something happened to remind us of our strange circumstances.

On January 18 the *Nautilus* lay in longitude 105° and latitude 15° south. The weather was threatening, the sea rough and billowy. The wind was blowing a strong gust from the east. The barometer, which had been falling for some days, forecast an approaching struggle of the elements.

I had climbed onto the platform just as the chief officer was taking his readings of hour angles. Out of habit I waited for him to pronounce his daily phrase. But that day it was replaced by a different phrase, just as incomprehensible. Almost at once

I saw Captain Nemo appear, lift his spyglass, and inspect the horizon.

For some minutes the captain stood motionless, rooted to the spot contained within the field of his lens. Then he lowered his spyglass and exchanged about ten words with his chief officer. The latter seemed to be in the grip of an excitement he tried in vain to control. More in command of himself, Captain Nemo remained cool. Furthermore, he seemed to be raising certain objections that his chief officer kept answering with flat assurances. At least that's what I gathered from their differences in tone and gesture.

As for me, I stared industriously in the direction under observation but without spotting a thing. Sky and water merged into a perfectly clean horizon line.

Meanwhile Captain Nemo strolled from one end of the platform to the other, not glancing at me, perhaps not even seeing me. His step was firm but less regular than usual. Sometimes he would stop, cross his arms over his chest, and observe the sea. What could he be looking for over that immense expanse? By then the *Nautilus* lay hundreds of miles from the nearest coast!

The chief officer kept lifting his spyglass and stubbornly examining the horizon, walking up and down, stamping his foot, in his nervous agitation a sharp contrast to his superior.

But this mystery would inevitably be cleared up, and soon, because Captain Nemo gave orders to increase speed; at once the engine stepped up its drive power, setting the propeller in swifter rotation.

Just then the chief officer drew the captain's attention anew. The latter interrupted his strolling and aimed his spyglass at the point indicated. He observed it a good while. As for me, deeply puzzled, I went below to the lounge and brought back an excellent long-range telescope I habitually used. Leaning my elbows on the beacon housing, which jutted from the stern of the platform, I got set to scour that whole stretch of sky and sea.

But no sooner had I peered into the eyepiece than the instrument was snatched from my hands.

I spun around. Captain Nemo was standing before me, but I almost didn't recognize him. His facial features were transfigured. Gleaming with dark fire, his eyes had shrunk beneath his frowning brow. His teeth were half bared. His rigid body, clenched fists, and head drawn between his shoulders, all attested to a fierce hate breathing from every pore. He didn't move. My spyglass fell from his hand and rolled at his feet.

Had I accidentally caused these symptoms of anger? Did this incomprehensible individual think I had detected some secret forbidden to guests on the *Nautilus*?

No! I wasn't the subject of his hate because he wasn't even looking at me; his eyes stayed stubbornly focused on that inscrutable point of the horizon.

Finally Captain Nemo regained his self-control. His facial appearance, so profoundly changed, now resumed its usual calm. He addressed a few words to his chief officer in their strange language, then he turned to me:

"Professor Aronnax," he told me in a tone of some urgency, "I ask that you now honor one of the binding agreements between us."

"Which one, Captain?"

"You and your companions must be placed in confinement until I see fit to set you free."

"You're in command," I answered, gaping at him. "But may I address a question to you?"

"You may not, sir."

After that, I stopped objecting and started obeying, since resistance was useless.

I went below to the cabin occupied by Ned Land and Conseil, and I informed them of the captain's decision. I'll let the reader decide how this news was received by the Canadian. In any case, there was no time for explanations. Four crewmen were waiting at the door, and they led us to the cell where we had spent our first night aboard the *Nautilus*.

Ned Land tried to lodge a complaint, but the only answer he got was a door shut in his face.

"Will master tell me what this means?" Conseil asked me.

I told my companions what had happened. They were as astonished as I was, but no wiser.

Then I sank into deep speculation, and Captain Nemo's strange facial seizure kept haunting me. I was incapable of connecting two ideas in logical order, and I had strayed into the most absurd hypotheses, when I was snapped out of my mental struggles by these words from Ned Land:

"Well, look here! Lunch is served!"

Indeed, the table had been laid. Apparently Captain Nemo had given this order at the same time he commanded the *Nautilus* to pick up speed.

"Will master allow me to make him a recommendation?" Conseil asked me.

"Yes, my boy," I replied.

"Well, master needs to eat his lunch! It's prudent, because we have no idea what the future holds."

"You're right, Conseil."

"Unfortunately," Ned Land said, "they've only given us the standard menu."

"Ned my friend," Conseil answered, "what would you say if they'd given us no lunch at all?"

This dose of sanity cut the harpooner's complaints clean off.

We sat down at the table. Our meal proceeded pretty much in silence. I ate very little. Conseil, everlastingly prudent, "force-fed" himself; and despite the menu, Ned Land didn't waste a bite. Then, lunch over, each of us propped himself in a corner.

Just then the luminous globe lighting our cell went out, leaving us in profound darkness. Ned Land soon dozed off, and to my astonishment, Conseil also fell into a heavy slumber. I was wondering what could have caused this urgent need for sleep, when I felt a dense torpor saturate my brain. I tried to keep my eyes open, but they closed in spite of me. I was in the grip of anguished hallucinations. Obviously some sleep–inducing substance had been laced into the food we'd just eaten! So imprisonment wasn't enough to conceal Captain Nemo's plans from us—sleep was needed as well!

Then I heard the hatches close. The sea's undulations, which had been creating a gentle rocking motion, now ceased. Had the *Nautilus* left the surface of the ocean? Was it re-entering the motionless strata deep in the sea?

I tried to fight off this drowsiness. It was impossible. My breathing grew weaker. I felt a mortal chill freeze my dull, nearly paralyzed limbs. Like little domes of lead, my lids fell over my eyes. I couldn't raise them. A morbid sleep, full of hallucinations, seized my whole being. Then the visions disappeared and left me in utter oblivion.

# CHAPTER 24

### The Coral Realm

THE NEXT DAY I woke up with my head unusually clear. Much to my surprise, I was in my stateroom. No doubt my companions had been put back in their cabin without noticing it any more than I had. Like me, they would have no idea what took place during the night, and to unravel this mystery I could count only on some future happenstance.

I then considered leaving my stateroom. Was I free or still a prisoner? Perfectly free. I opened my door, headed down the gangways, and climbed the central companionway. Hatches that had been closed the day before were now open. I arrived on the platform.

Ned Land and Conseil were there waiting for me. I questioned them. They knew nothing. Lost in a heavy sleep of which they had no memory, they were quite startled to be back in their cabin.

As for the *Nautilus*, it seemed as tranquil and mysterious as ever. It was cruising on the surface of the waves at a moderate speed. Nothing seemed to have changed on board.

Ned Land observed the sea with his penetrating eyes. It was deserted. The Canadian sighted nothing new on the horizon, neither sail nor shore. A breeze was blowing noisily from the west, and disheveled by the wind, long billows made the submersible roll very noticeably.

After renewing its air, the *Nautilus* stayed at an average depth of fifteen meters, enabling it to return quickly to the surface of the waves. And, contrary to custom, it executed such a maneuver several times during that day of January 19. The chief officer would then climb onto the platform, and his usual phrase would ring through the ship's interior.

As for Captain Nemo, he didn't appear. Of the other men on board, I saw only my emotionless steward, who served me with his usual mute efficiency.

Near two o'clock I was busy organizing my notes in the lounge, when the captain opened the door and appeared. I bowed to him. He gave me an almost imperceptible bow in return, without saying a word to me. I resumed my work, hoping he might give me some explanation of the previous afternoon's events. He did nothing of the sort. I stared at him. His face looked exhausted; his reddened eyes hadn't been refreshed by sleep; his facial features expressed profound sadness, real chagrin. He walked up and down, sat and stood, picked up a book at random, discarded it immediately, consulted his instruments without taking his customary notes, and seemed unable to rest easy for an instant.

Finally he came over to me and said:

"Are you a physician, Professor Aronnax?"

This inquiry was so unexpected that I stared at him a good while without replying.

"Are you a physician?" he repeated. "Several of your scientific colleagues took their degrees in medicine, such as Gratiolet, Moquin–Tandon, and others."

"That's right," I said, "I am a doctor, I used to be on call at the hospitals. I was in practice for several years before joining the museum."

"Excellent, sir."

My reply obviously pleased Captain Nemo. But not knowing what he was driving at, I waited for further questions, ready to reply as circumstances dictated.

"Professor Aronnax," the captain said to me, "would you

consent to give your medical attentions to one of my men?"

"Someone is sick?"

"Yes."

"I'm ready to go with you."

"Come."

I admit that my heart was pounding. Lord knows why, but I saw a definite connection between this sick crewman and yesterday's happenings, and the mystery of those events concerned me at least as much as the man's sickness.

Captain Nemo led me to the *Nautilus's* stern and invited me into a cabin located next to the sailors' quarters.

On a bed there lay a man some forty years old, with strongly molded features, the very image of an Anglo–Saxon.

I bent over him. Not only was he sick, he was wounded. Swathed in blood–soaked linen, his head was resting on a folded pillow. I undid the linen bandages, while the wounded man gazed with great staring eyes and let me proceed without making a single complaint.

It was a horrible wound. The cranium had been smashed open by some blunt instrument, leaving the naked brains exposed, and the cerebral matter had suffered deep abrasions. Blood clots had formed in this dissolving mass, taking on the color of wine dregs. Both contusion and concussion of the brain had occurred. The sick man's breathing was labored, and muscle spasms quivered in his face. Cerebral inflammation was complete and had brought on a paralysis of movement and sensation.

I took the wounded man's pulse. It was intermittent. The body's extremities were already growing cold, and I saw that death was approaching without any possibility of my holding it in check. After dressing the poor man's wound, I redid the linen bandages around his head, and I turned to Captain Nemo.

"How did he get this wound?" I asked him.

"That's not important," the captain replied evasively. "The *Nautilus* suffered a collision that cracked one of the engine levers, and it struck this man. My chief officer was standing beside him. This man leaped forward to intercept the blow. A brother lays down his life for his brother, a friend for his friend, what could be simpler? That's the law for everyone on board the *Nautilus*. But what's your diagnosis of his condition?"

I hesitated to speak my mind.

"You may talk freely," the captain told me. "This man doesn't understand French."

I took a last look at the wounded man, then I replied:

"This man will be dead in two hours."

"Nothing can save him?"

"Nothing."

Captain Nemo clenched his fists, and tears slid from his eyes, which I had thought incapable of weeping.

For a few moments more I observed the dying man, whose life was ebbing little by little. He grew still more pale under the electric light that bathed his deathbed. I looked at his intelligent head, furrowed with premature wrinkles that misfortune, perhaps misery, had etched long before. I was hoping to detect the secret of his life in the last words that might escape from his lips!

"You may go, Professor Aronnax," Captain Nemo told me.

I left the captain in the dying man's cabin and I repaired to my stateroom, very moved by this scene. All day long I was aquiver with gruesome forebodings. That night I slept poorly, and between my fitful dreams, I thought I heard a distant moaning, like a funeral dirge. Was it a prayer for the dead, murmured in that language I couldn't understand?

The next morning I climbed on deck. Captain Nemo was already there. As soon as he saw me, he came over.

"Professor," he said to me, "would it be convenient for you to make an underwater excursion today?"

"With my companions?" I asked.

"If they're agreeable."

"We're yours to command, Captain."

"Then kindly put on your diving suits."

As for the dead or dying man, he hadn't come into the picture. I rejoined Ned Land and Conseil. I informed them of Captain Nemo's proposition. Conseil was eager to accept, and this time the Canadian proved perfectly amenable to going with us.

It was eight o'clock in the morning. By 8:30 we were suited up for this new stroll and equipped with our two devices for lighting and breathing. The double door opened, and accompanied by Captain Nemo with a dozen crewmen following, we set foot on the firm seafloor where the *Nautilus* was resting, ten meters down.

A gentle slope gravitated to an uneven bottom whose depth was about fifteen fathoms. This bottom was completely different from the one I had visited during my first excursion under the waters of the Pacific Ocean. Here I saw no fine-grained sand, no underwater prairies, not one open-sea forest. I immediately recognized the wondrous region in which Captain Nemo did the honors that day. It was the coral realm.

In the zoophyte branch, class Alcyonaria, one finds the order Gorgonaria, which contains three groups: sea fans, isidian polyps, and coral polyps. It's in this last that precious coral belongs, an unusual substance that, at different times, has been classified in the mineral, vegetable, and animal kingdoms. Medicine to the ancients, jewelry to the moderns, it wasn't decisively placed in the animal kingdom until 1694, by Peysonnel of Marseilles.

A coral is a unit of tiny animals assembled over a polypary that's brittle and stony in nature. These polyps have a unique generating mechanism that reproduces them via the budding process, and they have an individual existence while also participating in a communal life. Hence they embody a sort of natural socialism. I was familiar with the latest research on this bizarre zoophyte—which turns to stone while taking on a tree form, as some naturalists have very aptly observed—and nothing could have been more fascinating to me than to visit one of these petrified forests that nature has planted on the bottom of the sea.

We turned on our Ruhmkorff devices and went along a coral shoal in the process of forming, which, given time, will someday close off this whole part of the Indian Ocean. Our path was bordered by hopelessly tangled bushes, formed from snarls of shrubs all covered with little star-shaped, white-streaked flowers. Only, contrary to plants on shore, these tree forms become attached to rocks on the seafloor by heading from top to bottom.

Our lights produced a thousand delightful effects while playing over these brightly colored boughs. I fancied I saw these cylindrical, membrane–filled tubes trembling beneath the water's undulations. I was tempted to gather their fresh petals, which were adorned with delicate tentacles, some newly in bloom, others barely opened, while nimble fish with fluttering fins brushed past them like flocks of birds. But if my hands came near the moving flowers of these sensitive, lively creatures, an alarm would instantly sound throughout the colony. The white petals retracted into their red sheaths, the flowers vanished before my eyes, and the bush changed into a chunk of stony nipples.

Sheer chance had placed me in the presence of the most valuable specimens of this zoophyte. This coral was the equal of those fished up from the Mediterranean off the Barbary Coast or the shores of France and Italy. With its bright colors, it lived up to those poetic names of blood flower and blood foam that the industry confers on its finest exhibits. Coral sells for as much as F500 per kilogram, and in this locality the liquid strata hid enough to make the fortunes of a whole host of coral fishermen. This valuable substance often merges with other polyparies, forming compact, hopelessly tangled units known as "macciota," and I noted some wonderful pink samples of this coral.

But as the bushes shrank, the tree forms magnified. Actual petrified thickets and long alcoves from some fantastic school of architecture kept opening up before our steps. Captain Nemo entered beneath a dark gallery whose gentle slope took us to a depth of 100 meters. The light from our glass coils produced magical effects at times, lingering on the wrinkled roughness of some natural arch, or some overhang suspended like a chandelier, which our lamps flecked with fiery sparks. Amid these shrubs of precious coral, I observed other polyps no less unusual: melita coral, rainbow coral with jointed outgrowths, then a few tufts of genus Corallina, some green and others red, actually a type of seaweed encrusted with limestone salts, which, after long disputes, naturalists have finally placed in the vegetable kingdom. But as one intellectual has remarked, "Here, perhaps, is the actual point where life rises humbly out of slumbering stone, but without breaking away from its crude starting point."

Finally, after two hours of walking, we reached a depth of about 300 meters, in other words, the lowermost limit at which coral can begin to form. But here it was no longer some isolated bush or a modest grove of low timber. It was an immense forest, huge mineral vegetation, enormous petrified trees linked by garlands of elegant hydras from the genus Plumularia, those tropical creepers of the sea, all decked out in shades and gleams. We passed freely under their lofty boughs, lost up in the shadows of the waves, while at our feet organ–pipe coral, stony coral, star coral, fungus coral, and sea anemone from the genus Caryophylia formed a carpet of flowers all strewn with dazzling gems.

What an indescribable sight! Oh, if only we could share our feelings! Why were we imprisoned behind these masks of metal and glass! Why were we forbidden to talk with each other! At least let us lead the lives of the fish that populate this liquid element, or better yet, the lives of amphibians, which can spend long hours either at sea or on shore, traveling through their double domain as their whims dictate!

Meanwhile Captain Nemo had called a halt. My companions and I stopped walking, and turning around, I saw the crewmen form a semicircle around their leader. Looking with greater care, I observed that four of them were carrying on their shoulders an object that was oblong in shape.

At this locality we stood in the center of a huge clearing surrounded by the tall tree forms of this underwater forest. Our lamps cast a sort of brilliant twilight over the area, making inordinately long shadows on the seafloor. Past the boundaries of the clearing, the darkness deepened again, relieved only by little sparkles given off by the sharp crests of coral.

Ned Land and Conseil stood next to me. We stared, and it dawned on me that I was about to witness a strange scene. Observing the seafloor, I saw that it swelled at certain points from low bulges that were encrusted with limestone deposits and arranged with a symmetry that betrayed the hand of man.

In the middle of the clearing, on a pedestal of roughly piled rocks, there stood a cross of coral, extending long arms you would have thought were made of petrified blood.

At a signal from Captain Nemo, one of his men stepped forward and, a few feet from this cross, detached a mattock from his belt and began to dig a hole.

I finally understood! This clearing was a cemetery, this hole a grave, that oblong object the body of the man who must have died during the night! Captain Nemo and his men had come to bury their companion in this communal resting place on the inaccessible ocean floor!

No! My mind was reeling as never before! Never had ideas of such impact raced through my brain! I didn't want to see what my eyes saw!

Meanwhile the grave digging went slowly. Fish fled here and there as their retreat was disturbed. I heard the pick ringing on the limestone soil, its iron tip sometimes giving off sparks when it hit a stray piece of flint on the sea bottom. The hole grew longer, wider, and soon was deep enough to receive the body.

Then the pallbearers approached. Wrapped in white fabric made from filaments of the fan mussel, the body was lowered into its watery grave. Captain Nemo, arms crossed over his chest, knelt in a posture of prayer, as did all the friends of him who had loved them. . . . My two companions and I bowed reverently.

The grave was then covered over with the rubble dug from the seafloor, and it formed a low mound.

When this was done, Captain Nemo and his men stood up; then they all approached the grave, sank again on bended knee, and extended their hands in a sign of final farewell. . . .

Then the funeral party went back up the path to the *Nautilus*, returning beneath the arches of the forest, through the thickets, along the coral bushes, going steadily higher.

Finally the ship's rays appeared. Their luminous trail guided us to the *Nautilus*. By one o'clock we had returned.

After changing clothes, I climbed onto the platform, and in the grip of dreadfully obsessive thoughts, I sat next to the beacon.

Captain Nemo rejoined me. I stood up and said to him:

"So, as I predicted, that man died during the night?"

"Yes, Professor Aronnax," Captain Nemo replied.

"And now he rests beside his companions in that coral cemetery?"

"Yes, forgotten by the world but not by us! We dig the

graves, then entrust the polyps with sealing away our dead for eternity!"

And with a sudden gesture, the captain hid his face in his clenched fists, vainly trying to hold back a sob. Then he added:

"There lies our peaceful cemetery, hundreds of feet beneath the surface of the waves!"

"At least, captain, your dead can sleep serenely there, out of the reach of sharks!"

"Yes, sir," Captain Nemo replied solemnly, "of sharks and men!"

## END OF THE FIRST PART

# SECOND PART

SECOND PART

# CHAPTER 1

## The Indian Ocean

NOW WE BEGIN the second part of this voyage under the seas. The first ended in that moving scene at the coral cemetery, which left a profound impression on my mind. And so Captain Nemo would live out his life entirely in the heart of this immense sea, and even his grave lay ready in its impenetrable depths. There the last sleep of the *Nautilus's* occupants, friends bound together in death as in life, would be disturbed by no monster of the deep! "No man either!" the captain had added.

Always that same fierce, implacable defiance of human society!

As for me, I was no longer content with the hypotheses that satisfied Conseil. That fine lad persisted in seeing the *Nautilus's* commander as merely one of those unappreciated scientists who repay humanity's indifference with contempt. For Conseil, the captain was still a misunderstood genius who, tired of the world's deceptions, had been driven to take refuge in this inaccessible environment where he was free to follow his instincts. But to my mind, this hypothesis explained only one side of Captain Nemo.

In fact, the mystery of that last afternoon when we were locked in prison and put to sleep, the captain's violent precaution of snatching from my grasp a spyglass poised to scour the horizon, and the fatal wound given that man during some unexplained collision suffered by the *Nautilus*, all led me down a plain trail. No! Captain Nemo wasn't content simply to avoid humanity! His fearsome submersible served not only his quest for freedom, but also, perhaps, it was used in Lord-knows-what schemes of dreadful revenge.

Right now, nothing is clear to me, I still glimpse only glimmers in the dark, and I must limit my pen, as it were, to taking dictation from events.

But nothing binds us to Captain Nemo. He believes that escaping from the *Nautilus* is impossible. We are not even constrained by our word of honor. No promises fetter us. We're simply captives, prisoners masquerading under the name "guests" for the sake of everyday courtesy. Even so, Ned Land hasn't given up all hope of recovering his freedom. He's sure to take advantage of the first chance that comes his way. No doubt I will do likewise. And yet I will feel some regret at making off with the *Nautilus's* secrets, so generously unveiled for us by Captain Nemo! Because, ultimately, should we detest or admire this man? Is he the persecutor or the persecuted? And in all honesty, before I leave him forever, I want to finish this underwater tour of the world, whose first stages have been so magnificent. I want to observe the full series of these wonders gathered under the seas of our globe. I want to see what no man has seen yet, even if I must pay for this insatiable curiosity with my life! What are my discoveries to date? Nothing, relatively speaking—since so far we've covered only 6,000 leagues across the Pacific!

Nevertheless, I'm well aware that the *Nautilus* is drawing near to populated shores, and if some chance for salvation becomes available to us, it would be sheer cruelty to sacrifice my companions to my passion for the unknown. I must go with them, perhaps even guide them. But will this opportunity ever arise? The human being, robbed of his free will, craves such an opportunity; but the scientist, forever inquisitive, dreads it.

That day, January 21, 1868, the chief officer went at noon

to take the sun's altitude. I climbed onto the platform, lit a cigar, and watched him at work. It seemed obvious to me that this man didn't understand French, because I made several remarks in a loud voice that were bound to provoke him to some involuntary show of interest had he understood them; but he remained mute and emotionless.

While he took his sights with his sextant, one of the Nautilus's sailors—that muscular man who had gone with us to Crespo Island during our first underwater excursion—came up to clean the glass panes of the beacon. I then examined the fittings of this mechanism, whose power was increased a hundredfold by biconvex lenses that were designed like those in a lighthouse and kept its rays productively focused. This electric lamp was so constructed as to yield its maximum illuminating power. In essence, its light was generated in a vacuum, insuring both its steadiness and intensity. Such a vacuum also reduced wear on the graphite points between which the luminous arc expanded. This was an important savings for Captain Nemo, who couldn't easily renew them. But under these conditions, wear and tear were almost nonexistent.

When the Nautilus was ready to resume its underwater travels, I went below again to the lounge. The hatches closed once more, and our course was set due west.

We then plowed the waves of the Indian Ocean, vast liquid plains with an area of 550,000,000 hectares, whose waters are so transparent it makes you dizzy to lean over their surface. There the Nautilus generally drifted at a depth between 100 and 200 meters. It behaved in this way for some days. To anyone without my grand passion for the sea, these hours would surely have seemed long and monotonous; but my daily strolls on the platform where I was revived by the life–giving ocean air, the sights in the rich waters beyond the lounge windows, the books to be read in the library, and the composition of my memoirs, took up all my time and left me without a moment of weariness or boredom.

All in all, we enjoyed a highly satisfactory state of health. The diet on board agreed with us perfectly, and for my part, I could easily have gone without those changes of pace that Ned Land, in a spirit of protest, kept taxing his ingenuity to supply us. What's more, in this constant temperature we didn't even have to worry about catching colds. Besides, the ship had a good stock of the madrepore Dendrophylia, known in Provence by the name sea fennel, and a poultice made from the dissolved flesh of its polyps will furnish an excellent cough medicine.

For some days we saw a large number of aquatic birds with webbed feet, known as gulls or sea mews. Some were skillfully slain, and when cooked in a certain fashion, they make a very acceptable platter of water game. Among the great wind riders—carried over long distances from every shore and resting on the waves from their exhausting flights—I spotted some magnificent albatross, birds belonging to the Longipennes (long-winged) family, whose discordant calls sound like the braying of an ass. The Totipalmes (fully webbed) family was represented by swift frigate birds, nimbly catching fish at the surface, and by numerous tropic birds of the genus Phaeton, among others the red-tailed tropic bird, the size of a pigeon, its white plumage shaded with pink tints that contrasted with its dark-hued wings.

The *Nautilus's* nets hauled up several types of sea turtle from the hawksbill genus with arching backs whose scales are highly prized. Diving easily, these reptiles can remain a good while underwater by closing the fleshy valves located at the external openings of their nasal passages. When they were captured, some hawksbills were still asleep inside their carapaces, a refuge from other marine animals. The flesh of these turtles was nothing memorable, but their eggs made an excellent feast.

As for fish, they always filled us with wonderment when, staring through the open panels, we could unveil the secrets of their aquatic lives. I noted several species I hadn't previously been able to observe.

I'll mention chiefly some trunkfish unique to the Red Sea, the sea of the East Indies, and that part of the ocean washing the coasts of equinoctial America. Like turtles, armadillos, sea urchins, and crustaceans, these fish are protected by armor plate that's neither chalky nor stony but actual bone. Sometimes this armor takes the shape of a solid triangle, sometimes that of a solid quadrangle. Among the triangular type, I noticed some half a decimeter long, with brown tails, yellow fins, and wholesome, exquisitely tasty flesh; I even recommend that they be acclimatized to fresh water, a change, incidentally, that a number of saltwater fish can make with ease. I'll also mention some quadrangular trunkfish topped by four large protuberances along the back; trunkfish sprinkled with white spots on the underside of the body, which make good house pets like certain birds; boxfish armed with stings formed by extensions of their bony crusts, and whose odd grunting has earned them the nickname "sea pigs"; then some trunkfish known as dromedaries, with tough, leathery flesh and big conical humps.

From the daily notes kept by Mr. Conseil, I also retrieve certain fish from the genus Tetradon unique to these seas: southern puffers with red backs and white chests distinguished by three lengthwise rows of filaments, and jugfish, seven inches long, decked out in the brightest colors. Then, as specimens of other genera, blowfish resembling a dark brown egg, furrowed with white bands, and lacking tails; globefish, genuine porcupines of the sea, armed with stings and able to inflate themselves until they look like a pin cushion bristling with needles; seahorses common to every ocean; flying dragonfish with long snouts and highly distended pectoral fins shaped like wings, which enable them, if not to fly, at least to spring into the air; spatula–shaped paddlefish whose tails are covered with many scaly rings; snipefish with long jaws, excellent animals twenty–five centimeters long and gleaming with the most cheerful colors; bluish gray dragonets with wrinkled heads; myriads of leaping blennies with black stripes and long pectoral fins, gliding over the surface of the water with prodigious speed; delicious sailfish that can hoist their fins in a favorable current like so many unfurled sails; splendid nurseryfish on which nature has lavished yellow, azure, silver, and gold; yellow-mackerel with wings made of filaments; bullheads forever spattered with mud, which make distinct hissing sounds; sea robins whose livers are thought to be poisonous; ladyfish that can flutter their eyelids; finally, archerfish with long, tubular snouts, real oceangoing flycatchers, armed with a rifle unforeseen by either Remington or Chassepot: it slays insects by shooting them with a simple drop of water.

From the eighty–ninth fish genus in Lacépède's system of classification, belonging to his second subclass of bony fish (characterized by gill covers and a bronchial membrane), I noted some scorpionfish whose heads are adorned with stings and which have only one dorsal fin; these animals are covered with small scales, or have none at all, depending on the subgenus to which they belong. The second subgenus gave us some Didactylus specimens three to four decimeters long, streaked with yellow, their heads having a phantasmagoric appearance. As for the first subgenus, it furnished several specimens of that bizarre fish aptly nicknamed "toadfish," whose big head is sometimes gouged with deep cavities, sometimes swollen with protuberances; bristling with stings and strewn with nodules, it sports hideously irregular horns; its body and tail are adorned with callosities; its stings can inflict dangerous injuries; it's repulsive and horrible.

From January 21 to the 23rd, the *Nautilus* traveled at the rate of 250 leagues in twenty–four hours, hence 540 miles at twenty–two miles per hour. If, during our trip, we were able to identify these different varieties of fish, it's because they were attracted by our electric light and tried to follow alongside; but most of them were outdistanced by our speed and soon fell behind; temporarily, however, a few managed to keep pace in the *Nautilus*'s waters.

On the morning of the 24th, in latitude 12° 5' south and longitude 94° 33', we raised Keeling Island, a madreporic upheaving planted with magnificent coconut trees, which had been visited by Mr. Darwin and Captain Fitzroy. The *Nautilus* cruised along a short distance off the shore of this desert island. Our dragnets brought up many specimens of polyps and echinoderms plus some unusual shells from the branch Mollusca. Captain Nemo's treasures were enhanced by some valuable exhibits from the delphinula snail species, to which I joined some pointed star coral, a sort of parasitic polypary that often attaches itself to seashells.

Soon Keeling Island disappeared below the horizon, and our course was set to the northwest, toward the tip of the Indian peninsula.

"Civilization!" Ned Land told me that day. "Much better than those Papuan Islands where we ran into more savages than venison! On this Indian shore, professor, there are roads and railways, English, French, and Hindu villages. We wouldn't go five miles without bumping into a fellow countryman. Come on now, isn't it time for our sudden departure from Captain Nemo?"

"No, no, Ned," I replied in a very firm tone. "Let's ride it out, as you seafaring fellows say. The *Nautilus* is approaching populated areas. It's going back toward Europe, let it take us there. After we arrive in home waters, we can do as we see fit. Besides, I don't imagine Captain Nemo will let us go hunting on the coasts of Malabar or Coromandel as he did in the forests of New Guinea."

"Well, sir, can't we manage without his permission?"

I didn't answer the Canadian. I wanted no arguments. Deep down, I was determined to fully exploit the good fortune that had put me on board the *Nautilus*.

After leaving Keeling Island, our pace got generally slower. It also got more unpredictable, often taking us to great depths. Several times we used our slanting fins, which internal levers could set at an oblique angle to our waterline. Thus we went as deep as two or three kilometers down but without ever verifying the lowest depths of this sea near India, which soundings of 13,000 meters have been unable to reach. As for the temperature in these lower strata, the thermometer always and invariably indicated 4° centigrade. I merely observed that in the upper layers, the water was always colder over shallows than in the open sea.

On January 25, the ocean being completely deserted, the *Nautilus* spent the day on the surface, churning the waves with its powerful propeller and making them spurt to great heights. Under these conditions, who wouldn't have mistaken it for a gigantic cetacean? I spent three-quarters of the day on the platform. I stared at the sea. Nothing on the horizon, except near four o'clock in the afternoon a long steamer to the west, running on our opposite tack. Its masting was visible for an instant, but it couldn't have seen the *Nautilus* because we were lying too low in the water. I imagine that steamboat belonged to the Peninsular & Oriental line, which provides service from the island of Ceylon to Sidney, also calling at King George Sound and Melbourne.

At five o'clock in the afternoon, just before that brief twilight that links day with night in tropical zones, Conseil and I marveled at an unusual sight.

It was a delightful animal whose discovery, according to

the ancients, is a sign of good luck. Aristotle, Athenaeus, Pliny, and Oppian studied its habits and lavished on its behalf all the scientific poetry of Greece and Italy. They called it "*Nautilus*" and "pompilius." But modern science has not endorsed these designations, and this mollusk is now known by the name argonaut.

Anyone consulting Conseil would soon learn from the gallant lad that the branch Mollusca is divided into five classes; that the first class features the Cephalopoda (whose members are sometimes naked, sometimes covered with a shell), which consists of two families, the Dibranchiata and the Tetrabranchiata, which are distinguished by their number of gills; that the family Dibranchiata includes three genera, the argonaut, the squid, and the cuttlefish, and that the family Tetrabranchiata contains only one genus, the *Nautilus*. After this catalog, if some recalcitrant listener confuses the argonaut, which is acetabuliferous (in other words, a bearer of suction tubes), with the *Nautilus*, which is tentaculiferous (a bearer of tentacles), it will be simply unforgivable.

Now, it was a school of argonauts then voyaging on the surface of the ocean. We could count several hundred of them. They belonged to that species of argonaut covered with protuberances and exclusive to the seas near India.

These graceful mollusks were swimming backward by means of their locomotive tubes, sucking water into these tubes and then expelling it. Six of their eight tentacles were long, thin, and floated on the water, while the other two were rounded into palms and spread to the wind like light sails. I could see perfectly their undulating, spiral–shaped shells, which Cuvier aptly compared to an elegant cockleboat. It's an actual boat indeed. It transports the animal that secretes it without the animal sticking to it.

"The argonaut is free to leave its shell," I told Conseil, "but it never does."

"Not unlike Captain Nemo," Conseil replied sagely. "Which is why he should have christened his ship the *Argonaut*."

For about an hour the *Nautilus* cruised in the midst of this school of mollusks. Then, lord knows why, they were gripped with a sudden fear. As if at a signal, every sail was abruptly lowered; arms folded, bodies contracted, shells turned over by changing their center of gravity, and the whole flotilla disappeared under the waves. It was instantaneous, and no squadron of ships ever maneuvered with greater togetherness.

Just then night fell suddenly, and the waves barely surged in the breeze, spreading placidly around the *Nautilus's* side plates.

The next day, January 26, we cut the equator on the 82nd meridian and we re-entered the northern hemisphere.

During that day a fearsome school of sharks provided us with an escort. Dreadful animals that teem in these seas and make them extremely dangerous. There were Port Jackson sharks with a brown back, a whitish belly, and eleven rows of teeth, bigeye sharks with necks marked by a large black spot encircled in white and resembling an eye, and Isabella sharks whose rounded snouts were strewn with dark speckles. Often these powerful animals rushed at the lounge window with a violence less than comforting. By this point Ned Land had lost all self-control. He wanted to rise to the surface of the waves and harpoon the monsters, especially certain smooth-hound sharks whose mouths were paved with teeth arranged like a mosaic, and some big five-meter tiger sharks that insisted on personally provoking him. But the *Nautilus* soon picked up speed and easily left astern the fastest of these man-eaters.

On January 27, at the entrance to the huge Bay of Bengal, we repeatedly encountered a gruesome sight: human corpses floating on the surface of the waves! Carried by the Ganges to the high seas, these were deceased Indian villagers who hadn't been fully devoured by vultures, the only morticians in these parts. But there was no shortage of sharks to assist them with their undertaking chores.

Near seven o'clock in the evening, the *Nautilus* lay half submerged, navigating in the midst of milky white waves. As far as the eye could see, the ocean seemed lactified. Was it an effect of the moon's rays? No, because the new moon was barely two days old and was still lost below the horizon in the sun's rays. The entire sky, although lit up by stellar radiation, seemed pitch-black in comparison with the whiteness of these waters.

Conseil couldn't believe his eyes, and he questioned me about the causes of this odd phenomenon. Luckily I was in a position to answer him.

"That's called a milk sea," I told him, "a vast expanse of white waves often seen along the coasts of Amboina and in these waterways."

"But," Conseil asked, "could master tell me the cause of this effect, because I presume this water hasn't really changed into milk!"

"No, my boy, and this whiteness that amazes you is merely due to the presence of myriads of tiny creatures called infusoria, a sort of diminutive glowworm that's colorless and gelatinous in appearance, as thick as a strand of hair, and no longer than one-fifth of a millimeter. Some of these tiny creatures stick together over an area of several leagues."

"Several leagues!" Conseil exclaimed.

"Yes, my boy, and don't even try to compute the number of these infusoria. You won't pull it off, because if I'm not mistaken, certain navigators have cruised through milk seas for more than forty miles."

I'm not sure that Conseil heeded my recommendation, because he seemed to be deep in thought, no doubt trying to calculate how many one-fifths of a millimeter are found in forty square miles. As for me, I continued to observe this phenomenon. For several hours the *Nautilus's* spur sliced through these whitish waves, and I watched it glide noiselessly over this soapy water, as if it were cruising through those foaming eddies that a bay's currents and countercurrents sometimes leave between each other.

Near midnight the sea suddenly resumed its usual hue, but behind us all the way to the horizon, the skies kept mirroring the whiteness of those waves and for a good while seemed imbued with the hazy glow of an aurora borealis.

# CHAPTER 2

A New Proposition from Captain Nemo

ON JANUARY 28, in latitude 9° 4' north, when the *Nautilus* returned at noon to the surface of the sea, it lay in sight of land some eight miles to the west. Right off, I observed a cluster of mountains about 2,000 feet high, whose shapes were very whimsically sculpted. After our position fix, I re-entered the lounge, and when our bearings were reported on the chart, I saw that we were off the island of Ceylon, that pearl dangling from the lower lobe of the Indian peninsula.

I went looking in the library for a book about this island, one of the most fertile in the world. Sure enough, I found a volume entitled *Ceylon and the Singhalese* by H. C. Sirr, Esq. Re-entering the lounge, I first noted the bearings of Ceylon, on which antiquity lavished so many different names. It was located between latitude 5° 55' and 9° 49' north, and between longitude 79° 42' and 82° 4' east of the meridian of Greenwich; its length is 275 miles; its maximum width, 150 miles; its circumference, 900 miles; its surface area, 24,448 square miles, in other words, a little smaller than that of Ireland.

Just then Captain Nemo and his chief officer appeared.

The captain glanced at the chart. Then, turning to me:

"The island of Ceylon," he said, "is famous for its pearl fisheries. Would you be interested, Professor Aronnax, in visiting one of those fisheries?"

"Certainly, Captain."

"Fine. It's easily done. Only, when we see the fisheries, we'll see no fishermen. The annual harvest hasn't yet begun. No matter. I'll give orders to make for the Gulf of Mannar, and we'll arrive there late tonight."

The captain said a few words to his chief officer who went out immediately. Soon the *Nautilus* re-entered its liquid element, and the pressure gauge indicated that it was staying at a depth of thirty feet.

With the chart under my eyes, I looked for the Gulf of Mannar. I found it by the 9th parallel off the northwestern shores of Ceylon. It was formed by the long curve of little Mannar Island. To reach it we had to go all the way up Ceylon's west coast.

"Professor," Captain Nemo then told me, "there are pearl fisheries in the Bay of Bengal, the seas of the East Indies, the seas of China and Japan, plus those seas south of the United States, the Gulf of Panama and the Gulf of California; but it's off Ceylon that such fishing reaps its richest rewards. No doubt we'll be arriving a little early. Fishermen gather in the Gulf of Mannar only during the month of March, and for thirty days some 300 boats concentrate on the lucrative harvest of these treasures from the sea. Each boat is manned by ten oarsmen and ten fishermen. The latter divide into two groups, dive in rotation, and descend to a depth of twelve meters with the help of a heavy stone clutched between their feet and attached by a rope to their boat."

"You mean," I said, "that such primitive methods are still all that they use?"

"All," Captain Nemo answered me, "although these fisheries belong to the most industrialized people in the world, the English, to whom the Treaty of Amiens granted them in 1802."

"Yet it strikes me that diving suits like yours could perform yeoman service in such work."

"Yes, since those poor fishermen can't stay long underwater. On his voyage to Ceylon, the Englishman

Percival made much of a Kaffir who stayed under five minutes without coming up to the surface, but I find that hard to believe. I know that some divers can last up to fifty-seven seconds, and highly skillful ones to eighty-seven; but such men are rare, and when the poor fellows climb back on board, the water coming out of their noses and ears is tinted with blood. I believe the average time underwater that these fishermen can tolerate is thirty seconds, during which they hastily stuff their little nets with all the pearl oysters they can tear loose. But these fishermen generally don't live to advanced age: their vision weakens, ulcers break out on their eyes, sores form on their bodies, and some are even stricken with apoplexy on the ocean floor."

"Yes," I said, "it's a sad occupation, and one that exists only to gratify the whims of fashion. But tell me, Captain, how many oysters can a boat fish up in a workday?"

"About 40,000 to 50,000. It's even said that in 1814, when the English government went fishing on its own behalf, its divers worked just twenty days and brought up 76,000,000 oysters."

"At least," I asked, "the fishermen are well paid, aren't they?"

"Hardly, professor. In Panama they make just $1.00 per week. In most places they earn only a penny for each oyster that has a pearl, and they bring up so many that have none!"

"Only one penny to those poor people who make their employers rich! That's atrocious!"

"On that note, professor," Captain Nemo told me, "you and your companions will visit the Mannar oysterbank, and if by chance some eager fisherman arrives early, well, we can watch him at work."

"That suits me, captain."

"By the way, Professor Aronnax, you aren't afraid of sharks, are you?"

"Sharks?" I exclaimed.

This struck me as a pretty needless question, to say the least.

"Well?" Captain Nemo went on.

"I admit, Captain, I'm not yet on very familiar terms with that genus of fish."

"We're used to them, the rest of us," Captain Nemo answered. "And in time you will be too. Anyhow, we'll be armed, and on our way we might hunt a man-eater or two. It's a fascinating sport. So, professor, I'll see you tomorrow, bright and early."

This said in a carefree tone, Captain Nemo left the lounge.

If you're invited to hunt bears in the Swiss mountains, you might say: "Oh good, I get to go bear hunting tomorrow!" If you're invited to hunt lions on the Atlas plains or tigers in the jungles of India, you might say: "Ha! Now's my chance to hunt lions and tigers!" But if you're invited to hunt sharks in their native element, you might want to think it over before accepting.

As for me, I passed a hand over my brow, where beads of cold sweat were busy forming.

"Let's think this over," I said to myself, "and let's take our time. Hunting otters in underwater forests, as we did in the forests of Crespo Island, is an acceptable activity. But to roam the bottom of the sea when you're almost certain to meet man-eaters in the neighborhood, that's another story! I know that in certain countries, particularly the Andaman Islands, Negroes don't hesitate to attack sharks, dagger in one hand and noose in the other; but I also know that many who face those fearsome animals don't come back alive. Besides, I'm not a Negro, and even if I were a Negro, in this instance I don't think a little hesitation on my part would be out of place."

And there I was, fantasizing about sharks, envisioning huge jaws armed with multiple rows of teeth and capable of cutting a man in half. I could already feel a definite pain around my pelvic girdle. And how I resented the offhand manner in which the captain had extended his deplorable invitation! You would have thought it was an issue of going into the woods on some harmless fox hunt!

"Thank heavens!" I said to myself. "Conseil will never want to come along, and that'll be my excuse for not going with the captain."

As for Ned Land, I admit I felt less confident of his wisdom. Danger, however great, held a perennial attraction for his aggressive nature.

I went back to reading Sirr's book, but I leafed through it mechanically. Between the lines I kept seeing fearsome, wide-open jaws.

Just then Conseil and the Canadian entered with a calm, even gleeful air. Little did they know what was waiting for them.

"Ye gods, sir!" Ned Land told me. "Your Captain Nemo—the devil take him—has just made us a very pleasant proposition!"

"Oh!" I said "You know about—"

"With all due respect to master," Conseil replied, "the *Nautilus's* commander has invited us, together with master, for a visit tomorrow to Ceylon's magnificent pearl fisheries. He did so in the most cordial terms and conducted himself like a true gentleman."

"He didn't tell you anything else?"

"Nothing, sir," the Canadian replied. "He said you'd already discussed this little stroll."

"Indeed," I said. "But didn't he give you any details on—"

"Not a one, Mr. Naturalist. You will be going with us, right?"

"Me? Why yes, certainly, of course! I can see that you like the idea, Mr. Land."

"Yes! It will be a really unusual experience!"

"And possibly dangerous!" I added in an insinuating tone.

"Dangerous?" Ned Land replied. "A simple trip to an oysterbank?"

Assuredly, Captain Nemo hadn't seen fit to plant the idea of sharks in the minds of my companions. For my part, I stared at them with anxious eyes, as if they were already missing a limb or two. Should I alert them? Yes, surely, but I hardly knew how to go about it.

"Would master," Conseil said to me, "give us some background on pearl fishing?"

"On the fishing itself?" I asked. "Or on the occupational hazards that—"

"On the fishing," the Canadian replied. "Before we tackle the terrain, it helps to be familiar with it."

"All right, sit down, my friends, and I'll teach you everything I myself have just been taught by the Englishman H. C. Sirr!"

Ned and Conseil took seats on a couch, and right off the Canadian said to me:

"Sir, just what is a pearl exactly?"

"My gallant Ned," I replied, "for poets a pearl is a tear from the sea; for Orientals it's a drop of solidified dew; for the ladies it's a jewel they can wear on their fingers, necks, and ears that's oblong in shape, glassy in luster, and formed from mother-of-pearl; for chemists it's a mixture of calcium phosphate and calcium carbonate with a little gelatin protein; and finally, for naturalists it's a simple festering secretion from the organ that produces mother-of-pearl in certain bivalves."

"Branch Mollusca," Conseil said, "class Acephala, order Testacea."

"Correct, my scholarly Conseil. Now then, those Testacea capable of producing pearls include rainbow abalone, turbo snails, giant clams, and saltwater scallops—briefly, all those that secrete mother-of-pearl, in other words, that blue, azure, violet, or white substance lining the insides of their valves."

"Are mussels included too?" the Canadian asked.

"Yes! The mussels of certain streams in Scotland, Wales, Ireland, Saxony, Bohemia, and France."

"Good!" the Canadian replied. "From now on we'll pay closer attention to 'em."

"But," I went on, "for secreting pearls, the ideal mollusk is the pearl oyster Meleagrina margaritifera, that valuable shellfish. Pearls result simply from mother–of–pearl solidifying into a globular shape. Either they stick to the oyster's shell, or they become embedded in the creature's folds. On the valves a pearl sticks fast; on the flesh it lies loose. But its nucleus is always some small, hard object, say a sterile egg or a grain of sand, around which the mother–of–pearl is deposited in thin, concentric layers over several years in succession."

"Can one find several pearls in the same oyster?" Conseil asked.

"Yes, my boy. There are some shellfish that turn into real jewel coffers. They even mention one oyster, about which I remain dubious, that supposedly contained at least 150 sharks."

"150 sharks!" Ned Land yelped.

"Did I say sharks?" I exclaimed hastily. "I meant 150 pearls. Sharks wouldn't make sense."

"Indeed," Conseil said. "But will master now tell us how one goes about extracting these pearls?"

"One proceeds in several ways, and often when pearls stick to the valves, fishermen even pull them loose with pliers. But usually the shellfish are spread out on mats made from the esparto grass that covers the beaches. Thus they die in the open air, and by the end of ten days they've rotted sufficiently. Next they're immersed in huge tanks of salt water, then they're opened up and washed. At this point the sorters begin their twofold task. First they remove the layers of mother–of–pearl, which are known in the industry by the names legitimate silver, bastard white, or bastard black, and these are shipped out in cases weighing 125 to 150 kilograms. Then they remove the oyster's meaty tissue, boil it, and finally strain it, in order to extract even the smallest pearls."

"Do the prices of these pearls differ depending on their size?" Conseil asked.

"Not only on their size," I replied, "but also according to their shape, their water—in other words, their color—and their orient—in other words, that dappled, shimmering glow that makes them so delightful to the eye. The finest pearls are called virgin pearls, or paragons; they form in isolation within the mollusk's tissue. They're white, often opaque but sometimes of opalescent transparency, and usually spherical or pear-shaped. The spherical ones are made into bracelets; the pear-shaped ones into earrings, and since they're the most valuable, they're priced individually. The other pearls that stick to the oyster's shell are more erratically shaped and are priced by weight. Finally, classed in the lowest order, the smallest pearls are known by the name seed pearls; they're priced by the measuring cup and are used mainly in the creation of embroidery for church vestments."

"But it must be a long, hard job, sorting out these pearls by size," the Canadian said.

"No, my friend. That task is performed with eleven strainers, or sieves, that are pierced with different numbers of holes. Those pearls staying in the strainers with twenty to eighty holes are in the first order. Those not slipping through the sieves pierced with 100 to 800 holes are in the second order. Finally, those pearls for which one uses strainers pierced with 900 to 1,000 holes make up the seed pearls."

"How ingenious," Conseil said, "to reduce dividing and classifying pearls to a mechanical operation. And could master tell us the profits brought in by harvesting these banks of pearl oysters?"

"According to Sirr's book," I replied, "these Ceylon fisheries are farmed annually for a total profit of 3,000,000 man-eaters."

"Francs!" Conseil rebuked.

"Yes, francs! F3,000,000!" I went on. "But I don't think these fisheries bring in the returns they once did. Similarly, the Central American fisheries used to make an annual profit of F4,000,000 during the reign of King Charles V, but now they bring in only two–thirds of that amount. All in all, it's estimated that F9,000,000 is the current yearly return for the whole pearl–harvesting industry."

"But," Conseil asked, "haven't certain famous pearls been quoted at extremely high prices?"

"Yes, my boy. They say Julius Caesar gave Servilia a pearl worth F120,000 in our currency."

"I've even heard stories," the Canadian said, "about some lady in ancient times who drank pearls in vinegar."

"Cleopatra," Conseil shot back.

"It must have tasted pretty bad," Ned Land added.

"Abominable, Ned my friend," Conseil replied. "But when a little glass of vinegar is worth F1,500,000, its taste is a small price to pay."

"I'm sorry I didn't marry the gal," the Canadian said, throwing up his hands with an air of discouragement.

"Ned Land married to Cleopatra?" Conseil exclaimed.

"But I was all set to tie the knot, Conseil," the Canadian replied in all seriousness, "and it wasn't my fault the whole business fell through. I even bought a pearl necklace for my fiancée, Kate Tender, but she married somebody else instead. Well, that necklace cost me only $1.50, but you can absolutely trust me on this, professor, its pearls were so big, they wouldn't have gone through that strainer with twenty holes."

"My gallant Ned," I replied, laughing, "those were artificial pearls, ordinary glass beads whose insides were coated with Essence of Orient."

"Wow!" the Canadian replied. "That Essence of Orient must sell for quite a large sum."

"As little as zero! It comes from the scales of a European carp, it's nothing more than a silver substance that collects in the water and is preserved in ammonia. It's worthless."

"Maybe that's why Kate Tender married somebody else," replied Mr. Land philosophically.

"But," I said, "getting back to pearls of great value, I don't think any sovereign ever possessed one superior to the pearl owned by Captain Nemo."

"This one?" Conseil said, pointing to a magnificent jewel in its glass case.

"Exactly. And I'm certainly not far off when I estimate its value at 2,000,000 . . . uh . . ."

"Francs!" Conseil said quickly.

"Yes," I said, "F2,000,000, and no doubt all it cost our captain was the effort to pick it up."

"Ha!" Ned Land exclaimed. "During our stroll tomorrow, who says we won't run into one just like it?"

"Bah!" Conseil put in.

"And why not?"

"What good would a pearl worth millions do us here on the *Nautilus*?"

"Here, no," Ned Land said. "But elsewhere. . . ."

"Oh! Elsewhere!" Conseil put in, shaking his head.

"In fact," I said, "Mr. Land is right. And if we ever brought back to Europe or America a pearl worth millions, it would make the story of our adventures more authentic—and much more rewarding."

"That's how I see it," the Canadian said.

"But," said Conseil, who perpetually returned to the didactic side of things, "is this pearl fishing ever dangerous?"

"No," I replied quickly, "especially if one takes certain precautions."

"What risks would you run in a job like that?" Ned Land said. "Swallowing a few gulps of salt water?"

"Whatever you say, Ned." Then, trying to imitate Captain Nemo's carefree tone, I asked, "By the way, gallant Ned, are you afraid of sharks?"

"Me?" the Canadian replied. "I'm a professional harpooner! It's my job to make a mockery of them!"

"It isn't an issue," I said, "of fishing for them with a swivel hook, hoisting them onto the deck of a ship, chopping off the tail with a sweep of the ax, opening the belly, ripping out the heart, and tossing it into the sea."

"So it's an issue of . . . ?"

"Yes, precisely."

"In the water?"

"In the water."

"Ye gods, just give me a good harpoon! You see, sir, these sharks are badly designed. They have to roll their bellies over to snap you up, and in the meantime . . ."

Ned Land had a way of pronouncing the word "snap" that sent chills down the spine.

"Well, how about you, Conseil? What are your feelings about these man-eaters?"

"Me?" Conseil said. "I'm afraid I must be frank with master."

Good for you, I thought.

"If master faces these sharks," Conseil said, "I think his loyal manservant should face them with him!"

# CHAPTER 3

## A Pearl Worth Ten Million

NIGHT FELL. I went to bed. I slept pretty poorly. Man-eaters played a major role in my dreams. And I found it more or less appropriate that the French word for shark, requin, has its linguistic roots in the word requiem.

The next day at four o'clock in the morning, I was awakened by the steward whom Captain Nemo had placed expressly at my service. I got up quickly, dressed, and went into the lounge.

Captain Nemo was waiting for me.

"Professor Aronnax," he said to me, "are you ready to start?"

"I'm ready."

"Kindly follow me."

"What about my companions, Captain?"

"They've been alerted and are waiting for us."

"Aren't we going to put on our diving suits?" I asked.

"Not yet. I haven't let the *Nautilus* pull too near the coast, and we're fairly well out from the Mannar oysterbank. But I have the skiff ready, and it will take us to the exact spot where we'll disembark, which will save us a pretty long trek. It's carrying our diving equipment, and we'll suit up just before we begin our underwater exploring."

Captain Nemo took me to the central companionway whose steps led to the platform. Ned and Conseil were there, enraptured with the "pleasure trip" getting under way. Oars in position, five of the *Nautilus's* sailors were waiting for us aboard the skiff, which was moored alongside. The night was still dark. Layers of clouds cloaked the sky and left only a few stars in view. My eyes flew to the side where land lay, but I saw only a blurred line covering three–quarters of the horizon from southwest to northwest. Going up Ceylon's west coast during the night, the *Nautilus* lay west of the bay, or rather that gulf formed by the mainland and Mannar Island. Under these dark waters there stretched the bank of shellfish, an inexhaustible field of pearls more than twenty miles long.

Captain Nemo, Conseil, Ned Land, and I found seats in the stern of the skiff. The longboat's coxswain took the tiller; his four companions leaned into their oars; the moorings were cast off and we pulled clear.

The skiff headed southward. The oarsmen took their time. I watched their strokes vigorously catch the water, and they always waited ten seconds before rowing again, following the practice used in most navies. While the longboat coasted, drops of liquid flicked from the oars and hit the dark troughs of the waves, pitter–pattering like splashes of molten lead. Coming from well out, a mild swell made the skiff roll gently, and a few cresting billows lapped at its bow.

We were silent. What was Captain Nemo thinking? Perhaps that this approaching shore was too close for comfort, contrary to the Canadian's views in which it still seemed too far away. As for Conseil, he had come along out of simple curiosity.

Near 5:30 the first glimmers of light on the horizon defined the upper lines of the coast with greater distinctness. Fairly flat to the east, it swelled a little toward the south. Five miles still separated it from us, and its beach merged with the misty waters. Between us and the shore, the sea was deserted. Not a boat, not a diver. Profound solitude reigned over this gathering place of pearl fishermen. As Captain Nemo had commented, we were arriving in these waterways a month too soon.

At six o'clock the day broke suddenly, with that speed unique to tropical regions, which experience no real dawn or dusk. The sun's rays pierced the cloud curtain gathered on the easterly horizon, and the radiant orb rose swiftly.

I could clearly see the shore, which featured a few sparse trees here and there.

The skiff advanced toward Mannar Island, which curved to the south. Captain Nemo stood up from his thwart and studied the sea.

At his signal the anchor was lowered, but its chain barely ran because the bottom lay no more than a meter down, and this locality was one of the shallowest spots near the bank of shellfish. Instantly the skiff wheeled around under the ebb tide's outbound thrust.

"Here we are, Professor Aronnax," Captain Nemo then said. "You observe this confined bay? A month from now in this very place, the numerous fishing boats of the harvesters will gather, and these are the waters their divers will ransack so daringly. This bay is felicitously laid out for their type of fishing. It's sheltered from the strongest winds, and the sea is never very turbulent here, highly favorable conditions for diving work. Now let's put on our underwater suits, and we'll begin our stroll."

I didn't reply, and while staring at these suspicious waves, I began to put on my heavy aquatic clothes, helped by the longboat's sailors. Captain Nemo and my two companions suited up as well. None of the Nautilus's men were to go with us on this new excursion.

Soon we were imprisoned up to the neck in india–rubber clothing, and straps fastened the air devices onto our backs. As for the Ruhmkorff device, it didn't seem to be in the picture. Before inserting my head into its copper capsule, I commented on this to the captain.

"Our lighting equipment would be useless to us," the captain answered me. "We won't be going very deep, and the sun's rays will be sufficient to light our way. Besides, it's unwise to carry electric lanterns under these waves. Their brightness might unexpectedly attract certain dangerous occupants of these waterways."

As Captain Nemo pronounced these words, I turned to Conseil and Ned Land. But my two friends had already encased their craniums in their metal headgear, and they could neither hear nor reply.

I had one question left to address to Captain Nemo.

"What about our weapons?" I asked him. "Our rifles?"

"Rifles! What for? Don't your mountaineers attack bears dagger in hand? And isn't steel surer than lead? Here's a sturdy blade. Slip it under your belt and let's be off."

I stared at my companions. They were armed in the same fashion, and Ned Land was also brandishing an enormous harpoon he had stowed in the skiff before leaving the *Nautilus*.

Then, following the captain's example, I let myself be crowned with my heavy copper sphere, and our air tanks immediately went into action.

An instant later, the longboat's sailors helped us overboard one after the other, and we set foot on level sand in a meter and a half of water. Captain Nemo gave us a hand signal. We followed him down a gentle slope and disappeared under the waves.

There the obsessive fears in my brain left me. I became surprisingly calm again. The ease with which I could move increased my confidence, and the many strange sights captivated my imagination.

The sun was already sending sufficient light under these waves. The tiniest objects remained visible. After ten minutes of walking, we were in five meters of water, and the terrain had become almost flat.

Like a covey of snipe over a marsh, there rose underfoot schools of unusual fish from the genus Monopterus, whose members have no fin but their tail. I recognized the Javanese eel, a genuine eight–decimeter serpent with a bluish gray belly, which, without the gold lines over its flanks, could easily be confused with the conger eel. From the butterfish genus, whose oval bodies are very flat, I observed several adorned in brilliant colors and sporting a dorsal fin like a sickle, edible fish that, when dried and marinated, make an excellent dish known by the name "karawade"; then some sea poachers, fish belonging to the genus Aspidophoroides, whose bodies are covered with scaly armor divided into eight lengthwise sections.

Meanwhile, as the sun got progressively higher, it lit up the watery mass more and more. The seafloor changed little by little. Its fine–grained sand was followed by a genuine causeway of smooth crags covered by a carpet of mollusks and zoophytes. Among other specimens in these two branches, I noted some windowpane oysters with thin valves of unequal size, a type of ostracod unique to the Red Sea and the Indian Ocean, then orange–hued lucina with circular shells, awl–shaped auger shells, some of those Persian murex snails that supply the *Nautilus* with such wonderful dye, spiky periwinkles fifteen centimeters long that rose under the waves like hands ready to grab you, turban snails with shells made of horn and bristling all over with spines, lamp shells, edible duck clams that feed the Hindu marketplace, subtly luminous jellyfish of the species Pelagia panopyra, and finally some wonderful Oculina flabelliforma, magnificent sea fans that fashion one of the most luxuriant tree forms in this ocean.

In the midst of this moving vegetation, under arbors of water plants, there raced legions of clumsy articulates, in particular some fanged frog crabs whose carapaces form a slightly rounded triangle, robber crabs exclusive to these waterways, and horrible parthenope crabs whose appearance was repulsive to the eye. One animal no less hideous, which I encountered several times, was the enormous crab that Mr. Darwin observed, to which nature has given the instinct and requisite strength to eat coconuts; it scrambles up trees on the beach and sends the coconuts tumbling; they fracture in their fall and are opened by its powerful pincers. Here, under these clear waves, this crab raced around with matchless agility, while green turtles from the species frequenting the Malabar coast moved sluggishly among the crumbling rocks.

Near seven o'clock we finally surveyed the bank of shellfish, where pearl oysters reproduce by the millions. These valuable mollusks stick to rocks, where they're strongly attached by a mass of brown filaments that forbids their moving about. In this respect oysters are inferior even to mussels, to whom nature has not denied all talent for locomotion.

The shellfish Meleagrina, that womb for pearls whose valves are nearly equal in size, has the shape of a round shell with thick walls and a very rough exterior. Some of these shells were furrowed with flaky, greenish bands that radiated down from the top. These were the young oysters. The others had rugged black surfaces, measured up to fifteen centimeters in width, and were ten or more years old.

Captain Nemo pointed to this prodigious heap of shellfish, and I saw that these mines were genuinely inexhaustible, since nature's creative powers are greater than man's destructive instincts. True to those instincts, Ned Land greedily stuffed the finest of these mollusks into a net he carried at his side.

But we couldn't stop. We had to follow the captain, who headed down trails seemingly known only to himself. The seafloor rose noticeably, and when I lifted my arms, sometimes they would pass above the surface of the sea. Then the level of the oysterbank would lower unpredictably. Often we went around tall, pointed rocks rising like pyramids. In their dark crevices huge crustaceans, aiming their long legs like heavy artillery, watched us with unblinking eyes, while underfoot there crept millipedes, bloodworms, aricia worms, and annelid worms, whose antennas and tubular tentacles were incredibly long.

Just then a huge cave opened up in our path, hollowed from a picturesque pile of rocks whose smooth heights were completely hung with underwater flora. At first this cave looked pitch–black to me. Inside, the sun's rays seemed to diminish by degrees. Their hazy transparency was nothing more than drowned light.

Captain Nemo went in. We followed him. My eyes soon grew accustomed to this comparative gloom. I distinguished the unpredictably contoured springings of a vault, supported by natural pillars firmly based on a granite foundation, like the weighty columns of Tuscan architecture. Why had our incomprehensible guide taken us into the depths of this underwater crypt? I would soon find out.

After going down a fairly steep slope, our feet trod the floor of a sort of circular pit. There Captain Nemo stopped, and his hand indicated an object that I hadn't yet noticed.

It was an oyster of extraordinary dimensions, a titanic giant clam, a holy–water font that could have held a whole lake, a basin more than two meters wide, hence even bigger than the one adorning the *Nautilus's* lounge.

I approached this phenomenal mollusk. Its mass of filaments attached it to a table of granite, and there it grew by itself in the midst of the cave's calm waters. I estimated the weight of this giant clam at 300 kilograms. Hence such an oyster held fifteen kilos of meat, and you'd need the stomach of King Gargantua to eat a couple dozen.

Captain Nemo was obviously familiar with this bivalve's existence. This wasn't the first time he'd paid it a visit, and I thought his sole reason for leading us to this locality was to show us a natural curiosity. I was mistaken. Captain Nemo had an explicit personal interest in checking on the current condition of this giant clam.

The mollusk's two valves were partly open. The captain approached and stuck his dagger vertically between the shells to discourage any ideas about closing; then with his hands he raised the fringed, membrane–filled tunic that made up the animal's mantle.

There, between its leaflike folds, I saw a loose pearl as big as a coconut. Its globular shape, perfect clarity, and wonderful orient made it a jewel of incalculable value. Carried away by curiosity, I stretched out my hand to take it, weigh it, fondle it! But the captain stopped me, signaled no, removed his dagger in one swift motion, and let the two valves snap shut.

I then understood Captain Nemo's intent. By leaving the pearl buried beneath the giant clam's mantle, he allowed it to grow imperceptibly. With each passing year the mollusk's secretions added new concentric layers. The captain alone was familiar with the cave where this wonderful fruit of nature was "ripening"; he alone reared it, so to speak, in order to transfer it one day to his dearly beloved museum. Perhaps, following the examples of oyster farmers in China and India, he had even predetermined the creation of this pearl by sticking under the mollusk's folds some piece of glass or metal that was gradually covered with mother–of–pearl. In any case, comparing this pearl to others I already knew about, and to those shimmering in the captain's collection, I estimated that it was worth at least F10,000,000. It was a superb natural curiosity rather than a luxurious piece of jewelry, because I don't know of any female ear that could handle it.

Our visit to this opulent giant clam came to an end. Captain Nemo left the cave, and we climbed back up the bank of shellfish in the midst of these clear waters not yet disturbed by divers at work.

We walked by ourselves, genuine loiterers stopping or straying as our fancies dictated. For my part, I was no longer worried about those dangers my imagination had so ridiculously exaggerated. The shallows drew noticeably closer to the surface of the sea, and soon, walking in only a meter of water, my head passed well above the level of the ocean. Conseil rejoined me, and gluing his huge copper capsule to mine, his eyes gave me a friendly greeting. But this lofty plateau measured only a few fathoms, and soon we re-entered Our Element. I think I've now earned the right to dub it that.

Ten minutes later, Captain Nemo stopped suddenly. I thought he'd called a halt so that we could turn and start back. No. With a gesture he ordered us to crouch beside him at the foot of a wide crevice. His hand motioned toward a spot within the liquid mass, and I looked carefully.

Five meters away a shadow appeared and dropped to the seafloor. The alarming idea of sharks crossed my mind. But I was mistaken, and once again we didn't have to deal with monsters of the deep.

It was a man, a living man, a black Indian fisherman, a poor devil who no doubt had come to gather what he could before harvest time. I saw the bottom of his dinghy, moored a few feet above his head. He would dive and go back up in quick succession. A stone cut in the shape of a sugar loaf, which he gripped between his feet while a rope connected it to his boat, served to lower him more quickly to the ocean floor. This was the extent of his equipment. Arriving on the seafloor at a depth of about five meters, he fell to his knees and stuffed his sack with shellfish gathered at random. Then he went back up, emptied his sack, pulled up his stone, and started all over again, the whole process lasting only thirty seconds.

This diver didn't see us. A shadow cast by our crag hid us from his view. And besides, how could this poor Indian ever have guessed that human beings, creatures like himself, were near him under the waters, eavesdropping on his movements, not missing a single detail of his fishing!

So he went up and down several times. He gathered only about ten shellfish per dive, because he had to tear them from the banks where each clung with its tough mass of filaments.

And how many of these oysters for which he risked his life would have no pearl in them!

I observed him with great care. His movements were systematically executed, and for half an hour no danger seemed to threaten him. So I had gotten used to the sight of this fascinating fishing when all at once, just as the Indian was kneeling on the seafloor, I saw him make a frightened gesture, stand, and gather himself to spring back to the surface of the waves.

I understood his fear. A gigantic shadow appeared above the poor diver. It was a shark of huge size, moving in diagonally, eyes ablaze, jaws wide open!

I was speechless with horror, unable to make a single movement.

With one vigorous stroke of its fins, the voracious animal shot toward the Indian, who jumped aside and avoided the shark's bite but not the thrashing of its tail, because that tail struck him across the chest and stretched him out on the seafloor.

This scene lasted barely a few seconds. The shark returned, rolled over on its back, and was getting ready to cut the Indian in half, when Captain Nemo, who was stationed beside me, suddenly stood up. Then he strode right toward the monster, dagger in hand, ready to fight it at close quarters.

Just as it was about to snap up the poor fisherman, the man–eater saw its new adversary, repositioned itself on its belly, and headed swiftly toward him.

I can see Captain Nemo's bearing to this day. Bracing himself, he waited for the fearsome man–eater with wonderful composure, and when the latter rushed at him, the captain leaped aside with prodigious quickness, avoided a collision, and sank his dagger into its belly. But that wasn't the end of the story. A dreadful battle was joined.

The shark bellowed, so to speak. Blood was pouring into

the waves from its wounds. The sea was dyed red, and through this opaque liquid I could see nothing else.

Nothing else until the moment when, through a rift in the clouds, I saw the daring captain clinging to one of the animal's fins, fighting the monster at close quarters, belaboring his enemy's belly with stabs of the dagger yet unable to deliver the deciding thrust, in other words, a direct hit to the heart. In its struggles the man–eater churned the watery mass so furiously, its eddies threatened to knock me over.

I wanted to run to the captain's rescue. But I was transfixed with horror, unable to move.

I stared, wild–eyed. I saw the fight enter a new phase. The captain fell to the seafloor, toppled by the enormous mass weighing him down. Then the shark's jaws opened astoundingly wide, like a pair of industrial shears, and that would have been the finish of Captain Nemo had not Ned Land, quick as thought, rushed forward with his harpoon and driven its dreadful point into the shark's underside.

The waves were saturated with masses of blood. The waters shook with the movements of the man–eater, which thrashed about with indescribable fury. Ned Land hadn't missed his target. This was the monster's death rattle. Pierced to the heart, it was struggling with dreadful spasms whose aftershocks knocked Conseil off his feet.

Meanwhile Ned Land pulled the captain clear. Uninjured, the latter stood up, went right to the Indian, quickly cut the rope binding the man to his stone, took the fellow in his arms, and with a vigorous kick of the heel, rose to the surface of the sea.

The three of us followed him, and a few moments later, miraculously safe, we reached the fisherman's longboat.

Captain Nemo's first concern was to revive this unfortunate man. I wasn't sure he would succeed. I hoped so, since the poor devil hadn't been under very long. But that stroke from the shark's tail could have been his deathblow.

Fortunately, after vigorous massaging by Conseil and the captain, I saw the nearly drowned man regain consciousness little by little. He opened his eyes. How startled he must have felt, how frightened even, at seeing four huge, copper craniums leaning over him!

And above all, what must he have thought when Captain Nemo pulled a bag of pearls from a pocket in his diving suit and placed it in the fisherman's hands? This magnificent benefaction from the Man of the Waters to the poor Indian from Ceylon was accepted by the latter with trembling hands. His bewildered eyes indicated that he didn't know to what superhuman creatures he owed both his life and his fortune.

At the captain's signal we returned to the bank of shellfish, and retracing our steps, we walked for half an hour until we encountered the anchor connecting the seafloor with the *Nautilus's* skiff.

Back on board, the sailors helped divest us of our heavy copper carapaces.

Captain Nemo's first words were spoken to the Canadian.

"Thank you, Mr. Land," he told him.

"Tit for tat, Captain," Ned Land replied. "I owed it to you."

The ghost of a smile glided across the captain's lips, and that was all.

"To the *Nautilus*," he said.

The longboat flew over the waves. A few minutes later we encountered the shark's corpse again, floating.

From the black markings on the tips of its fins, I recognized the dreadful Squalus melanopterus from the seas of the East Indies, a variety in the species of sharks proper. It was more than twenty-five feet long; its enormous mouth occupied a third of its body. It was an adult, as could be seen from the six rows of teeth forming an isosceles triangle in its upper jaw.

Conseil looked at it with purely scientific fascination, and

I'm sure he placed it, not without good reason, in the class of cartilaginous fish, order Chondropterygia with fixed gills, family Selacia, genus Squalus.

While I was contemplating this inert mass, suddenly a dozen of these voracious melanoptera appeared around our longboat; but, paying no attention to us, they pounced on the corpse and quarreled over every scrap of it.

By 8:30 we were back on board the *Nautilus*.

There I fell to thinking about the incidents that marked our excursion over the Mannar oysterbank. Two impressions inevitably stood out. One concerned Captain Nemo's matchless bravery, the other his devotion to a human being, a representative of that race from which he had fled beneath the seas. In spite of everything, this strange man hadn't yet succeeded in completely stifling his heart.

When I shared these impressions with him, he answered me in a tone touched with emotion:

"That Indian, professor, lives in the land of the oppressed, and I am to this day, and will be until my last breath, a native of that same land!"

# CHAPTER 4

## The Red Sea

DURING THE DAY of January 29, the island of Ceylon disappeared below the horizon, and at a speed of twenty miles per hour, the *Nautilus* glided into the labyrinthine channels that separate the Maldive and Laccadive Islands. It likewise hugged Kiltan Island, a shore of madreporic origin discovered by Vasco da Gama in 1499 and one of nineteen chief islands in the island group of the Laccadives, located between latitude 10° and 14° 30' north, and between longitude 50° 72' and 69° east.

By then we had fared 16,220 miles, or 7,500 leagues, from our starting point in the seas of Japan.

The next day, January 30, when the *Nautilus* rose to the surface of the ocean, there was no more land in sight. Setting its course to the north–northwest, the ship headed toward the Gulf of Oman, carved out between Arabia and the Indian peninsula and providing access to the Persian Gulf.

This was obviously a blind alley with no possible outlet. So where was Captain Nemo taking us? I was unable to say. Which didn't satisfy the Canadian, who that day asked me where we were going.

"We're going, Mr. Ned, where the Captain's fancy takes us."

"His fancy," the Canadian replied, "won't take us very far. The Persian Gulf has no outlet, and if we enter those waters, it won't be long before we return in our tracks."

"All right, we'll return, Mr. Land, and after the Persian Gulf, if the *Nautilus* wants to visit the Red Sea, the Strait of Bab el Mandeb is still there to let us in!"

"I don't have to tell you, sir," Ned Land replied, "that the Red Sea is just as landlocked as the gulf, since the Isthmus of Suez hasn't been cut all the way through yet; and even if it was, a boat as secretive as ours wouldn't risk a canal intersected with locks. So the Red Sea won't be our way back to Europe either."

"But I didn't say we'd return to Europe."

"What do you figure, then?"

"I figure that after visiting these unusual waterways of Arabia and Egypt, the *Nautilus* will go back down to the Indian Ocean, perhaps through Mozambique Channel, perhaps off the Mascarene Islands, and then make for the Cape of Good Hope."

"And once we're at the Cape of Good Hope?" the Canadian asked with typical persistence.

"Well then, we'll enter that Atlantic Ocean with which we aren't yet familiar. What's wrong, Ned my friend? Are you tired of this voyage under the seas? Are you bored with the constantly changing sight of these underwater wonders? Speaking for myself, I'll be extremely distressed to see the end of a voyage so few men will ever have a chance to make."

"But don't you realize, Professor Aronnax," the Canadian replied, "that soon we'll have been imprisoned for three whole months aboard this *Nautilus*?"

"No, Ned, I didn't realize it, I don't want to realize it, and I don't keep track of every day and every hour."

"But when will it be over?"

"In its appointed time. Meanwhile there's nothing we can do about it, and our discussions are futile. My gallant Ned, if you come and tell me, 'A chance to escape is available to us,' then I'll discuss it with you. But that isn't the case, and in all honesty, I don't think Captain Nemo ever ventures into European seas."

This short dialogue reveals that in my mania for the *Nautilus*, I was turning into the spitting image of its commander.

As for Ned Land, he ended our talk in his best speechifying style: "That's all fine and dandy. But in my humble opinion, a life in jail is a life without joy."

For four days until February 3, the *Nautilus* inspected the Gulf of Oman at various speeds and depths. It seemed to be traveling at random, as if hesitating over which course to follow, but it never crossed the Tropic of Cancer.

After leaving this gulf we raised Muscat for an instant, the most important town in the country of Oman. I marveled at its strange appearance in the midst of the black rocks surrounding it, against which the white of its houses and forts stood out sharply. I spotted the rounded domes of its mosques, the elegant tips of its minarets, and its fresh, leafy terraces. But it was only a fleeting vision, and the *Nautilus* soon sank beneath the dark waves of these waterways.

Then our ship went along at a distance of six miles from the Arabic coasts of Mahra and Hadhramaut, their undulating lines of mountains relieved by a few ancient ruins. On February 5 we finally put into the Gulf of Aden, a genuine funnel stuck into the neck of Bab el Mandeb and bottling these Indian waters in the Red Sea.

On February 6 the *Nautilus* cruised in sight of the city of Aden, perched on a promontory connected to the continent by a narrow isthmus, a sort of inaccessible Gibraltar whose fortifications the English rebuilt after capturing it in 1839. I glimpsed the octagonal minarets of this town, which used to be one of the wealthiest, busiest commercial centers along this coast, as the Arab historian Idrisi tells it.

I was convinced that when Captain Nemo reached this point, he would back out again; but I was mistaken, and much to my surprise, he did nothing of the sort.

The next day, February 7, we entered the Strait of Bab el

Mandeb, whose name means "Gate of Tears" in the Arabic language. Twenty miles wide, it's only fifty-two kilometers long, and with the *Nautilus* launched at full speed, clearing it was the work of barely an hour. But I didn't see a thing, not even Perim Island where the British government built fortifications to strengthen Aden's position. There were many English and French steamers plowing this narrow passageway, liners going from Suez to Bombay, Calcutta, Melbourne, Réunion Island, and Mauritius; far too much traffic for the *Nautilus* to make an appearance on the surface. So it wisely stayed in midwater.

Finally, at noon, we were plowing the waves of the Red Sea.

The Red Sea: that great lake so famous in biblical traditions, seldom replenished by rains, fed by no important rivers, continually drained by a high rate of evaporation, its water level dropping a meter and a half every year! If it were fully landlocked like a lake, this odd gulf might dry up completely; on this score it's inferior to its neighbors, the Caspian Sea and the Dead Sea, whose levels lower only to the point where their evaporation exactly equals the amounts of water they take to their hearts.

This Red Sea is 2,600 kilometers long with an average width of 240. In the days of the Ptolemies and the Roman emperors, it was a great commercial artery for the world, and when its isthmus has been cut through, it will completely regain that bygone importance that the Suez railways have already brought back in part.

I would not even attempt to understand the whim that induced Captain Nemo to take us into this gulf. But I wholeheartedly approved of the *Nautilus's* entering it. It adopted a medium pace, sometimes staying on the surface, sometimes diving to avoid some ship, and so I could observe both the inside and topside of this highly unusual sea.

On February 8, as early as the first hours of daylight, Mocha appeared before us: a town now in ruins, whose walls would collapse at the mere sound of a cannon, and which shelters a few leafy date trees here and there. This once-important city used to contain six public marketplaces plus twenty-six mosques, and its walls, protected by fourteen forts, fashioned a three-kilometer girdle around it.

Then the *Nautilus* drew near the beaches of Africa, where the sea is considerably deeper. There, through the open panels and in a midwater of crystal clarity, our ship enabled us to study wonderful bushes of shining coral and huge chunks of rock wrapped in splendid green furs of algae and fucus. What an indescribable sight, and what a variety of settings and scenery where these reefs and volcanic islands leveled off by the Libyan coast! But soon the *Nautilus* hugged the eastern shore where these tree forms appeared in all their glory. This was off the coast of Tihama, and there such zoophyte displays not only flourished below sea level but they also fashioned picturesque networks that unreeled as high as ten fathoms above it; the latter were more whimsical but less colorful than the former, which kept their bloom thanks to the moist vitality of the waters.

How many delightful hours I spent in this way at the lounge window! How many new specimens of underwater flora and fauna I marveled at beneath the light of our electric beacon! Mushroom-shaped fungus coral, some slate-colored sea anemone including the species Thalassianthus aster among others, organ-pipe coral arranged like flutes and just begging for a puff from the god Pan, shells unique to this sea that dwell in madreporic cavities and whose bases are twisted into squat spirals, and finally a thousand samples of a polypary I hadn't observed until then: the common sponge.

First division in the polyp group, the class Spongiaria has been created by scientists precisely for this unusual exhibit whose usefulness is beyond dispute. The sponge is definitely not a plant, as some naturalists still believe, but an animal of the lowest order, a polypary inferior even to coral. Its animal nature isn't in doubt, and we can't accept even the views of the ancients, who regarded it as halfway between plant and animal. But I must say that naturalists are not in agreement on the structural mode of sponges. For some it's a polypary, and for others, such as Professor Milne-Edwards, it's a single, solitary individual.

The class Spongiaria contains about 300 species that are encountered in a large number of seas and even in certain streams, where they've been given the name freshwater sponges. But their waters of choice are the Red Sea and the Mediterranean near the Greek Islands or the coast of Syria. These waters witness the reproduction and growth of soft, delicate bath sponges whose prices run as high as F150 apiece: the yellow sponge from Syria, the horn sponge from Barbary, etc. But since I had no hope of studying these zoophytes in the seaports of the Levant, from which we were separated by the insuperable Isthmus of Suez, I had to be content with observing them in the waters of the Red Sea.

So I called Conseil to my side, while at an average depth of eight to nine meters, the *Nautilus* slowly skimmed every beautiful rock on the easterly coast.

There sponges grew in every shape, globular, stalklike, leaflike, fingerlike. With reasonable accuracy, they lived up to their nicknames of basket sponges, chalice sponges, distaff sponges, elkhorn sponges, lion's paws, peacock's tails, and Neptune's gloves—designations bestowed on them by fishermen, more poetically inclined than scientists. A gelatinous, semifluid substance coated the fibrous tissue of these sponges, and from this tissue there escaped a steady trickle of water that, after carrying sustenance to each cell, was being expelled by a contracting movement. This jellylike substance disappears when the polyp dies, emitting ammonia as it rots. Finally nothing remains but the fibers, either gelatinous or made of horn, that constitute your household sponge, which takes on a russet hue and is used for various tasks depending on its degree of elasticity, permeability, or resistance to saturation.

These polyparies were sticking to rocks, shells of mollusks, and even the stalks of water plants. They adorned the smallest crevices, some sprawling, others standing or hanging like coral outgrowths. I told Conseil that sponges are fished up in two ways, either by dragnet or by hand. The latter method calls for the services of a diver, but it's preferable because it spares the polypary's tissue, leaving it with a much higher market value.

Other zoophytes swarming near the sponges consisted chiefly of a very elegant species of jellyfish; mollusks were represented by varieties of squid that, according to Professor Orbigny, are unique to the Red Sea; and reptiles by virgata turtles belonging to the genus Chelonia, which furnished our table with a dainty but wholesome dish.

As for fish, they were numerous and often remarkable. Here are the ones that the Nautilus's nets most frequently hauled on board: rays, including spotted rays that were oval in shape and brick red in color, their bodies strewn with erratic blue speckles and identifiable by their jagged double stings, silver-backed skates, common stingrays with stippled tails, butterfly rays that looked like huge two-meter cloaks flapping at middepth, toothless guitarfish that were a type of cartilaginous fish closer to the shark, trunkfish known as dromedaries that were one and a half feet long and had humps ending in backward-curving stings, serpentine moray eels with silver tails and bluish backs plus brown pectorals trimmed in gray piping, a species of butterfish called the fiatola decked out in thin gold stripes and the three colors of the French flag, Montague blennies four decimeters long, superb jacks handsomely embellished by seven black crosswise streaks with blue and yellow fins plus gold and silver scales, snooks, standard mullet with yellow heads, parrotfish, wrasse, triggerfish, gobies, etc., plus a thousand other fish common to the oceans we had already crossed.

On February 9 the *Nautilus* cruised in the widest part of the Red Sea, measuring 190 miles straight across from Suakin on the west coast to Qunfidha on the east coast.

At noon that day after our position fix, Captain Nemo climbed onto the platform, where I happened to be. I vowed not to let him go below again without at least sounding him out on his future plans. As soon as he saw me, he came over, graciously offered me a cigar, and said to me:

"Well, professor, are you pleased with this Red Sea? Have you seen enough of its hidden wonders, its fish and zoophytes, its gardens of sponges and forests of coral? Have you glimpsed the towns built on its shores?"

"Yes, Captain Nemo," I replied, "and the *Nautilus* is wonderfully suited to this whole survey. Ah, it's a clever boat!"

"Yes, sir, clever, daring, and invulnerable! It fears neither the Red Sea's dreadful storms nor its currents and reefs."

"Indeed," I said, "this sea is mentioned as one of the worst, and in the days of the ancients, if I'm not mistaken, it had an abominable reputation."

"Thoroughly abominable, Professor Aronnax. The Greek and Latin historians can find nothing to say in its favor, and the Greek geographer Strabo adds that it's especially rough during the rainy season and the period of summer prevailing winds. The Arab Idrisi, referring to it by the name Gulf of Colzoum, relates that ships perished in large numbers on its sandbanks and that no one risked navigating it by night. This, he claims, is a sea subject to fearful hurricanes, strewn with inhospitable islands, and 'with nothing good to offer,' either on its surface or in its depths. As a matter of fact, the same views can also be found in Arrian, Agatharchides, and Artemidorus."

"One can easily see," I answered, "that those historians

didn't navigate aboard the *Nautilus*."

"Indeed," the captain replied with a smile, "and in this respect, the moderns aren't much farther along than the ancients. It took many centuries to discover the mechanical power of steam! Who knows whether we'll see a second *Nautilus* within the next 100 years! Progress is slow, Professor Aronnax."

"It's true," I replied. "Your ship is a century ahead of its time, perhaps several centuries. It would be most unfortunate if such a secret were to die with its inventor!"

Captain Nemo did not reply. After some minutes of silence:

"We were discussing," he said, "the views of ancient historians on the dangers of navigating this Red Sea?"

"True," I replied. "But weren't their fears exaggerated?"

"Yes and no, Professor Aronnax," answered Captain Nemo, who seemed to know "his Red Sea" by heart. "To a modern ship, well rigged, solidly constructed, and in control of its course thanks to obedient steam, some conditions are no longer hazardous that offered all sorts of dangers to the vessels of the ancients. Picture those early navigators venturing forth in sailboats built from planks lashed together with palm–tree ropes, caulked with powdered resin, and coated with dogfish grease. They didn't even have instruments for taking their bearings, they went by guesswork in the midst of currents they barely knew. Under such conditions, shipwrecks had to be numerous. But nowadays steamers providing service between Suez and the South Seas have nothing to fear from the fury of this gulf, despite the contrary winds of its monsoons. Their captains and passengers no longer prepare for departure with sacrifices to placate the gods, and after returning, they don't traipse in wreaths and gold ribbons to say thanks at the local temple."

"Agreed," I said. "And steam seems to have killed off all gratitude in seamen's hearts. But since you seem to have made a special study of this sea, Captain, can you tell me how it got its name?"

"Many explanations exist on the subject, Professor Aronnax. Would you like to hear the views of one chronicler in the 14th century?"

"Gladly."

"This fanciful fellow claims the sea was given its name after the crossing of the Israelites, when the Pharaoh perished in those waves that came together again at Moses' command:

To mark that miraculous sequel, the sea turned a red without equal.

Thus no other course would do but to name it for its hue."

"An artistic explanation, Captain Nemo," I replied, "but I'm unable to rest content with it. So I'll ask you for your own personal views."

"Here they come. To my thinking, Professor Aronnax, this 'Red Sea' designation must be regarded as a translation of the Hebrew word Edrom, and if the ancients gave it that name, it was because of the unique color of its waters."

"Until now, however, I've seen only clear waves, without any unique hue."

"Surely, but as we move ahead to the far end of this gulf, you'll note its odd appearance. I recall seeing the bay of El Tur completely red, like a lake of blood."

"And you attribute this color to the presence of microscopic algae?"

"Yes. It's a purplish, mucilaginous substance produced by those tiny buds known by the name trichodesmia, 40,000 of which are needed to occupy the space of one square millimeter. Perhaps you'll encounter them when we reach El Tur."

"Hence, Captain Nemo, this isn't the first time you've gone through the Red Sea aboard the Nautilus?"

"No, sir."

"Then, since you've already mentioned the crossing of the

Israelites and the catastrophe that befell the Egyptians, I would ask if you've ever discovered any traces under the waters of that great historic event?"

"No, professor, and for an excellent reason."

"What's that?"

"It's because that same locality where Moses crossed with all his people is now so clogged with sand, camels can barely get their legs wet. You can understand that my *Nautilus* wouldn't have enough water for itself."

"And that locality is . . . ?" I asked.

"That locality lies a little above Suez in a sound that used to form a deep estuary when the Red Sea stretched as far as the Bitter Lakes. Now, whether or not their crossing was literally miraculous, the Israelites did cross there in returning to the Promised Land, and the Pharaoh's army did perish at precisely that locality. So I think that excavating those sands would bring to light a great many weapons and tools of Egyptian origin."

"Obviously," I replied. "And for the sake of archaeology, let's hope that sooner or later such excavations do take place, once new towns are settled on the isthmus after the Suez Canal has been cut through—a canal, by the way, of little use to a ship such as the *Nautilus*!"

"Surely, but of great use to the world at large," Captain Nemo said. "The ancients well understood the usefulness to commerce of connecting the Red Sea with the Mediterranean, but they never dreamed of cutting a canal between the two, and instead they picked the Nile as their link. If we can trust tradition, it was probably Egypt's King Sesostris who started digging the canal needed to join the Nile with the Red Sea. What's certain is that in 615 B.C. King Necho II was hard at work on a canal that was fed by Nile water and ran through the Egyptian plains opposite Arabia. This canal could be traveled in four days, and it was so wide, two triple-tiered galleys could pass through it abreast. Its construction was continued by Darius the Great, son of Hystaspes, and probably completed by King Ptolemy II. Strabo saw it used for shipping; but the weakness of its slope between its starting point, near Bubastis, and the Red Sea left it navigable only a few months out of the year. This canal served commerce until the century of Rome's Antonine emperors; it was then abandoned and covered with sand, subsequently reinstated by Arabia's Caliph Omar I, and finally filled in for good in 761 or 762 A.D. by Caliph Al–Mansur, in an effort to prevent supplies from reaching Mohammed ibn Abdullah, who had rebelled against him. During his Egyptian campaign, your General Napoleon Bonaparte discovered traces of this old canal in the Suez desert, and when the tide caught him by surprise, he wellnigh perished just a few hours before rejoining his regiment at Hadjaroth, the very place where Moses had pitched camp 3,300 years before him."

"Well, Captain, what the ancients hesitated to undertake, Mr. de Lesseps is now finishing up; his joining of these two seas will shorten the route from Cadiz to the East Indies by 9,000 kilometers, and he'll soon change Africa into an immense island."

"Yes, Professor Aronnax, and you have every right to be proud of your fellow countryman. Such a man brings a nation more honor than the greatest commanders! Like so many others, he began with difficulties and setbacks, but he triumphed because he has the volunteer spirit. And it's sad to think that this deed, which should have been an international deed, which would have insured that any administration went down in history, will succeed only through the efforts of one man. So all hail to Mr. de Lesseps!"

"Yes, all hail to that great French citizen," I replied, quite startled by how emphatically Captain Nemo had just spoken.

"Unfortunately," he went on, "I can't take you through that Suez Canal, but the day after tomorrow, you'll be able to see the long jetties of Port Said when we're in the Mediterranean."

"In the Mediterranean!" I exclaimed.

"Yes, professor. Does that amaze you?"

"What amazes me is thinking we'll be there the day after tomorrow."

"Oh really?"

"Yes, captain, although since I've been aboard your vessel, I should have formed the habit of not being amazed by anything!"

"But what is it that startles you?"

"The thought of how hideously fast the *Nautilus* will need to go, if it's to double the Cape of Good Hope, circle around Africa, and lie in the open Mediterranean by the day after tomorrow."

"And who says it will circle Africa, professor? What's this talk about doubling the Cape of Good Hope?"

"But unless the *Nautilus* navigates on dry land and crosses over the isthmus—"

"Or under it, Professor Aronnax."

"Under it?"

"Surely," Captain Nemo replied serenely. "Under that tongue of land, nature long ago made what man today is making on its surface."

"What! There's a passageway?"

"Yes, an underground passageway that I've named the Arabian Tunnel. It starts below Suez and leads to the Bay of Pelusium."

"But isn't that isthmus only composed of quicksand?"

"To a certain depth. But at merely fifty meters, one encounters a firm foundation of rock."

"And it's by luck that you discovered this passageway?" I asked, more and more startled.

"Luck plus logic, professor, and logic even more than luck."

"Captain, I hear you, but I can't believe my ears."

"Oh, sir! The old saying still holds good: *Aures habent et non audient!* Not only does this passageway exist, but I've taken advantage of it on several occasions. Without it, I wouldn't have ventured today into such a blind alley as the Red Sea."

"Is it indiscreet to ask how you discovered this tunnel?"

"Sir," the captain answered me, "there can be no secrets between men who will never leave each other."

I ignored this innuendo and waited for Captain Nemo's explanation.

"Professor," he told me, "the simple logic of the naturalist led me to discover this passageway, and I alone am familiar with it. I'd noted that in the Red Sea and the Mediterranean there exist a number of absolutely identical species of fish: eels, butterfish, greenfish, bass, jewelfish, flying fish. Certain of this fact, I wondered if there weren't a connection between the two seas. If there were, its underground current had to go from the Red Sea to the Mediterranean simply because of their difference in level. So I caught a large number of fish in the vicinity of Suez. I slipped copper rings around their tails and tossed them back into the sea. A few months later off the coast of Syria, I recaptured a few specimens of my fish, adorned with their telltale rings. So this proved to me that some connection existed between the two seas. I searched for it with my *Nautilus*, I discovered it, I ventured into it; and soon, professor, you also will have cleared my Arabic tunnel!"

# CHAPTER 5

## Arabian Tunnel

THE SAME DAY, I reported to Conseil and Ned Land that part of the foregoing conversation directly concerning them. When I told them we would be lying in Mediterranean waters within two days, Conseil clapped his hands, but the Canadian shrugged his shoulders.

"An underwater tunnel!" he exclaimed. "A connection between two seas! Who ever heard of such malarkey!"

"Ned my friend," Conseil replied, "had you ever heard of the *Nautilus*? No, yet here it is! So don't shrug your shoulders so blithely, and don't discount something with the feeble excuse that you've never heard of it."

"We'll soon see!" Ned Land shot back, shaking his head. "After all, I'd like nothing better than to believe in your captain's little passageway, and may Heaven grant it really does take us to the Mediterranean."

The same evening, at latitude 21° 30' north, the *Nautilus* was afloat on the surface of the sea and drawing nearer to the Arab coast. I spotted Jidda, an important financial center for Egypt, Syria, Turkey, and the East Indies. I could distinguish with reasonable clarity the overall effect of its buildings, the ships made fast along its wharves, and those bigger vessels whose draft of water required them to drop anchor at the port's offshore mooring. The sun, fairly low on the horizon, struck full force on the houses in this town, accenting their whiteness. Outside the city limits, some wood or reed huts indicated the quarter where the bedouins lived.

Soon Jidda faded into the shadows of evening, and the *Nautilus* went back beneath the mildly phosphorescent waters.

The next day, February 10, several ships appeared, running on our opposite tack. The *Nautilus* resumed its underwater navigating; but at the moment of our noon sights, the sea was deserted and the ship rose again to its waterline.

With Ned and Conseil, I went to sit on the platform. The coast to the east looked like a slightly blurred mass in a damp fog.

Leaning against the sides of the skiff, we were chatting of one thing and another, when Ned Land stretched his hand toward a point in the water, saying to me:

"See anything out there, professor?"

"No, Ned," I replied, "but you know I don't have your eyes."

"Take a good look," Ned went on. "There, ahead to starboard, almost level with the beacon! Don't you see a mass that seems to be moving around?"

"Right," I said after observing carefully, "I can make out something like a long, blackish object on the surface of the water."

"A second *Nautilus*?" Conseil said.

"No," the Canadian replied, "unless I'm badly mistaken, that's some marine animal."

"Are there whales in the Red Sea?" Conseil asked.

"Yes, my boy," I replied, "they're sometimes found here."

"That's no whale," continued Ned Land, whose eyes never strayed from the object they had sighted. "We're old chums, whales and I, and I couldn't mistake their little ways."

"Let's wait and see," Conseil said. "The *Nautilus* is heading that direction, and we'll soon know what we're in for."

In fact, that blackish object was soon only a mile away from us. It looked like a huge reef stranded in midocean. What was it? I still couldn't make up my mind.

"Oh, it's moving off! It's diving!" Ned Land exclaimed. "Damnation! What can that animal be? It doesn't have a forked tail like baleen whales or sperm whales, and its fins look like sawed–off limbs."

"But in that case—" I put in.

"Good lord," the Canadian went on, "it's rolled over on its back, and it's raising its breasts in the air!"

"It's a siren!" Conseil exclaimed. "With all due respect to master, it's an actual mermaid!"

That word "siren" put me back on track, and I realized that the animal belonged to the order Sirenia: marine creatures that legends have turned into mermaids, half woman, half fish.

"No," I told Conseil, "that's no mermaid, it's an unusual creature of which only a few specimens are left in the Red Sea. That's a dugong."

"Order Sirenia, group Pisciforma, subclass Monodelphia, class Mammalia, branch Vertebrata," Conseil replied.

And when Conseil has spoken, there's nothing else to be said.

Meanwhile Ned Land kept staring. His eyes were gleaming with desire at the sight of that animal. His hands were ready to hurl a harpoon. You would have thought he was waiting for the right moment to jump overboard and attack the creature in its own element.

"Oh, sir," he told me in a voice trembling with excitement, "I've never killed anything like that!"

His whole being was concentrated in this last word.

Just then Captain Nemo appeared on the platform. He spotted the dugong. He understood the Canadian's frame of mind and addressed him directly:

"If you held a harpoon, Mr. Land, wouldn't your hands be itching to put it to work?"

"Positively, sir."

"And just for one day, would it displease you to return to

your fisherman's trade and add this cetacean to the list of those you've already hunted down?"

"It wouldn't displease me one bit."

"All right, you can try your luck!"

"Thank you, sir," Ned Land replied, his eyes ablaze.

"Only," the captain went on, "I urge you to aim carefully at this animal, in your own personal interest."

"Is the dugong dangerous to attack?" I asked, despite the Canadian's shrug of the shoulders.

"Yes, sometimes," the captain replied. "These animals have been known to turn on their assailants and capsize their longboats. But with Mr. Land that danger isn't to be feared. His eye is sharp, his arm is sure. If I recommend that he aim carefully at this dugong, it's because the animal is justly regarded as fine game, and I know Mr. Land doesn't despise a choice morsel."

"Aha!" the Canadian put in. "This beast offers the added luxury of being good to eat?"

"Yes, Mr. Land. Its flesh is actual red meat, highly prized, and set aside throughout Malaysia for the tables of aristocrats. Accordingly, this excellent animal has been hunted so bloodthirstily that, like its manatee relatives, it has become more and more scarce."

"In that case, Captain," Conseil said in all seriousness, "on the offchance that this creature might be the last of its line, wouldn't it be advisable to spare its life, in the interests of science?"

"Maybe," the Canadian answered, "it would be better to hunt it down, in the interests of mealtime."

"Then proceed, Mr. Land," Captain Nemo replied.

Just then, as mute and emotionless as ever, seven crewmen climbed onto the platform. One carried a harpoon and line similar to those used in whale fishing. Its deck paneling opened, the skiff was wrenched from its socket and launched to sea. Six rowers sat on the thwarts, and the coxswain took the tiller. Ned, Conseil, and I found seats in the stern.

"Aren't you coming, Captain?" I asked.

"No, sir, but I wish you happy hunting."

The skiff pulled clear, and carried off by its six oars, it headed swiftly toward the dugong, which by then was floating two miles from the *Nautilus*.

Arriving within a few cable lengths of the cetacean, our longboat slowed down, and the sculls dipped noiselessly into the tranquil waters. Harpoon in hand, Ned Land went to take his stand in the skiff's bow. Harpoons used for hunting whales are usually attached to a very long rope that pays out quickly when the wounded animal drags it with him. But this rope measured no more than about ten fathoms, and its end had simply been fastened to a small barrel that, while floating, would indicate the dugong's movements beneath the waters.

I stood up and could clearly observe the Canadian's adversary. This dugong—which also boasts the name halicore—closely resembled a manatee. Its oblong body ended in a very long caudal fin and its lateral fins in actual fingers. It differs from the manatee in that its upper jaw is armed with two long, pointed teeth that form diverging tusks on either side.

This dugong that Ned Land was preparing to attack was of colossal dimensions, easily exceeding seven meters in length. It didn't stir and seemed to be sleeping on the surface of the waves, a circumstance that should have made it easier to capture.

The skiff approached cautiously to within three fathoms of the animal. The oars hung suspended above their rowlocks. I was crouching. His body leaning slightly back, Ned Land brandished his harpoon with expert hands.

Suddenly a hissing sound was audible, and the dugong disappeared. Although the harpoon had been forcefully hurled, it apparently had hit only water.

"Damnation!" exclaimed the furious Canadian. "I missed it!"

"No," I said, "the animal's wounded, there's its blood; but your weapon didn't stick in its body."

"My harpoon! Get my harpoon!" Ned Land exclaimed.

The sailors went back to their sculling, and the coxswain steered the longboat toward the floating barrel. We fished up the harpoon, and the skiff started off in pursuit of the animal.

The latter returned from time to time to breathe at the surface of the sea. Its wound hadn't weakened it because it went with tremendous speed. Driven by energetic arms, the longboat flew on its trail. Several times we got within a few fathoms of it, and the Canadian hovered in readiness to strike; but then the dugong would steal away with a sudden dive, and it proved impossible to overtake the beast.

I'll let you assess the degree of anger consuming our impatient Ned Land. He hurled at the hapless animal the most potent swearwords in the English language. For my part, I was simply distressed to see this dugong outwit our every scheme.

We chased it unflaggingly for a full hour, and I'd begun to think it would prove too difficult to capture, when the animal got the untimely idea of taking revenge on us, a notion it would soon have cause to regret. It wheeled on the skiff, to assault us in its turn.

This maneuver did not escape the Canadian.

"Watch out!" he said.

The coxswain pronounced a few words in his bizarre language, and no doubt he alerted his men to keep on their guard.

Arriving within twenty feet of the skiff, the dugong stopped, sharply sniffing the air with its huge nostrils, pierced not at the tip of its muzzle but on its topside. Then it gathered itself and sprang at us.

The skiff couldn't avoid the collision. Half overturned, it shipped a ton or two of water that we had to bail out. But thanks to our skillful coxswain, we were fouled on the bias rather than broadside, so we didn't capsize. Clinging to the stempost, Ned Land thrust his harpoon again and again into the gigantic animal, which imbedded its teeth in our gunwale and lifted the longboat out of the water as a lion would lift a deer. We were thrown on top of each other, and I have no idea how the venture would have ended had not the Canadian, still thirsting for the beast's blood, finally pierced it to the heart.

I heard its teeth grind on sheet iron, and the dugong disappeared, taking our harpoon along with it. But the barrel soon popped up on the surface, and a few moments later the animal's body appeared and rolled over on its back. Our skiff rejoined it, took it in tow, and headed to the *Nautilus*.

It took pulleys of great strength to hoist this dugong onto the platform. The beast weighed 5,000 kilograms. It was carved up in sight of the Canadian, who remained to watch every detail of the operation. At dinner the same day, my steward served me some slices of this flesh, skillfully dressed by the ship's cook. I found it excellent, even better than veal if not beef.

The next morning, February 11, the *Nautilus's* pantry was enriched by more dainty game. A covey of terns alighted on the *Nautilus*. They were a species of Sterna nilotica unique to Egypt: beak black, head gray and stippled, eyes surrounded by white dots, back, wings, and tail grayish, belly and throat white, feet red. Also caught were a couple dozen Nile duck, superior–tasting wildfowl whose neck and crown of the head are white speckled with black.

By then the *Nautilus* had reduced speed. It moved ahead at a saunter, so to speak. I observed that the Red Sea's water was becoming less salty the closer we got to Suez.

Near five o'clock in the afternoon, we sighted Cape Ras

Mohammed to the north. This cape forms the tip of Arabia Petraea, which lies between the Gulf of Suez and the Gulf of Aqaba.

The *Nautilus* entered the Strait of Jubal, which leads to the Gulf of Suez. I could clearly make out a high mountain crowning Ras Mohammed between the two gulfs. It was Mt. Horeb, that biblical Mt. Sinai on whose summit Moses met God face to face, that summit the mind's eye always pictures as wreathed in lightning.

At six o'clock, sometimes afloat and sometimes submerged, the *Nautilus* passed well out from El Tur, which sat at the far end of a bay whose waters seemed to be dyed red, as Captain Nemo had already mentioned. Then night fell in the midst of a heavy silence occasionally broken by the calls of pelicans and nocturnal birds, by the sound of surf chafing against rocks, or by the distant moan of a steamer churning the waves of the gulf with noisy blades.

From eight to nine o'clock, the *Nautilus* stayed a few meters beneath the waters. According to my calculations, we had to be quite close to Suez. Through the panels in the lounge, I spotted rocky bottoms brightly lit by our electric rays. It seemed to me that the strait was getting narrower and narrower.

At 9:15 when our boat returned to the surface, I climbed onto the platform. I was quite impatient to clear Captain Nemo's tunnel, couldn't sit still, and wanted to breathe the fresh night air.

Soon, in the shadows, I spotted a pale signal light glimmering a mile away, half discolored by mist.

"A floating lighthouse," said someone next to me.

I turned and discovered the captain.

"That's the floating signal light of Suez," he went on. "It won't be long before we reach the entrance to the tunnel."

"It can't be very easy to enter it."

"No, sir. Accordingly, I'm in the habit of staying in the

pilothouse and directing maneuvers myself. And now if you'll kindly go below, Professor Aronnax, the *Nautilus* is about to sink beneath the waves, and it will only return to the surface after we've cleared the Arabian Tunnel."

I followed Captain Nemo. The hatch closed, the ballast tanks filled with water, and the submersible sank some ten meters down.

Just as I was about to repair to my stateroom, the captain stopped me.

"Professor," he said to me, "would you like to go with me to the wheelhouse?"

"I was afraid to ask," I replied.

"Come along, then. This way, you'll learn the full story about this combination underwater and underground navigating."

Captain Nemo led me to the central companionway. In midstair he opened a door, went along the upper gangways, and arrived at the wheelhouse, which, as you know, stands at one end of the platform.

It was a cabin measuring six feet square and closely resembling those occupied by the helmsmen of steamboats on the Mississippi or Hudson rivers. In the center stood an upright wheel geared to rudder cables running to the *Nautilus's* stern. Set in the cabin's walls were four deadlights, windows of biconvex glass that enabled the man at the helm to see in every direction.

The cabin was dark; but my eyes soon grew accustomed to its darkness and I saw the pilot, a muscular man whose hands rested on the pegs of the wheel. Outside, the sea was brightly lit by the beacon shining behind the cabin at the other end of the platform.

"Now," Captain Nemo said, "let's look for our passageway."

Electric wires linked the pilothouse with the engine room, and from this cabin the captain could simultaneously signal heading and speed to his *Nautilus*. He pressed a metal button and at once the propeller slowed down significantly.

I stared in silence at the high, sheer wall we were skirting just then, the firm base of the sandy mountains on the coast. For an hour we went along it in this fashion, staying only a few meters away. Captain Nemo never took his eyes off the two concentric circles of the compass hanging in the cabin. At a mere gesture from him, the helmsman would instantly change the *Nautilus's* heading.

Standing by the port deadlight, I spotted magnificent coral substructures, zoophytes, algae, and crustaceans with enormous quivering claws that stretched forth from crevices in the rock.

At 10:15 Captain Nemo himself took the helm. Dark and deep, a wide gallery opened ahead of us. The *Nautilus* was brazenly swallowed up. Strange rumblings were audible along our sides. It was the water of the Red Sea, hurled toward the Mediterranean by the tunnel's slope. Our engines tried to offer resistance by churning the waves with propeller in reverse, but the *Nautilus* went with the torrent, as swift as an arrow.

Along the narrow walls of this passageway, I saw only brilliant streaks, hard lines, fiery furrows, all scrawled by our speeding electric light. With my hand I tried to curb the pounding of my heart.

At 10:35 Captain Nemo left the steering wheel and turned to me:

"The Mediterranean," he told me.

In less than twenty minutes, swept along by the torrent, the *Nautilus* had just cleared the Isthmus of Suez.

# CHAPTER 6

## The Greek Islands

A T SUNRISE the next morning, February 12, the *Nautilus* rose to the surface of the waves.

I rushed onto the platform. The hazy silhouette of Pelusium was outlined three miles to the south. A torrent had carried us from one sea to the other. But although that tunnel was easy to descend, going back up must have been impossible.

Near seven o'clock Ned and Conseil joined me. Those two inseparable companions had slept serenely, utterly unaware of the *Nautilus's* feat.

"Well, Mr. Naturalist," the Canadian asked in a gently mocking tone, "and how about that Mediterranean?"

"We're floating on its surface, Ned my friend."

"What!" Conseil put in. "Last night . . . ?"

"Yes, last night, in a matter of minutes, we cleared that insuperable isthmus."

"I don't believe a word of it," the Canadian replied.

"And you're in the wrong, Mr. Land," I went on. "That flat coastline curving southward is the coast of Egypt."

"Tell it to the marines, sir," answered the stubborn Canadian.

"But if Master says so," Conseil told him, "then so be it."

"What's more, Ned," I said, "Captain Nemo himself did the honors in his tunnel, and I stood beside him in the pilothouse while he steered the *Nautilus* through that narrow passageway."

"You hear, Ned?" Conseil said.

"And you, Ned, who have such good eyes," I added, "you can spot the jetties of Port Said stretching out to sea."

The Canadian looked carefully.

"Correct," he said. "You're right, Professor, and your captain's a superman. We're in the Mediterranean. Fine. So now let's have a chat about our little doings, if you please, but in such a way that nobody overhears."

I could easily see what the Canadian was driving at. In any event, I thought it best to let him have his chat, and we all three went to sit next to the beacon, where we were less exposed to the damp spray from the billows.

"Now, Ned, we're all ears," I said. "What have you to tell us?"

"What I've got to tell you is very simple," the Canadian replied. "We're in Europe, and before Captain Nemo's whims take us deep into the polar seas or back to Oceania, I say we should leave this *Nautilus*."

I confess that such discussions with the Canadian always baffled me. I didn't want to restrict my companions' freedom in any way, and yet I had no desire to leave Captain Nemo. Thanks to him and his submersible, I was finishing my undersea research by the day, and I was rewriting my book on the great ocean depths in the midst of its very element. Would I ever again have such an opportunity to observe the ocean's wonders? Absolutely not! So I couldn't entertain this idea of leaving the *Nautilus* before completing our course of inquiry.

"Ned my friend," I said, "answer me honestly. Are you bored with this ship? Are you sorry that fate has cast you into Captain Nemo's hands?"

The Canadian paused for a short while before replying. Then, crossing his arms:

"Honestly," he said, "I'm not sorry about this voyage under the seas. I'll be glad to have done it, but in order to have done it, it has to finish. That's my feeling."

"It will finish, Ned."

"Where and when?"

"Where? I don't know. When? I can't say. Or, rather, I suppose it will be over when these seas have nothing more to teach us. Everything that begins in this world must inevitably come to an end."

"I think as Master does," Conseil replied, "and it's extremely possible that after crossing every sea on the globe, Captain Nemo will bid the three of us a fond farewell."

"Bid us a fond farewell?" the Canadian exclaimed. "You mean beat us to a fare–thee–well!"

"Let's not exaggerate, Mr. Land," I went on. "We have nothing to fear from the captain, but neither do I share Conseil's views. We're privy to the *Nautilus's* secrets, and I don't expect that its commander, just to set us free, will meekly stand by while we spread those secrets all over the world."

"But in that case what do you expect?" the Canadian asked.

"That we'll encounter advantageous conditions for escaping just as readily in six months as now."

"Great Scott!" Ned Land put in. "And where, if you please, will we be in six months, Mr. Naturalist?"

"Perhaps here, perhaps in China. You know how quickly the *Nautilus* moves. It crosses oceans like swallows cross the air or express trains continents. It doesn't fear heavily traveled seas. Who can say it won't hug the coasts of France, England, or America, where an escape attempt could be carried out just as effectively as here."

"Professor Aronnax," the Canadian replied, "your arguments are rotten to the core. You talk way off in the future: 'We'll be here, we'll be there!' Me, I'm talking about right now: we are here, and we must take advantage of it!"

I was hard pressed by Ned Land's common sense, and I felt myself losing ground. I no longer knew what arguments to put forward on my behalf.

"Sir," Ned went on, "let's suppose that by some impossibility, Captain Nemo offered your freedom to you this very day. Would you accept?"

"I don't know," I replied.

"And suppose he adds that this offer he's making you today won't ever be repeated, then would you accept?"

I did not reply.

"And what thinks our friend Conseil?" Ned Land asked.

"Your friend Conseil," the fine lad replied serenely, "has nothing to say for himself. He's a completely disinterested party on this question. Like his master, like his comrade Ned, he's a bachelor. Neither wife, parents, nor children are waiting for him back home. He's in Master's employ, he thinks like Master, he speaks like Master, and much to his regret, he can't be counted on to form a majority. Only two persons face each other here: Master on one side, Ned Land on the other. That said, your friend Conseil is listening, and he's ready to keep score."

I couldn't help smiling as Conseil wiped himself out of existence. Deep down, the Canadian must have been overjoyed at not having to contend with him.

"Then, sir," Ned Land said, "since Conseil is no more, we'll have this discussion between just the two of us. I've talked, you've listened. What's your reply?"

It was obvious that the matter had to be settled, and evasions were distasteful to me.

"Ned my friend," I said, "here's my reply. You have right on your side and my arguments can't stand up to yours. It will never do to count on Captain Nemo's benevolence. The most ordinary good sense would forbid him to set us free. On the other hand, good sense decrees that we take advantage of our first opportunity to leave the *Nautilus*."

"Fine, Professor Aronnax, that's wisely said."

"But one proviso," I said, "just one. The opportunity must

be the real thing. Our first attempt to escape must succeed, because if it misfires, we won't get a second chance, and Captain Nemo will never forgive us."

"That's also well put," the Canadian replied. "But your proviso applies to any escape attempt, whether it happens in two years or two days. So this is still the question: if a promising opportunity comes up, we have to grab it."

"Agreed. And now, Ned, will you tell me what you mean by a promising opportunity?"

"One that leads the *Nautilus* on a cloudy night within a short distance of some European coast."

"And you'll try to get away by swimming?"

"Yes, if we're close enough to shore and the ship's afloat on the surface. No, if we're well out and the ship's navigating under the waters."

"And in that event?"

"In that event I'll try to get hold of the skiff. I know how to handle it. We'll stick ourselves inside, undo the bolts, and rise to the surface, without the helmsman in the bow seeing a thing."

"Fine, Ned. Stay on the lookout for such an opportunity, but don't forget, one slipup will finish us."

"I won't forget, sir."

"And now, Ned, would you like to know my overall thinking on your plan?"

"Gladly, Professor Aronnax."

"Well then, I think—and I don't mean 'I hope'—that your promising opportunity won't ever arise."

"Why not?"

"Because Captain Nemo recognizes that we haven't given up all hope of recovering our freedom, and he'll keep on his guard, above all in seas within sight of the coasts of Europe."

"I'm of Master's opinion," Conseil said.

"We'll soon see," Ned Land replied, shaking his head with a

determined expression.

"And now, Ned Land," I added, "let's leave it at that. Not another word on any of this. The day you're ready, alert us and we're with you. I turn it all over to you."

That's how we ended this conversation, which later was to have such serious consequences. At first, I must say, events seemed to confirm my forecasts, much to the Canadian's despair. Did Captain Nemo view us with distrust in these heavily traveled seas, or did he simply want to hide from the sight of those ships of every nation that plowed the Mediterranean? I have no idea, but usually he stayed in midwater and well out from any coast. Either the *Nautilus* surfaced only enough to let its pilothouse emerge, or it slipped away to the lower depths, although, between the Greek Islands and Asia Minor, we didn't find bottom even at 2,000 meters down.

Accordingly, I became aware of the isle of Karpathos, one of the Sporades Islands, only when Captain Nemo placed his finger over a spot on the world map and quoted me this verse from Virgil:

Est in Carpathio Neptuni gurgite vates
Caeruleus Proteus . . .

It was indeed that bygone abode of Proteus, the old shepherd of King Neptune's flocks: an island located between Rhodes and Crete, which Greeks now call Karpathos, Italians Scarpanto. Through the lounge window I could see only its granite bedrock.

The next day, February 14, I decided to spend a few hours studying the fish of this island group; but for whatever reason, the panels remained hermetically sealed. After determining the *Nautilus's* heading, I noted that it was proceeding toward the ancient island of Crete, also called Candia. At the time I had shipped aboard the *Abraham Lincoln*, this whole island was in rebellion against its tyrannical rulers, the Ottoman Empire of Turkey. But since then I had absolutely no idea what happened to this revolution, and Captain Nemo, deprived of all contact with the shore, was hardly the man to keep me informed.

So I didn't allude to this event when, that evening, I chanced to be alone with the captain in the lounge. Besides, he seemed silent and preoccupied. Then, contrary to custom, he ordered that both panels in the lounge be opened, and going from the one to the other, he carefully observed the watery mass. For what purpose? I hadn't a guess, and for my part, I spent my time studying the fish that passed before my eyes.

Among others I noted that sand goby mentioned by Aristotle and commonly known by the name sea loach, which is encountered exclusively in the salty waters next to the Nile Delta. Near them some semiphosphorescent red porgy rolled by, a variety of gilthead that the Egyptians ranked among their sacred animals, lauding them in religious ceremonies when their arrival in the river's waters announced the fertile flood season. I also noticed some wrasse known as the tapiro, three decimeters long, bony fish with transparent scales whose bluish gray color is mixed with red spots; they're enthusiastic eaters of marine vegetables, which gives them an exquisite flavor; hence these tapiro were much in demand by the epicures of ancient Rome, and their entrails were dressed with brains of peacock, tongue of flamingo, and testes of moray to make that divine platter that so enraptured the Roman emperor Vitellius.

Another resident of these seas caught my attention and revived all my memories of antiquity. This was the remora, which travels attached to the bellies of sharks; as the ancients tell it, when these little fish cling to the undersides of a ship, they can bring it to a halt, and by so impeding Mark Antony's vessel during the Battle of Actium, one of them facilitated the victory of Augustus Caesar. From such slender threads hang the destinies of nations! I also observed some wonderful snappers belonging to the order Lutianida, sacred fish for the Greeks, who claimed they could drive off sea monsters from the waters they frequent; their Greek name anthias means "flower," and they live up to it in the play of their colors and in those fleeting reflections that turn their dorsal fins into watered silk; their hues are confined to a gamut of reds, from the pallor of pink to the glow of ruby. I couldn't take my eyes off these marine wonders, when I was suddenly jolted by an unexpected apparition.

In the midst of the waters, a man appeared, a diver carrying a little leather bag at his belt. It was no corpse lost in the waves. It was a living man, swimming vigorously, sometimes disappearing to breathe at the surface, then instantly diving again.

I turned to Captain Nemo, and in an agitated voice:

"A man! A castaway!" I exclaimed. "We must rescue him at all cost!"

The captain didn't reply but went to lean against the window.

The man drew near, and gluing his face to the panel, he stared at us.

To my deep astonishment, Captain Nemo gave him a signal. The diver answered with his hand, immediately swam up to the surface of the sea, and didn't reappear.

"Don't be alarmed," the captain told me. "That's Nicolas from Cape Matapan, nicknamed 'Il Pesce.' He's well known throughout the Cyclades Islands. A bold diver! Water is his true element, and he lives in the sea more than on shore, going constantly from one island to another, even to Crete."

"You know him, captain?"

"Why not, Professor Aronnax?"

This said, Captain Nemo went to a cabinet standing near the lounge's left panel. Next to this cabinet I saw a chest bound with hoops of iron, its lid bearing a copper plaque that displayed the *Nautilus's* monogram with its motto Mobilis in Mobili.

Just then, ignoring my presence, the captain opened this cabinet, a sort of safe that contained a large number of ingots.

They were gold ingots. And they represented an enormous sum of money. Where had this precious metal come from? How had the captain amassed this gold, and what was he about to do with it?

I didn't pronounce a word. I gaped. Captain Nemo took out the ingots one by one and arranged them methodically inside the chest, filling it to the top. At which point I estimate that it held more than 1,000 kilograms of gold, in other words, close to F5,000,000.

After securely fastening the chest, Captain Nemo wrote an address on its lid in characters that must have been modern Greek.

This done, the captain pressed a button whose wiring was in communication with the crew's quarters. Four men appeared and, not without difficulty, pushed the chest out of the lounge. Then I heard them hoist it up the iron companionway by means of pulleys.

Just then Captain Nemo turned to me:

"You were saying, Professor?" he asked me.

"I wasn't saying a thing, Captain."

"Then, sir, with your permission, I'll bid you good evening."

And with that, Captain Nemo left the lounge.

I re-entered my stateroom, very puzzled, as you can imagine. I tried in vain to fall asleep. I kept searching for a relationship between the appearance of the diver and that chest filled with gold. Soon, from certain rolling and pitching movements, I sensed that the *Nautilus* had left the lower strata and was back on the surface of the water.

Then I heard the sound of footsteps on the platform. I realized that the skiff was being detached and launched to sea.

For an instant it bumped the *Nautilus's* side, then all sounds ceased.

Two hours later, the same noises, the same comings and goings, were repeated. Hoisted on board, the longboat was readjusted into its socket, and the *Nautilus* plunged back beneath the waves.

So those millions had been delivered to their address. At what spot on the continent? Who was the recipient of Captain Nemo's gold?

The next day I related the night's events to Conseil and the Canadian, events that had aroused my curiosity to a fever pitch. My companions were as startled as I was.

"But where does he get those millions?" Ned Land asked.

To this no reply was possible. After breakfast I made my way to the lounge and went about my work. I wrote up my notes until five o'clock in the afternoon. Just then—was it due to some personal indisposition?—I felt extremely hot and had to take off my jacket made of fan mussel fabric. A perplexing circumstance because we weren't in the low latitudes, and besides, once the *Nautilus* was submerged, it shouldn't be subject to any rise in temperature. I looked at the pressure gauge. It marked a depth of sixty feet, a depth beyond the reach of atmospheric heat.

I kept on working, but the temperature rose to the point of becoming unbearable.

"Could there be a fire on board?" I wondered.

I was about to leave the lounge when Captain Nemo entered. He approached the thermometer, consulted it, and turned to me:

"42° centigrade," he said.

"I've detected as much, Captain," I replied, "and if it gets even slightly hotter, we won't be able to stand it."

"Oh, professor, it won't get any hotter unless we want it to!"

"You mean you can control this heat?"

"No, but I can back away from the fireplace producing it."

"So it's outside?"

"Surely. We're cruising in a current of boiling water."

"It can't be!" I exclaimed.

"Look."

The panels had opened, and I could see a completely white sea around the *Nautilus*. Steaming sulfurous fumes uncoiled in the midst of waves bubbling like water in a boiler. I leaned my hand against one of the windows, but the heat was so great, I had to snatch it back.

"Where are we?" I asked.

"Near the island of Santorini, professor," the captain answered me, "and right in the channel that separates the volcanic islets of Nea Kameni and Palea Kameni. I wanted to offer you the unusual sight of an underwater eruption."

"I thought," I said, "that the formation of such new islands had come to an end."

"Nothing ever comes to an end in these volcanic waterways," Captain Nemo replied, "and thanks to its underground fires, our globe is continuously under construction in these regions. According to the Latin historians Cassiodorus and Pliny, by the year 19 of the Christian era, a new island, the divine Thera, had already appeared in the very place these islets have more recently formed. Then Thera sank under the waves, only to rise and sink once more in the year 69 A.D. From that day to this, such plutonic construction work has been in abeyance. But on February 3, 1866, a new islet named George Island emerged in the midst of sulfurous steam near Nea Kameni and was fused to it on the 6th of the same month. Seven days later, on February 13, the islet of Aphroessa appeared, leaving a ten-meter channel between itself and Nea Kameni. I was in these seas when that phenomenon occurred and I was able to observe its every phase. The islet of Aphroessa was circular in shape, measuring 300 feet in diameter and thirty feet in height.

It was made of black, glassy lava mixed with bits of feldspar. Finally, on March 10, a smaller islet called Reka appeared next to Nea Kameni, and since then, these three islets have fused to form one single, selfsame island."

"What about this channel we're in right now?" I asked.

"Here it is," Captain Nemo replied, showing me a chart of the Greek Islands. "You observe that I've entered the new islets in their place."

"But will this channel fill up one day?"

"Very likely, Professor Aronnax, because since 1866 eight little lava islets have surged up in front of the port of St. Nicolas on Palea Kameni. So it's obvious that Nea and Palea will join in days to come. In the middle of the Pacific, tiny infusoria build continents, but here they're built by volcanic phenomena. Look, sir! Look at the construction work going on under these waves."

I returned to the window. The *Nautilus* was no longer moving. The heat had become unbearable. From the white it had recently been, the sea was turning red, a coloration caused by the presence of iron salts. Although the lounge was hermetically sealed, it was filling with an intolerable stink of sulfur, and I could see scarlet flames of such brightness, they overpowered our electric light.

I was swimming in perspiration, I was stifling, I was about to be cooked. Yes, I felt myself cooking in actual fact!

"We can't stay any longer in this boiling water," I told the captain.

"No, it wouldn't be advisable," replied Nemo the Emotionless.

He gave an order. The *Nautilus* tacked about and retreated from this furnace it couldn't brave with impunity. A quarter of an hour later, we were breathing fresh air on the surface of the waves.

It then occurred to me that if Ned had chosen these

waterways for our escape attempt, we wouldn't have come out alive from this sea of fire.

The next day, February 16, we left this basin, which tallies depths of 3,000 meters between Rhodes and Alexandria, and passing well out from Cerigo Island after doubling Cape Matapan, the *Nautilus* left the Greek Islands behind.

# CHAPTER 7

The Mediterranean in Forty-Eight Hours

THE MEDITERRANEAN, your ideal blue sea: to Greeks simply "the sea," to Hebrews "the great sea," to Romans mare nostrum. Bordered by orange trees, aloes, cactus, and maritime pine trees, perfumed with the scent of myrtle, framed by rugged mountains, saturated with clean, transparent air but continuously under construction by fires in the earth, this sea is a genuine battlefield where Neptune and Pluto still struggle for world domination. Here on these beaches and waters, says the French historian Michelet, a man is revived by one of the most invigorating climates in the world.

But as beautiful as it was, I could get only a quick look at this basin whose surface area comprises 2,000,000 square kilometers. Even Captain Nemo's personal insights were denied me, because that mystifying individual didn't appear one single time during our high-speed crossing. I estimate that the *Nautilus* covered a track of some 600 leagues under the waves of this sea, and this voyage was accomplished in just twenty-four hours times two. Departing from the waterways of Greece on the morning of February 16, we cleared the Strait of Gibraltar by sunrise on the 18th.

It was obvious to me that this Mediterranean, pinned in the middle of those shores he wanted to avoid, gave Captain Nemo no pleasure. Its waves and breezes brought back too many memories, if not too many regrets. Here he no longer had the ease of movement and freedom of maneuver that the oceans allowed him, and his *Nautilus* felt cramped so close to the coasts of both Africa and Europe.

Accordingly, our speed was twenty–five miles (that is, twelve four–kilometer leagues) per hour. Needless to say, Ned Land had to give up his escape plans, much to his distress. Swept along at the rate of twelve to thirteen meters per second, he could hardly make use of the skiff. Leaving the *Nautilus* under these conditions would have been like jumping off a train racing at this speed, a rash move if there ever was one. Moreover, to renew our air supply, the submersible rose to the surface of the waves only at night, and relying solely on compass and log, it steered by dead reckoning.

Inside the Mediterranean, then, I could catch no more of its fast–passing scenery than a traveler might see from an express train; in other words, I could view only the distant horizons because the foregrounds flashed by like lightning. But Conseil and I were able to observe those Mediterranean fish whose powerful fins kept pace for a while in the *Nautilus's* waters. We stayed on watch before the lounge windows, and our notes enable me to reconstruct, in a few words, the ichthyology of this sea.

Among the various fish inhabiting it, some I viewed, others I glimpsed, and the rest I missed completely because of the *Nautilus's* speed. Kindly allow me to sort them out using this whimsical system of classification. It will at least convey the quickness of my observations.

In the midst of the watery mass, brightly lit by our electric beams, there snaked past those one–meter lampreys that are common to nearly every clime. A type of ray from the genus Oxyrhynchus, five feet wide, had a white belly with a spotted, ash–gray back and was carried along by the currents like a huge, wide–open shawl. Other rays passed by so quickly I couldn't tell if they deserved that name "eagle ray" coined by the ancient Greeks, or those designations of "rat ray," "bat ray," and "toad ray" that modern fishermen have inflicted on them. Dogfish known as topes, twelve feet long and especially feared by divers, were racing with each other. Looking like big bluish shadows, thresher sharks went by, eight feet long and gifted with an extremely acute sense of smell. Dorados from the genus Sparus, some measuring up to thirteen decimeters, appeared in silver and azure costumes encircled with ribbons, which contrasted with the dark color of their fins; fish sacred to the goddess Venus, their eyes set in brows of gold; a valuable species that patronizes all waters fresh or salt, equally at home in rivers, lakes, and oceans, living in every clime, tolerating any temperature, their line dating back to prehistoric times on this earth yet preserving all its beauty from those far-off days. Magnificent sturgeons, nine to ten meters long and extremely fast, banged their powerful tails against the glass of our panels, showing bluish backs with small brown spots; they resemble sharks, without equaling their strength, and are encountered in every sea; in the spring they delight in swimming up the great rivers, fighting the currents of the Volga, Danube, Po, Rhine, Loire, and Oder, while feeding on herring, mackerel, salmon, and codfish; although they belong to the class of cartilaginous fish, they rate as a delicacy; they're eaten fresh, dried, marinated, or salt-preserved, and in olden times they were borne in triumph to the table of the Roman epicure Lucullus.

But whenever the *Nautilus* drew near the surface, those denizens of the Mediterranean I could observe most productively belonged to the sixty-third genus of bony fish. These were tuna from the genus Scomber, blue-black on top, silver on the belly armor, their dorsal stripes giving off a golden gleam. They are said to follow ships in search of refreshing shade from the hot tropical sun, and they did just that with the *Nautilus*, as they had once done with the vessels of the Count de La Pérouse. For long hours they competed in speed with our submersible. I couldn't stop marveling at these animals so perfectly cut out for racing, their heads small, their bodies sleek, spindle–shaped, and in some cases over three meters long, their pectoral fins gifted with remarkable strength, their caudal fins forked. Like certain flocks of birds, whose speed they equal, these tuna swim in triangle formation, which prompted the ancients to say they'd boned up on geometry and military strategy. And yet they can't escape the Provençal fishermen, who prize them as highly as did the ancient inhabitants of Turkey and Italy; and these valuable animals, as oblivious as if they were deaf and blind, leap right into the Marseilles tuna nets and perish by the thousands.

Just for the record, I'll mention those Mediterranean fish that Conseil and I barely glimpsed. There were whitish eels of the species Gymnotus fasciatus that passed like elusive wisps of steam, conger eels three to four meters long that were tricked out in green, blue, and yellow, three–foot hake with a liver that makes a dainty morsel, wormfish drifting like thin seaweed, sea robins that poets call lyrefish and seamen pipers and whose snouts have two jagged triangular plates shaped like old Homer's lyre, swallowfish swimming as fast as the bird they're named after, redheaded groupers whose dorsal fins are trimmed with filaments, some shad (spotted with black, gray, brown, blue, yellow, and green) that actually respond to tinkling handbells, splendid diamond–shaped turbot that were like aquatic pheasants with yellowish fins stippled in brown and the left topside mostly marbled in brown and yellow, finally schools of wonderful red mullet, real oceanic birds of paradise that ancient Romans bought for as much as 10,000 sesterces apiece, and which they killed at the table, so they could heartlessly watch it change color from cinnabar red when alive to pallid white when dead.

And as for other fish common to the Atlantic and Mediterranean, I was unable to observe miralets, triggerfish, puffers, seahorses, jewelfish, trumpetfish, blennies, gray mullet, wrasse, smelt, flying fish, anchovies, sea bream, porgies, garfish, or any of the chief representatives of the order Pleuronecta, such as sole, flounder, plaice, dab, and brill, simply because of the dizzying speed with which the *Nautilus* hustled through these opulent waters.

As for marine mammals, on passing by the mouth of the Adriatic Sea, I thought I recognized two or three sperm whales equipped with the single dorsal fin denoting the genus Physeter, some pilot whales from the genus Globicephalus exclusive to the Mediterranean, the forepart of the head striped with small distinct lines, and also a dozen seals with white bellies and black coats, known by the name monk seals and just as solemn as if they were three-meter Dominicans.

For his part, Conseil thought he spotted a turtle six feet wide and adorned with three protruding ridges that ran lengthwise. I was sorry to miss this reptile, because from Conseil's description, I believe I recognized the leatherback turtle, a pretty rare species. For my part, I noted only some loggerhead turtles with long carapaces.

As for zoophytes, for a few moments I was able to marvel at a wonderful, orange-hued hydra from the genus Galeolaria that clung to the glass of our port panel; it consisted of a long, lean filament that spread out into countless branches and ended in the most delicate lace ever spun by the followers of Arachne. Unfortunately I couldn't fish up this wonderful specimen, and surely no other Mediterranean zoophytes would have been offered to my gaze, if, on the evening of the 16th, the *Nautilus* hadn't slowed down in an odd fashion. This was the situation.

By then we were passing between Sicily and the coast of Tunisia. In the cramped space between Cape Bon and the Strait of Messina, the sea bottom rises almost all at once. It forms an actual ridge with only seventeen meters of water remaining above it, while the depth on either side is 170 meters.

Consequently, the *Nautilus* had to maneuver with caution so as not to bump into this underwater barrier.

I showed Conseil the position of this long reef on our chart of the Mediterranean.

"But with all due respect to Master," Conseil ventured to observe, "it's like an actual isthmus connecting Europe to Africa."

"Yes, my boy," I replied, "it cuts across the whole Strait of Sicily, and Smith's soundings prove that in the past, these two continents were genuinely connected between Cape Boeo and Cape Farina."

"I can easily believe it," Conseil said.

"I might add," I went on, "that there's a similar barrier between Gibraltar and Ceuta, and in prehistoric times it closed off the Mediterranean completely."

"Gracious!" Conseil put in. "Suppose one day some volcanic upheaval raises these two barriers back above the waves!"

"That's most unlikely, Conseil."

"If Master will allow me to finish, I mean that if this phenomenon occurs, it might prove distressing to Mr. de Lesseps, who has gone to such pains to cut through his isthmus!"

"Agreed, but I repeat, Conseil: such a phenomenon won't occur. The intensity of these underground forces continues to diminish. Volcanoes were quite numerous in the world's early days, but they're going extinct one by one; the heat inside the earth is growing weaker, the temperature in the globe's lower strata is cooling appreciably every century, and to our globe's detriment, because its heat is its life."

"But the sun—"

"The sun isn't enough, Conseil. Can it restore heat to a corpse?"

"Not that I've heard."

"Well, my friend, someday the earth will be just such a cold corpse. Like the moon, which long ago lost its vital heat, our globe will become lifeless and unlivable."

"In how many centuries?" Conseil asked.

"In hundreds of thousands of years, my boy."

"Then we have ample time to finish our voyage," Conseil replied, "if Ned Land doesn't mess things up!"

Thus reassured, Conseil went back to studying the shallows that the *Nautilus* was skimming at moderate speed.

On the rocky, volcanic seafloor, there bloomed quite a collection of moving flora: sponges, sea cucumbers, jellyfish called sea gooseberries that were adorned with reddish tendrils and gave off a subtle phosphorescence, members of the genus Beroe that are commonly known by the name melon jellyfish and are bathed in the shimmer of the whole solar spectrum, free-swimming crinoids one meter wide that reddened the waters with their crimson hue, treelike basket stars of the greatest beauty, sea fans from the genus Pavonacea with long stems, numerous edible sea urchins of various species, plus green sea anemones with a grayish trunk and a brown disk lost beneath the olive-colored tresses of their tentacles.

Conseil kept especially busy observing mollusks and articulates, and although his catalog is a little dry, I wouldn't want to wrong the gallant lad by leaving out his personal observations.

From the branch Mollusca, he mentions numerous comb-shaped scallops, hooflike spiny oysters piled on top of each other, triangular coquina, three-pronged glass snails with yellow fins and transparent shells, orange snails from the genus Pleurobranchus that looked like eggs spotted or speckled with greenish dots, members of the genus Aplysia also known by the name sea hares, other sea hares from the genus Dolabella, plump paper-bubble shells, umbrella shells exclusive to the Mediterranean, abalone whose shell produces a mother-of-pearl much in demand, pilgrim scallops, saddle shells that

diners in the French province of Languedoc are said to like
better than oysters, some of those cockleshells so dear to the
citizens of Marseilles, fat white venus shells that are among
the clams so abundant off the coasts of North America and
eaten in such quantities by New Yorkers, variously colored
comb shells with gill covers, burrowing date mussels with a
peppery flavor I relish, furrowed heart cockles whose shells
have riblike ridges on their arching summits, triton shells
pocked with scarlet bumps, carniaira snails with backward-
curving tips that make them resemble flimsy gondolas,
crowned ferola snails, atlanta snails with spiral shells, gray
nudibranchs from the genus Tethys that were spotted with
white and covered by fringed mantles, nudibranchs from the
suborder Eolidea that looked like small slugs, sea butterflies
crawling on their backs, seashells from the genus Auricula
including the oval-shaped Auricula myosotis, tan wentletrap
snails, common periwinkles, violet snails, cineraira snails,
rock borers, ear shells, cabochon snails, pandora shells, etc.

As for the articulates, in his notes Conseil has very
appropriately divided them into six classes, three of which
belong to the marine world. These classes are the Crustacea,
Cirripedia, and Annelida.

Crustaceans are subdivided into nine orders, and the first
of these consists of the decapods, in other words, animals
whose head and thorax are usually fused, whose cheek-and-
mouth mechanism is made up of several pairs of appendages,
and whose thorax has four, five, or six pairs of walking
legs. Conseil used the methods of our mentor Professor
Milne-Edwards, who puts the decapods in three divisions:
Brachyura, Macrura, and Anomura. These names may look
a tad fierce, but they're accurate and appropriate. Among the
Brachyura, Conseil mentions some amanthia crabs whose
fronts were armed with two big diverging tips, those inachus
scorpions that—lord knows why—symbolized wisdom to the

ancient Greeks, spider crabs of the massena and spinimane varieties that had probably gone astray in these shallows because they usually live in the lower depths, xanthid crabs, pilumna crabs, rhomboid crabs, granular box crabs (easy on the digestion, as Conseil ventured to observe), toothless masked crabs, ebalia crabs, cymopolia crabs, woolly–handed crabs, etc. Among the Macrura (which are subdivided into five families: hardshells, burrowers, crayfish, prawns, and ghost crabs) Conseil mentions some common spiny lobsters whose females supply a meat highly prized, slipper lobsters or common shrimp, waterside gebia shrimp, and all sorts of edible species, but he says nothing of the crayfish subdivision that includes the true lobster, because spiny lobsters are the only type in the Mediterranean. Finally, among the Anomura, he saw common drocina crabs dwelling inside whatever abandoned seashells they could take over, homola crabs with spiny fronts, hermit crabs, hairy porcelain crabs, etc.

There Conseil's work came to a halt. He didn't have time to finish off the class Crustacea through an examination of its stomatopods, amphipods, homopods, isopods, trilobites, branchiopods, ostracods, and entomostraceans. And in order to complete his study of marine articulates, he needed to mention the class Cirripedia, which contains water fleas and carp lice, plus the class Annelida, which he would have divided without fail into tubifex worms and dorsibranchian worms. But having gone past the shallows of the Strait of Sicily, the *Nautilus* resumed its usual deep–water speed. From then on, no more mollusks, no more zoophytes, no more articulates. Just a few large fish sweeping by like shadows.

During the night of February 16–17, we entered the second Mediterranean basin, whose maximum depth we found at 3,000 meters. The *Nautilus*, driven downward by its propeller and slanting fins, descended to the lowest strata of this sea.

There, in place of natural wonders, the watery mass offered some thrilling and dreadful scenes to my eyes. In essence, we were then crossing that part of the whole Mediterranean so fertile in casualties. From the coast of Algiers to the beaches of Provence, how many ships have wrecked, how many vessels have vanished! Compared to the vast liquid plains of the Pacific, the Mediterranean is a mere lake, but it's an unpredictable lake with fickle waves, today kindly and affectionate to those frail single-masters drifting between a double ultramarine of sky and water, tomorrow bad-tempered and turbulent, agitated by the winds, demolishing the strongest ships beneath sudden waves that smash down with a headlong wallop.

So, in our swift cruise through these deep strata, how many vessels I saw lying on the seafloor, some already caked with coral, others clad only in a layer of rust, plus anchors, cannons, shells, iron fittings, propeller blades, parts of engines, cracked cylinders, staved-in boilers, then hulls floating in midwater, here upright, there overturned.

Some of these wrecked ships had perished in collisions, others from hitting granite reefs. I saw a few that had sunk straight down, their masting still upright, their rigging stiffened by the water. They looked like they were at anchor by some immense, open, offshore mooring where they were waiting for their departure time. When the *Nautilus* passed between them, covering them with sheets of electricity, they seemed ready to salute us with their colors and send us their serial numbers! But no, nothing but silence and death filled this field of catastrophes!

I observed that these Mediterranean depths became more and more cluttered with such gruesome wreckage as the *Nautilus* drew nearer to the Strait of Gibraltar. By then the shores of Africa and Europe were converging, and in this narrow space collisions were commonplace. There I saw numerous iron undersides, the phantasmagoric ruins of steamers, some lying down, others rearing up like fearsome animals. One of these boats made a dreadful first impression: sides torn open, funnel bent, paddle wheels stripped to the mountings, rudder separated from the sternpost and still hanging from an iron chain, the board on its stern eaten away by marine salts! How many lives were dashed in this shipwreck! How many victims were swept under the waves! Had some sailor on board lived to tell the story of this dreadful disaster, or do the waves still keep this casualty a secret? It occurred to me, lord knows why, that this boat buried under the sea might have been the Atlas, lost with all hands some twenty years ago and never heard from again! Oh, what a gruesome tale these Mediterranean depths could tell, this huge boneyard where so much wealth has been lost, where so many victims have met their deaths!

Meanwhile, briskly unconcerned, the *Nautilus* ran at full propeller through the midst of these ruins. On February 18, near three o'clock in the morning, it hove before the entrance to the Strait of Gibraltar.

There are two currents here: an upper current, long known to exist, that carries the ocean's waters into the Mediterranean basin; then a lower countercurrent, the only present–day proof of its existence being logic. In essence, the Mediterranean receives a continual influx of water not only from the Atlantic but from rivers emptying into it; since local evaporation isn't enough to restore the balance, the total amount of added water should make this sea's level higher every year. Yet this isn't the case, and we're naturally forced to believe in the existence of some lower current that carries the Mediterranean's surplus through the Strait of Gibraltar and into the Atlantic basin.

And so it turned out. The *Nautilus* took full advantage of this countercurrent. It advanced swiftly through this narrow passageway. For an instant I could glimpse the wonderful ruins of the Temple of Hercules, buried undersea, as Pliny and Avianus have mentioned, together with the flat island they stand on; and a few minutes later, we were floating on the waves of the Atlantic.

# CHAPTER 8

The Bay of Vigo

THE ATLANTIC! A vast expanse of water whose surface area is 25,000,000 square miles, with a length of 9,000 miles and an average width of 2,700. A major sea nearly unknown to the ancients, except perhaps the Carthaginians, those Dutchmen of antiquity who went along the west coasts of Europe and Africa on their commercial junkets! An ocean whose parallel winding shores form an immense perimeter fed by the world's greatest rivers: the St. Lawrence, Mississippi, Amazon, Plata, Orinoco, Niger, Senegal, Elbe, Loire, and Rhine, which bring it waters from the most civilized countries as well as the most undeveloped areas! A magnificent plain of waves plowed continuously by ships of every nation, shaded by every flag in the world, and ending in those two dreadful headlands so feared by navigators, Cape Horn and the Cape of Tempests!

The *Nautilus* broke these waters with the edge of its spur after doing nearly 10,000 leagues in three and a half months, a track longer than a great circle of the earth. Where were we heading now, and what did the future have in store for us?

Emerging from the Strait of Gibraltar, the *Nautilus* took to the high seas. It returned to the surface of the waves, so our daily strolls on the platform were restored to us.

I climbed onto it instantly, Ned Land and Conseil along with me. Twelve miles away, Cape St. Vincent was hazily visible, the southwestern tip of the Hispanic peninsula. The wind was blowing a pretty strong gust from the south. The sea was swelling and surging. Its waves made the *Nautilus* roll and jerk violently. It was nearly impossible to stand up on the platform, which was continuously buffeted by this enormously heavy sea. After inhaling a few breaths of air, we went below once more.

I repaired to my stateroom. Conseil returned to his cabin; but the Canadian, looking rather worried, followed me. Our quick trip through the Mediterranean hadn't allowed him to put his plans into execution, and he could barely conceal his disappointment.

After the door to my stateroom was closed, he sat and stared at me silently.

"Ned my friend," I told him, "I know how you feel, but you mustn't blame yourself. Given the way the *Nautilus* was navigating, it would have been sheer insanity to think of escaping!"

Ned Land didn't reply. His pursed lips and frowning brow indicated that he was in the grip of his monomania.

"Look here," I went on, "as yet there's no cause for despair. We're going up the coast of Portugal. France and England aren't far off, and there we'll easily find refuge. Oh, I grant you, if the *Nautilus* had emerged from the Strait of Gibraltar and made for that cape in the south, if it were taking us toward those regions that have no continents, then I'd share your alarm. But we now know that Captain Nemo doesn't avoid the seas of civilization, and in a few days I think we can safely take action."

Ned Land stared at me still more intently and finally unpursed his lips:

"We'll do it this evening," he said.

I straightened suddenly. I admit that I was less than ready for this announcement. I wanted to reply to the Canadian, but words failed me.

"We agreed to wait for the right circumstances," Ned Land

went on. "Now we've got those circumstances. This evening we'll be just a few miles off the coast of Spain. It'll be cloudy tonight. The wind's blowing toward shore. You gave me your promise, Professor Aronnax, and I'm counting on you."

Since I didn't say anything, the Canadian stood up and approached me:

"We'll do it this evening at nine o'clock," he said. "I've alerted Conseil. By that time Captain Nemo will be locked in his room and probably in bed. Neither the mechanics or the crewmen will be able to see us. Conseil and I will go to the central companionway. As for you, Professor Aronnax, you'll stay in the library two steps away and wait for my signal. The oars, mast, and sail are in the skiff. I've even managed to stow some provisions inside. I've gotten hold of a monkey wrench to unscrew the nuts bolting the skiff to the *Nautilus's* hull. So everything's ready. I'll see you this evening."

"The sea is rough," I said.

"Admitted," the Canadian replied, "but we've got to risk it. Freedom is worth paying for. Besides, the longboat's solidly built, and a few miles with the wind behind us is no big deal. By tomorrow, who knows if this ship won't be 100 leagues out to sea? If circumstances are in our favor, between ten and eleven this evening we'll be landing on some piece of solid ground, or we'll be dead. So we're in God's hands, and I'll see you this evening!"

This said, the Canadian withdrew, leaving me close to dumbfounded. I had imagined that if it came to this, I would have time to think about it, to talk it over. My stubborn companion hadn't granted me this courtesy. But after all, what would I have said to him? Ned Land was right a hundred times over. These were near–ideal circumstances, and he was taking full advantage of them. In my selfish personal interests, could I go back on my word and be responsible for ruining the future lives of my companions? Tomorrow, might not Captain Nemo take us far away from any shore?

Just then a fairly loud hissing told me that the ballast tanks were filling, and the *Nautilus* sank beneath the waves of the Atlantic.

I stayed in my stateroom. I wanted to avoid the captain, to hide from his eyes the agitation overwhelming me. What an agonizing day I spent, torn between my desire to regain my free will and my regret at abandoning this marvelous *Nautilus*, leaving my underwater research incomplete! How could I relinquish this ocean—"my own Atlantic," as I liked to call it—without observing its lower strata, without wresting from it the kinds of secrets that had been revealed to me by the seas of the East Indies and the Pacific! I was putting down my novel half read, I was waking up as my dream neared its climax! How painfully the hours passed, as I sometimes envisioned myself safe on shore with my companions, or, despite my better judgment, as I sometimes wished that some unforeseen circumstances would prevent Ned Land from carrying out his plans.

Twice I went to the lounge. I wanted to consult the compass. I wanted to see if the *Nautilus's* heading was actually taking us closer to the coast or spiriting us farther away. But no. The *Nautilus* was still in Portuguese waters. Heading north, it was cruising along the ocean's beaches.

So I had to resign myself to my fate and get ready to escape. My baggage wasn't heavy. My notes, nothing more.

As for Captain Nemo, I wondered what he would make of our escaping, what concern or perhaps what distress it might cause him, and what he would do in the twofold event of our attempt either failing or being found out! Certainly I had no complaints to register with him, on the contrary. Never was hospitality more wholehearted than his. Yet in leaving him I couldn't be accused of ingratitude. No solemn promises bound us to him. In order to keep us captive, he had counted only on the force of circumstances and not on our word of honor. But his avowed intention to imprison us forever on his ship justified our every effort.

I hadn't seen the captain since our visit to the island of Santorini. Would fate bring me into his presence before our departure? I both desired and dreaded it. I listened for footsteps in the stateroom adjoining mine. Not a sound reached my ear. His stateroom had to be deserted.

Then I began to wonder if this eccentric individual was even on board. Since that night when the skiff had left the Nautilus on some mysterious mission, my ideas about him had subtly changed. In spite of everything, I thought that Captain Nemo must have kept up some type of relationship with the shore. Did he himself never leave the Nautilus? Whole weeks had often gone by without my encountering him. What was he doing all the while? During all those times I'd thought he was convalescing in the grip of some misanthropic fit, was he instead far away from the ship, involved in some secret activity whose nature still eluded me?

All these ideas and a thousand others assaulted me at the same time. In these strange circumstances the scope for conjecture was unlimited. I felt an unbearable queasiness. This day of waiting seemed endless. The hours struck too slowly to keep up with my impatience.

As usual, dinner was served me in my stateroom. Full of anxiety, I ate little. I left the table at seven o'clock. 120 minutes—I was keeping track of them—still separated me from the moment I was to rejoin Ned Land. My agitation increased. My pulse was throbbing violently. I couldn't stand still. I walked up and down, hoping to calm my troubled mind with movement. The possibility of perishing in our reckless undertaking was the least of my worries; my heart was pounding at the thought that our plans might be discovered before we had left the Nautilus, at the thought of being hauled in front of Captain Nemo and finding him angered, or worse, saddened by my deserting him.

I wanted to see the lounge one last time. I went down the gangways and arrived at the museum where I had spent so many pleasant and productive hours. I stared at all its wealth, all its treasures, like a man on the eve of his eternal exile, a man departing to return no more. For so many days now, these natural wonders and artistic masterworks had been central to my life, and I was about to leave them behind forever. I wanted to plunge my eyes through the lounge window and into these Atlantic waters; but the panels were hermetically sealed, and a mantle of sheet iron separated me from this ocean with which I was still unfamiliar.

Crossing through the lounge, I arrived at the door, contrived in one of the canted corners, that opened into the captain's stateroom. Much to my astonishment, this door was ajar. I instinctively recoiled. If Captain Nemo was in his stateroom, he might see me. But, not hearing any sounds, I approached. The stateroom was deserted. I pushed the door open. I took a few steps inside. Still the same austere, monastic appearance.

Just then my eye was caught by some etchings hanging on the wall, which I hadn't noticed during my first visit. They were portraits of great men of history who had spent their lives in perpetual devotion to a great human ideal: Thaddeus Kosciusko, the hero whose dying words had been Finis Poloniae; Markos Botzaris, for modern Greece the reincarnation of Sparta's King Leonidas; Daniel O'Connell, Ireland's defender; George Washington, founder of the American Union; Daniele Manin, the Italian patriot; Abraham Lincoln, dead from the bullet of a believer in slavery; and finally, that martyr for the redemption of the black race, John Brown, hanging from his gallows as Victor Hugo's pencil has so terrifyingly depicted.

What was the bond between these heroic souls and the

soul of Captain Nemo? From this collection of portraits could I finally unravel the mystery of his existence? Was he a fighter for oppressed peoples, a liberator of enslaved races? Had he figured in the recent political or social upheavals of this century? Was he a hero of that dreadful civil war in America, a war lamentable yet forever glorious . . . ?

Suddenly the clock struck eight. The first stroke of its hammer on the chime snapped me out of my musings. I shuddered as if some invisible eye had plunged into my innermost thoughts, and I rushed outside the stateroom.

There my eyes fell on the compass. Our heading was still northerly. The log indicated a moderate speed, the pressure gauge a depth of about sixty feet. So circumstances were in favor of the Canadian's plans.

I stayed in my stateroom. I dressed warmly: fishing boots, otter cap, coat of fan–mussel fabric lined with sealskin. I was ready. I was waiting. Only the propeller's vibrations disturbed the deep silence reigning on board. I cocked an ear and listened. Would a sudden outburst of voices tell me that Ned Land's escape plans had just been detected? A ghastly uneasiness stole through me. I tried in vain to recover my composure.

A few minutes before nine o'clock, I glued my ear to the captain's door. Not a sound. I left my stateroom and returned to the lounge, which was deserted and plunged in near darkness.

I opened the door leading to the library. The same inadequate light, the same solitude. I went to man my post near the door opening into the well of the central companionway. I waited for Ned Land's signal.

At this point the propeller's vibrations slowed down appreciably, then they died out altogether. Why was the *Nautilus* stopping? Whether this layover would help or hinder Ned Land's schemes I couldn't have said.

The silence was further disturbed only by the pounding of my heart.

Suddenly I felt a mild jolt. I realized the *Nautilus* had come to rest on the ocean floor. My alarm increased. The Canadian's signal hadn't reached me. I longed to rejoin Ned Land and urge him to postpone his attempt. I sensed that we were no longer navigating under normal conditions.

Just then the door to the main lounge opened and Captain Nemo appeared. He saw me, and without further preamble:

"Ah, Professor," he said in an affable tone, "I've been looking for you. Do you know your Spanish history?"

Even if he knew it by heart, a man in my disturbed, befuddled condition couldn't have quoted a syllable of his own country's history.

"Well?" Captain Nemo went on. "Did you hear my question? Do you know the history of Spain?"

"Very little of it," I replied.

"The most learned men," the captain said, "still have much to learn. Have a seat," he added, "and I'll tell you about an unusual episode in this body of history."

The captain stretched out on a couch, and I mechanically took a seat near him, but half in the shadows.

"Professor," he said, "listen carefully. This piece of history concerns you in one definite respect, because it will answer a question you've no doubt been unable to resolve."

"I'm listening, Captain," I said, not knowing what my partner in this dialogue was driving at, and wondering if this incident related to our escape plans.

"Professor," Captain Nemo went on, "if you're amenable, we'll go back in time to 1702. You're aware of the fact that in those days your King Louis XIV thought an imperial gesture would suffice to humble the Pyrenees in the dust, so he inflicted his grandson, the Duke of Anjou, on the Spaniards. Reigning more or less poorly under the name King Philip V, this aristocrat had to deal with mighty opponents abroad.

"In essence, the year before, the royal houses of Holland,

Austria, and England had signed a treaty of alliance at The Hague, aiming to wrest the Spanish crown from King Philip V and to place it on the head of an archduke whom they prematurely dubbed King Charles III.

"Spain had to withstand these allies. But the country had practically no army or navy. Yet it wasn't short of money, provided that its galleons, laden with gold and silver from America, could enter its ports. Now then, late in 1702 Spain was expecting a rich convoy, which France ventured to escort with a fleet of twenty-three vessels under the command of Admiral de Chateau-Renault, because by that time the allied navies were roving the Atlantic.

"This convoy was supposed to put into Cadiz, but after learning that the English fleet lay across those waterways, the admiral decided to make for a French port.

"The Spanish commanders in the convoy objected to this decision. They wanted to be taken to a Spanish port, if not to Cadiz, then to the Bay of Vigo, located on Spain's northwest coast and not blockaded.

"Admiral de Chateau-Renault was so indecisive as to obey this directive, and the galleons entered the Bay of Vigo.

"Unfortunately this bay forms an open, offshore mooring that's impossible to defend. So it was essential to hurry and empty the galleons before the allied fleets arrived, and there would have been ample time for this unloading, if a wretched question of trade agreements hadn't suddenly come up.

"Are you clear on the chain of events?" Captain Nemo asked me.

"Perfectly clear," I said, not yet knowing why I was being given this history lesson.

"Then I'll continue. Here's what came to pass. The tradesmen of Cadiz had negotiated a charter whereby they were to receive all merchandise coming from the West Indies. Now then, unloading the ingots from those galleons at the port of Vigo would have been a violation of their rights. So they lodged a complaint in Madrid, and they obtained an order from the indecisive King Philip V: without unloading, the convoy would stay in custody at the offshore mooring of Vigo until the enemy fleets had retreated.

"Now then, just as this decision was being handed down, English vessels arrived in the Bay of Vigo on October 22, 1702. Despite his inferior forces, Admiral de Chateau–Renault fought courageously. But when he saw that the convoy's wealth was about to fall into enemy hands, he burned and scuttled the galleons, which went to the bottom with their immense treasures."

Captain Nemo stopped. I admit it: I still couldn't see how this piece of history concerned me.

"Well?" I asked him.

"Well, Professor Aronnax," Captain Nemo answered me, "we're actually in that Bay of Vigo, and all that's left is for you to probe the mysteries of the place."

The captain stood up and invited me to follow him. I'd had time to collect myself. I did so. The lounge was dark, but the sea's waves sparkled through the transparent windows. I stared.

Around the *Nautilus* for a half–mile radius, the waters seemed saturated with electric light. The sandy bottom was clear and bright. Dressed in diving suits, crewmen were busy clearing away half–rotted barrels and disemboweled trunks in the midst of the dingy hulks of ships. Out of these trunks and kegs spilled ingots of gold and silver, cascades of jewels, pieces of eight. The sand was heaped with them. Then, laden with these valuable spoils, the men returned to the *Nautilus*, dropped off their burdens inside, and went to resume this inexhaustible fishing for silver and gold.

I understood. This was the setting of that battle on October 22, 1702. Here, in this very place, those galleons carrying treasure to the Spanish government had gone to the bottom.

Here, whenever he needed, Captain Nemo came to withdraw these millions to ballast his *Nautilus*. It was for him, for him alone, that America had yielded up its precious metals. He was the direct, sole heir to these treasures wrested from the Incas and those peoples conquered by Hernando Cortez!

"Did you know, professor," he asked me with a smile, "that the sea contained such wealth?"

"I know it's estimated," I replied, "that there are 2,000,000 metric tons of silver held in suspension in seawater."

"Surely, but in extracting that silver, your expenses would outweigh your profits. Here, by contrast, I have only to pick up what other men have lost, and not only in this Bay of Vigo but at a thousand other sites where ships have gone down, whose positions are marked on my underwater chart. Do you understand now that I'm rich to the tune of billions?"

"I understand, Captain. Nevertheless, allow me to inform you that by harvesting this very Bay of Vigo, you're simply forestalling the efforts of a rival organization."

"What organization?"

"A company chartered by the Spanish government to search for these sunken galleons. The company's investors were lured by the bait of enormous gains, because this scuttled treasure is estimated to be worth F500,000,000."

"It was 500,000,000 francs," Captain Nemo replied, "but no more!"

"Right," I said. "Hence a timely warning to those investors would be an act of charity. Yet who knows if it would be well received? Usually what gamblers regret the most isn't the loss of their money so much as the loss of their insane hopes. But ultimately I feel less sorry for them than for the thousands of unfortunate people who would have benefited from a fair distribution of this wealth, whereas now it will be of no help to them!"

No sooner had I voiced this regret than I felt it must have

wounded Captain Nemo.

"No help!" he replied with growing animation. "Sir, what makes you assume this wealth goes to waste when I'm the one amassing it? Do you think I toil to gather this treasure out of selfishness? Who says I don't put it to good use? Do you think I'm unaware of the suffering beings and oppressed races living on this earth, poor people to comfort, victims to avenge? Don't you understand . . . ?"

Captain Nemo stopped on these last words, perhaps sorry that he had said too much. But I had guessed. Whatever motives had driven him to seek independence under the seas, he remained a human being before all else! His heart still throbbed for suffering humanity, and his immense philanthropy went out both to downtrodden races and to individuals!

And now I knew where Captain Nemo had delivered those millions, when the *Nautilus* navigated the waters where Crete was in rebellion against the Ottoman Empire!

# CHAPTER 9

## A Lost Continent

THE NEXT MORNING, February 19, I beheld the Canadian entering my stateroom. I was expecting this visit. He wore an expression of great disappointment.

"Well, sir?" he said to me.

"Well, Ned, the fates were against us yesterday."

"Yes! That damned captain had to call a halt just as we were going to escape from his boat."

"Yes, Ned, he had business with his bankers."

"His bankers?"

"Or rather his bank vaults. By which I mean this ocean, where his wealth is safer than in any national treasury."

I then related the evening's incidents to the Canadian, secretly hoping he would come around to the idea of not deserting the captain; but my narrative had no result other than Ned's voicing deep regret that he hadn't strolled across the Vigo battlefield on his own behalf.

"Anyhow," he said, "it's not over yet! My first harpoon missed, that's all! We'll succeed the next time, and as soon as this evening, if need be . . ."

"What's the *Nautilus's* heading?" I asked.

"I've no idea," Ned replied.

"All right, at noon we'll find out what our position is!"

The Canadian returned to Conseil's side. As soon as I was dressed, I went into the lounge. The compass wasn't encouraging. The *Nautilus's* course was south-southwest. We were turning our backs on Europe.

I could hardly wait until our position was reported on the chart. Near 11:30 the ballast tanks emptied, and the submersible rose to the surface of the ocean. I leaped onto the platform. Ned Land was already there.

No more shore in sight. Nothing but the immenseness of the sea. A few sails were on the horizon, no doubt ships going as far as Cape São Roque to find favorable winds for doubling the Cape of Good Hope. The sky was overcast. A squall was on the way.

Furious, Ned tried to see through the mists on the horizon. He still hoped that behind all that fog there lay those shores he longed for.

At noon the sun made a momentary appearance. Taking advantage of this rift in the clouds, the chief officer took the orb's altitude. Then the sea grew turbulent, we went below again, and the hatch closed once more.

When I consulted the chart an hour later, I saw that the *Nautilus*'s position was marked at longitude 16° 17' and latitude 33° 22', a good 150 leagues from the nearest coast. It wouldn't do to even dream of escaping, and I'll let the reader decide how promptly the Canadian threw a tantrum when I ventured to tell him our situation.

As for me, I wasn't exactly grief–stricken. I felt as if a heavy weight had been lifted from me, and I was able to resume my regular tasks in a state of comparative calm.

Near eleven o'clock in the evening, I received a most unexpected visit from Captain Nemo. He asked me very graciously if I felt exhausted from our vigil the night before. I said no.

"Then, Professor Aronnax, I propose an unusual excursion."

"Propose away, Captain."

"So far you've visited the ocean depths only by day and under sunlight. Would you like to see these depths on a dark night?"

"Very much."

"I warn you, this will be an exhausting stroll. We'll need to walk long hours and scale a mountain. The roads aren't terribly well kept up."

"Everything you say, Captain, just increases my curiosity. I'm ready to go with you."

"Then come along, professor, and we'll go put on our diving suits."

Arriving at the wardrobe, I saw that neither my companions nor any crewmen would be coming with us on this excursion. Captain Nemo hadn't even suggested my fetching Ned or Conseil.

In a few moments we had put on our equipment. Air tanks, abundantly charged, were placed on our backs, but the electric lamps were not in readiness. I commented on this to the captain.

"They'll be useless to us," he replied.

I thought I hadn't heard him right, but I couldn't repeat my comment because the captain's head had already disappeared into its metal covering. I finished harnessing myself, I felt an alpenstock being placed in my hand, and a few minutes later, after the usual procedures, we set foot on the floor of the Atlantic, 300 meters down.

Midnight was approaching. The waters were profoundly dark, but Captain Nemo pointed to a reddish spot in the distance, a sort of wide glow shimmering about two miles from the *Nautilus*. What this fire was, what substances fed it, how and why it kept burning in the liquid mass, I couldn't say. Anyhow it lit our way, although hazily, but I soon grew accustomed to this unique gloom, and in these circumstances I understood the uselessness of the Ruhmkorff device.

Side by side, Captain Nemo and I walked directly toward this conspicuous flame. The level seafloor rose imperceptibly. We took long strides, helped by our alpenstocks; but in general our progress was slow, because our feet kept sinking into a kind of slimy mud mixed with seaweed and assorted flat stones.

As we moved forward, I heard a kind of pitter–patter above my head. Sometimes this noise increased and became a continuous crackle. I soon realized the cause. It was a heavy rainfall rattling on the surface of the waves. Instinctively I worried that I might get soaked! By water in the midst of water! I couldn't help smiling at this outlandish notion. But to tell the truth, wearing these heavy diving suits, you no longer feel the liquid element, you simply think you're in the midst of air a little denser than air on land, that's all.

After half an hour of walking, the seafloor grew rocky. Jellyfish, microscopic crustaceans, and sea–pen coral lit it faintly with their phosphorescent glimmers. I glimpsed piles of stones covered by a couple million zoophytes and tangles of algae. My feet often slipped on this viscous seaweed carpet, and without my alpenstock I would have fallen more than once. When I turned around, I could still see the *Nautilus's* whitish beacon, which was starting to grow pale in the distance.

Those piles of stones just mentioned were laid out on the ocean floor with a distinct but inexplicable symmetry. I spotted gigantic furrows trailing off into the distant darkness, their length incalculable. There also were other peculiarities I couldn't make sense of. It seemed to me that my heavy lead soles were crushing a litter of bones that made a dry crackling noise. So what were these vast plains we were now crossing? I wanted to ask the captain, but I still didn't grasp that sign language that allowed him to chat with his companions when they went with him on his underwater excursions.

Meanwhile the reddish light guiding us had expanded and inflamed the horizon. The presence of this furnace under the waters had me extremely puzzled. Was it some sort of electrical discharge? Was I approaching some natural phenomenon still unknown to scientists on shore? Or, rather (and this thought did cross my mind), had the hand of man intervened in that blaze? Had human beings fanned those flames? In these deep strata would I meet up with more of Captain Nemo's companions, friends he was about to visit who led lives as strange as his own? Would I find a whole colony of exiles down here, men tired of the world's woes, men who had sought and found independence in the ocean's lower depths? All these insane, inadmissible ideas dogged me, and in this frame of mind, continually excited by the series of wonders passing before my eyes, I wouldn't have been surprised to find on this sea bottom one of those underwater towns Captain Nemo dreamed about!

Our path was getting brighter and brighter. The red glow had turned white and was radiating from a mountain peak about 800 feet high. But what I saw was simply a reflection produced by the crystal waters of these strata. The furnace that was the source of this inexplicable light occupied the far side of the mountain.

In the midst of the stone mazes furrowing this Atlantic seafloor, Captain Nemo moved forward without hesitation. He knew this dark path. No doubt he had often traveled it and was incapable of losing his way. I followed him with unshakeable confidence. He seemed like some Spirit of the Sea, and as he walked ahead of me, I marveled at his tall figure, which stood out in black against the glowing background of the horizon.

It was one o'clock in the morning. We arrived at the mountain's lower gradients. But in grappling with them, we had to venture up difficult trails through a huge thicket.

Yes, a thicket of dead trees! Trees without leaves, without sap, turned to stone by the action of the waters, and crowned here and there by gigantic pines. It was like a still–erect coalfield, its roots clutching broken soil, its boughs clearly outlined against the ceiling of the waters like thin, black, paper cutouts. Picture a forest clinging to the sides of a peak in the Harz Mountains, but a submerged forest. The trails were cluttered with algae and fucus plants, hosts of crustaceans swarming among them. I plunged on, scaling rocks, straddling fallen tree trunks, snapping marine creepers that swayed from one tree to another, startling the fish that flitted from branch to branch. Carried away, I didn't feel exhausted any more. I followed a guide who was immune to exhaustion.

What a sight! How can I describe it! How can I portray these woods and rocks in this liquid setting, their lower parts dark and sullen, their upper parts tinted red in this light whose intensity was doubled by the reflecting power of the waters! We scaled rocks that crumbled behind us, collapsing in enormous sections with the hollow rumble of an avalanche. To our right and left there were carved gloomy galleries where the eye lost its way. Huge glades opened up, seemingly cleared by the hand of man, and I sometimes wondered whether some residents of these underwater regions would suddenly appear before me.

But Captain Nemo kept climbing. I didn't want to fall behind. I followed him boldly. My alpenstock was a great help. One wrong step would have been disastrous on the narrow paths cut into the sides of these chasms, but I walked along with a firm tread and without the slightest feeling of dizziness. Sometimes I leaped over a crevasse whose depth would have made me recoil had I been in the midst of glaciers on shore; sometimes I ventured out on a wobbling tree trunk fallen across a gorge, without looking down, having eyes only for marveling at the wild scenery of this region. There, leaning on erratically cut foundations, monumental rocks seemed to defy the laws of balance. From between their stony knees, trees sprang up like jets under fearsome pressure, supporting other trees that supported them in turn. Next, natural towers with wide, steeply carved battlements leaned at angles that, on dry land, the laws of gravity would never have authorized.

And I too could feel the difference created by the water's

powerful density—despite my heavy clothing, copper headpiece, and metal soles, I climbed the most impossibly steep gradients with all the nimbleness, I swear it, of a chamois or a Pyrenees mountain goat!

As for my account of this excursion under the waters, I'm well aware that it sounds incredible! I'm the chronicler of deeds seemingly impossible and yet incontestably real. This was no fantasy. This was what I saw and felt!

Two hours after leaving the *Nautilus*, we had cleared the timberline, and 100 feet above our heads stood the mountain peak, forming a dark silhouette against the brilliant glare that came from its far slope. Petrified shrubs rambled here and there in sprawling zigzags. Fish rose in a body at our feet like birds startled in tall grass. The rocky mass was gouged with impenetrable crevices, deep caves, unfathomable holes at whose far ends I could hear fearsome things moving around. My blood would curdle as I watched some enormous antenna bar my path, or saw some frightful pincer snap shut in the shadow of some cavity! A thousand specks of light glittered in the midst of the gloom. They were the eyes of gigantic crustaceans crouching in their lairs, giant lobsters rearing up like spear carriers and moving their claws with a scrap-iron clanking, titanic crabs aiming their bodies like cannons on their carriages, and hideous devilfish intertwining their tentacles like bushes of writhing snakes.

What was this astounding world that I didn't yet know? In what order did these articulates belong, these creatures for which the rocks provided a second carapace? Where had nature learned the secret of their vegetating existence, and for how many centuries had they lived in the ocean's lower strata?

But I couldn't linger. Captain Nemo, on familiar terms with these dreadful animals, no longer minded them. We arrived at a preliminary plateau where still other surprises were waiting for me. There picturesque ruins took shape, betraying the hand of man, not our Creator. They were huge stacks of stones in which you could distinguish the indistinct forms of palaces and temples, now arrayed in hosts of blossoming zoophytes, and over it all, not ivy but a heavy mantle of algae and fucus plants.

But what part of the globe could this be, this land swallowed by cataclysms? Who had set up these rocks and stones like the dolmens of prehistoric times? Where was I, where had Captain Nemo's fancies taken me?

I wanted to ask him. Unable to, I stopped him. I seized his arm. But he shook his head, pointed to the mountain's topmost peak, and seemed to tell me:

"Come on! Come with me! Come higher!"

I followed him with one last burst of energy, and in a few minutes I had scaled the peak, which crowned the whole rocky mass by some ten meters.

I looked back down the side we had just cleared. There the mountain rose only 700 to 800 feet above the plains; but on its far slope it crowned the receding bottom of this part of the Atlantic by a height twice that. My eyes scanned the distance and took in a vast area lit by intense flashes of light. In essence, this mountain was a volcano. Fifty feet below its peak, amid a shower of stones and slag, a wide crater vomited torrents of lava that were dispersed in fiery cascades into the heart of the liquid mass. So situated, this volcano was an immense torch that lit up the lower plains all the way to the horizon.

As I said, this underwater crater spewed lava, but not flames. Flames need oxygen from the air and are unable to spread underwater; but a lava flow, which contains in itself the principle of its incandescence, can rise to a white heat, overpower the liquid element, and turn it into steam on contact. Swift currents swept away all this diffuse gas, and torrents of lava slid to the foot of the mountain, like the disgorgings of a Mt. Vesuvius over the city limits of a second Torre del Greco.

In fact, there beneath my eyes was a town in ruins, demolished, overwhelmed, laid low, its roofs caved in, its temples pulled down, its arches dislocated, its columns stretching over the earth; in these ruins you could still detect the solid proportions of a sort of Tuscan architecture; farther off, the remains of a gigantic aqueduct; here, the caked heights of an acropolis along with the fluid forms of a Parthenon; there, the remnants of a wharf, as if some bygone port had long ago harbored merchant vessels and triple-tiered war galleys on the shores of some lost ocean; still farther off, long rows of collapsing walls, deserted thoroughfares, a whole Pompeii buried under the waters, which Captain Nemo had resurrected before my eyes!

Where was I? Where was I? I had to find out at all cost, I wanted to speak, I wanted to rip off the copper sphere imprisoning my head.

But Captain Nemo came over and stopped me with a gesture. Then, picking up a piece of chalky stone, he advanced to a black basaltic rock and scrawled this one word:

ATLANTIS

What lightning flashed through my mind! Atlantis, that ancient land of Meropis mentioned by the historian Theopompus; Plato's Atlantis; the continent whose very existence has been denied by such philosophers and scientists as Origen, Porphyry, Iamblichus, d'Anville, Malte-Brun, and Humboldt, who entered its disappearance in the ledger of myths and folk tales; the country whose reality has nevertheless been accepted by such other thinkers as Posidonius, Pliny, Ammianus Marcellinus, Tertullian, Engel, Scherer, Tournefort, Buffon, and d'Avezac; I had this land right under my eyes, furnishing its own unimpeachable evidence of the catastrophe that had overtaken it! So this was the submerged region that had existed outside Europe, Asia, and Libya, beyond the Pillars of Hercules, home of those powerful Atlantean people against whom ancient Greece had waged its earliest wars!

The writer whose narratives record the lofty deeds of those heroic times is Plato himself. His dialogues Timæus and Critias were drafted with the poet and legislator Solon as their inspiration, as it were.

One day Solon was conversing with some elderly wise men in the Egyptian capital of Sais, a town already 8,000 years of age, as documented by the annals engraved on the sacred walls of its temples. One of these elders related the history of another town 1,000 years older still. This original city of Athens, ninety centuries old, had been invaded and partly destroyed by the Atlanteans. These Atlanteans, he said, resided on an immense continent greater than Africa and Asia combined, taking in an area that lay between latitude 12° and 40° north. Their dominion extended even to Egypt. They tried to enforce their rule as far as Greece, but they had to retreat before the indomitable resistance of the Hellenic people. Centuries passed. A cataclysm occurred—floods, earthquakes. A single night and day were enough to obliterate this Atlantis, whose highest peaks (Madeira, the Azores, the Canaries, the Cape Verde Islands) still emerge above the waves.

These were the historical memories that Captain Nemo's scrawl sent rushing through my mind. Thus, led by the strangest of fates, I was treading underfoot one of the mountains of that continent! My hands were touching ruins many thousands of years old, contemporary with prehistoric times! I was walking in the very place where contemporaries of early man had walked! My heavy soles were crushing the skeletons of animals from the age of fable, animals that used to take cover in the shade of these trees now turned to stone!

Oh, why was I so short of time! I would have gone down the steep slopes of this mountain, crossed this entire immense continent, which surely connects Africa with America, and visited its great prehistoric cities. Under my eyes there perhaps lay the warlike town of Makhimos or the pious village of Eusebes, whose gigantic inhabitants lived for whole centuries and had the strength to raise blocks of stone that still withstood the action of the waters. One day perhaps, some volcanic phenomenon will bring these sunken ruins back to the surface of the waves! Numerous underwater volcanoes have been sighted in this part of the ocean, and many ships have felt terrific tremors when passing over these turbulent depths. A few have heard hollow noises that announced some struggle of the elements far below, others have hauled in volcanic ash hurled above the waves. As far as the equator this whole seafloor is still under construction by plutonic forces. And in some remote epoch, built up by volcanic disgorgings and successive layers of lava, who knows whether the peaks of these fire–belching mountains may reappear above the surface of the Atlantic!

As I mused in this way, trying to establish in my memory every detail of this impressive landscape, Captain Nemo was leaning his elbows on a moss–covered monument, motionless as if petrified in some mute trance. Was he dreaming of those lost generations, asking them for the secret of human destiny? Was it here that this strange man came to revive himself, basking in historical memories, reliving that bygone life, he who had no desire for our modern one? I would have given anything to know his thoughts, to share them, understand them!

We stayed in this place an entire hour, contemplating its vast plains in the lava's glow, which sometimes took on a startling intensity. Inner boilings sent quick shivers running through the mountain's crust. Noises from deep underneath, clearly transmitted by the liquid medium, reverberated with majestic amplitude.

Just then the moon appeared for an instant through the watery mass, casting a few pale rays over this submerged continent. It was only a fleeting glimmer, but its effect was indescribable. The captain stood up and took one last look at these immense plains; then his hand signaled me to follow him.

We went swiftly down the mountain. Once past the petrified forest, I could see the *Nautilus's* beacon twinkling like a star. The captain walked straight toward it, and we were back on board just as the first glimmers of dawn were whitening the surface of the ocean.

# CHAPTER 10

## The Underwater Coalfields

THE NEXT DAY, February 20, I overslept. I was so exhausted from the night before, I didn't get up until eleven o'clock. I dressed quickly. I hurried to find out the *Nautilus's* heading. The instruments indicated that it was running southward at a speed of twenty miles per hour and a depth of 100 meters.

Conseil entered. I described our nocturnal excursion to him, and since the panels were open, he could still catch a glimpse of this submerged continent.

In fact, the *Nautilus* was skimming only ten meters over the soil of these Atlantis plains. The ship scudded along like an air balloon borne by the wind over some prairie on land; but it would be more accurate to say that we sat in the lounge as if we were riding in a coach on an express train. As for the foregrounds passing before our eyes, they were fantastically carved rocks, forests of trees that had crossed over from the vegetable kingdom into the mineral kingdom, their motionless silhouettes sprawling beneath the waves. There also were stony masses buried beneath carpets of axidia and sea anemone, bristling with long, vertical water plants, then strangely contoured blocks of lava that testified to all the fury of those plutonic developments.

While this bizarre scenery was glittering under our electric beams, I told Conseil the story of the Atlanteans, who had inspired the old French scientist Jean Bailly to write so many entertaining—albeit utterly fictitious—pages. I told the lad about the wars of these heroic people. I discussed the question of Atlantis with the fervor of a man who no longer had any doubts. But Conseil was so distracted he barely heard me, and his lack of interest in any commentary on this historical topic was soon explained.

In essence, numerous fish had caught his eye, and when fish pass by, Conseil vanishes into his world of classifying and leaves real life behind. In which case I could only tag along and resume our ichthyological research.

Even so, these Atlantic fish were not noticeably different from those we had observed earlier. There were rays of gigantic size, five meters long and with muscles so powerful they could leap above the waves, sharks of various species including a fifteen-foot glaucous shark with sharp triangular teeth and so transparent it was almost invisible amid the waters, brown lantern sharks, prism-shaped humantin sharks armored with protuberant hides, sturgeons resembling their relatives in the Mediterranean, trumpet-snouted pipefish a foot and a half long, yellowish brown with small gray fins and no teeth or tongue, unreeling like slim, supple snakes.

Among bony fish, Conseil noticed some blackish marlin three meters long with a sharp sword jutting from the upper jaw, bright-colored weevers known in Aristotle's day as sea dragons and whose dorsal stingers make them quite dangerous to pick up, then dolphinfish with brown backs striped in blue and edged in gold, handsome dorados, moonlike opahs that look like azure disks but which the sun's rays turn into spots of silver, finally eight-meter swordfish from the genus Xiphias, swimming in schools, sporting yellowish sickle-shaped fins and six-foot broadswords, stalwart animals, plant eaters rather than fish eaters, obeying the tiniest signals from their females like henpecked husbands.

But while observing these different specimens of marine fauna, I didn't stop examining the long plains of Atlantis.

Sometimes an unpredictable irregularity in the seafloor would force the *Nautilus* to slow down, and then it would glide into the narrow channels between the hills with a cetacean's dexterity. If the labyrinth became hopelessly tangled, the submersible would rise above it like an airship, and after clearing the obstacle, it would resume its speedy course just a few meters above the ocean floor. It was an enjoyable and impressive way of navigating that did indeed recall the maneuvers of an airship ride, with the major difference that the *Nautilus* faithfully obeyed the hands of its helmsman.

The terrain consisted mostly of thick slime mixed with petrified branches, but it changed little by little near four o'clock in the afternoon; it grew rockier and seemed to be strewn with pudding stones and a basaltic gravel called "tuff," together with bits of lava and sulfurous obsidian. I expected these long plains to change into mountain regions, and in fact, as the *Nautilus* was executing certain turns, I noticed that the southerly horizon was blocked by a high wall that seemed to close off every exit. Its summit obviously poked above the level of the ocean. It had to be a continent or at least an island, either one of the Canaries or one of the Cape Verde Islands. Our bearings hadn't been marked on the chart—perhaps deliberately—and I had no idea what our position was. In any case this wall seemed to signal the end of Atlantis, of which, all in all, we had crossed only a small part.

Nightfall didn't interrupt my observations. I was left to myself. Conseil had repaired to his cabin. The *Nautilus* slowed down, hovering above the muddled masses on the seafloor, sometimes grazing them as if wanting to come to rest, sometimes rising unpredictably to the surface of the waves. Then I glimpsed a few bright constellations through the crystal waters, specifically five or six of those zodiacal stars trailing from the tail end of Orion.

I would have stayed longer at my window, marveling at

these beauties of sea and sky, but the panels closed. Just then the *Nautilus* had arrived at the perpendicular face of that high wall. How the ship would maneuver I hadn't a guess. I repaired to my stateroom. The *Nautilus* did not stir. I fell asleep with the firm intention of waking up in just a few hours.

But it was eight o'clock the next day when I returned to the lounge. I stared at the pressure gauge. It told me that the *Nautilus* was afloat on the surface of the ocean. Furthermore, I heard the sound of footsteps on the platform. Yet there were no rolling movements to indicate the presence of waves undulating above me.

I climbed as far as the hatch. It was open. But instead of the broad daylight I was expecting, I found that I was surrounded by total darkness. Where were we? Had I been mistaken? Was it still night? No! Not one star was twinkling, and nighttime is never so utterly black.

I wasn't sure what to think, when a voice said to me:

"Is that you, Professor?"

"Ah, Captain Nemo!" I replied. "Where are we?"

"Underground, Professor."

"Underground!" I exclaimed. "And the *Nautilus* is still floating?"

"It always floats."

"But I don't understand!"

"Wait a little while. Our beacon is about to go on, and if you want some light on the subject, you'll be satisfied."

I set foot on the platform and waited. The darkness was so profound I couldn't see even Captain Nemo. However, looking at the zenith directly overhead, I thought I caught sight of a feeble glimmer, a sort of twilight filtering through a circular hole. Just then the beacon suddenly went on, and its intense brightness made that hazy light vanish.

This stream of electricity dazzled my eyes, and after momentarily shutting them, I looked around. The *Nautilus* was stationary. It was floating next to an embankment shaped like a wharf. As for the water now buoying the ship, it was a lake completely encircled by an inner wall about two miles in diameter, hence six miles around. Its level—as indicated by the pressure gauge—would be the same as the outside level, because some connection had to exist between this lake and the sea. Slanting inward over their base, these high walls converged to form a vault shaped like an immense upside–down funnel that measured 500 or 600 meters in height. At its summit there gaped the circular opening through which I had detected that faint glimmer, obviously daylight.

Before more carefully examining the interior features of this enormous cavern, and before deciding if it was the work of nature or humankind, I went over to Captain Nemo.

"Where are we?" I said.

"In the very heart of an extinct volcano," the captain answered me, "a volcano whose interior was invaded by the sea after some convulsion in the earth. While you were sleeping, professor, the Nautilus entered this lagoon through a natural channel that opens ten meters below the surface of the ocean. This is our home port, secure, convenient, secret, and sheltered against winds from any direction! Along the coasts of your continents or islands, show me any offshore mooring that can equal this safe refuge for withstanding the fury of hurricanes."

"Indeed," I replied, "here you're in perfect safety, Captain Nemo. Who could reach you in the heart of a volcano? But don't I see an opening at its summit?"

"Yes, its crater, a crater formerly filled with lava, steam, and flames, but which now lets in this life–giving air we're breathing."

"But which volcanic mountain is this?" I asked.

"It's one of the many islets with which this sea is strewn. For ships a mere reef, for us an immense cavern. I discovered it by chance, and chance served me well."

"But couldn't someone enter through the mouth of its crater?"

"No more than I could exit through it. You can climb about 100 feet up the inner base of this mountain, but then the walls overhang, they lean too far in to be scaled."

"I can see, Captain, that nature is your obedient servant, any time or any place. You're safe on this lake, and nobody else can visit its waters. But what's the purpose of this refuge? The *Nautilus* doesn't need a harbor."

"No, professor, but it needs electricity to run, batteries to generate its electricity, sodium to feed its batteries, coal to make its sodium, and coalfields from which to dig its coal. Now then, right at this spot the sea covers entire forests that sank underwater in prehistoric times; today, turned to stone, transformed into carbon fuel, they offer me inexhaustible coal mines."

"So, Captain, your men practice the trade of miners here?"

"Precisely. These mines extend under the waves like the coalfields at Newcastle. Here, dressed in diving suits, pick and mattock in hand, my men go out and dig this carbon fuel for which I don't need a single mine on land. When I burn this combustible to produce sodium, the smoke escaping from the mountain's crater gives it the appearance of a still-active volcano."

"And will we see your companions at work?"

"No, at least not this time, because I'm eager to continue our underwater tour of the world. Accordingly, I'll rest content with drawing on my reserve stock of sodium. We'll stay here long enough to load it on board, in other words, a single workday, then we'll resume our voyage. So, Professor Aronnax, if you'd like to explore this cavern and circle its lagoon, seize the day."

I thanked the captain and went to look for my two companions, who hadn't yet left their cabin. I invited them to follow me, not telling them where we were.

They climbed onto the platform. Conseil, whom nothing could startle, saw it as a perfectly natural thing to fall asleep under the waves and wake up under a mountain. But Ned Land had no idea in his head other than to see if this cavern offered some way out.

After breakfast near ten o'clock, we went down onto the embankment.

"So here we are, back on shore," Conseil said.

"I'd hardly call this shore," the Canadian replied. "And besides, we aren't on it but under it."

A sandy beach unfolded before us, measuring 500 feet at its widest point between the waters of the lake and the foot of the mountain's walls. Via this strand you could easily circle the lake. But the base of these high walls consisted of broken soil over which there lay picturesque piles of volcanic blocks and enormous pumice stones. All these crumbling masses were covered with an enamel polished by the action of underground fires, and they glistened under the stream of electric light from our beacon. Stirred up by our footsteps, the mica–rich dust on this beach flew into the air like a cloud of sparks.

The ground rose appreciably as it moved away from the sand flats by the waves, and we soon arrived at some long, winding gradients, genuinely steep paths that allowed us to climb little by little; but we had to tread cautiously in the midst of pudding stones that weren't cemented together, and our feet kept skidding on glassy trachyte, made of feldspar and quartz crystals.

The volcanic nature of this enormous pit was apparent all around us. I ventured to comment on it to my companions.

"Can you picture," I asked them, "what this funnel must have been like when it was filled with boiling lava, and the level of that incandescent liquid rose right to the mountain's mouth, like cast iron up the insides of a furnace?"

"I can picture it perfectly," Conseil replied. "But will Master tell me why this huge smelter suspended operations, and how it is that an oven was replaced by the tranquil waters of a lake?"

"In all likelihood, Conseil, because some convulsion created an opening below the surface of the ocean, the opening that serves as a passageway for the *Nautilus*. Then the waters of the Atlantic rushed inside the mountain. There ensued a dreadful struggle between the elements of fire and water, a struggle ending in King Neptune's favor. But many centuries have passed since then, and this submerged volcano has changed into a peaceful cavern."

"That's fine," Ned Land answered. "I accept the explanation, but in our personal interests, I'm sorry this opening the professor mentions wasn't made above sea level."

"But Ned my friend," Conseil answered, "if it weren't an underwater passageway, the *Nautilus* couldn't enter it!"

"And I might add, Mr. Land," I said, "that the waters wouldn't have rushed under the mountain, and the volcano would still be a volcano. So you have nothing to be sorry about."

Our climb continued. The gradients got steeper and narrower. Sometimes they were cut across by deep pits that had to be cleared. Masses of overhanging rock had to be gotten around. You slid on your knees, you crept on your belly. But helped by the Canadian's strength and Conseil's dexterity, we overcame every obstacle.

At an elevation of about thirty meters, the nature of the terrain changed without becoming any easier. Pudding stones and trachyte gave way to black basaltic rock: here, lying in slabs all swollen with blisters; there, shaped like actual prisms and arranged into a series of columns that supported the springings of this immense vault, a wonderful sample of natural architecture. Then, among this basaltic rock, there snaked long, hardened lava flows inlaid with veins of bituminous coal and in places covered by wide carpets of sulfur. The sunshine coming through the crater had grown stronger, shedding a hazy light over all the volcanic waste forever buried in the heart of this extinct mountain.

But when we had ascended to an elevation of about 250 feet, we were stopped by insurmountable obstacles. The converging inside walls changed into overhangs, and our climb into a circular stroll. At this topmost level the vegetable kingdom began to challenge the mineral kingdom. Shrubs, and even a few trees, emerged from crevices in the walls. I recognized some spurges that let their caustic, purgative sap trickle out. There were heliotropes, very remiss at living up to their sun–worshipping reputations since no sunlight ever reached them; their clusters of flowers drooped sadly, their colors and scents were faded. Here and there chrysanthemums sprouted timidly at the feet of aloes with long, sad, sickly leaves. But between these lava flows I spotted little violets that still gave off a subtle fragrance, and I confess that I inhaled it with delight. The soul of a flower is its scent, and those splendid water plants, flowers of the sea, have no souls!

We had arrived at the foot of a sturdy clump of dragon trees, which were splitting the rocks with exertions of their muscular roots, when Ned Land exclaimed:

"Oh, sir, a hive!"

"A hive?" I answered, with a gesture of utter disbelief.

"Yes, a hive," the Canadian repeated, "with bees buzzing around!"

I went closer and was forced to recognize the obvious. At the mouth of a hole cut in the trunk of a dragon tree, there swarmed thousands of these ingenious insects so common to all the Canary Islands, where their output is especially prized.

Naturally enough, the Canadian wanted to lay in a supply of honey, and it would have been ill–mannered of me to say no. He mixed sulfur with some dry leaves, set them on fire with a spark from his tinderbox, and proceeded to smoke the bees out. Little by little the buzzing died down and the disemboweled hive yielded several pounds of sweet honey. Ned Land stuffed his haversack with it.

"When I've mixed this honey with our breadfruit batter," he told us, "I'll be ready to serve you a delectable piece of cake."

"But of course," Conseil put in, "it will be gingerbread!"

"I'm all for gingerbread," I said, "but let's resume this fascinating stroll."

At certain turns in the trail we were going along, the lake appeared in its full expanse. The ship's beacon lit up that whole placid surface, which experienced neither ripples nor undulations. The *Nautilus* lay perfectly still. On its platform and on the embankment, crewmen were bustling around, black shadows that stood out clearly in the midst of the luminous air.

Just then we went around the highest ridge of these rocky foothills that supported the vault. Then I saw that bees weren't the animal kingdom's only representatives inside this volcano. Here and in the shadows, birds of prey soared and whirled, flying away from nests perched on tips of rock. There were sparrow hawks with white bellies, and screeching kestrels. With all the speed their stiltlike legs could muster, fine fat bustards scampered over the slopes. I'll let the reader decide whether the Canadian's appetite was aroused by the sight of this tasty game, and whether he regretted having no rifle in his hands. He tried to make stones do the work of bullets, and after several fruitless attempts, he managed to wound one of these magnificent bustards. To say he risked his life twenty times in order to capture this bird is simply the unadulterated truth; but he fared so well, the animal went into his sack to join the honeycombs.

By then we were forced to go back down to the beach because the ridge had become impossible. Above us, the yawning crater looked like the wide mouth of a well. From where we stood, the sky was pretty easy to see, and I watched clouds race by, disheveled by the west wind, letting tatters of mist trail over the mountain's summit. Proof positive that those clouds kept at a moderate altitude, because this volcano didn't rise more than 1,800 feet above the level of the ocean.

Half an hour after the Canadian's latest exploits, we were back on the inner beach. There the local flora was represented by a wide carpet of samphire, a small umbelliferous plant that keeps quite nicely, which also boasts the names glasswort, saxifrage, and sea fennel. Conseil picked a couple bunches. As for the local fauna, it included thousands of crustaceans of every type: lobsters, hermit crabs, prawns, mysid shrimps, daddy longlegs, rock crabs, and a prodigious number of seashells, such as cowries, murex snails, and limpets.

In this locality there gaped the mouth of a magnificent cave. My companions and I took great pleasure in stretching out on its fine-grained sand. Fire had polished the sparkling enamel of its inner walls, sprinkled all over with mica-rich dust. Ned Land tapped these walls and tried to probe their thickness. I couldn't help smiling. Our conversation then turned to his everlasting escape plans, and without going too far, I felt I could offer him this hope: Captain Nemo had gone down south only to replenish his sodium supplies. So I hoped he would now hug the coasts of Europe and America, which would allow the Canadian to try again with a greater chance of success.

We were stretched out in this delightful cave for an hour. Our conversation, lively at the outset, then languished. A definite drowsiness overcame us. Since I saw no good reason to resist the call of sleep, I fell into a heavy doze. I dreamed—one doesn't choose his dreams—that my life had been reduced to the vegetating existence of a simple mollusk. It seemed to me that this cave made up my double-valved shell. . . .

Suddenly Conseil's voice startled me awake.

"Get up! Get up!" shouted the fine lad.

"What is it?" I asked, in a sitting position.

"The water's coming up to us!"

I got back on my feet. Like a torrent the sea was rushing into our retreat, and since we definitely were not mollusks, we had to clear out.

In a few seconds we were safe on top of the cave.

"What happened?" Conseil asked. "Some new phenomenon?"

"Not quite, my friends!" I replied. "It was the tide, merely the tide, which wellnigh caught us by surprise just as it did Sir Walter Scott's hero! The ocean outside is rising, and by a perfectly natural law of balance, the level of this lake is also rising. We've gotten off with a mild dunking. Let's go change clothes on the *Nautilus*."

Three-quarters of an hour later, we had completed our circular stroll and were back on board. Just then the crewmen finished loading the sodium supplies, and the *Nautilus* could have departed immediately.

But Captain Nemo gave no orders. Would he wait for nightfall and exit through his underwater passageway in secrecy? Perhaps.

Be that as it may, by the next day the *Nautilus* had left its home port and was navigating well out from any shore, a few meters beneath the waves of the Atlantic.

# CHAPTER 11

The Sargasso Sea

THE *Nautilus* didn't change direction. For the time being, then, we had to set aside any hope of returning to European seas. Captain Nemo kept his prow pointing south. Where was he taking us? I was afraid to guess.

That day the *Nautilus* crossed an odd part of the Atlantic Ocean. No one is unaware of the existence of that great warm–water current known by name as the Gulf Stream. After emerging from channels off Florida, it heads toward Spitzbergen. But before entering the Gulf of Mexico near latitude 44° north, this current divides into two arms; its chief arm makes for the shores of Ireland and Norway while the second flexes southward at the level of the Azores; then it hits the coast of Africa, sweeps in a long oval, and returns to the Caribbean Sea.

Now then, this second arm—more accurately, a collar—forms a ring of warm water around a section of cool, tranquil, motionless ocean called the Sargasso Sea. This is an actual lake in the open Atlantic, and the great current's waters take at least three years to circle it.

Properly speaking, the Sargasso Sea covers every submerged part of Atlantis. Certain authors have even held that the many weeds strewn over this sea were torn loose from the prairies of that ancient continent. But it's more likely that these grasses, algae, and fucus plants were carried off from the beaches of Europe and America, then taken as far as this zone by the Gulf

Stream. This is one of the reasons why Christopher Columbus assumed the existence of a New World. When the ships of that bold investigator arrived in the Sargasso Sea, they had great difficulty navigating in the midst of these weeds, which, much to their crews' dismay, slowed them down to a halt; and they wasted three long weeks crossing this sector.

Such was the region our *Nautilus* was visiting just then: a genuine prairie, a tightly woven carpet of algae, gulfweed, and bladder wrack so dense and compact a craft's stempost couldn't tear through it without difficulty. Accordingly, not wanting to entangle his propeller in this weed–choked mass, Captain Nemo stayed at a depth some meters below the surface of the waves.

The name Sargasso comes from the Spanish word sargazo, meaning gulfweed. This gulfweed, the swimming gulfweed or berry carrier, is the chief substance making up this immense shoal. And here's why these water plants collect in this placid Atlantic basin, according to the expert on the subject, Commander Maury, author of *The Physical Geography of the Sea*.

The explanation he gives seems to entail a set of conditions that everybody knows: "Now," Maury says, "if bits of cork or chaff, or any floating substance, be put into a basin, and a circular motion be given to the water, all the light substances will be found crowding together near the center of the pool, where there is the least motion. Just such a basin is the Atlantic Ocean to the Gulf Stream, and the Sargasso Sea is the center of the whirl."

I share Maury's view, and I was able to study the phenomenon in this exclusive setting where ships rarely go. Above us, huddled among the brown weeds, there floated objects originating from all over: tree trunks ripped from the Rocky Mountains or the Andes and sent floating down the Amazon or the Mississippi, numerous pieces of wreckage, remnants of keels or undersides, bulwarks staved in and so weighed down with seashells and barnacles, they couldn't rise to the surface of the ocean. And the passing years will someday bear out Maury's other view that by collecting in this way over the centuries, these substances will be turned to stone by the action of the waters and will then form inexhaustible coalfields. Valuable reserves prepared by farseeing nature for that time when man will have exhausted his mines on the continents.

In the midst of this hopelessly tangled fabric of weeds and fucus plants, I noted some delightful pink–colored, star–shaped alcyon coral, sea anemone trailing the long tresses of their tentacles, some green, red, and blue jellyfish, and especially those big rhizostome jellyfish that Cuvier described, whose bluish parasols are trimmed with violet festoons.

We spent the whole day of February 22 in the Sargasso Sea, where fish that dote on marine plants and crustaceans find plenty to eat. The next day the ocean resumed its usual appearance.

From this moment on, for nineteen days from February 23 to March 12, the *Nautilus* stayed in the middle of the Atlantic, hustling us along at a constant speed of 100 leagues every twenty–four hours. It was obvious that Captain Nemo wanted to carry out his underwater program, and I had no doubt that he intended, after doubling Cape Horn, to return to the Pacific South Seas.

So Ned Land had good reason to worry. In these wide seas empty of islands, it was no longer feasible to jump ship. Nor did we have any way to counter Captain Nemo's whims. We had no choice but to acquiesce; but if we couldn't attain our end through force or cunning, I liked to think we might achieve it through persuasion. Once this voyage was over, might not Captain Nemo consent to set us free in return for our promise never to reveal his existence? Our word of honor, which we sincerely would have kept. However, this delicate question would have to be negotiated with the captain. But how would he receive our demands for freedom? At the very outset and in no uncertain terms, hadn't he declared that the secret of his life required that we be permanently imprisoned on board the *Nautilus*? Wouldn't he see my four–month silence as a tacit acceptance of this situation? Would my returning to this subject arouse suspicions that could jeopardize our escape plans, if we had promising circumstances for trying again later on? I weighed all these considerations, turned them over in my mind, submitted them to Conseil, but he was as baffled as I was. In short, although I'm not easily discouraged, I realized that my chances of ever seeing my fellow men again were shrinking by the day, especially at a time when Captain Nemo was recklessly racing toward the south Atlantic!

During those nineteen days just mentioned, no unique incidents distinguished our voyage. I saw little of the captain. He was at work. In the library I often found books he had left open, especially books on natural history. He had thumbed through my work on the great ocean depths, and the margins were covered with his notes, which sometimes contradicted my theories and formulations. But the captain remained content with this method of refining my work, and he rarely discussed it with me. Sometimes I heard melancholy sounds reverberating from the organ, which he played very expressively, but only at night in the midst of the most secretive darkness, while the *Nautilus* slumbered in the wilderness of the ocean.

During this part of our voyage, we navigated on the surface of the waves for entire days. The sea was nearly deserted. A few sailing ships, laden for the East Indies, were heading toward the Cape of Good Hope. One day we were chased by the longboats of a whaling vessel, which undoubtedly viewed us as some enormous baleen whale of great value. But Captain Nemo didn't want these gallant gentlemen wasting their time and energy, so he ended the hunt by diving beneath the waters.

This incident seemed to fascinate Ned Land intensely. I'm sure the Canadian was sorry that these fishermen couldn't harpoon our sheet–iron cetacean and mortally wound it.

During this period the fish Conseil and I observed differed little from those we had already studied in other latitudes. Chief among them were specimens of that dreadful cartilaginous genus that's divided into three subgenera numbering at least thirty–two species: striped sharks five meters long, the head squat and wider than the body, the caudal fin curved, the back with seven big, black, parallel lines running lengthwise; then perlon sharks, ash gray, pierced with seven gill openings, furnished with a single dorsal fin placed almost exactly in the middle of the body.

Some big dogfish also passed by, a voracious species of shark if there ever was one. With some justice, fishermen's yarns aren't to be trusted, but here's what a few of them relate. Inside the corpse of one of these animals there were found a buffalo head and a whole calf; in another, two tuna and a sailor in uniform; in yet another, a soldier with his saber; in another, finally, a horse with its rider. In candor, none of these sounds like divinely inspired truth. But the fact remains that not a single dogfish let itself get caught in the Nautilus's nets, so I can't vouch for their voracity.

Schools of elegant, playful dolphin swam alongside for entire days. They went in groups of five or six, hunting in packs like wolves over the countryside; moreover, they're just as voracious as dogfish, if I can believe a certain Copenhagen professor who says that from one dolphin's stomach, he removed thirteen porpoises and fifteen seals. True, it was a killer whale, belonging to the biggest known species, whose length sometimes exceeds twenty–four feet. The family Delphinia numbers ten genera, and the dolphins I saw were akin to the genus Delphinorhynchus, remarkable for an extremely narrow muzzle four times as long as the cranium. Measuring three meters, their bodies were black on top, underneath a pinkish white strewn with small, very scattered spots.

From these seas I'll also mention some unusual specimens of croakers, fish from the order Acanthopterygia, family Scienidea. Some authors—more artistic than scientific— claim that these fish are melodious singers, that their voices in unison put on concerts unmatched by human choristers. I don't say nay, but to my regret these croakers didn't serenade us as we passed.

Finally, to conclude, Conseil classified a large number of flying fish. Nothing could have made a more unusual sight than the marvelous timing with which dolphins hunt these fish. Whatever the range of its flight, however evasive its trajectory (even up and over the *Nautilus*), the hapless flying fish always found a dolphin to welcome it with open mouth. These were either flying gurnards or kitelike sea robins, whose lips glowed in the dark, at night scrawling fiery streaks in the air before plunging into the murky waters like so many shooting stars.

Our navigating continued under these conditions until March 13. That day the *Nautilus* was put to work in some depth–sounding experiments that fascinated me deeply.

By then we had fared nearly 13,000 leagues from our starting point in the Pacific high seas. Our position fix placed us in latitude 45° 37' south and longitude 37° 53' west. These were the same waterways where Captain Denham, aboard the *Herald,* payed out 14,000 meters of sounding line without finding bottom. It was here too that Lieutenant Parker, aboard the American frigate *Congress*, was unable to reach the underwater soil at 15,149 meters.

Captain Nemo decided to take his *Nautilus* down to the lowest depths in order to double–check these different soundings. I got ready to record the results of this experiment. The panels in the lounge opened, and maneuvers began for reaching those strata so prodigiously far removed.

It was apparently considered out of the question to dive by filling the ballast tanks. Perhaps they wouldn't sufficiently increase the *Nautilus's* specific gravity. Moreover, in order to come back up, it would be necessary to expel the excess water, and our pumps might not have been strong enough to overcome the outside pressure.

Captain Nemo decided to make for the ocean floor by submerging on an appropriately gradual diagonal with the help of his side fins, which were set at a 45° angle to the *Nautilus's* waterline. Then the propeller was brought to its maximum speed, and its four blades churned the waves with indescribable violence.

Under this powerful thrust the *Nautilus's* hull quivered like a resonating chord, and the ship sank steadily under the waters. Stationed in the lounge, the captain and I watched the needle swerving swiftly over the pressure gauge. Soon we had gone below the livable zone where most fish reside. Some of these animals can thrive only at the surface of seas or rivers, but a minority can dwell at fairly great depths. Among the latter I observed a species of dogfish called the cow shark that's equipped with six respiratory slits, the telescope fish with its enormous eyes, the armored gurnard with gray thoracic fins plus black pectoral fins and a breastplate protected by pale red slabs of bone, then finally the grenadier, living at a depth of 1,200 meters, by that point tolerating a pressure of 120 atmospheres.

I asked Captain Nemo if he had observed any fish at more considerable depths.

"Fish? Rarely!" he answered me. "But given the current state of marine science, who are we to presume, what do we really know of these depths?"

"Just this, Captain. In going toward the ocean's lower strata, we know that vegetable life disappears more quickly than animal life. We know that moving creatures can still be encountered where water plants no longer grow. We know that oysters and pilgrim scallops live in 2,000 meters of water, and that Admiral McClintock, England's hero of the polar seas, pulled in a live sea star from a depth of 2,500 meters. We know that the crew of the Royal Navy's *Bulldog* fished up a starfish from 2,620 fathoms, hence from a depth of more than one vertical league. Would you still say, Captain Nemo, that we really know nothing?"

"No, Professor," the captain replied, "I wouldn't be so discourteous. Yet I'll ask you to explain how these creatures can live at such depths?"

"I explain it on two grounds," I replied. "In the first place, because vertical currents, which are caused by differences in the water's salinity and density, can produce enough motion to sustain the rudimentary lifestyles of sea lilies and starfish."

"True," the captain put in.

"In the second place, because oxygen is the basis of life, and we know that the amount of oxygen dissolved in salt water increases rather than decreases with depth, that the pressure in these lower strata helps to concentrate their oxygen content."

"Oho! We know that, do we?" Captain Nemo replied in a tone of mild surprise. "Well, Professor, we have good reason to know it because it's the truth. I might add, in fact, that the air bladders of fish contain more nitrogen than oxygen when these animals are caught at the surface of the water, and conversely, more oxygen than nitrogen when they're pulled up from the lower depths. Which bears out your formulation. But let's continue our observations."

My eyes flew back to the pressure gauge. The instrument indicated a depth of 6,000 meters. Our submergence had been going on for an hour. The *Nautilus* slid downward on its slanting fins, still sinking. These deserted waters were wonderfully clear, with a transparency impossible to convey. An hour later we were at 13,000 meters—about three and a quarter vertical leagues—and the ocean floor was nowhere in sight.

However, at 14,000 meters I saw blackish peaks rising in the midst of the waters. But these summits could have belonged to mountains as high or even higher than the Himalayas or Mt. Blanc, and the extent of these depths remained incalculable.

Despite the powerful pressures it was undergoing, the *Nautilus* sank still deeper. I could feel its sheet-iron plates trembling down to their riveted joins; metal bars arched; bulkheads groaned; the lounge windows seemed to be warping inward under the water's pressure. And this whole sturdy mechanism would surely have given way, if, as its captain had said, it weren't capable of resisting like a solid block.

While grazing these rocky slopes lost under the waters, I still spotted some seashells, tube worms, lively annelid worms from the genus Spirorbis, and certain starfish specimens.

But soon these last representatives of animal life vanished, and three vertical leagues down, the *Nautilus* passed below the limits of underwater existence just as an air balloon rises above the breathable zones in the sky. We reached a depth of 16,000 meters—four vertical leagues—and by then the *Nautilus's* plating was tolerating a pressure of 1,600 atmospheres, in other words, 1,600 kilograms per each square centimeter on its surface!

"What an experience!" I exclaimed. "Traveling these deep regions where no man has ever ventured before! Look, captain! Look at these magnificent rocks, these uninhabited caves, these last global haunts where life is no longer possible! What unheard-of scenery, and why are we reduced to preserving it only as a memory?"

"Would you like," Captain Nemo asked me, "to bring back more than just a memory?"

"What do you mean?"

"I mean that nothing could be easier than taking a

photograph of this underwater region!"

Before I had time to express the surprise this new proposition caused me, a camera was carried into the lounge at Captain Nemo's request. The liquid setting, electrically lit, unfolded with perfect clarity through the wide–open panels. No shadows, no blurs, thanks to our artificial light. Not even sunshine could have been better for our purposes. With the thrust of its propeller curbed by the slant of its fins, the *Nautilus* stood still. The camera was aimed at the scenery on the ocean floor, and in a few seconds we had a perfect negative.

I attach a print of the positive. In it you can view these primordial rocks that have never seen the light of day, this nether granite that forms the powerful foundation of our globe, the deep caves cut into the stony mass, the outlines of incomparable distinctness whose far edges stand out in black as if from the brush of certain Flemish painters. In the distance is a mountainous horizon, a wondrously undulating line that makes up the background of this landscape. The general effect of these smooth rocks is indescribable: black, polished, without moss or other blemish, carved into strange shapes, sitting firmly on a carpet of sand that sparkled beneath our streams of electric light.

Meanwhile, his photographic operations over, Captain Nemo told me:

"Let's go back up, professor. We mustn't push our luck and expose the *Nautilus* too long to these pressures."

"Let's go back up!" I replied.

"Hold on tight."

Before I had time to realize why the captain made this recommendation, I was hurled to the carpet.

Its fins set vertically, its propeller thrown in gear at the captain's signal, the *Nautilus* rose with lightning speed, shooting upward like an air balloon into the sky. Vibrating resonantly, it knifed through the watery mass. Not a single detail was visible. In four minutes it had cleared the four vertical leagues separating it from the surface of the ocean, and after emerging like a flying fish, it fell back into the sea, making the waves leap to prodigious heights.

# CHAPTER 12

### Sperm Whales and Baleen Whales

DURING THE NIGHT of March 13–14, the *Nautilus* resumed its southward heading. Once it was abreast of Cape Horn, I thought it would strike west of the cape, make for Pacific seas, and complete its tour of the world. It did nothing of the sort and kept moving toward the southernmost regions. So where was it bound? The pole? That was insanity. I was beginning to think that the captain's recklessness more than justified Ned Land's worst fears.

For a good while the Canadian had said nothing more to me about his escape plans. He had become less sociable, almost sullen. I could see how heavily this protracted imprisonment was weighing on him. I could feel the anger building in him. Whenever he encountered the captain, his eyes would flicker with dark fire, and I was in constant dread that his natural vehemence would cause him to do something rash.

That day, March 14, he and Conseil managed to find me in my stateroom. I asked them the purpose of their visit.

"To put a simple question to you, sir," the Canadian answered me.

"Go on, Ned."

"How many men do you think are on board the *Nautilus*?"

"I'm unable to say, my friend."

"It seems to me," Ned Land went on, "that it wouldn't take much of a crew to run a ship like this one."

"Correct," I replied. "Under existing conditions some ten

men at the most should be enough to operate it."

"All right," the Canadian said, "then why should there be any more than that?"

"Why?" I answered.

I stared at Ned Land, whose motives were easy to guess.

"Because," I said, "if I can trust my hunches, if I truly understand the captain's way of life, his *Nautilus* isn't simply a ship. It's meant to be a refuge for people like its commander, people who have severed all ties with the shore."

"Perhaps," Conseil said, "but in a nutshell, the *Nautilus* can hold only a certain number of men, so couldn't Master estimate their maximum?"

"How, Conseil?"

"By calculating it. Master is familiar with the ship's capacity, hence the amount of air it contains; on the other hand, Master knows how much air each man consumes in the act of breathing, and he can compare this data with the fact that the *Nautilus* must rise to the surface every twenty–four hours . . ."

Conseil didn't finish his sentence, but I could easily see what he was driving at.

"I follow you," I said. "But while they're simple to do, such calculations can give only a very uncertain figure."

"No problem," the Canadian went on insistently.

"Then here's how to calculate it," I replied. "In one hour each man consumes the oxygen contained in 100 liters of air, hence during twenty–four hours the oxygen contained in 2,400 liters. Therefore, we must look for the multiple of 2,400 liters of air that gives us the amount found in the *Nautilus*."

"Precisely," Conseil said.

"Now then," I went on, "the *Nautilus*'s capacity is 1,500 metric tons, and that of a ton is 1,000 liters, so the *Nautilus* holds 1,500,000 liters of air, which, divided by 2,400 . . ."

I did a quick pencil calculation.

". . . gives us the quotient of 625. Which is tantamount to

saying that the air contained in the *Nautilus* would be exactly enough for 625 men over twenty-four hours."

"625!" Ned repeated.

"But rest assured," I added, "that between passengers, seamen, or officers, we don't total one-tenth of that figure."

"Which is still too many for three men!" Conseil muttered.

"So, my poor Ned, I can only counsel patience."

"And," Conseil replied, "even more than patience, resignation."

Conseil had said the true word.

"Even so," he went on, "Captain Nemo can't go south forever! He'll surely have to stop, if only at the Ice Bank, and he'll return to the seas of civilization! Then it will be time to resume Ned Land's plans."

The Canadian shook his head, passed his hand over his brow, made no reply, and left us.

"With Master's permission, I'll make an observation to him," Conseil then told me. "Our poor Ned broods about all the things he can't have. He's haunted by his former life. He seems to miss everything that's denied us. He's obsessed by his old memories and it's breaking his heart. We must understand him. What does he have to occupy him here? Nothing. He isn't a scientist like Master, and he doesn't share our enthusiasm for the sea's wonders. He would risk anything just to enter a tavern in his own country!"

To be sure, the monotony of life on board must have seemed unbearable to the Canadian, who was accustomed to freedom and activity. It was a rare event that could excite him. That day, however, a development occurred that reminded him of his happy years as a harpooner.

Near eleven o'clock in the morning, while on the surface of the ocean, the *Nautilus* fell in with a herd of baleen whales. This encounter didn't surprise me, because I knew these animals were being hunted so relentlessly that they took refuge in the ocean basins of the high latitudes.

In the maritime world and in the realm of geographic exploration, whales have played a major role. This is the animal that first dragged the Basques in its wake, then Asturian Spaniards, Englishmen, and Dutchmen, emboldening them against the ocean's perils, and leading them to the ends of the earth. Baleen whales like to frequent the southernmost and northernmost seas. Old legends even claim that these cetaceans led fishermen to within a mere seven leagues of the North Pole. Although this feat is fictitious, it will someday come true, because it's likely that by hunting whales in the Arctic or Antarctic regions, man will finally reach this unknown spot on the globe.

We were seated on the platform next to a tranquil sea. The month of March, since it's the equivalent of October in these latitudes, was giving us some fine autumn days. It was the Canadian—on this topic he was never mistaken—who sighted a baleen whale on the eastern horizon. If you looked carefully, you could see its blackish back alternately rise and fall above the waves, five miles from the *Nautilus*.

"Wow!" Ned Land exclaimed. "If I were on board a whaler, there's an encounter that would be great fun! That's one big animal! Look how high its blowholes are spouting all that air and steam! Damnation! Why am I chained to this hunk of sheet iron!"

"Why, Ned!" I replied. "You still aren't over your old fishing urges?"

"How could a whale fisherman forget his old trade, sir? Who could ever get tired of such exciting hunting?"

"You've never fished these seas, Ned?"

"Never, sir. Just the northernmost seas, equally in the Bering Strait and the Davis Strait."

"So the southern right whale is still unknown to you. Until now it's the bowhead whale you've hunted, and it won't risk going past the warm waters of the equator."

"Oh, professor, what are you feeding me?" the Canadian answered in a tolerably skeptical tone.

"I'm feeding you the facts."

"By thunder! In '65, just two and a half years ago, I to whom you speak, I myself stepped onto the carcass of a whale near Greenland, and its flank still carried the marked harpoon of a whaling ship from the Bering Sea. Now I ask you, after it had been wounded west of America, how could this animal be killed in the east, unless it had cleared the equator and doubled Cape Horn or the Cape of Good Hope?"

"I agree with our friend Ned," Conseil said, "and I'm waiting to hear how Master will reply to him."

"Master will reply, my friends, that baleen whales are localized, according to species, within certain seas that they never leave. And if one of these animals went from the Bering Strait to the Davis Strait, it's quite simply because there's some passageway from the one sea to the other, either along the coasts of Canada or Siberia."

"You expect us to fall for that?" the Canadian asked, tipping me a wink.

"If Master says so," Conseil replied.

"Which means," the Canadian went on, "since I've never fished these waterways, I don't know the whales that frequent them?"

"That's what I've been telling you, Ned."

"All the more reason to get to know them," Conseil answered.

"Look! Look!" the Canadian exclaimed, his voice full of excitement. "It's approaching! It's coming toward us! It's thumbing its nose at me! It knows I can't do a blessed thing to it!"

Ned stamped his foot. Brandishing an imaginary harpoon, his hands positively trembled.

"These cetaceans," he asked, "are they as big as the ones in the northernmost seas?"

"Pretty nearly, Ned."

"Because I've seen big baleen whales, sir, whales measuring up to 100 feet long! I've even heard that those rorqual whales off the Aleutian Islands sometimes get over 150 feet."

"That strikes me as exaggerated," I replied. "Those animals are only members of the genus Balaenoptera furnished with dorsal fins, and like sperm whales, they're generally smaller than the bowhead whale."

"Oh!" exclaimed the Canadian, whose eyes hadn't left the ocean. "It's getting closer, it's coming into the *Nautilus's* waters!"

Then, going on with his conversation:

"You talk about sperm whales," he said, "as if they were little beasts! But there are stories of gigantic sperm whales. They're shrewd cetaceans. I hear that some will cover themselves with algae and fucus plants. People mistake them for islets. They pitch camp on top, make themselves at home, light a fire—"

"Build houses," Conseil said.

"Yes, funny man," Ned Land replied. "Then one fine day the animal dives and drags all its occupants down into the depths."

"Like in the voyages of Sinbad the Sailor," I answered, laughing. "Oh, Mr. Land, you're addicted to tall tales! What sperm whales you're handing us! I hope you don't really believe in them!"

"Mr. Naturalist," the Canadian replied in all seriousness, "when it comes to whales, you can believe anything! (Look at that one move! Look at it stealing away!) People claim these animals can circle around the world in just fifteen days."

"I don't say nay."

"But what you undoubtedly don't know, Professor Aronnax, is that at the beginning of the world, whales traveled even quicker."

"Oh really, Ned! And why so?"

"Because in those days their tails moved side to side, like those on fish, in other words, their tails were straight up, thrashing the water from left to right, right to left. But spotting that they swam too fast, our Creator twisted their tails, and ever since they've been thrashing the waves up and down, at the expense of their speed."

"Fine, Ned," I said, then resurrected one of the Canadian's expressions. "You expect us to fall for that?"

"Not too terribly," Ned Land replied, "and no more than if I told you there are whales that are 300 feet long and weigh 1,000,000 pounds."

"That's indeed considerable," I said. "But you must admit that certain cetaceans do grow to significant size, since they're said to supply as much as 120 metric tons of oil."

"That I've seen," the Canadian said.

"I can easily believe it, Ned, just as I can believe that certain baleen whales equal 100 elephants in bulk. Imagine the impact of such a mass if it were launched at full speed!"

"Is it true," Conseil asked, "that they can sink ships?"

"Ships? I doubt it," I replied. "However, they say that in 1820, right in these southern seas, a baleen whale rushed at the Essex and pushed it backward at a speed of four meters per second. Its stern was flooded, and the Essex went down fast."

Ned looked at me with a bantering expression.

"Speaking for myself," he said, "I once got walloped by a whale's tail—in my longboat, needless to say. My companions and I were launched to an altitude of six meters. But next to the Professor's whale, mine was just a baby."

"Do these animals live a long time?" Conseil asked.

"A thousand years," the Canadian replied without hesitation.

"And how, Ned," I asked, "do you know that's so?"

"Because people say so."

"And why do people say so?"

"Because people know so."

"No, Ned! People don't know so, they suppose so, and here's the logic with which they back up their beliefs. When fishermen first hunted whales 400 years ago, these animals grew to bigger sizes than they do today. Reasonably enough, it's assumed that today's whales are smaller because they haven't had time to reach their full growth. That's why the Count de Buffon's encyclopedia says that cetaceans can live, and even must live, for a thousand years. You understand?"

Ned Land didn't understand. He no longer even heard me. That baleen whale kept coming closer. His eyes devoured it.

"Oh!" he exclaimed. "It's not just one whale, it's ten, twenty, a whole gam! And I can't do a thing! I'm tied hand and foot!"

"But Ned my friend," Conseil said, "why not ask Captain Nemo for permission to hunt—"

Before Conseil could finish his sentence, Ned Land scooted down the hatch and ran to look for the captain. A few moments later, the two of them reappeared on the platform.

Captain Nemo observed the herd of cetaceans cavorting on the waters a mile from the *Nautilus*.

"They're southern right whales," he said. "There goes the fortune of a whole whaling fleet."

"Well, sir," the Canadian asked, "couldn't I hunt them, just so I don't forget my old harpooning trade?"

"Hunt them? What for?" Captain Nemo replied. "Simply to destroy them? We have no use for whale oil on this ship."

"But, sir," the Canadian went on, "in the Red Sea you authorized us to chase a dugong!"

"There it was an issue of obtaining fresh meat for my crew. Here it would be killing for the sake of killing. I'm well aware that's a privilege reserved for mankind, but I don't allow such murderous pastimes. When your peers, Mr. Land, destroy decent, harmless creatures like the southern right whale or the bowhead whale, they commit a reprehensible offense.

Thus they've already depopulated all of Baffin Bay, and they'll wipe out a whole class of useful animals. So leave these poor cetaceans alone. They have quite enough natural enemies, such as sperm whales, swordfish, and sawfish, without you meddling with them."

I'll let the reader decide what faces the Canadian made during this lecture on hunting ethics. Furnishing such arguments to a professional harpooner was a waste of words. Ned Land stared at Captain Nemo and obviously missed his meaning. But the captain was right. Thanks to the mindless, barbaric bloodthirstiness of fishermen, the last baleen whale will someday disappear from the ocean.

Ned Land whistled "Yankee Doodle" between his teeth, stuffed his hands in his pockets, and turned his back on us.

Meanwhile Captain Nemo studied the herd of cetaceans, then addressed me:

"I was right to claim that baleen whales have enough natural enemies without counting man. These specimens will soon have to deal with mighty opponents. Eight miles to leeward, Professor Aronnax, can you see those blackish specks moving about?"

"Yes, Captain," I replied.

"Those are sperm whales, dreadful animals that I've sometimes encountered in herds of 200 or 300! As for them, they're cruel, destructive beasts, and they deserve to be exterminated."

The Canadian turned swiftly at these last words.

"Well, Captain," I said, "on behalf of the baleen whales, there's still time—"

"It's pointless to run any risks, professor. The Nautilus will suffice to disperse these sperm whales. It's armed with a steel spur quite equal to Mr. Land's harpoon, I imagine."

The Canadian didn't even bother shrugging his shoulders. Attacking cetaceans with thrusts from a spur! Who ever heard of such malarkey!

"Wait and see, Professor Aronnax," Captain Nemo said. "We'll show you a style of hunting with which you aren't yet familiar. We'll take no pity on these ferocious cetaceans. They're merely mouth and teeth!"

Mouth and teeth! There's no better way to describe the long–skulled sperm whale, whose length sometimes exceeds twenty–five meters. The enormous head of this cetacean occupies about a third of its body. Better armed than a baleen whale, whose upper jaw is adorned solely with whalebone, the sperm whale is equipped with twenty–five huge teeth that are twenty centimeters high, have cylindrical, conical summits, and weigh two pounds each. In the top part of this enormous head, inside big cavities separated by cartilage, you'll find 300 to 400 kilograms of that valuable oil called "spermaceti." The sperm whale is an awkward animal, more tadpole than fish, as Professor Frédol has noted. It's poorly constructed, being "defective," so to speak, over the whole left side of its frame, with good eyesight only in its right eye.

Meanwhile that monstrous herd kept coming closer. It had seen the baleen whales and was preparing to attack. You could tell in advance that the sperm whales would be victorious, not only because they were better built for fighting than their harmless adversaries, but also because they could stay longer underwater before returning to breathe at the surface.

There was just time to run to the rescue of the baleen whales. The *Nautilus* proceeded to midwater. Conseil, Ned, and I sat in front of the lounge windows. Captain Nemo made his way to the helmsman's side to operate his submersible as an engine of destruction. Soon I felt the beats of our propeller getting faster, and we picked up speed.

The battle between sperm whales and baleen whales had already begun when the *Nautilus* arrived. It maneuvered to cut into the herd of long–skulled predators. At first the latter showed little concern at the sight of this new monster meddling in the battle. But they soon had to sidestep its thrusts.

What a struggle! Ned Land quickly grew enthusiastic and even ended up applauding. Brandished in its captain's hands, the *Nautilus* was simply a fearsome harpoon. He hurled it at those fleshy masses and ran them clean through, leaving behind two squirming animal halves. As for those daunting strokes of the tail hitting our sides, the ship never felt them. No more than the collisions it caused. One sperm whale exterminated, it ran at another, tacked on the spot so as not to miss its prey, went ahead or astern, obeyed its rudder, dived when the cetacean sank to deeper strata, rose with it when it returned to the surface, struck it head–on or slantwise, hacked at it or tore it, and from every direction and at any speed, skewered it with its dreadful spur.

What bloodshed! What a hubbub on the surface of the waves! What sharp hisses and snorts unique to these frightened animals! Their tails churned the normally peaceful strata into actual billows.

This Homeric slaughter dragged on for an hour, and the long–skulled predators couldn't get away. Several times ten or twelve of them teamed up, trying to crush the *Nautilus* with their sheer mass. Through the windows you could see their enormous mouths paved with teeth, their fearsome eyes. Losing all self–control, Ned Land hurled threats and insults at them. You could feel them clinging to the submersible like hounds atop a wild boar in the underbrush. But by forcing the pace of its propeller, the *Nautilus* carried them off, dragged them under, or brought them back to the upper level of the waters, untroubled by their enormous weight or their powerful grip.

Finally this mass of sperm whales thinned out. The waves grew tranquil again. I felt us rising to the surface of the ocean. The hatch opened and we rushed onto the platform.

The sea was covered with mutilated corpses. A fearsome explosion couldn't have slashed, torn, or shredded these fleshy masses with greater violence. We were floating in the midst of gigantic bodies, bluish on the back, whitish on the belly, and all deformed by enormous protuberances. A few frightened sperm whales were fleeing toward the horizon. The waves were dyed red over an area of several miles, and the *Nautilus* was floating in the middle of a sea of blood.

Captain Nemo rejoined us.

"Well, Mr. Land?" he said.

"Well, sir," replied the Canadian, whose enthusiasm had subsided, "it's a dreadful sight for sure. But I'm a hunter not a butcher, and this is plain butchery."

"It was a slaughter of destructive animals," the captain replied, "and the *Nautilus* is no butcher knife."

"I prefer my harpoon," the Canadian answered.

"To each his own," the captain replied, staring intently at Ned Land.

I was in dread the latter would give way to some violent outburst that might have had deplorable consequences. But his anger was diverted by the sight of a baleen whale that the *Nautilus* had pulled alongside of just then.

This animal had been unable to escape the teeth of those sperm whales. I recognized the southern right whale, its head squat, its body dark all over. Anatomically, it's distinguished from the white whale and the black right whale by the fusion of its seven cervical vertebrae, and it numbers two more ribs than its relatives. Floating on its side, its belly riddled with bites, the poor cetacean was dead. Still hanging from the tip of its mutilated fin was a little baby whale that it had been unable to rescue from the slaughter. Its open mouth let water flow through its whalebone like a murmuring surf.

Captain Nemo guided the *Nautilus* next to the animal's corpse. Two of his men climbed onto the whale's flank, and to my astonishment, I saw them draw from its udders all the milk they held, in other words, enough to fill two or three casks.

The captain offered me a cup of this still–warm milk. I couldn't help showing my distaste for such a beverage. He assured me that this milk was excellent, no different from cow's milk.

I sampled it and agreed. So this milk was a worthwhile reserve ration for us, because in the form of salt butter or cheese, it would provide a pleasant change of pace from our standard fare.

From that day on, I noted with some uneasiness that Ned Land's attitudes toward Captain Nemo grew worse and worse, and I decided to keep a close watch on the Canadian's movements and activities.

# CHAPTER 13

## The Ice Bank

THE *Nautilus* resumed its unruffled southbound heading. It went along the 50th meridian with considerable speed. Would it go to the pole? I didn't think so, because every previous attempt to reach this spot on the globe had failed. Besides, the season was already quite advanced, since March 13 on Antarctic shores corresponds with September 13 in the northernmost regions, which marks the beginning of the equinoctial period.

On March 14 at latitude 55°, I spotted floating ice, plain pale bits of rubble twenty to twenty-five feet long, which formed reefs over which the sea burst into foam. The *Nautilus* stayed on the surface of the ocean. Having fished in the Arctic seas, Ned Land was already familiar with the sight of icebergs. Conseil and I were marveling at them for the first time.

In the sky toward the southern horizon, there stretched a dazzling white band. English whalers have given this the name "ice blink." No matter how heavy the clouds may be, they can't obscure this phenomenon. It announces the presence of a pack, or shoal, of ice.

Indeed, larger blocks of ice soon appeared, their brilliance varying at the whim of the mists. Some of these masses displayed green veins, as if scrawled with undulating lines of copper sulfate. Others looked like enormous amethysts, letting the light penetrate their insides. The latter reflected the sun's rays from the thousand facets of their crystals. The former, tinted with a bright limestone sheen, would have supplied enough building material to make a whole marble town.

The farther down south we went, the more these floating islands grew in numbers and prominence. Polar birds nested on them by the thousands. These were petrels, cape pigeons, or puffins, and their calls were deafening. Mistaking the *Nautilus* for the corpse of a whale, some of them alighted on it and prodded its resonant sheet iron with pecks of their beaks.

During this navigating in the midst of the ice, Captain Nemo often stayed on the platform. He observed these deserted waterways carefully. I saw his calm eyes sometimes perk up. In these polar seas forbidden to man, did he feel right at home, the lord of these unreachable regions? Perhaps. But he didn't say. He stood still, reviving only when his pilot's instincts took over. Then, steering his *Nautilus* with consummate dexterity, he skillfully dodged the masses of ice, some of which measured several miles in length, their heights varying from seventy to eighty meters. Often the horizon seemed completely closed off. Abreast of latitude 60°, every passageway had disappeared. Searching with care, Captain Nemo soon found a narrow opening into which he brazenly slipped, well aware, however, that it would close behind him.

Guided by his skillful hands, the *Nautilus* passed by all these different masses of ice, which are classified by size and shape with a precision that enraptured Conseil: "icebergs," or mountains; "ice fields," or smooth, limitless tracts; "drift ice," or floating floes; "packs," or broken tracts, called "patches" when they're circular and "streams" when they form long strips.

The temperature was fairly low. Exposed to the outside air, the thermometer marked −2° to −3° centigrade. But we were warmly dressed in furs, for which seals and aquatic bears had paid the price. Evenly heated by all its electric equipment, the *Nautilus's* interior defied the most intense cold. Moreover, to find a bearable temperature, the ship had only to sink just a few meters beneath the waves.

Two months earlier we would have enjoyed perpetual daylight in this latitude; but night already fell for three or four hours, and later it would cast six months of shadow over these circumpolar regions.

On March 15 we passed beyond the latitude of the South Shetland and South Orkney Islands. The captain told me that many tribes of seals used to inhabit these shores; but English and American whalers, in a frenzy of destruction, slaughtered all the adults, including pregnant females, and where life and activity once existed, those fishermen left behind only silence and death.

Going along the 55th meridian, the *Nautilus* cut the Antarctic Circle on March 16 near eight o'clock in the morning. Ice completely surrounded us and closed off the horizon. Nevertheless, Captain Nemo went from passageway to passageway, always proceeding south.

"But where's he going?" I asked.

"Straight ahead," Conseil replied. "Ultimately, when he can't go any farther, he'll stop."

"I wouldn't bet on it!" I replied.

And in all honesty, I confess that this venturesome excursion was far from displeasing to me. I can't express the intensity of my amazement at the beauties of these new regions. The ice struck superb poses. Here, its general effect suggested an oriental town with countless minarets and mosques. There, a city in ruins, flung to the ground by convulsions in the earth. These views were varied continuously by the sun's oblique rays, or were completely swallowed up by gray mists in the middle of blizzards. Then explosions, cave-ins, and great iceberg somersaults would occur all around us, altering the scenery like the changing landscape in a diorama.

If the *Nautilus* was submerged during these losses of balance, we heard the resulting noises spread under the waters with frightful intensity, and the collapse of these masses created daunting eddies down to the ocean's lower strata. The *Nautilus* then rolled and pitched like a ship left to the fury of the elements.

Often, no longer seeing any way out, I thought we were imprisoned for good, but Captain Nemo, guided by his instincts, discovered new passageways from the tiniest indications. He was never wrong when he observed slender threads of bluish water streaking through these ice fields. Accordingly, I was sure that he had already risked his *Nautilus* in the midst of the Antarctic seas.

However, during the day of March 16, these tracts of ice completely barred our path. It wasn't the Ice Bank as yet, just huge ice fields cemented together by the cold. This obstacle couldn't stop Captain Nemo, and he launched his ship against the ice fields with hideous violence. The *Nautilus* went into these brittle masses like a wedge, splitting them with dreadful cracklings. It was an old–fashioned battering ram propelled with infinite power. Hurled aloft, ice rubble fell back around us like hail. Through brute force alone, the submersible carved out a channel for itself. Carried away by its momentum, the ship sometimes mounted on top of these tracts of ice and crushed them with its weight, or at other times, when cooped up beneath the ice fields, it split them with simple pitching movements, creating wide punctures.

Violent squalls assaulted us during the daytime. Thanks to certain heavy mists, we couldn't see from one end of the platform to the other. The wind shifted abruptly to every point on the compass. The snow was piling up in such packed layers, it had to be chipped loose with blows from picks. Even in a temperature of merely –5° centigrade, every outside part of the *Nautilus* was covered with ice. A ship's rigging would have been unusable, because all its tackle would have jammed in the grooves of the pulleys. Only a craft without sails, driven by an electric motor that needed no coal, could face such high latitudes.

Under these conditions the barometer generally stayed quite low. It fell as far as 73.5 centimeters. Our compass indications no longer offered any guarantees. The deranged needles would mark contradictory directions as we approached the southern magnetic pole, which doesn't coincide with the South Pole proper. In fact, according to the astronomer Hansteen, this magnetic pole is located fairly close to latitude 70° and longitude 130°, or abiding by the observations of Louis–Isidore Duperrey, in longitude 135° and latitude 70° 30'. Hence we had to transport compasses to different parts of the ship, take many readings, and strike an average. Often we could chart our course only by guesswork, a less than satisfactory method in the midst of these winding passageways whose landmarks change continuously.

At last on March 18, after twenty futile assaults, the *Nautilus* was decisively held in check. No longer was it an ice stream, patch, or field—it was an endless, immovable barrier formed by ice mountains fused to each other.

"The Ice Bank!" the Canadian told me.

For Ned Land, as well as for every navigator before us, I knew that this was the great insurmountable obstacle. When the sun appeared for an instant near noon, Captain Nemo took a reasonably accurate sight that gave our position as longitude 51° 30' and latitude 67° 39' south. This was a position already well along in these Antarctic regions.

As for the liquid surface of the sea, there was no longer any semblance of it before our eyes. Before the *Nautilus's* spur there lay vast broken plains, a tangle of confused chunks with all the helter–skelter unpredictability typical of a river's surface a short while before its ice breakup; but in this case the proportions were gigantic. Here and there stood sharp peaks, lean spires that rose as high as 200 feet; farther off, a succession of steeply cut cliffs sporting a grayish tint, huge mirrors that reflected the sparse rays of a sun half drowned in mist. Beyond, a stark silence reigned in this desolate natural setting, a silence barely broken by the flapping wings of petrels or puffins. By this point everything was frozen, even sound.

So the *Nautilus* had to halt in its venturesome course among these tracts of ice.

"Sir," Ned Land told me that day, "if your captain goes any farther . . ."

"Yes?"

"He'll be a superman."

"How so, Ned?"

"Because nobody can clear the Ice Bank. Your captain's a powerful man, but damnation, he isn't more powerful than nature. If she draws a boundary line, there you stop, like it or not!"

"Correct, Ned Land, but I still want to know what's behind this Ice Bank! Behold my greatest source of irritation—a wall!"

"Master is right," Conseil said. "Walls were invented simply to frustrate scientists. All walls should be banned."

"Fine!" the Canadian put in. "But we already know what's behind this Ice Bank."

"What?" I asked.

"Ice, ice, and more ice."

"You may be sure of that, Ned," I answered, "but I'm not. That's why I want to see for myself."

"Well, Professor," the Canadian replied, "you can just drop that idea! You've made it to the Ice Bank, which is already far enough, but you won't get any farther, neither your Captain Nemo or his *Nautilus*. And whether he wants to or not, we'll head north again, in other words, to the land of sensible people."

I had to agree that Ned Land was right, and until ships are built to navigate over tracts of ice, they'll have to stop at the Ice Bank.

Indeed, despite its efforts, despite the powerful methods it used to split this ice, the *Nautilus* was reduced to immobility. Ordinarily, when someone can't go any farther, he still has the option of returning in his tracks. But here it was just as impossible to turn back as to go forward, because every passageway had closed behind us, and if our submersible remained even slightly stationary, it would be frozen in without delay. Which is exactly what happened near two o'clock in the afternoon, and fresh ice kept forming over the ship's sides with astonishing speed. I had to admit that Captain Nemo's leadership had been most injudicious.

Just then I was on the platform. Observing the situation for some while, the captain said to me:

"Well, Professor! What think you?"

"I think we're trapped, Captain."

"Trapped! What do you mean?"

"I mean we can't go forward, backward, or sideways. I think that's the standard definition of 'trapped,' at least in the civilized world."

"So, Professor Aronnax, you think the *Nautilus* won't be able to float clear?"

"Only with the greatest difficulty, Captain, since the season is already too advanced for you to depend on an ice breakup."

"Oh, Professor," Captain Nemo replied in an ironic tone, "you never change! You see only impediments and obstacles! I promise you, not only will the *Nautilus* float clear, it will go farther still!"

"Farther south?" I asked, gaping at the captain.

"Yes, sir, it will go to the pole."

"To the pole!" I exclaimed, unable to keep back a movement of disbelief.

"Yes," the captain replied coolly, "the Antarctic pole, that unknown spot crossed by every meridian on the globe. As you know, I do whatever I like with my *Nautilus*."

Yes, I did know that! I knew this man was daring to the point of being foolhardy. But to overcome all the obstacles around the South Pole—even more unattainable than the North Pole, which still hadn't been reached by the boldest navigators—wasn't this an absolutely insane undertaking, one that could occur only in the brain of a madman?

It then dawned on me to ask Captain Nemo if he had already discovered this pole, which no human being had ever trod underfoot.

"No, sir," he answered me, "but we'll discover it together. Where others have failed, I'll succeed. Never before has my *Nautilus* cruised so far into these southernmost seas, but I repeat: it will go farther still."

"I'd like to believe you, Captain," I went on in a tone of some sarcasm. "Oh I do believe you! Let's forge ahead! There are no obstacles for us! Let's shatter this Ice Bank! Let's blow it up, and if it still resists, let's put wings on the *Nautilus* and fly over it!"

"Over it, Professor?" Captain Nemo replied serenely. "No, not over it, but under it."

"Under it!" I exclaimed.

A sudden insight into Captain Nemo's plans had just flashed through my mind. I understood. The marvelous talents of his *Nautilus* would be put to work once again in this superhuman undertaking!

"I can see we're starting to understand each other, Professor," Captain Nemo told me with a half smile. "You already glimpse the potential—myself, I'd say the success—of this attempt. Maneuvers that aren't feasible for an ordinary ship are easy for the *Nautilus*. If a continent emerges at the pole, we'll stop at that continent. But on the other hand, if open sea washes the pole, we'll go to that very place!"

"Right," I said, carried away by the captain's logic. "Even though the surface of the sea has solidified into ice, its lower strata are still open, thanks to that divine justice that puts the maximum density of salt water one degree above its freezing point. And if I'm not mistaken, the submerged part of this Ice Bank is in a four–to–one ratio to its emerging part."

"Very nearly, Professor. For each foot of iceberg above the sea, there are three more below. Now then, since these ice mountains don't exceed a height of 100 meters, they sink only to a depth of 300 meters. And what are 300 meters to the Nautilus?"

"A mere nothing, sir."

"We could even go to greater depths and find that temperature layer common to all ocean water, and there we'd brave with impunity the –30° or –40° cold on the surface."

"True, sir, very true," I replied with growing excitement.

"Our sole difficulty," Captain Nemo went on, "lies in our staying submerged for several days without renewing our air supply."

"That's all?" I answered. "The Nautilus has huge air tanks; we'll fill them up and they'll supply all the oxygen we need."

"Good thinking, Professor Aronnax," the captain replied with a smile. "But since I don't want to be accused of foolhardiness, I'm giving you all my objections in advance."

"You have more?"

"Just one. If a sea exists at the South Pole, it's possible this sea may be completely frozen over, so we couldn't come up to the surface!"

"My dear sir, have you forgotten that the Nautilus is armed with a fearsome spur? Couldn't it be launched diagonally against those tracts of ice, which would break open from the impact?"

"Ah, Professor, you're full of ideas today!"

"Besides, Captain," I added with still greater enthusiasm, "why wouldn't we find open sea at the South Pole just as at the North Pole? The cold–temperature poles and the geographical poles don't coincide in either the northern or southern hemispheres, and until proof to the contrary, we can assume these two spots on the earth feature either a continent or an ice-free ocean."

"I think as you do, Professor Aronnax," Captain Nemo replied. "I'll only point out that after raising so many objections against my plan, you're now crushing me under arguments in its favor."

Captain Nemo was right. I was outdoing him in daring! It was I who was sweeping him to the pole. I was leading the way, I was out in front . . . but no, you silly fool! Captain Nemo already knew the pros and cons of this question, and it amused him to see you flying off into impossible fantasies!

Nevertheless, he didn't waste an instant. At his signal, the chief officer appeared. The two men held a quick exchange in their incomprehensible language, and either the chief officer had been alerted previously or he found the plan feasible, because he showed no surprise.

But as unemotional as he was, he couldn't have been more impeccably emotionless than Conseil when I told the fine lad our intention of pushing on to the South Pole. He greeted my announcement with the usual "As Master wishes," and I had to be content with that. As for Ned Land, no human shoulders ever executed a higher shrug than the pair belonging to our Canadian.

"Honestly, sir," he told me. "You and your Captain Nemo, I pity you both!"

"But we will go to the pole, Mr. Land."

"Maybe, but you won't come back!"

And Ned Land re-entered his cabin, "to keep from doing something desperate," he said as he left me.

Meanwhile preparations for this daring attempt were getting under way. The *Nautilus's* powerful pumps forced air down into the tanks and stored it under high pressure. Near four o'clock Captain Nemo informed me that the platform hatches were about to be closed. I took a last look at the dense Ice Bank we were going to conquer. The weather was fair, the skies reasonably clear, the cold quite brisk, namely –12° centigrade; but after the wind had lulled, this temperature didn't seem too unbearable.

Equipped with picks, some ten men climbed onto the *Nautilus's* sides and cracked loose the ice around the ship's lower plating, which was soon set free. This operation was swiftly executed because the fresh ice was still thin. We all re-entered the interior. The main ballast tanks were filled with the water that hadn't yet congealed at our line of flotation. The *Nautilus* submerged without delay.

I took a seat in the lounge with Conseil. Through the open window we stared at the lower strata of this southernmost ocean. The thermometer rose again. The needle on the pressure gauge swerved over its dial.

About 300 meters down, just as Captain Nemo had predicted, we cruised beneath the undulating surface of the Ice Bank. But the *Nautilus* sank deeper still. It reached a depth of 800 meters. At the surface this water gave a temperature of –12° centigrade, but now it gave no more than –10°. Two degrees had already been gained. Thanks to its heating equipment, the *Nautilus's* temperature, needless to say, stayed at a much higher degree. Every maneuver was accomplished with extraordinary precision.

"With all due respect to Master," Conseil told me, "we'll pass it by."

"I fully expect to!" I replied in a tone of deep conviction.

Now in open water, the *Nautilus* took a direct course to the pole without veering from the 52nd meridian. From 67° 30' to 90°, twenty-two and a half ° of latitude were left to cross, in other words, slightly more than 500 leagues. The *Nautilus* adopted an average speed of twenty-six miles per hour, the speed of an express train. If it kept up this pace, forty hours would do it for reaching the pole.

For part of the night, the novelty of our circumstances kept Conseil and me at the lounge window. The sea was lit by our beacon's electric rays. But the depths were deserted. Fish didn't linger in these imprisoned waters. Here they found merely a passageway for going from the Antarctic Ocean to open sea at the pole. Our progress was swift. You could feel it in the vibrations of the long steel hull.

Near two o'clock in the morning, I went to snatch a few hours of sleep. Conseil did likewise. I didn't encounter Captain Nemo while going down the gangways. I assumed that he was keeping to the pilothouse.

The next day, March 19, at five o'clock in the morning, I was back at my post in the lounge. The electric log indicated that the *Nautilus* had reduced speed. By then it was rising to the surface, but cautiously, while slowly emptying its ballast tanks.

My heart was pounding. Would we emerge into the open and find the polar air again?

No. A jolt told me that the *Nautilus* had bumped the underbelly of the Ice Bank, still quite thick to judge from the hollowness of the accompanying noise. Indeed, we had "struck bottom," to use nautical terminology, but in the opposite direction and at a depth of 3,000 feet. That gave us 4,000 feet of ice overhead, of which 1,000 feet emerged above water. So the Ice Bank was higher here than we had found it on the outskirts. A circumstance less than encouraging.

Several times that day, the *Nautilus* repeated the same experiment and always it bumped against this surface that formed a ceiling above it. At certain moments the ship encountered ice at a depth of 900 meters, denoting a thickness of 1,200 meters, of which 300 meters rose above the level of the ocean. This height had tripled since the moment the *Nautilus* had dived beneath the waves.

I meticulously noted these different depths, obtaining the

underwater profile of this upside–down mountain chain that stretched beneath the sea.

By evening there was still no improvement in our situation. The ice stayed between 400 and 500 meters deep. It was obviously shrinking, but what a barrier still lay between us and the surface of the ocean!

By then it was eight o'clock. The air inside the *Nautilus* should have been renewed four hours earlier, following daily practice on board. But I didn't suffer very much, although Captain Nemo hadn't yet made demands on the supplementary oxygen in his air tanks.

That night my sleep was fitful. Hope and fear besieged me by turns. I got up several times. The *Nautilus* continued groping. Near three o'clock in the morning, I observed that we encountered the Ice Bank's underbelly at a depth of only fifty meters. So only 150 feet separated us from the surface of the water. Little by little the Ice Bank was turning into an ice field again. The mountains were changing back into plains.

My eyes didn't leave the pressure gauge. We kept rising on a diagonal, going along this shiny surface that sparkled beneath our electric rays. Above and below, the Ice Bank was subsiding in long gradients. Mile after mile it was growing thinner.

Finally, at six o'clock in the morning on that memorable day of March 19, the lounge door opened. Captain Nemo appeared.

"Open sea!" he told me.

# CHAPTER 14

### The South Pole

I RUSHED UP onto the platform. Yes, open sea! Barely a few sparse floes, some moving icebergs; a sea stretching into the distance; hosts of birds in the air and myriads of fish under the waters, which varied from intense blue to olive green depending on the depth. The thermometer marked 3° centigrade. It was as if a comparative springtime had been locked up behind that Ice Bank, whose distant masses were outlined on the northern horizon.

"Are we at the pole?" I asked the captain, my heart pounding.

"I've no idea," he answered me. "At noon we'll fix our position."

"But will the sun show through this mist?" I said, staring at the grayish sky.

"No matter how faintly it shines, it will be enough for me," the captain replied.

To the south, ten miles from the *Nautilus*, a solitary islet rose to a height of 200 meters. We proceeded toward it, but cautiously, because this sea could have been strewn with reefs.

In an hour we had reached the islet. Two hours later we had completed a full circle around it. It measured four to five miles in circumference. A narrow channel separated it from a considerable shore, perhaps a continent whose limits we couldn't see. The existence of this shore seemed to bear out Commander Maury's hypotheses. In essence, this ingenious

American has noted that between the South Pole and the 60th parallel, the sea is covered with floating ice of dimensions much greater than any found in the north Atlantic. From this fact he drew the conclusion that the Antarctic Circle must contain considerable shores, since icebergs can't form on the high seas but only along coastlines. According to his calculations, this frozen mass enclosing the southernmost pole forms a vast ice cap whose width must reach 4,000 kilometers.

Meanwhile, to avoid running aground, the *Nautilus* halted three cable lengths from a strand crowned by superb piles of rocks. The skiff was launched to sea. Two crewmen carrying instruments, the captain, Conseil, and I were on board. It was ten o'clock in the morning. I hadn't seen Ned Land. No doubt, in the presence of the South Pole, the Canadian hated having to eat his words.

A few strokes of the oar brought the skiff to the sand, where it ran aground. Just as Conseil was about to jump ashore, I held him back.

"Sir," I told Captain Nemo, "to you belongs the honor of first setting foot on this shore."

"Yes, sir," the captain replied, "and if I have no hesitation in treading this polar soil, it's because no human being until now has left a footprint here."

So saying, he leaped lightly onto the sand. His heart must have been throbbing with intense excitement. He scaled an overhanging rock that ended in a small promontory and there, mute and motionless, with crossed arms and blazing eyes, he seemed to be laying claim to these southernmost regions. After spending five minutes in this trance, he turned to us.

"Whenever you're ready, sir," he called to me.

I got out, Conseil at my heels, leaving the two men in the skiff.

Over an extensive area, the soil consisted of that igneous gravel called "tuff," reddish in color as if made from crushed bricks. The ground was covered with slag, lava flows, and pumice stones. Its volcanic origin was unmistakable. In certain localities thin smoke holes gave off a sulfurous odor, showing that the inner fires still kept their wide–ranging power. Nevertheless, when I scaled a high escarpment, I could see no volcanoes within a radius of several miles. In these Antarctic districts, as is well known, Sir James Clark Ross had found the craters of Mt. Erebus and Mt. Terror in fully active condition on the 167th meridian at latitude 77° 32'.

The vegetation on this desolate continent struck me as quite limited. A few lichens of the species Usnea melanoxanthra sprawled over the black rocks. The whole meager flora of this region consisted of certain microscopic buds, rudimentary diatoms made up of a type of cell positioned between two quartz–rich shells, plus long purple and crimson fucus plants, buoyed by small air bladders and washed up on the coast by the surf.

The beach was strewn with mollusks: small mussels, limpets, smooth heart–shaped cockles, and especially some sea butterflies with oblong, membrane–filled bodies whose heads are formed from two rounded lobes. I also saw myriads of those northernmost sea butterflies three centimeters long, which a baleen whale can swallow by the thousands in one gulp. The open waters at the shoreline were alive with these delightful pteropods, true butterflies of the sea.

Among other zoophytes present in these shallows, there were a few coral tree forms that, according to Sir James Clark Ross, live in these Antarctic seas at depths as great as 1,000 meters; then small alcyon coral belonging to the species Procellaria pelagica, also a large number of starfish unique to these climes, plus some feather stars spangling the sand.

But it was in the air that life was superabundant. There various species of birds flew and fluttered by the thousands, deafening us with their calls. Crowding the rocks, other fowl watched without fear as we passed and pressed familiarly against our feet. These were auks, as agile and supple in water, where they are sometimes mistaken for fast bonito, as they are clumsy and heavy on land. They uttered outlandish calls and participated in numerous public assemblies that featured much noise but little action.

Among other fowl I noted some sheathbills from the wading-bird family, the size of pigeons, white in color, the beak short and conical, the eyes framed by red circles. Conseil laid in a supply of them, because when they're properly cooked, these winged creatures make a pleasant dish. In the air there passed sooty albatross with four-meter wingspans, birds aptly dubbed "vultures of the ocean," also gigantic petrels including several with arching wings, enthusiastic eaters of seal that are known as quebrantahuesos, and cape pigeons, a sort of small duck, the tops of their bodies black and white—in short, a whole series of petrels, some whitish with wings trimmed in brown, others blue and exclusive to these Antarctic seas, the former "so oily," I told Conseil, "that inhabitants of the Faroe Islands simply fit the bird with a wick, then light it up."

"With that minor addition," Conseil replied, "these fowl would make perfect lamps! After this, we should insist that nature equip them with wicks in advance!"

Half a mile farther on, the ground was completely riddled with penguin nests, egg-laying burrows from which numerous birds emerged. Later Captain Nemo had hundreds of them hunted because their black flesh is highly edible. They brayed like donkeys. The size of a goose with slate-colored bodies, white undersides, and lemon-colored neck bands, these animals let themselves be stoned to death without making any effort to get away.

Meanwhile the mists didn't clear, and by eleven o'clock the sun still hadn't made an appearance. Its absence disturbed me. Without it, no sights were possible. Then how could we tell whether we had reached the pole?

When I rejoined Captain Nemo, I found him leaning silently against a piece of rock and staring at the sky. He seemed impatient, baffled. But what could we do? This daring and powerful man couldn't control the sun as he did the sea.

Noon arrived without the orb of day appearing for a single instant. You couldn't even find its hiding place behind the curtain of mist. And soon this mist began to condense into snow.

"Until tomorrow," the captain said simply; and we went back to the *Nautilus*, amid flurries in the air.

During our absence the nets had been spread, and I observed with fascination the fish just hauled on board. The Antarctic seas serve as a refuge for an extremely large number of migratory fish that flee from storms in the subpolar zones, in truth only to slide down the gullets of porpoises and seals. I noted some one-decimeter southern bullhead, a species of whitish cartilaginous fish overrun with bluish gray stripes and armed with stings, then some Antarctic rabbitfish three feet long, the body very slender, the skin a smooth silver white, the head rounded, the topside furnished with three fins, the snout ending in a trunk that curved back toward the mouth. I sampled its flesh but found it tasteless, despite Conseil's views, which were largely approving.

The blizzard lasted until the next day. It was impossible to stay on the platform. From the lounge, where I was writing up the incidents of this excursion to the polar continent, I could hear the calls of petrel and albatross cavorting in the midst of the turmoil. The *Nautilus* didn't stay idle, and cruising along the coast, it advanced some ten miles farther south amid the half light left by the sun as it skimmed the edge of the horizon.

The next day, March 20, it stopped snowing. The cold was a little more brisk. The thermometer marked −2° centigrade.

The mist had cleared, and on that day I hoped our noon sights could be accomplished.

Since Captain Nemo hadn't yet appeared, only Conseil and I were taken ashore by the skiff. The soil's nature was still the same: volcanic. Traces of lava, slag, and basaltic rock were everywhere, but I couldn't find the crater that had vomited them up. There as yonder, myriads of birds enlivened this part of the polar continent. But they had to share their dominion with huge herds of marine mammals that looked at us with gentle eyes. These were seals of various species, some stretched out on the ground, others lying on drifting ice floes, several leaving or re-entering the sea. Having never dealt with man, they didn't run off at our approach, and I counted enough of them thereabouts to provision a couple hundred ships.

"Ye gods," Conseil said, "it's fortunate that Ned Land didn't come with us!"

"Why so, Conseil?"

"Because that madcap hunter would kill every animal here."

"Every animal may be overstating it, but in truth I doubt we could keep our Canadian friend from harpooning some of these magnificent cetaceans. Which would be an affront to Captain Nemo, since he hates to slay harmless beasts needlessly."

"He's right."

"Certainly, Conseil. But tell me, haven't you finished classifying these superb specimens of marine fauna?"

"Master is well aware," Conseil replied, "that I'm not seasoned in practical application. When master has told me these animals' names . . ."

"They're seals and walruses."

"Two genera," our scholarly Conseil hastened to say, "that belong to the family Pinnipedia, order Carnivora, group Unguiculata, subclass Monodelphia, class Mammalia, branch Vertebrata."

"Very nice, Conseil," I replied, "but these two genera of seals and walruses are each divided into species, and if I'm not mistaken, we now have a chance to actually look at them. Let's."

It was eight o'clock in the morning. We had four hours to ourselves before the sun could be productively observed. I guided our steps toward a huge bay that made a crescent-shaped incision in the granite cliffs along the beach.

There, all about us, I swear that the shores and ice floes were crowded with marine mammals as far as the eye could see, and I involuntarily looked around for old Proteus, that mythological shepherd who guarded King Neptune's immense flocks. To be specific, these were seals. They formed distinct male–and–female groups, the father watching over his family, the mother suckling her little ones, the stronger youngsters emancipated a few paces away. When these mammals wanted to relocate, they moved in little jumps made by contracting their bodies, clumsily helped by their imperfectly developed flippers, which, as with their manatee relatives, form actual forearms. In the water, their ideal element, I must say these animals swim wonderfully thanks to their flexible backbones, narrow pelvises, close–cropped hair, and webbed feet. Resting on shore, they assumed extremely graceful positions. Consequently, their gentle features, their sensitive expressions equal to those of the loveliest women, their soft, limpid eyes, their charming poses, led the ancients to glorify them by metamorphosing the males into sea gods and the females into mermaids.

I drew Conseil's attention to the considerable growth of the cerebral lobes found in these intelligent cetaceans. No mammal except man has more abundant cerebral matter. Accordingly, seals are quite capable of being educated; they make good pets, and together with certain other naturalists, I think these animals can be properly trained to perform yeoman service as hunting dogs for fishermen.

Most of these seals were sleeping on the rocks or the sand. Among those properly termed seals—which have no external ears, unlike sea lions whose ears protrude—I observed several varieties of the species stenorhynchus, three meters long, with white hair, bulldog heads, and armed with ten teeth in each jaw: four incisors in both the upper and lower, plus two big canines shaped like the fleur–de–lis. Among them slithered some sea elephants, a type of seal with a short, flexible trunk; these are the giants of the species, with a circumference of twenty feet and a length of ten meters. They didn't move as we approached.

"Are these animals dangerous?" Conseil asked me.

"Only if they're attacked," I replied. "But when these giant seals defend their little ones, their fury is dreadful, and it isn't rare for them to smash a fisherman's longboat to bits."

"They're within their rights," Conseil answered.

"I don't say nay."

Two miles farther on, we were stopped by a promontory that screened the bay from southerly winds. It dropped straight down to the sea, and surf foamed against it. From beyond this ridge there came fearsome bellows, such as a herd of cattle might produce.

"Gracious," Conseil put in, "a choir of bulls?"

"No," I said, "a choir of walruses."

"Are they fighting with each other?"

"Either fighting or playing."

"With all due respect to Master, this we must see."

"Then see it we must, Conseil."

And there we were, climbing these blackish rocks amid sudden landslides and over stones slippery with ice. More than once I took a tumble at the expense of my backside. Conseil, more cautious or more stable, barely faltered and would help me up, saying:

"If Master's legs would kindly adopt a wider stance, Master

will keep his balance."

Arriving at the topmost ridge of this promontory, I could see vast white plains covered with walruses. These animals were playing among themselves. They were howling not in anger but in glee.

Walruses resemble seals in the shape of their bodies and the arrangement of their limbs. But their lower jaws lack canines and incisors, and as for their upper canines, they consist of two tusks eighty centimeters long with a circumference of thirty-three centimeters at the socket. Made of solid ivory, without striations, harder than elephant tusks, and less prone to yellowing, these teeth are in great demand. Accordingly, walruses are the victims of a mindless hunting that soon will destroy them all, since their hunters indiscriminately slaughter pregnant females and youngsters, and over 4,000 individuals are destroyed annually.

Passing near these unusual animals, I could examine them at my leisure since they didn't stir. Their hides were rough and heavy, a tan color leaning toward a reddish brown; their coats were short and less than abundant. Some were four meters long. More tranquil and less fearful than their northern relatives, they posted no sentinels on guard duty at the approaches to their campsite.

After examining this community of walruses, I decided to return in my tracks. It was eleven o'clock, and if Captain Nemo found conditions favorable for taking his sights, I wanted to be present at the operation. But I held no hopes that the sun would make an appearance that day. It was hidden from our eyes by clouds squeezed together on the horizon. Apparently the jealous orb didn't want to reveal this inaccessible spot on the globe to any human being.

Yet I decided to return to the Nautilus. We went along a steep, narrow path that ran over the cliff's summit. By 11:30 we had arrived at our landing place. The beached skiff had brought the captain ashore. I spotted him standing on a chunk of basalt. His instruments were beside him. His eyes were focused on the northern horizon, along which the sun was sweeping in its extended arc.

I found a place near him and waited without speaking. Noon arrived, and just as on the day before, the sun didn't put in an appearance.

It was sheer bad luck. Our noon sights were still lacking. If we couldn't obtain them tomorrow, we would finally have to give up any hope of fixing our position.

In essence, it was precisely March 20. Tomorrow, the 21st, was the day of the equinox; the sun would disappear below the horizon for six months not counting refraction, and after its disappearance the long polar night would begin. Following the September equinox, the sun had emerged above the northerly horizon, rising in long spirals until December 21. At that time, the summer solstice of these southernmost districts, the sun had started back down, and tomorrow it would cast its last rays.

I shared my thoughts and fears with Captain Nemo.

"You're right, Professor Aronnax," he told me. "If I can't take the sun's altitude tomorrow, I won't be able to try again for another six months. But precisely because sailors' luck has led me into these seas on March 21, it will be easy to get our bearings if the noonday sun does appear before our eyes."

"Why easy, Captain?"

"Because when the orb of day sweeps in such long spirals, it's difficult to measure its exact altitude above the horizon, and our instruments are open to committing serious errors."

"Then what can you do?"

"I use only my chronometer," Captain Nemo answered me. "At noon tomorrow, March 21, if, after accounting for refraction, the sun's disk is cut exactly in half by the northern horizon, that will mean I'm at the South Pole."

"Right," I said. "Nevertheless, it isn't mathematically exact proof, because the equinox needn't fall precisely at noon."

"No doubt, sir, but the error will be under 100 meters, and that's close enough for us. Until tomorrow then."

Captain Nemo went back on board. Conseil and I stayed behind until five o'clock, surveying the beach, observing and studying. The only unusual object I picked up was an auk's egg of remarkable size, for which a collector would have paid more than F1,000. Its cream–colored tint, plus the streaks and markings that decorated it like so many hieroglyphics, made it a rare trinket. I placed it in Conseil's hands, and holding it like precious porcelain from China, that cautious, sure–footed lad got it back to the *Nautilus* in one piece.

There I put this rare egg inside one of the glass cases in the museum. I ate supper, feasting with appetite on an excellent piece of seal liver whose flavor reminded me of pork. Then I went to bed; but not without praying, like a good Hindu, for the favors of the radiant orb.

The next day, March 21, bright and early at five o'clock in the morning, I climbed onto the platform. I found Captain Nemo there.

"The weather is clearing a bit," he told me. "I have high hopes. After breakfast we'll make our way ashore and choose an observation post."

This issue settled, I went to find Ned Land. I wanted to take him with me. The obstinate Canadian refused, and I could clearly see that his tight–lipped mood and his bad temper were growing by the day. Under the circumstances I ultimately wasn't sorry that he refused. In truth, there were too many seals ashore, and it would never do to expose this impulsive fisherman to such temptations.

Breakfast over, I made my way ashore. The *Nautilus* had gone a few more miles during the night. It lay well out, a good league from the coast, which was crowned by a sharp peak 400 to 500 meters high. In addition to me, the skiff carried Captain Nemo, two crewmen, and the instruments—in other words, a chronometer, a spyglass, and a barometer.

During our crossing I saw numerous baleen whales belonging to the three species unique to these southernmost seas: the bowhead whale (or "right whale," according to the English), which has no dorsal fin; the humpback whale from the genus Balaenoptera (in other words, "winged whales"), beasts with wrinkled bellies and huge whitish fins that, genus name regardless, do not yet form wings; and the finback whale, yellowish brown, the swiftest of all cetaceans. This powerful animal is audible from far away when it sends up towering spouts of air and steam that resemble swirls of smoke. Herds of these different mammals were playing about in the tranquil waters, and I could easily see that this Antarctic polar basin now served as a refuge for those cetaceans too relentlessly pursued by hunters.

I also noted long, whitish strings of salps, a type of mollusk found in clusters, and some jellyfish of large size that swayed in the eddies of the billows.

By nine o'clock we had pulled up to shore. The sky was growing brighter. Clouds were fleeing to the south. Mists were rising from the cold surface of the water. Captain Nemo headed toward the peak, which he no doubt planned to make his observatory. It was an arduous climb over sharp lava and pumice stones in the midst of air often reeking with sulfurous fumes from the smoke holes. For a man out of practice at treading land, the captain scaled the steepest slopes with a supple agility I couldn't equal, and which would have been envied by hunters of Pyrenees mountain goats.

It took us two hours to reach the summit of this half–crystal, half–basalt peak. From there our eyes scanned a vast sea, which scrawled its boundary line firmly against the background of the northern sky. At our feet: dazzling tracts of white. Over our heads: a pale azure, clear of mists. North of us: the sun's disk, like a ball of fire already cut into by the edge of the horizon. From the heart of the waters: jets of liquid rising like hundreds of magnificent bouquets. Far off, like a sleeping cetacean: the *Nautilus*. Behind us to the south and east: an immense shore, a chaotic heap of rocks and ice whose limits we couldn't see.

Arriving at the summit of this peak, Captain Nemo carefully determined its elevation by means of his barometer, since he had to take this factor into account in his noon sights.

At 11:45 the sun, by then seen only by refraction, looked like a golden disk, dispersing its last rays over this deserted continent and down to these seas not yet plowed by the ships of man.

Captain Nemo had brought a spyglass with a reticular eyepiece, which corrected the sun's refraction by means of a mirror, and he used it to observe the orb sinking little by little along a very extended diagonal that reached below the horizon. I held the chronometer. My heart was pounding mightily. If the lower half of the sun's disk disappeared just as the chronometer said noon, we were right at the pole.

"Noon!" I called.

"The South Pole!" Captain Nemo replied in a solemn voice, handing me the spyglass, which showed the orb of day cut into two exactly equal parts by the horizon.

I stared at the last rays wreathing this peak, while shadows were gradually climbing its gradients.

Just then, resting his hand on my shoulder, Captain Nemo said to me:

"In 1600, sir, the Dutchman Gheritk was swept by storms and currents, reaching latitude 64° south and discovering the South Shetland Islands. On January 17, 1773, the famous Captain Cook went along the 38th meridian, arriving at latitude 67° 30'; and on January 30, 1774, along the 109th meridian, he reached latitude 71° 15'. In 1819 the Russian Bellinghausen lay on the 69th parallel, and in 1821 on the 66th at longitude 111° west. In 1820 the Englishman Bransfield stopped at 65°. That same year the American Morrel, whose reports are dubious, went along the 42nd meridian, finding open sea at latitude 70° 14'. In 1825 the Englishman Powell was unable to get beyond 62°. That same year a humble seal fisherman, the Englishman Weddell, went as far as latitude 72° 14' on the 35th meridian, and as far as 74° 15' on the 36th. In 1829 the Englishman Forster, commander of the *Chanticleer*, laid claim to the Antarctic continent in latitude 63° 26' and longitude 66° 26'. On February 1, 1831, the Englishman Biscoe discovered Enderby Land at latitude 68° 50', Adelaide Land at latitude 67° on February 5, 1832, and Graham Land at latitude 64° 45' on February 21. In 1838 the Frenchman Dumont d'Urville stopped at the Ice Bank in latitude 62° 57', sighting the Louis–Philippe Peninsula; on January 21 two years later, at a new southerly position of 66° 30', he named the Adélie Coast and eight days later, the Clarie Coast at 64° 40'. In 1838 the American Wilkes advanced as far as the 69th parallel on the 100th meridian. In 1839 the Englishman Balleny discovered the Sabrina Coast at the edge of the polar circle. Lastly, on January 12, 1842, with his ships, the *Erebus* and the *Terror*, the Englishman Sir James Clark Ross found Victoria Land in latitude 70° 56' and longitude 171° 7' east; on the 23rd of that same month, he reached the 74th parallel, a position denoting the Farthest South attained until then; on the 27th he lay at 76° 8'; on the 28th at 77° 32'; on February 2 at 78° 4'; and late in 1842 he returned to 71° but couldn't get beyond it. Well now! In 1868, on this 21st day of March, I myself, Captain Nemo, have reached the South Pole at 90°, and I hereby claim this entire part of the globe, equal to one–sixth of the known continents."

"In the name of which sovereign, Captain?"

"In my own name, sir!"

So saying, Captain Nemo unfurled a black flag bearing a gold "N" on its quartered bunting. Then, turning toward the orb of day, whose last rays were licking at the sea's horizon:

"Farewell, O sun!" he called. "Disappear, O radiant orb! Retire beneath this open sea, and let six months of night spread their shadows over my new domains!"

# CHAPTER 15

Accident or Incident?

THE NEXT DAY, March 22, at six o'clock in the morning, preparations for departure began. The last gleams of twilight were melting into night. The cold was brisk. The constellations were glittering with startling intensity. The wonderful Southern Cross, polar star of the Antarctic regions, twinkled at its zenith.

The thermometer marked –12° centigrade, and a fresh breeze left a sharp nip in the air. Ice floes were increasing over the open water. The sea was starting to congeal everywhere. Numerous blackish patches were spreading over its surface, announcing the imminent formation of fresh ice. Obviously this southernmost basin froze over during its six-month winter and became utterly inaccessible. What happened to the whales during this period? No doubt they went beneath the Ice Bank to find more feasible seas. As for seals and walruses, they were accustomed to living in the harshest climates and stayed on in these icy waterways. These animals know by instinct how to gouge holes in the ice fields and keep them continually open; they go to these holes to breathe. Once the birds have migrated northward to escape the cold, these marine mammals remain as sole lords of the polar continent.

Meanwhile the ballast tanks filled with water and the *Nautilus* sank slowly. At a depth of 1,000 feet, it stopped. Its propeller churned the waves and it headed due north at a speed of fifteen miles per hour. Near the afternoon it was already cruising under the immense frozen carapace of the Ice Bank.

As a precaution, the panels in the lounge stayed closed, because the *Nautilus's* hull could run afoul of some submerged block of ice. So I spent the day putting my notes into final form. My mind was completely wrapped up in my memories of the pole. We had reached that inaccessible spot without facing exhaustion or danger, as if our seagoing passenger carriage had glided there on railroad tracks. And now we had actually started our return journey. Did it still have comparable surprises in store for me? I felt sure it did, so inexhaustible is this series of underwater wonders! As it was, in the five and a half months since fate had brought us on board, we had cleared 14,000 leagues, and over this track longer than the earth's equator, so many fascinating or frightening incidents had beguiled our voyage: that hunting trip in the Crespo forests, our running aground in the Torres Strait, the coral cemetery, the pearl fisheries of Ceylon, the Arabic tunnel, the fires of Santorini, those millions in the Bay of Vigo, Atlantis, the South Pole! During the night all these memories crossed over from one dream to the next, not giving my brain a moment's rest.

At three o'clock in the morning, I was awakened by a violent collision. I sat up in bed, listening in the darkness, and then was suddenly hurled into the middle of my stateroom. Apparently the *Nautilus* had gone aground, then heeled over sharply.

Leaning against the walls, I dragged myself down the gangways to the lounge, whose ceiling lights were on. The furniture had been knocked over. Fortunately the glass cases were solidly secured at the base and had stood fast. Since we were no longer vertical, the starboard pictures were glued to the tapestries, while those to port had their lower edges hanging a foot away from the wall. So the *Nautilus* was lying on its starboard side, completely stationary to boot.

In its interior I heard the sound of footsteps and muffled

voices. But Captain Nemo didn't appear. Just as I was about to leave the lounge, Ned Land and Conseil entered.

"What happened?" I instantly said to them.

"I came to ask Master that," Conseil replied.

"Damnation!" the Canadian exclaimed. "I know full well what happened! The *Nautilus* has gone aground, and judging from the way it's listing, I don't think it'll pull through like that first time in the Torres Strait."

"But," I asked, "are we at least back on the surface of the sea?"

"We have no idea," Conseil replied.

"It's easy to find out," I answered.

I consulted the pressure gauge. Much to my surprise, it indicated a depth of 360 meters.

"What's the meaning of this?" I exclaimed.

"We must confer with Captain Nemo," Conseil said.

"But where do we find him?" Ned Land asked.

"Follow me," I told my two companions.

We left the lounge. Nobody in the library. Nobody by the central companionway or the crew's quarters. I assumed that Captain Nemo was stationed in the pilothouse. Best to wait. The three of us returned to the lounge.

I'll skip over the Canadian's complaints. He had good grounds for an outburst. I didn't answer him back, letting him blow off all the steam he wanted.

We had been left to ourselves for twenty minutes, trying to detect the tiniest noises inside the *Nautilus*, when Captain Nemo entered. He didn't seem to see us. His facial features, usually so emotionless, revealed a certain uneasiness. He studied the compass and pressure gauge in silence, then went and put his finger on the world map at a spot in the sector depicting the southernmost seas.

I hesitated to interrupt him. But some moments later, when he turned to me, I threw back at him a phrase he had used in the Torres Strait:

"An incident, Captain?"

"No, sir," he replied, "this time an accident."

"Serious?"

"Perhaps."

"Is there any immediate danger?"

"No."

"The *Nautilus* has run aground?"

"Yes."

"And this accident came about . . . ?"

"Through nature's unpredictability not man's incapacity. No errors were committed in our maneuvers. Nevertheless, we can't prevent a loss of balance from taking its toll. One may defy human laws, but no one can withstand the laws of nature."

Captain Nemo had picked an odd time to philosophize. All in all, this reply told me nothing.

"May I learn, sir," I asked him, "what caused this accident?"

"An enormous block of ice, an entire mountain, has toppled over," he answered me. "When an iceberg is eroded at the base by warmer waters or by repeated collisions, its center of gravity rises. Then it somersaults, it turns completely upside down. That's what happened here. When it overturned, one of these blocks hit the *Nautilus* as it was cruising under the waters. Sliding under our hull, this block then raised us with irresistible power, lifting us into less congested strata where we now lie on our side."

"But can't we float the *Nautilus* clear by emptying its ballast tanks, to regain our balance?"

"That, sir, is being done right now. You can hear the pumps working. Look at the needle on the pressure gauge. It indicates that the *Nautilus* is rising, but this block of ice is rising with us, and until some obstacle halts its upward movement, our position won't change."

Indeed, the *Nautilus* kept the same heel to starboard. No

doubt it would straighten up once the block came to a halt. But before that happened, who knew if we might not hit the underbelly of the Ice Bank and be hideously squeezed between two frozen surfaces?

I mused on all the consequences of this situation. Captain Nemo didn't stop studying the pressure gauge. Since the toppling of this iceberg, the *Nautilus* had risen about 150 feet, but it still stayed at the same angle to the perpendicular.

Suddenly a slight movement could be felt over the hull. Obviously the *Nautilus* was straightening a bit. Objects hanging in the lounge were visibly returning to their normal positions. The walls were approaching the vertical. Nobody said a word. Hearts pounding, we could see and feel the ship righting itself. The floor was becoming horizontal beneath our feet. Ten minutes went by.

"Finally, we're upright!" I exclaimed.

"Yes," Captain Nemo said, heading to the lounge door.

"But will we float off?" I asked him.

"Certainly," he replied, "since the ballast tanks aren't yet empty, and when they are, the *Nautilus* must rise to the surface of the sea."

The captain went out, and soon I saw that at his orders, the *Nautilus* had halted its upward movement. In fact, it soon would have hit the underbelly of the Ice Bank, but it had stopped in time and was floating in midwater.

"That was a close call!" Conseil then said.

"Yes. We could have been crushed between these masses of ice, or at least imprisoned between them. And then, with no way to renew our air supply. . . . Yes, that was a close call!"

"If it's over with!" Ned Land muttered.

I was unwilling to get into a pointless argument with the Canadian and didn't reply. Moreover, the panels opened just then, and the outside light burst through the uncovered windows.

We were fully afloat, as I have said; but on both sides of the Nautilus, about ten meters away, there rose dazzling walls of ice. There also were walls above and below. Above, because the Ice Bank's underbelly spread over us like an immense ceiling. Below, because the somersaulting block, shifting little by little, had found points of purchase on both side walls and had gotten jammed between them. The Nautilus was imprisoned in a genuine tunnel of ice about twenty meters wide and filled with quiet water. So the ship could easily exit by going either ahead or astern, sinking a few hundred meters deeper, and then taking an open passageway beneath the Ice Bank.

The ceiling lights were off, yet the lounge was still brightly lit. This was due to the reflecting power of the walls of ice, which threw the beams of our beacon right back at us. Words cannot describe the effects produced by our galvanic rays on these huge, whimsically sculpted blocks, whose every angle, ridge, and facet gave off a different glow depending on the nature of the veins running inside the ice. It was a dazzling mine of gems, in particular sapphires and emeralds, whose jets of blue and green crisscrossed. Here and there, opaline hues of infinite subtlety raced among sparks of light that were like so many fiery diamonds, their brilliance more than any eye could stand. The power of our beacon was increased a hundredfold, like a lamp shining through the biconvex lenses of a world–class lighthouse.

"How beautiful!" Conseil exclaimed.

"Yes," I said, "it's a wonderful sight! Isn't it, Ned?"

"Oh damnation, yes!" Ned Land shot back. "It's superb! I'm furious that I have to admit it. Nobody has ever seen the like. But this sight could cost us dearly. And in all honesty, I think we're looking at things God never intended for human eyes."

Ned was right. It was too beautiful. All at once a yell from Conseil made me turn around.

"What is it?" I asked.

"Master must close his eyes! Master mustn't look!"

With that, Conseil clapped his hands over his eyes.

"But what's wrong, my boy?"

"I've been dazzled, struck blind!"

Involuntarily my eyes flew to the window, but I couldn't stand the fire devouring it.

I realized what had happened. The *Nautilus* had just started off at great speed. All the tranquil glimmers of the ice walls had then changed into blazing streaks. The sparkles from these myriads of diamonds were merging with each other. Swept along by its propeller, the *Nautilus* was traveling through a sheath of flashing light.

Then the panels in the lounge closed. We kept our hands over our eyes, which were utterly saturated with those concentric gleams that swirl before the retina when sunlight strikes it too intensely. It took some time to calm our troubled vision.

Finally we lowered our hands.

"Ye gods, I never would have believed it," Conseil said.

"And I still don't believe it!" the Canadian shot back.

"When we return to shore, jaded from all these natural wonders," Conseil added, "think how we'll look down on those pitiful land masses, those puny works of man! No, the civilized world won't be good enough for us!"

Such words from the lips of this emotionless Flemish boy showed that our enthusiasm was near the boiling point. But the Canadian didn't fail to throw his dram of cold water over us.

"The civilized world!" he said, shaking his head. "Don't worry, Conseil my friend, we're never going back to that world!"

By this point it was five o'clock in the morning. Just then there was a collision in the *Nautilus's* bow. I realized that its spur had just bumped a block of ice. It must have been a faulty maneuver because this underwater tunnel was obstructed by such blocks and didn't make for easy navigating. So I had assumed that Captain Nemo, in adjusting his course, would go around each obstacle or would hug the walls and follow the windings of the tunnel. In either case our forward motion wouldn't receive an absolute check. Nevertheless, contrary to my expectations, the *Nautilus* definitely began to move backward.

"We're going astern?" Conseil said.

"Yes," I replied. "Apparently the tunnel has no way out at this end."

"And so . . . ?"

"So," I said, "our maneuvers are quite simple. We'll return in our tracks and go out the southern opening. That's all."

As I spoke, I tried to sound more confident than I really felt. Meanwhile the *Nautilus* accelerated its backward movement, and running with propeller in reverse, it swept us along at great speed.

"This'll mean a delay," Ned said.

"What are a few hours more or less, so long as we get out."

"Yes," Ned Land repeated, "so long as we get out!"

I strolled for a little while from the lounge into the library. My companions kept their seats and didn't move. Soon I threw myself down on a couch and picked up a book, which my eyes skimmed mechanically.

A quarter of an hour later, Conseil approached me, saying:

"Is it deeply fascinating, this volume Master is reading?"

"Tremendously fascinating," I replied.

"I believe it. Master is reading his own book!"

"My own book?"

Indeed, my hands were holding my own work on the great ocean depths. I hadn't even suspected. I closed the book and resumed my strolling. Ned and Conseil stood up to leave.

"Stay here, my friends," I said, stopping them. "Let's stay

together until we're out of this blind alley."

"As Master wishes," Conseil replied.

The hours passed. I often studied the instruments hanging on the lounge wall. The pressure gauge indicated that the *Nautilus* stayed at a constant depth of 300 meters, the compass that it kept heading south, the log that it was traveling at a speed of twenty miles per hour, an excessive speed in such a cramped area. But Captain Nemo knew that by this point there was no such thing as too fast, since minutes were now worth centuries.

At 8:25 a second collision took place. This time astern. I grew pale. My companions came over. I clutched Conseil's hand. Our eyes questioned each other, and more directly than if our thoughts had been translated into words.

Just then the captain entered the lounge. I went to him.

"Our path is barred to the south?" I asked him.

"Yes, sir. When it overturned, that iceberg closed off every exit."

"We're boxed in?"

"Yes."

# CHAPTER 16

## Shortage of Air

CONSEQUENTLY, above, below, and around the *Nautilus*, there were impenetrable frozen walls. We were the Ice Bank's prisoners! The Canadian banged a table with his fearsome fist. Conseil kept still. I stared at the captain. His face had resumed its usual emotionlessness. He crossed his arms. He pondered. The *Nautilus* did not stir.

The captain then broke into speech:

"Gentlemen," he said in a calm voice, "there are two ways of dying under the conditions in which we're placed."

This inexplicable individual acted like a mathematics professor working out a problem for his pupils.

"The first way," he went on, "is death by crushing. The second is death by asphyxiation. I don't mention the possibility of death by starvation because the *Nautilus's* provisions will certainly last longer than we will. Therefore, let's concentrate on our chances of being crushed or asphyxiated."

"As for asphyxiation, Captain," I replied, "that isn't a cause for alarm, because the air tanks are full."

"True," Captain Nemo went on, "but they'll supply air for only two days. Now then, we've been buried beneath the waters for thirty-six hours, and the *Nautilus's* heavy atmosphere already needs renewing. In another forty-eight hours, our reserve air will be used up."

"Well then, Captain, let's free ourselves within forty-eight hours!"

"We'll try to at least, by cutting through one of these walls surrounding us."

"Which one?" I asked.

"Borings will tell us that. I'm going to ground the *Nautilus* on the lower shelf, then my men will put on their diving suits and attack the thinnest of these ice walls."

"Can the panels in the lounge be left open?"

"Without ill effect. We're no longer in motion."

Captain Nemo went out. Hissing sounds soon told me that water was being admitted into the ballast tanks. The *Nautilus* slowly settled and rested on the icy bottom at a depth of 350 meters, the depth at which the lower shelf of ice lay submerged.

"My friends," I said, "we're in a serious predicament, but I'm counting on your courage and energy."

"Sir," the Canadian replied, "this is no time to bore you with my complaints. I'm ready to do anything I can for the common good."

"Excellent, Ned," I said, extending my hand to the Canadian.

"I might add," he went on, "that I'm as handy with a pick as a harpoon. If I can be helpful to the captain, he can use me any way he wants."

"He won't turn down your assistance. Come along, Ned."

I led the Canadian to the room where the *Nautilus's* men were putting on their diving suits. I informed the captain of Ned's proposition, which was promptly accepted. The Canadian got into his underwater costume and was ready as soon as his fellow workers. Each of them carried on his back a Rouquayrol device that the air tanks had supplied with a generous allowance of fresh oxygen. A considerable but necessary drain on the *Nautilus's* reserves. As for the Ruhmkorff lamps, they were unnecessary in the midst of these brilliant waters saturated with our electric rays.

After Ned was dressed, I re-entered the lounge, whose windows had been uncovered; stationed next to Conseil, I examined the strata surrounding and supporting the *Nautilus*.

Some moments later, we saw a dozen crewmen set foot on the shelf of ice, among them Ned Land, easily recognized by his tall figure. Captain Nemo was with them.

Before digging into the ice, the captain had to obtain borings, to insure working in the best direction. Long bores were driven into the side walls; but after fifteen meters, the instruments were still impeded by the thickness of those walls. It was futile to attack the ceiling since that surface was the Ice Bank itself, more than 400 meters high. Captain Nemo then bored into the lower surface. There we were separated from the sea by a ten–meter barrier. That's how thick the iceberg was. From this point on, it was an issue of cutting out a piece equal in surface area to the *Nautilus's* waterline. This meant detaching about 6,500 cubic meters, to dig a hole through which the ship could descend below this tract of ice.

Work began immediately and was carried on with tireless tenacity. Instead of digging all around the *Nautilus*, which would have entailed even greater difficulties, Captain Nemo had an immense trench outlined on the ice, eight meters from our port quarter. Then his men simultaneously staked it off at several points around its circumference. Soon their picks were vigorously attacking this compact matter, and huge chunks were loosened from its mass. These chunks weighed less than the water, and by an unusual effect of specific gravity, each chunk took wing, as it were, to the roof of the tunnel, which thickened above by as much as it diminished below. But this hardly mattered so long as the lower surface kept growing thinner.

After two hours of energetic work, Ned Land re-entered, exhausted. He and his companions were replaced by new workmen, including Conseil and me. The *Nautilus's* chief officer supervised us.

The water struck me as unusually cold, but I warmed up

promptly while wielding my pick. My movements were quite free, although they were executed under a pressure of thirty atmospheres.

After two hours of work, re-entering to snatch some food and rest, I found a noticeable difference between the clean elastic fluid supplied me by the Rouquayrol device and the *Nautilus's* atmosphere, which was already charged with carbon dioxide. The air hadn't been renewed in forty–eight hours, and its life–giving qualities were considerably weakened. Meanwhile, after twelve hours had gone by, we had removed from the outlined surface area a slice of ice only one meter thick, hence about 600 cubic meters. Assuming the same work would be accomplished every twelve hours, it would still take five nights and four days to see the undertaking through to completion.

"Five nights and four days!" I told my companions. "And we have oxygen in the air tanks for only two days."

"Without taking into account," Ned answered, "that once we're out of this damned prison, we'll still be cooped up beneath the Ice Bank, without any possible contact with the open air!"

An apt remark. For who could predict the minimum time we would need to free ourselves? Before the *Nautilus* could return to the surface of the waves, couldn't we all die of asphyxiation? Were this ship and everyone on board doomed to perish in this tomb of ice? It was a dreadful state of affairs. But we faced it head–on, each one of us determined to do his duty to the end.

During the night, in line with my forecasts, a new one–meter slice was removed from this immense socket. But in the morning, wearing my diving suit, I was crossing through the liquid mass in a temperature of $-6°$ to $-7°$ centigrade, when I noted that little by little the side walls were closing in on each other. The liquid strata farthest from the trench, not warmed by the movements of workmen and tools, were showing a tendency to solidify. In the face of this imminent new danger, what would happen to our chances for salvation, and how could we prevent this liquid medium from solidifying, then cracking the *Nautilus's* hull like glass?

I didn't tell my two companions about this new danger. There was no point in dampening the energy they were putting into our arduous rescue work. But when I returned on board, I mentioned this serious complication to Captain Nemo.

"I know," he told me in that calm tone the most dreadful outlook couldn't change. "It's one more danger, but I don't know any way of warding it off. Our sole chance for salvation is to work faster than the water solidifies. We've got to get there first, that's all."

Get there first! By then I should have been used to this type of talk!

For several hours that day, I wielded my pick doggedly. The work kept me going. Besides, working meant leaving the *Nautilus*, which meant breathing the clean oxygen drawn from the air tanks and supplied by our equipment, which meant leaving the thin, foul air behind.

Near evening one more meter had been dug from the trench. When I returned on board, I was wellnigh asphyxiated by the carbon dioxide saturating the air. Oh, if only we had the chemical methods that would enable us to drive out this noxious gas! There was no lack of oxygen. All this water contained a considerable amount, and after it was decomposed by our powerful batteries, this life–giving elastic fluid could have been restored to us. I had thought it all out, but to no avail because the carbon dioxide produced by our breathing permeated every part of the ship. To absorb it, we would need to fill containers with potassium hydroxide and shake them continually. But this substance was missing on board and nothing else could replace it.

That evening Captain Nemo was forced to open the spigots of his air tanks and shoot a few spouts of fresh oxygen through the *Nautilus's* interior. Without this precaution we wouldn't have awakened the following morning.

The next day, March 26, I returned to my miner's trade, working to remove the fifth meter. The Ice Bank's side walls and underbelly had visibly thickened. Obviously they would come together before the *Nautilus* could break free. For an instant I was gripped by despair. My pick nearly slipped from my hands. What was the point of this digging if I was to die smothered and crushed by this water turning to stone, a torture undreamed of by even the wildest savages! I felt like I was lying in the jaws of a fearsome monster, jaws irresistibly closing.

Supervising our work, working himself, Captain Nemo passed near me just then. I touched him with my hand and pointed to the walls of our prison. The starboard wall had moved forward to a point less than four meters from the *Nautilus's* hull.

The captain understood and gave me a signal to follow him. We returned on board. My diving suit removed, I went with him to the lounge.

"Professor Aronnax," he told me, "this calls for heroic measures, or we'll be sealed up in this solidified water as if it were cement."

"Yes!" I said. "But what can we do?"

"Oh," he exclaimed, "if only my *Nautilus* were strong enough to stand that much pressure without being crushed!"

"Well?" I asked, not catching the captain's meaning.

"Don't you understand," he went on, "that the congealing of this water could come to our rescue? Don't you see that by solidifying, it could burst these tracts of ice imprisoning us, just as its freezing can burst the hardest stones? Aren't you aware that this force could be the instrument of our salvation rather than our destruction?"

"Yes, Captain, maybe so. But whatever resistance to crushing the *Nautilus* may have, it still couldn't stand such dreadful pressures, and it would be squashed as flat as a piece of sheet iron."

"I know it, sir. So we can't rely on nature to rescue us, only our own efforts. We must counteract this solidification. We must hold it in check. Not only are the side walls closing in, but there aren't ten feet of water ahead or astern of the *Nautilus*. All around us, this freeze is gaining fast."

"How long," I asked, "will the oxygen in the air tanks enable us to breathe on board?"

The captain looked me straight in the eye.

"After tomorrow," he said, "the air tanks will be empty!"

I broke out in a cold sweat. But why should I have been startled by this reply? On March 22 the *Nautilus* had dived under the open waters at the pole. It was now the 26th. We had lived off the ship's stores for five days! And all remaining breathable air had to be saved for the workmen. Even today as I write these lines, my sensations are so intense that an involuntary terror sweeps over me, and my lungs still seem short of air!

Meanwhile, motionless and silent, Captain Nemo stood lost in thought. An idea visibly crossed his mind. But he seemed to brush it aside. He told himself no. At last these words escaped his lips:

"Boiling water!" he muttered.

"Boiling water?" I exclaimed.

"Yes, sir. We're shut up in a relatively confined area. If the *Nautilus's* pumps continually injected streams of boiling water into this space, wouldn't that raise its temperature and delay its freezing?"

"It's worth trying!" I said resolutely.

"So let's try it, Professor."

By then the thermometer gave −7° centigrade outside.

Captain Nemo led me to the galley where a huge distilling mechanism was at work, supplying drinking water via evaporation. The mechanism was loaded with water, and the full electric heat of our batteries was thrown into coils awash in liquid. In a few minutes the water reached 100° centigrade. It was sent to the pumps while new water replaced it in the process. The heat generated by our batteries was so intense that after simply going through the mechanism, water drawn cold from the sea arrived boiling hot at the body of the pump.

The steaming water was injected into the icy water outside, and after three hours had passed, the thermometer gave the exterior temperature as -6° centigrade. That was one degree gained. Two hours later the thermometer gave only -4°.

After I monitored the operation's progress, double-checking it with many inspections, I told the captain, "It's working."

"I think so," he answered me. "We've escaped being crushed. Now we have only asphyxiation to fear."

During the night the water temperature rose to -1° centigrade. The injections couldn't get it to go a single degree higher. But since salt water freezes only at -2°, I was finally assured that there was no danger of it solidifying.

By the next day, March 27, six meters of ice had been torn from the socket. Only four meters were left to be removed. That still meant forty-eight hours of work. The air couldn't be renewed in the *Nautilus's* interior. Accordingly, that day it kept getting worse.

An unbearable heaviness weighed me down. Near three o'clock in the afternoon, this agonizing sensation affected me to an intense degree. Yawns dislocated my jaws. My lungs were gasping in their quest for that enkindling elastic fluid required for breathing, now growing scarcer and scarcer. My mind was in a daze. I lay outstretched, strength gone, nearly unconscious. My gallant Conseil felt the same symptoms, suffered the same sufferings, yet never left my side. He held my hand, he kept encouraging me, and I even heard him mutter:

"Oh, if only I didn't have to breathe, to leave more air for Master!"

It brought tears to my eyes to hear him say these words.

Since conditions inside were universally unbearable, how eagerly, how happily, we put on our diving suits to take our turns working! Picks rang out on that bed of ice. Arms grew weary, hands were rubbed raw, but who cared about exhaustion, what difference were wounds? Life-sustaining air reached our lungs! We could breathe! We could breathe!

And yet nobody prolonged his underwater work beyond the time allotted him. His shift over, each man surrendered to a gasping companion the air tank that would revive him. Captain Nemo set the example and was foremost in submitting to this strict discipline. When his time was up, he yielded his equipment to another and re-entered the foul air on board, always calm, unflinching, and uncomplaining.

That day the usual work was accomplished with even greater energy. Over the whole surface area, only two meters were left to be removed. Only two meters separated us from the open sea. But the ship's air tanks were nearly empty. The little air that remained had to be saved for the workmen. Not an atom for the *Nautilus*!

When I returned on board, I felt half suffocated. What a night! I'm unable to depict it. Such sufferings are indescribable. The next day I was short-winded. Headaches and staggering fits of dizziness made me reel like a drunk. My companions were experiencing the same symptoms. Some crewmen were at their last gasp.

That day, the sixth of our imprisonment, Captain Nemo concluded that picks and mattocks were too slow to deal with the ice layer still separating us from open water—and he decided to crush this layer. The man had kept his energy and composure. He had subdued physical pain with moral strength. He could still think, plan, and act.

At his orders the craft was eased off, in other words, it was raised from its icy bed by a change in its specific gravity. When it was afloat, the crew towed it, leading it right above the immense trench outlined to match the ship's waterline. Next the ballast tanks filled with water, the boat sank, and was fitted into its socket.

Just then the whole crew returned on board, and the double outside door was closed. By this point the *Nautilus* was resting on a bed of ice only one meter thick and drilled by bores in a thousand places.

The stopcocks of the ballast tanks were then opened wide, and 100 cubic meters of water rushed in, increasing the *Nautilus's* weight by 100,000 kilograms.

We waited, we listened, we forgot our sufferings, we hoped once more. We had staked our salvation on this one last gamble.

Despite the buzzing in my head, I soon could hear vibrations under the *Nautilus's* hull. We tilted. The ice cracked with an odd ripping sound, like paper tearing, and the *Nautilus* began settling downward.

"We're going through!" Conseil muttered in my ear.

I couldn't answer him. I clutched his hand. I squeezed it in an involuntary convulsion.

All at once, carried away by its frightful excess load, the *Nautilus* sank into the waters like a cannonball, in other words, dropping as if in a vacuum!

Our full electric power was then put on the pumps, which instantly began to expel water from the ballast tanks. After a few minutes we had checked our fall. The pressure gauge soon indicated an ascending movement. Brought to full speed, the propeller made the sheet–iron hull tremble down to its rivets, and we sped northward.

But how long would it take to navigate under the Ice Bank to the open sea? Another day? I would be dead first!

Half lying on a couch in the library, I was suffocating. My face was purple, my lips blue, my faculties in abeyance. I could no longer see or hear. I had lost all sense of time. My muscles had no power to contract.

I'm unable to estimate the hours that passed in this way. But I was aware that my death throes had begun. I realized that I was about to die . . .

Suddenly I regained consciousness. A few whiffs of air had entered my lungs. Had we risen to the surface of the waves? Had we cleared the Ice Bank?

No! Ned and Conseil, my two gallant friends, were sacrificing themselves to save me. A few atoms of air were still left in the depths of one Rouquayrol device. Instead of breathing it themselves, they had saved it for me, and while they were suffocating, they poured life into me drop by drop! I tried to push the device away. They held my hands, and for a few moments I could breathe luxuriously.

My eyes flew toward the clock. It was eleven in the morning. It had to be March 28. The *Nautilus* was traveling at the frightful speed of forty miles per hour. It was writhing in the waters.

Where was Captain Nemo? Had he perished? Had his companions died with him?

Just then the pressure gauge indicated we were no more than twenty feet from the surface. Separating us from the open air was a mere tract of ice. Could we break through it?

Perhaps! In any event the *Nautilus* was going to try. In fact, I could feel it assuming an oblique position, lowering its stern and raising its spur. The admission of additional water was enough to shift its balance. Then, driven by its powerful propeller, it attacked this ice field from below like a fearsome battering ram. It split the barrier little by little, backing up, then putting on full speed against the punctured tract of ice; and finally, carried away by its supreme momentum, it lunged through and onto this frozen surface, crushing the ice beneath its weight.

The hatches were opened—or torn off, if you prefer—and waves of clean air were admitted into every part of the *Nautilus*.

# CHAPTER 17

### From Cape Horn to the Amazon

HOW I GOT ONTO the platform I'm unable to say. Perhaps the Canadian transferred me there. But I could breathe, I could inhale the life–giving sea air. Next to me my two companions were getting tipsy on the fresh oxygen particles. Poor souls who have suffered from long starvation mustn't pounce heedlessly on the first food given them. We, on the other hand, didn't have to practice such moderation: we could suck the atoms from the air by the lungful, and it was the breeze, the breeze itself, that poured into us this luxurious intoxication!

"Ahhh!" Conseil was putting in. "What fine oxygen! Let Master have no fears about breathing. There's enough for everyone."

As for Ned Land, he didn't say a word, but his wide–open jaws would have scared off a shark. And what powerful inhalations! The Canadian "drew" like a furnace going full blast.

Our strength returned promptly, and when I looked around, I saw that we were alone on the platform. No crewmen. Not even Captain Nemo. Those strange seamen on the *Nautilus* were content with the oxygen circulating inside. Not one of them had come up to enjoy the open air.

The first words I pronounced were words of appreciation and gratitude to my two companions. Ned and Conseil had kept me alive during the final hours of our long death throes.

But no expression of thanks could repay them fully for such devotion.

"Good lord, Professor," Ned Land answered me, "don't mention it! What did we do that's so praiseworthy? Not a thing. It was a question of simple arithmetic. Your life is worth more than ours. So we had to save it."

"No, Ned," I replied, "it isn't worth more. Nobody could be better than a kind and generous man like yourself!"

"All right, all right!" the Canadian repeated in embarrassment.

"And you, my gallant Conseil, you suffered a great deal."

"Not too much, to be candid with Master. I was lacking a few throatfuls of air, but I would have gotten by. Besides, when I saw Master fainting, it left me without the slightest desire to breathe. It took my breath away, in a manner of . . ."

Confounded by this lapse into banality, Conseil left his sentence hanging.

"My friends," I replied, very moved, "we're bound to each other forever, and I'm deeply indebted to you—"

"Which I'll take advantage of," the Canadian shot back.

"Eh?" Conseil put in.

"Yes," Ned Land went on. "You can repay your debt by coming with me when I leave this infernal *Nautilus*."

"By the way," Conseil said, "are we going in a favorable direction?"

"Yes," I replied, "because we're going in the direction of the sun, and here the sun is due north."

"Sure," Ned Land went on, "but it remains to be seen whether we'll make for the Atlantic or the Pacific, in other words, whether we'll end up in well-traveled or deserted seas."

I had no reply to this, and I feared that Captain Nemo wouldn't take us homeward but rather into that huge ocean washing the shores of both Asia and America. In this way he would complete his underwater tour of the world, going back to those seas where the *Nautilus* enjoyed the greatest freedom. But if we returned to the Pacific, far from every populated shore, what would happen to Ned Land's plans?

We would soon settle this important point. The *Nautilus* traveled swiftly. Soon we had cleared the Antarctic Circle plus the promontory of Cape Horn. We were abreast of the tip of South America by March 31 at seven o'clock in the evening.

By then all our past sufferings were forgotten. The memory of that imprisonment under the ice faded from our minds. We had thoughts only of the future. Captain Nemo no longer appeared, neither in the lounge nor on the platform. The positions reported each day on the world map were put there by the chief officer, and they enabled me to determine the *Nautilus's* exact heading. Now then, that evening it became obvious, much to my satisfaction, that we were returning north by the Atlantic route.

I shared the results of my observations with the Canadian and Conseil.

"That's good news," the Canadian replied, "but where's the *Nautilus* going?"

"I'm unable to say, Ned."

"After the South Pole, does our captain want to tackle the North Pole, then go back to the Pacific by the notorious Northwest Passage?"

"I wouldn't double dare him," Conseil replied.

"Oh well," the Canadian said, "we'll give him the slip long before then."

"In any event," Conseil added, "he's a superman, that Captain Nemo, and we'll never regret having known him."

"Especially once we've left him," Ned Land shot back.

The next day, April 1, when the *Nautilus* rose to the surface of the waves a few minutes before noon, we raised land to the west. It was Tierra del Fuego, the Land of Fire, a name given it by early navigators after they saw numerous curls of smoke rising from the natives' huts. This Land of Fire forms a huge cluster of islands over thirty leagues long and eighty leagues wide, extending between latitude 53° and 56° south, and between longitude 67° 50' and 77° 15' west. Its coastline looked flat, but high mountains rose in the distance. I even thought I glimpsed Mt. Sarmiento, whose elevation is 2,070 meters above sea level: a pyramid–shaped block of shale with a very sharp summit, which, depending on whether it's clear or veiled in vapor, "predicts fair weather or foul," as Ned Land told me.

"A first–class barometer, my friend."

"Yes, sir, a natural barometer that didn't let me down when I navigated the narrows of the Strait of Magellan."

Just then its peak appeared before us, standing out distinctly against the background of the skies. This forecast fair weather. And so it proved.

Going back under the waters, the *Nautilus* drew near the coast, cruising along it for only a few miles. Through the lounge windows I could see long creepers and gigantic fucus plants, bulb–bearing seaweed of which the open sea at the pole had revealed a few specimens; with their smooth, viscous filaments, they measured as much as 300 meters long; genuine cables more than an inch thick and very tough, they're often used as mooring lines for ships. Another weed, known by the name velp and boasting four–foot leaves, was crammed into the coral concretions and carpeted the ocean floor. It served as both nest and nourishment for myriads of crustaceans and mollusks, for crabs and cuttlefish. Here seals and otters could indulge in a sumptuous meal, mixing meat from fish with vegetables from the sea, like the English with their Irish stews.

The *Nautilus* passed over these lush, luxuriant depths with tremendous speed. Near evening it approached the Falkland Islands, whose rugged summits I recognized the next day. The sea was of moderate depth. So not without good reason, I assumed that these two islands, plus the many islets surrounding them, used to be part of the Magellan coastline. The Falkland Islands were probably discovered by the famous navigator John Davis, who gave them the name Davis Southern Islands. Later Sir Richard Hawkins called them the Maidenland, after the Blessed Virgin. Subsequently, at the beginning of the 18th century, they were named the Malouines by fishermen from Saint–Malo in Brittany, then finally dubbed the Falklands by the English, to whom they belong today.

In these waterways our nets brought up fine samples of algae, in particular certain fucus plants whose roots were laden with the world's best mussels. Geese and duck alighted by the dozens on the platform and soon took their places in the ship's pantry. As for fish, I specifically observed some bony fish belonging to the goby genus, especially some gudgeon two decimeters long, sprinkled with whitish and yellow spots.

I likewise marveled at the numerous medusas, including the most beautiful of their breed, the compass jellyfish, unique to the Falkland seas. Some of these jellyfish were shaped like very smooth, semispheric parasols with russet stripes and fringes of twelve neat festoons. Others looked like upside–down baskets from which wide leaves and long red twigs were gracefully trailing. They swam with quiverings of their four leaflike arms, letting the opulent tresses of their tentacles dangle in the drift. I wanted to preserve a few specimens of these delicate zoophytes, but they were merely clouds, shadows, illusions, melting and evaporating outside their native element.

When the last tips of the Falkland Islands had disappeared below the horizon, the *Nautilus* submerged to a depth between twenty and twenty–five meters and went along the South American coast. Captain Nemo didn't put in an appearance.

We didn't leave these Patagonian waterways until April 3, sometimes cruising under the ocean, sometimes on its surface. The *Nautilus* passed the wide estuary formed by the mouth of the Rio de la Plata, and on April 4 we lay abreast of Uruguay, albeit fifty miles out. Keeping to its northerly heading, it followed the long windings of South America. By then we had fared 16,000 leagues since coming on board in the seas of Japan.

Near eleven o'clock in the morning, we cut the Tropic of Capricorn on the 37th meridian, passing well out from Cape Frio. Much to Ned Land's displeasure, Captain Nemo had no liking for the neighborhood of Brazil's populous shores, because he shot by with dizzying speed. Not even the swiftest fish or birds could keep up with us, and the natural curiosities in these seas completely eluded our observation.

This speed was maintained for several days, and on the evening of April 9, we raised South America's easternmost tip, Cape São Roque. But then the Nautilus veered away again and went looking for the lowest depths of an underwater valley gouged between this cape and Sierra Leone on the coast of Africa. Abreast of the West Indies, this valley forks into two arms, and to the north it ends in an enormous depression 9,000 meters deep. From this locality to the Lesser Antilles, the ocean's geologic profile features a steeply cut cliff six kilometers high, and abreast of the Cape Verde Islands, there's another wall just as imposing; together these two barricades confine the whole submerged continent of Atlantis. The floor of this immense valley is made picturesque by mountains that furnish these underwater depths with scenic views. This description is based mostly on certain hand–drawn charts kept in the Nautilus's library, charts obviously rendered by Captain Nemo himself from his own personal observations.

For two days we visited these deep and deserted waters by means of our slanting fins. The Nautilus would do long, diagonal dives that took us to every level. But on April 11 it rose suddenly, and the shore reappeared at the mouth of the Amazon River, a huge estuary whose outflow is so considerable, it desalts the sea over an area of several leagues.

We cut the Equator. Twenty miles to the west lay Guiana, French territory where we could easily have taken refuge. But the wind was blowing a strong gust, and the furious billows would not allow us to face them in a mere skiff. No doubt Ned Land understood this because he said nothing to me. For my part, I made no allusion to his escape plans because I didn't want to push him into an attempt that was certain to misfire.

I was readily compensated for this delay by fascinating research. During those two days of April 11–12, the *Nautilus* didn't leave the surface of the sea, and its trawl brought up a simply miraculous catch of zoophytes, fish, and reptiles.

Some zoophytes were dredged up by the chain of our trawl. Most were lovely sea anemone belonging to the family Actinidia, including among other species, the Phyctalis protexta, native to this part of the ocean: a small cylindrical trunk adorned with vertical lines, mottled with red spots, and crowned by a wondrous blossoming of tentacles. As for mollusks, they consisted of exhibits I had already observed: turret snails, olive shells of the "tent olive" species with neatly intersecting lines and russet spots standing out sharply against a flesh-colored background, fanciful spider conchs that looked like petrified scorpions, transparent glass snails, argonauts, some highly edible cuttlefish, and certain species of squid that the naturalists of antiquity classified with the flying fish, which are used chiefly as bait for catching cod.

As for the fish in these waterways, I noted various species that I hadn't yet had the opportunity to study. Among cartilaginous fish: some brook lamprey, a type of eel fifteen inches long, head greenish, fins violet, back bluish gray, belly a silvery brown strewn with bright spots, iris of the eye encircled in gold, unusual animals that the Amazon's current must have swept out to sea because their natural habitat is fresh water; sting rays, the snout pointed, the tail long, slender, and armed with an extensive jagged sting; small one-meter sharks with gray and whitish hides, their teeth arranged in several backward-curving rows, fish commonly known by the name carpet shark; batfish, a sort of reddish isosceles triangle half a meter long, whose pectoral fins are attached by fleshy extensions that make these fish look like bats, although an appendage made of horn, located near the nostrils, earns them the nickname of sea unicorns; lastly, a couple species of triggerfish, the cucuyo whose stippled flanks glitter with a sparkling gold color, and the bright purple leatherjacket whose hues glisten like a pigeon's throat.

I'll finish up this catalog, a little dry but quite accurate, with the series of bony fish I observed: eels belonging to the genus Apteronotus whose snow-white snout is very blunt, the body painted a handsome black and armed with a very long, slender, fleshy whip; long sardines from the genus Odontognathus, like three-decimeter pike, shining with a bright silver glow; Guaranian mackerel furnished with two anal fins; black-tinted rudderfish that you catch by using torches, fish measuring two meters and boasting white, firm, plump meat that, when fresh, tastes like eel, when dried, like smoked salmon; semired wrasse sporting scales only at the bases of their dorsal and anal fins; grunts on which gold and silver mingle their luster with that of ruby and topaz; yellow-tailed gilthead whose flesh is extremely dainty and whose phosphorescent properties give them away in the midst of the waters; porgies tinted orange, with slender tongues; croakers with gold caudal fins; black surgeonfish; four-eyed fish from Surinam, etc.

This "et cetera" won't keep me from mentioning one more fish that Conseil, with good reason, will long remember.

One of our nets had hauled up a type of very flat ray that weighed some twenty kilograms; with its tail cut off, it would have formed a perfect disk. It was white underneath and reddish on top, with big round spots of deep blue encircled in black, its hide quite smooth and ending in a double-lobed fin.

Laid out on the platform, it kept struggling with convulsive movements, trying to turn over, making such efforts that its final lunge was about to flip it into the sea. But Conseil, being very possessive of his fish, rushed at it, and before I could stop him, he seized it with both hands.

Instantly there he was, thrown on his back, legs in the air, his body half paralyzed, and yelling:

"Oh, sir, sir! Will you help me!"

For once in his life, the poor lad didn't address me "in the third person."

The Canadian and I sat him up; we massaged his contracted arms, and when he regained his five senses, that eternal classifier mumbled in a broken voice:

"Class of cartilaginous fish, order Chondropterygia with fixed gills, suborder Selacia, family Rajiiforma, genus electric ray."

"Yes, my friend," I answered, "it was an electric ray that put you in this deplorable state."

"Oh, Master can trust me on this," Conseil shot back. "I'll be revenged on that animal!"

"How?"

"I'll eat it."

Which he did that same evening, but strictly as retaliation. Because, frankly, it tasted like leather.

Poor Conseil had assaulted an electric ray of the most dangerous species, the cumana. Living in a conducting medium such as water, this bizarre animal can electrocute other fish from several meters away, so great is the power of its electric organ, an organ whose two chief surfaces measure at least twenty-seven square feet.

During the course of the next day, April 12, the *Nautilus* drew near the coast of Dutch Guiana, by the mouth of the Maroni River. There several groups of sea cows were living in family units. These were manatees, which belong to the order

Sirenia, like the dugong and Steller's sea cow. Harmless and unaggressive, these fine animals were six to seven meters long and must have weighed at least 4,000 kilograms each. I told Ned Land and Conseil that farseeing nature had given these mammals a major role to play. In essence, manatees, like seals, are designed to graze the underwater prairies, destroying the clusters of weeds that obstruct the mouths of tropical rivers.

"And do you know," I added, "what happened since man has almost completely wiped out these beneficial races? Rotting weeds have poisoned the air, and this poisoned air causes the yellow fever that devastates these wonderful countries. This toxic vegetation has increased beneath the seas of the Torrid Zone, so the disease spreads unchecked from the mouth of the Rio de la Plata to Florida!"

And if Professor Toussenel is correct, this plague is nothing compared to the scourge that will strike our descendants once the seas are depopulated of whales and seals. By then, crowded with jellyfish, squid, and other devilfish, the oceans will have become huge centers of infection, because their waves will no longer possess "these huge stomachs that God has entrusted with scouring the surface of the sea."

Meanwhile, without scorning these theories, the *Nautilus's* crew captured half a dozen manatees. In essence, it was an issue of stocking the larder with excellent red meat, even better than beef or veal. Their hunting was not a fascinating sport. The manatees let themselves be struck down without offering any resistance. Several thousand kilos of meat were hauled below, to be dried and stored.

The same day an odd fishing practice further increased the *Nautilus's* stores, so full of game were these seas. Our trawl brought up in its meshes a number of fish whose heads were topped by little oval slabs with fleshy edges. These were suckerfish from the third family of the subbrachian Malacopterygia. These flat disks on their heads consist of crosswise plates of movable cartilage, between which the animals can create a vacuum, enabling them to stick to objects like suction cups.

The remoras I had observed in the Mediterranean were related to this species. But the creature at issue here was an Echeneis osteochara, unique to this sea. Right after catching them, our seamen dropped them in buckets of water.

Its fishing finished, the *Nautilus* drew nearer to the coast. In this locality a number of sea turtles were sleeping on the surface of the waves. It would have been difficult to capture these valuable reptiles, because they wake up at the slightest sound, and their solid carapaces are harpoon–proof. But our suckerfish would effect their capture with extraordinary certainty and precision. In truth, this animal is a living fishhook, promising wealth and happiness to the greenest fisherman in the business.

The *Nautilus's* men attached to each fish's tail a ring that was big enough not to hamper its movements, and to this ring a long rope whose other end was moored on board.

Thrown into the sea, the suckerfish immediately began to play their roles, going and fastening themselves onto the breastplates of the turtles. Their tenacity was so great, they would rip apart rather than let go. They were hauled in, still sticking to the turtles that came aboard with them.

In this way we caught several loggerheads, reptiles a meter wide and weighing 200 kilos. They're extremely valuable because of their carapaces, which are covered with big slabs of horn, thin, brown, transparent, with white and yellow markings. Besides, they were excellent from an edible viewpoint, with an exquisite flavor comparable to the green turtle.

This fishing ended our stay in the waterways of the Amazon, and that evening the *Nautilus* took to the high seas once more.

# CHAPTER 18

## The Devilfish

FOR SOME DAYS the *Nautilus* kept veering away from the American coast. It obviously didn't want to frequent the waves of the Gulf of Mexico or the Caribbean Sea. Yet there was no shortage of water under its keel, since the average depth of these seas is 1,800 meters; but these waterways, strewn with islands and plowed by steamers, probably didn't agree with Captain Nemo.

On April 16 we raised Martinique and Guadalupe from a distance of about thirty miles. For one instant I could see their lofty peaks.

The Canadian was quite disheartened, having counted on putting his plans into execution in the gulf, either by reaching shore or by pulling alongside one of the many boats plying a coastal trade from one island to another. An escape attempt would have been quite feasible, assuming Ned Land managed to seize the skiff without the captain's knowledge. But in midocean it was unthinkable.

The Canadian, Conseil, and I had a pretty long conversation on this subject. For six months we had been prisoners aboard the *Nautilus*. We had fared 17,000 leagues, and as Ned Land put it, there was no end in sight. So he made me a proposition I hadn't anticipated. We were to ask Captain Nemo this question straight out: did the captain mean to keep us on board his vessel permanently?

This measure was distasteful to me. To my mind it would

lead nowhere. We could hope for nothing from the *Nautilus's* commander but could depend only on ourselves. Besides, for some time now the man had been gloomier, more withdrawn, less sociable. He seemed to be avoiding me. I encountered him only at rare intervals. He used to take pleasure in explaining the underwater wonders to me; now he left me to my research and no longer entered the lounge.

What changes had come over him? From what cause? I had no reason to blame myself. Was our presence on board perhaps a burden to him? Even so, I cherished no hopes that the man would set us free.

So I begged Ned to let me think about it before taking action. If this measure proved fruitless, it could arouse the captain's suspicions, make our circumstances even more arduous, and jeopardize the Canadian's plans. I might add that I could hardly use our state of health as an argument. Except for that grueling ordeal under the Ice Bank at the South Pole, we had never felt better, neither Ned, Conseil, nor I. The nutritious food, life–giving air, regular routine, and uniform temperature kept illness at bay; and for a man who didn't miss his past existence on land, for a Captain Nemo who was at home here, who went where he wished, who took paths mysterious to others if not himself in attaining his ends, I could understand such a life. But we ourselves hadn't severed all ties with humanity. For my part, I didn't want my new and unusual research to be buried with my bones. I had now earned the right to pen the definitive book on the sea, and sooner or later I wanted that book to see the light of day.

There once more, through the panels opening into these Caribbean waters ten meters below the surface of the waves, I found so many fascinating exhibits to describe in my daily notes! Among other zoophytes there were Portuguese men–of–war known by the name Physalia pelagica, like big, oblong bladders with a pearly sheen, spreading their membranes to the wind, letting their blue tentacles drift like silken threads; to the eye delightful jellyfish, to the touch actual nettles that ooze a corrosive liquid. Among the articulates there were annelid worms one and a half meters long, furnished with a pink proboscis, equipped with 1,700 organs of locomotion, snaking through the waters, and as they went, throwing off every gleam in the solar spectrum. From the fish branch there were manta rays, enormous cartilaginous fish ten feet long and weighing 600 pounds, their pectoral fin triangular, their midback slightly arched, their eyes attached to the edges of the face at the front of the head; they floated like wreckage from a ship, sometimes fastening onto our windows like opaque shutters. There were American triggerfish for which nature has ground only black and white pigments, feather–shaped gobies that were long and plump with yellow fins and jutting jaws, sixteen–decimeter mackerel with short, sharp teeth, covered with small scales, and related to the albacore species. Next came swarms of red mullet corseted in gold stripes from head to tail, their shining fins all aquiver, genuine masterpieces of jewelry, formerly sacred to the goddess Diana, much in demand by rich Romans, and about which the old saying goes: "He who catches them doesn't eat them!" Finally, adorned with emerald ribbons and dressed in velvet and silk, golden angelfish passed before our eyes like courtiers in the paintings of Veronese; spurred gilthead stole by with their swift thoracic fins; thread herring fifteen inches long were wrapped in their phosphorescent glimmers; gray mullet thrashed the sea with their big fleshy tails; red salmon seemed to mow the waves with their slicing pectorals; and silver moonfish, worthy of their name, rose on the horizon of the waters like the whitish reflections of many moons.

How many other marvelous new specimens I still could have observed if, little by little, the *Nautilus* hadn't settled to the lower strata! Its slanting fins drew it to depths of 2,000 and

3,500 meters. There animal life was represented by nothing more than sea lilies, starfish, delightful crinoids with bell-shaped heads like little chalices on straight stems, top-shell snails, blood-red tooth shells, and fissurella snails, a large species of coastal mollusk.

By April 20 we had risen to an average level of 1,500 meters. The nearest land was the island group of the Bahamas, scattered like a batch of cobblestones over the surface of the water. There high underwater cliffs reared up, straight walls made of craggy chunks arranged like big stone foundations, among which there gaped black caves so deep our electric rays couldn't light them to the far ends.

These rocks were hung with huge weeds, immense sea tangle, gigantic fucus—a genuine trellis of water plants fit for a world of giants.

In discussing these colossal plants, Conseil, Ned, and I were naturally led into mentioning the sea's gigantic animals. The former were obviously meant to feed the latter. However, through the windows of our almost motionless Nautilus, I could see nothing among these long filaments other than the chief articulates of the division Brachyura: long-legged spider crabs, violet crabs, and sponge crabs unique to the waters of the Caribbean.

It was about eleven o'clock when Ned Land drew my attention to a fearsome commotion out in this huge seaweed.

"Well," I said, "these are real devilfish caverns, and I wouldn't be surprised to see some of those monsters hereabouts."

"What!" Conseil put in. "Squid, ordinary squid from the class Cephalopoda?"

"No," I said, "devilfish of large dimensions. But friend Land is no doubt mistaken, because I don't see a thing."

"That's regrettable," Conseil answered. "I'd like to come face to face with one of those devilfish I've heard so much about, which can drag ships down into the depths. Those beasts go by the name of krake—"

"Fake is more like it," the Canadian replied sarcastically.

"Krakens!" Conseil shot back, finishing his word without wincing at his companion's witticism.

"Nobody will ever make me believe," Ned Land said, "that such animals exist."

"Why not?" Conseil replied. "We sincerely believed in Master's narwhale."

"We were wrong, Conseil."

"No doubt, but there are others with no doubts who believe to this day!"

"Probably, Conseil. But as for me, I'm bound and determined not to accept the existence of any such monster till I've dissected it with my own two hands."

"Yet," Conseil asked me, "doesn't Master believe in gigantic devilfish?"

"Yikes! Who in Hades ever believed in them?" the Canadian exclaimed.

"Many people, Ned my friend," I said.

"No fishermen. Scientists maybe!"

"Pardon me, Ned. Fishermen and scientists!"

"Why, I to whom you speak," Conseil said with the world's straightest face, "I recall perfectly seeing a large boàt dragged under the waves by the arms of a cephalopod."

"You saw that?" the Canadian asked.

"Yes, Ned."

"With your own two eyes?"

"With my own two eyes."

"Where, may I ask?"

"In Saint–Malo," Conseil returned unflappably.

"In the harbor?" Ned Land said sarcastically.

"No, in a church," Conseil replied.

"In a church!" the Canadian exclaimed.

"Yes, Ned my friend. It had a picture that portrayed the

devilfish in question."

"Oh good!" Ned Land exclaimed with a burst of laughter. "Mr. Conseil put one over on me!"

"Actually he's right," I said. "I've heard about that picture. But the subject it portrays is taken from a legend, and you know how to rate legends in matters of natural history! Besides, when it's an issue of monsters, the human imagination always tends to run wild. People not only claimed these devilfish could drag ships under, but a certain Olaus Magnus tells of a cephalopod a mile long that looked more like an island than an animal. There's also the story of how the Bishop of Trondheim set up an altar one day on an immense rock. After he finished saying mass, this rock started moving and went back into the sea. The rock was a devilfish."

"And that's everything we know?" the Canadian asked.

"No," I replied, "another bishop, Pontoppidan of Bergen, also tells of a devilfish so large a whole cavalry regiment could maneuver on it."

"They sure did go on, those oldtime bishops!" Ned Land said.

"Finally, the naturalists of antiquity mention some monsters with mouths as big as a gulf, which were too huge to get through the Strait of Gibraltar."

"Good work, men!" the Canadian put in.

"But in all these stories, is there any truth?" Conseil asked.

"None at all, my friends, at least in those that go beyond the bounds of credibility and fly off into fable or legend. Yet for the imaginings of these storytellers there had to be, if not a cause, at least an excuse. It can't be denied that some species of squid and other devilfish are quite large, though still smaller than cetaceans. Aristotle put the dimensions of one squid at five cubits, or 3.1 meters. Our fishermen frequently see specimens over 1.8 meters long. The museums in Trieste and Montpellier have preserved some devilfish carcasses measuring two meters.

Besides, according to the calculations of naturalists, one of these animals only six feet long would have tentacles as long as twenty–seven. Which is enough to make a fearsome monster."

"Does anybody fish for 'em nowadays?" the Canadian asked.

"If they don't fish for them, sailors at least sight them. A friend of mine, Captain Paul Bos of Le Havre, has often sworn to me that he encountered one of these monsters of colossal size in the seas of the East Indies. But the most astonishing event, which proves that these gigantic animals undeniably exist, took place a few years ago in 1861."

"What event was that?" Ned Land asked.

"Just this. In 1861, to the northeast of Tenerife and fairly near the latitude where we are right now, the crew of the gunboat Alecto spotted a monstrous squid swimming in their waters. Commander Bouguer approached the animal and attacked it with blows from harpoons and blasts from rifles, but without much success because bullets and harpoons crossed its soft flesh as if it were semiliquid jelly. After several fruitless attempts, the crew managed to slip a noose around the mollusk's body. This noose slid as far as the caudal fins and came to a halt. Then they tried to haul the monster on board, but its weight was so considerable that when they tugged on the rope, the animal parted company with its tail; and deprived of this adornment, it disappeared beneath the waters."

"Finally, an actual event," Ned Land said.

"An indisputable event, my gallant Ned. Accordingly, people have proposed naming this devilfish Bouguer's Squid."

"And how long was it?" the Canadian asked.

"Didn't it measure about six meters?" said Conseil, who was stationed at the window and examining anew the crevices in the cliff.

"Precisely," I replied.

"Wasn't its head," Conseil went on, "crowned by eight

tentacles that quivered in the water like a nest of snakes?"

"Precisely."

"Weren't its eyes prominently placed and considerably enlarged?"

"Yes, Conseil."

"And wasn't its mouth a real parrot's beak but of fearsome size?"

"Correct, Conseil."

"Well, with all due respect to Master," Conseil replied serenely, "if this isn't Bouguer's Squid, it's at least one of his close relatives!"

I stared at Conseil. Ned Land rushed to the window.

"What an awful animal!" he exclaimed.

I stared in my turn and couldn't keep back a movement of revulsion. Before my eyes there quivered a horrible monster worthy of a place among the most farfetched teratological legends.

It was a squid of colossal dimensions, fully eight meters long. It was traveling backward with tremendous speed in the same direction as the *Nautilus*. It gazed with enormous, staring eyes that were tinted sea green. Its eight arms (or more accurately, feet) were rooted in its head, which has earned these animals the name cephalopod; its arms stretched a distance twice the length of its body and were writhing like the serpentine hair of the Furies. You could plainly see its 250 suckers, arranged over the inner sides of its tentacles and shaped like semispheric capsules. Sometimes these suckers fastened onto the lounge window by creating vacuums against it. The monster's mouth—a beak made of horn and shaped like that of a parrot—opened and closed vertically. Its tongue, also of horn substance and armed with several rows of sharp teeth, would flicker out from between these genuine shears. What a freak of nature! A bird's beak on a mollusk! Its body was spindle-shaped and swollen in the middle, a fleshy mass that must have weighed 20,000 to 25,000 kilograms. Its unstable color would change with tremendous speed as the animal grew irritated, passing successively from bluish gray to reddish brown.

What was irritating this mollusk? No doubt the presence of the *Nautilus*, even more fearsome than itself, and which it couldn't grip with its mandibles or the suckers on its arms. And yet what monsters these devilfish are, what vitality our Creator has given them, what vigor in their movements, thanks to their owning a triple heart!

Sheer chance had placed us in the presence of this squid, and I didn't want to lose this opportunity to meticulously study such a cephalopod specimen. I overcame the horror that its appearance inspired in me, picked up a pencil, and began to sketch it.

"Perhaps this is the same as the Alecto's," Conseil said.

"Can't be," the Canadian replied, "because this one's complete while the other one lost its tail!"

"That doesn't necessarily follow," I said. "The arms and tails of these animals grow back through regeneration, and in seven years the tail on Bouguer's Squid has surely had time to sprout again."

"Anyhow," Ned shot back, "if it isn't this fellow, maybe it's one of those!"

Indeed, other devilfish had appeared at the starboard window. I counted seven of them. They provided the *Nautilus* with an escort, and I could hear their beaks gnashing on the sheet–iron hull. We couldn't have asked for a more devoted following.

I continued sketching. These monsters kept pace in our waters with such precision, they seemed to be standing still, and I could have traced their outlines in miniature on the window. But we were moving at a moderate speed.

All at once the *Nautilus* stopped. A jolt made it tremble

through its entire framework.

"Did we strike bottom?" I asked.

"In any event we're already clear," the Canadian replied, "because we're afloat."

The *Nautilus* was certainly afloat, but it was no longer in motion. The blades of its propeller weren't churning the waves. A minute passed. Followed by his chief officer, Captain Nemo entered the lounge.

I hadn't seen him for a good while. He looked gloomy to me. Without speaking to us, without even seeing us perhaps, he went to the panel, stared at the devilfish, and said a few words to his chief officer.

The latter went out. Soon the panels closed. The ceiling lit up.

I went over to the captain.

"An unusual assortment of devilfish," I told him, as carefree as a collector in front of an aquarium.

"Correct, Mr. Naturalist," he answered me, "and we're going to fight them at close quarters."

I gaped at the captain. I thought my hearing had gone bad.

"At close quarters?" I repeated.

"Yes, sir. Our propeller is jammed. I think the horn-covered mandibles of one of these squid are entangled in the blades. That's why we aren't moving."

"And what are you going to do?"

"Rise to the surface and slaughter the vermin."

"A difficult undertaking."

"Correct. Our electric bullets are ineffective against such soft flesh, where they don't meet enough resistance to go off. But we'll attack the beasts with axes."

"And harpoons, sir," the Canadian said, "if you don't turn down my help."

"I accept it, Mr. Land."

"We'll go with you," I said. And we followed Captain Nemo,

heading to the central companionway.

There some ten men were standing by for the assault, armed with boarding axes. Conseil and I picked up two more axes. Ned Land seized a harpoon.

By then the *Nautilus* had returned to the surface of the waves. Stationed on the top steps, one of the seamen undid the bolts of the hatch. But he had scarcely unscrewed the nuts when the hatch flew up with tremendous violence, obviously pulled open by the suckers on a devilfish's arm.

Instantly one of those long arms glided like a snake into the opening, and twenty others were quivering above. With a sweep of the ax, Captain Nemo chopped off this fearsome tentacle, which slid writhing down the steps.

Just as we were crowding each other to reach the platform, two more arms lashed the air, swooped on the seaman stationed in front of Captain Nemo, and carried the fellow away with irresistible violence.

Captain Nemo gave a shout and leaped outside. We rushed after him.

What a scene! Seized by the tentacle and glued to its suckers, the unfortunate man was swinging in the air at the mercy of this enormous appendage. He gasped, he choked, he yelled: "Help! Help!" These words, pronounced in French, left me deeply stunned! So I had a fellow countryman on board, perhaps several! I'll hear his harrowing plea the rest of my life!

The poor fellow was done for. Who could tear him from such a powerful grip? Even so, Captain Nemo rushed at the devilfish and with a sweep of the ax hewed one more of its arms. His chief officer struggled furiously with other monsters crawling up the *Nautilus's* sides. The crew battled with flailing axes. The Canadian, Conseil, and I sank our weapons into these fleshy masses. An intense, musky odor filled the air. It was horrible.

For an instant I thought the poor man entwined by the

devilfish might be torn loose from its powerful suction. Seven arms out of eight had been chopped off. Brandishing its victim like a feather, one lone tentacle was writhing in the air. But just as Captain Nemo and his chief officer rushed at it, the animal shot off a spout of blackish liquid, secreted by a pouch located in its abdomen. It blinded us. When this cloud had dispersed, the squid was gone, and so was my poor fellow countryman!

What rage then drove us against these monsters! We lost all self-control. Ten or twelve devilfish had overrun the *Nautilus's* platform and sides. We piled helter-skelter into the thick of these sawed-off snakes, which darted over the platform amid waves of blood and sepia ink. It seemed as if these viscous tentacles grew back like the many heads of Hydra. At every thrust Ned Land's harpoon would plunge into a squid's sea-green eye and burst it. But my daring companion was suddenly toppled by the tentacles of a monster he could not avoid.

Oh, my heart nearly exploded with excitement and horror! The squid's fearsome beak was wide open over Ned Land. The poor man was about to be cut in half. I ran to his rescue. But Captain Nemo got there first. His ax disappeared between the two enormous mandibles, and the Canadian, miraculously saved, stood and plunged his harpoon all the way into the devilfish's triple heart.

"Tit for tat," Captain Nemo told the Canadian. "I owed it to myself!"

Ned bowed without answering him.

This struggle had lasted a quarter of an hour. Defeated, mutilated, battered to death, the monsters finally yielded to us and disappeared beneath the waves.

Red with blood, motionless by the beacon, Captain Nemo stared at the sea that had swallowed one of his companions, and large tears streamed from his eyes.

# CHAPTER 19

## The Gulf Stream

THIS DREADFUL SCENE on April 20 none of us will ever be able to forget. I wrote it up in a state of intense excitement. Later I reviewed my narrative. I read it to Conseil and the Canadian. They found it accurate in detail but deficient in impact. To convey such sights, it would take the pen of our most famous poet, Victor Hugo, author of *The Toilers of the Sea*.

As I said, Captain Nemo wept while staring at the waves. His grief was immense. This was the second companion he had lost since we had come aboard. And what a way to die! Smashed, strangled, crushed by the fearsome arms of a devilfish, ground between its iron mandibles, this friend would never rest with his companions in the placid waters of their coral cemetery!

As for me, what had harrowed my heart in the thick of this struggle was the despairing yell given by this unfortunate man. Forgetting his regulation language, this poor Frenchman had reverted to speaking his own mother tongue to fling out one supreme plea! Among the *Nautilus's* crew, allied body and soul with Captain Nemo and likewise fleeing from human contact, I had found a fellow countryman! Was he the only representative of France in this mysterious alliance, obviously made up of individuals from different nationalities? This was just one more of those insoluble problems that kept welling up in my mind!

Captain Nemo re-entered his stateroom, and I saw no

more of him for a good while. But how sad, despairing, and irresolute he must have felt, to judge from this ship whose soul he was, which reflected his every mood! The *Nautilus* no longer kept to a fixed heading. It drifted back and forth, riding with the waves like a corpse. Its propeller had been disentangled but was barely put to use. It was navigating at random. It couldn't tear itself away from the setting of this last struggle, from this sea that had devoured one of its own!

Ten days went by in this way. It was only on May 1 that the *Nautilus* openly resumed its northbound course, after raising the Bahamas at the mouth of Old Bahama Channel. We then went with the current of the sea's greatest river, which has its own banks, fish, and temperature. I mean the Gulf Stream.

It is indeed a river that runs independently through the middle of the Atlantic, its waters never mixing with the ocean's waters. It's a salty river, saltier than the sea surrounding it. Its average depth is 3,000 feet, its average width sixty miles. In certain localities its current moves at a speed of four kilometers per hour. The unchanging volume of its waters is greater than that of all the world's rivers combined.

As discovered by Commander Maury, the true source of the Gulf Stream, its starting point, if you prefer, is located in the Bay of Biscay. There its waters, still weak in temperature and color, begin to form. It goes down south, skirts equatorial Africa, warms its waves in the rays of the Torrid Zone, crosses the Atlantic, reaches Cape São Roque on the coast of Brazil, and forks into two branches, one going to the Caribbean Sea for further saturation with heat particles. Then, entrusted with restoring the balance between hot and cold temperatures and with mixing tropical and northern waters, the Gulf Stream begins to play its stabilizing role. Attaining a white heat in the Gulf of Mexico, it heads north up the American coast, advances as far as Newfoundland, swerves away under the thrust of a cold current from the Davis Strait, and resumes its ocean course by going along a great circle of the earth on a rhumb line; it then divides into two arms near the 43rd parallel; one, helped by the northeast trade winds, returns to the Bay of Biscay and the Azores; the other washes the shores of Ireland and Norway with lukewarm water, goes beyond Spitzbergen, where its temperature falls to 4° centigrade, and fashions the open sea at the pole.

It was on this oceanic river that the *Nautilus* was then navigating. Leaving Old Bahama Channel, which is fourteen leagues wide by 350 meters deep, the Gulf Stream moves at the rate of eight kilometers per hour. Its speed steadily decreases as it advances northward, and we must pray that this steadiness continues, because, as experts agree, if its speed and direction were to change, the climates of Europe would undergo disturbances whose consequences are incalculable.

Near noon I was on the platform with Conseil. I shared with him the relevant details on the Gulf Stream. When my explanation was over, I invited him to dip his hands into its current.

Conseil did so, and he was quite astonished to experience no sensation of either hot or cold.

"That comes," I told him, "from the water temperature of the Gulf Stream, which, as it leaves the Gulf of Mexico, is barely different from your blood temperature. This Gulf Stream is a huge heat generator that enables the coasts of Europe to be decked in eternal greenery. And if Commander Maury is correct, were one to harness the full warmth of this current, it would supply enough heat to keep molten a river of iron solder as big as the Amazon or the Missouri."

Just then the Gulf Stream's speed was 2.25 meters per second. So distinct is its current from the surrounding sea, its confined waters stand out against the ocean and operate on a different level from the colder waters. Murky as well, and very rich in saline material, their pure indigo contrasts with the green waves surrounding them. Moreover, their line of demarcation is so clear that abreast of the Carolinas, the *Nautilus's* spur cut the waves of the Gulf Stream while its propeller was still churning those belonging to the ocean.

This current swept along with it a whole host of moving creatures. Argonauts, so common in the Mediterranean, voyaged here in schools of large numbers. Among cartilaginous fish, the most remarkable were rays whose ultra slender tails made up nearly a third of the body, which was shaped like a huge diamond twenty–five feet long; then little one–meter sharks, the head large, the snout short and rounded, the teeth sharp and arranged in several rows, the body seemingly covered with scales.

Among bony fish, I noted grizzled wrasse unique to these seas, deep–water gilthead whose iris has a fiery gleam, one–meter croakers whose large mouths bristle with small teeth and which let out thin cries, black rudderfish like those I've already discussed, blue dorados accented with gold and silver, rainbow–hued parrotfish that can rival the loveliest tropical birds in coloring, banded blennies with triangular heads, bluish flounder without scales, toadfish covered with a crosswise yellow band in the shape of a T, swarms of little freckled gobies stippled with brown spots, lungfish with silver heads and yellow tails, various specimens of salmon, mullet with slim figures and a softly glowing radiance that Lacépède dedicated to the memory of his wife, and finally the American cavalla, a handsome fish decorated by every honorary order, bedizened with their every ribbon, frequenting the shores of this great nation where ribbons and orders are held in such low esteem.

I might add that during the night, the Gulf Stream's phosphorescent waters rivaled the electric glow of our beacon, especially in the stormy weather that frequently threatened us.

On May 8, while abreast of North Carolina, we were

across from Cape Hatteras once more. There the Gulf Stream is seventy-five miles wide and 210 meters deep. The *Nautilus* continued to wander at random. Seemingly, all supervision had been jettisoned. Under these conditions I admit that we could easily have gotten away. In fact, the populous shores offered ready refuge everywhere. The sea was plowed continuously by the many steamers providing service between the Gulf of Mexico and New York or Boston, and it was crossed night and day by little schooners engaged in coastal trade over various points on the American shore. We could hope to be picked up. So it was a promising opportunity, despite the thirty miles that separated the *Nautilus* from these Union coasts.

But one distressing circumstance totally thwarted the Canadian's plans. The weather was thoroughly foul. We were approaching waterways where storms are commonplace, the very homeland of tornadoes and cyclones specifically engendered by the Gulf Stream's current. To face a frequently raging sea in a frail skiff was a race to certain disaster. Ned Land conceded this himself. So he champed at the bit, in the grip of an intense homesickness that could be cured only by our escape.

"Sir," he told me that day, "it's got to stop. I want to get to the bottom of this. Your Nemo's veering away from shore and heading up north. But believe you me, I had my fill at the South Pole and I'm not going with him to the North Pole."

"What can we do, Ned, since it isn't feasible to escape right now?"

"I keep coming back to my idea. We've got to talk to the captain. When we were in your own country's seas, you didn't say a word. Now that we're in mine, I intend to speak up. Before a few days are out, I figure the *Nautilus* will lie abreast of Nova Scotia, and from there to Newfoundland is the mouth of a large gulf, and the St. Lawrence empties into that gulf, and the St. Lawrence is my own river, the river running by Quebec, my hometown—and when I think about all this, my gorge rises and my hair stands on end! Honestly, sir, I'd rather jump overboard! I can't stay here any longer! I'm suffocating!"

The Canadian was obviously at the end of his patience. His vigorous nature couldn't adapt to this protracted imprisonment. His facial appearance was changing by the day. His moods grew gloomier and gloomier. I had a sense of what he was suffering because I also was gripped by homesickness. Nearly seven months had gone by without our having any news from shore. Moreover, Captain Nemo's reclusiveness, his changed disposition, and especially his total silence since the battle with the devilfish all made me see things in a different light. I no longer felt the enthusiasm of our first days on board. You needed to be Flemish like Conseil to accept these circumstances, living in a habitat designed for cetaceans and other denizens of the deep. Truly, if that gallant lad had owned gills instead of lungs, I think he would have made an outstanding fish!

"Well, sir?" Ned Land went on, seeing that I hadn't replied.

"Well, Ned, you want me to ask Captain Nemo what he intends to do with us?"

"Yes, sir."

"Even though he has already made that clear?"

"Yes. I want it settled once and for all. Speak just for me, strictly on my behalf, if you want."

"But I rarely encounter him. He positively avoids me."

"All the more reason you should go look him up."

"I'll confer with him, Ned."

"When?" the Canadian asked insistently.

"When I encounter him."

"Professor Aronnax, would you like me to go find him myself?"

"No, let me do it. Tomorrow—"

"Today," Ned Land said.

"So be it. I'll see him today," I answered the Canadian, who, if he took action himself, would certainly have ruined everything.

I was left to myself. His request granted, I decided to dispose of it immediately. I like things over and done with.

I re-entered my stateroom. From there I could hear movements inside Captain Nemo's quarters. I couldn't pass up this chance for an encounter. I knocked on his door. I received no reply. I knocked again, then tried the knob. The door opened.

I entered. The captain was there. He was bending over his worktable and hadn't heard me. Determined not to leave without questioning him, I drew closer. He looked up sharply, with a frowning brow, and said in a pretty stern tone:

"Oh, it's you! What do you want?"

"To speak with you, Captain."

"But I'm busy, sir, I'm at work. I give you the freedom to enjoy your privacy, can't I have the same for myself?"

This reception was less than encouraging. But I was determined to give as good as I got.

"Sir," I said coolly, "I need to speak with you on a matter that simply can't wait."

"Whatever could that be, sir?" he replied sarcastically. "Have you made some discovery that has escaped me? Has the sea yielded up some novel secret to you?"

We were miles apart. But before I could reply, he showed me a manuscript open on the table and told me in a more serious tone:

"Here, Professor Aronnax, is a manuscript written in several languages. It contains a summary of my research under the sea, and God willing, it won't perish with me. Signed with my name, complete with my life story, this manuscript will be enclosed in a small, unsinkable contrivance. The last surviving man on the *Nautilus* will throw this contrivance into the sea, and it will go wherever the waves carry it."

The man's name! His life story written by himself! So the secret of his existence might someday be unveiled? But just then I saw this announcement only as a lead-in to my topic.

"Captain," I replied, "I'm all praise for this idea you're putting into effect. The fruits of your research must not be lost. But the methods you're using strike me as primitive. Who knows where the winds will take that contrivance, into whose hands it may fall? Can't you find something better? Can't you or one of your men—"

"Never, sir," the captain said, swiftly interrupting me.

"But my companions and I would be willing to safeguard this manuscript, and if you give us back our freedom—"

"Your freedom!" Captain Nemo put in, standing up.

"Yes, sir, and that's the subject on which I wanted to confer with you. For seven months we've been aboard your vessel, and I ask you today, in the name of my companions as well as myself, if you intend to keep us here forever."

"Professor Aronnax," Captain Nemo said, "I'll answer you today just as I did seven months ago: whomever boards the *Nautilus* must never leave it."

"What you're inflicting on us is outright slavery!"

"Call it anything you like."

"But every slave has the right to recover his freedom! By any worthwhile, available means!"

"Who has denied you that right?" Captain Nemo replied. "Did I ever try to bind you with your word of honor?"

The captain stared at me, crossing his arms.

"Sir," I told him, "to take up this subject a second time would be distasteful to both of us. So let's finish what we've started. I repeat: it isn't just for myself that I raise this issue. To me, research is a relief, a potent diversion, an enticement, a passion that can make me forget everything else. Like you, I'm a man neglected and unknown, living in the faint hope that someday I can pass on to future generations the fruits of my labors—figuratively speaking, by means of some contrivance left to the luck of winds and waves. In short, I can admire you and comfortably go with you while playing a role I only partly understand; but I still catch glimpses of other aspects of your life that are surrounded by involvements and secrets that, alone on board, my companions and I can't share. And even when our hearts could beat with yours, moved by some of your griefs or stirred by your deeds of courage and genius, we've had to stifle even the slightest token of that sympathy that arises at the sight of something fine and good, whether it comes from friend or enemy. All right then! It's this feeling of being alien to your deepest concerns that makes our situation unacceptable, impossible, even impossible for me but especially for Ned Land. Every man, by virtue of his very humanity, deserves fair treatment. Have you considered how a love of freedom and hatred of slavery could lead to plans of vengeance in a temperament like the Canadian's, what he might think, attempt, endeavor . . . ?"

I fell silent. Captain Nemo stood up.

"Ned Land can think, attempt, or endeavor anything he wants, what difference is it to me? I didn't go looking for him! I don't keep him on board for my pleasure! As for you, Professor Aronnax, you're a man able to understand anything, even silence. I have nothing more to say to you. Let this first time you've come to discuss this subject also be the last, because a second time I won't even listen."

I withdrew. From that day forward our position was very strained. I reported this conversation to my two companions.

"Now we know," Ned said, "that we can't expect a thing from this man. The Nautilus is nearing Long Island. We'll escape, no matter what the weather."

But the skies became more and more threatening. There were conspicuous signs of a hurricane on the way. The atmosphere was turning white and milky. Slender sheaves of cirrus clouds were followed on the horizon by layers of nimbocumulus. Other low clouds fled swiftly. The sea grew towering, inflated by long swells. Every bird had disappeared except a few petrels, friends of the storms. The barometer fell significantly, indicating a tremendous tension in the surrounding haze. The mixture in our stormglass decomposed under the influence of the electricity charging the air. A struggle of the elements was approaching.

The storm burst during the daytime of May 13, just as the *Nautilus* was cruising abreast of Long Island, a few miles from the narrows to Upper New York Bay. I'm able to describe this struggle of the elements because Captain Nemo didn't flee into the ocean depths; instead, from some inexplicable whim, he decided to brave it out on the surface.

The wind was blowing from the southwest, initially a stiff breeze, in other words, with a speed of fifteen meters per second, which built to twenty–five meters near three o'clock in the afternoon. This is the figure for major storms.

Unshaken by these squalls, Captain Nemo stationed himself on the platform. He was lashed around the waist to withstand the monstrous breakers foaming over the deck. I hoisted and attached myself to the same place, dividing my wonderment between the storm and this incomparable man who faced it head–on.

The raging sea was swept with huge tattered clouds drenched by the waves. I saw no more of the small intervening billows that form in the troughs of the big crests. Just long, soot–colored undulations with crests so compact they didn't foam. They kept growing taller. They were spurring each other on. The *Nautilus*, sometimes lying on its side, sometimes standing on end like a mast, rolled and pitched frightfully.

Near five o'clock a torrential rain fell, but it lulled neither wind nor sea. The hurricane was unleashed at a speed of forty–

five meters per second, hence almost forty leagues per hour. Under these conditions houses topple, roof tiles puncture doors, iron railings snap in two, and twenty–four–pounder cannons relocate. And yet in the midst of this turmoil, the *Nautilus* lived up to that saying of an expert engineer: "A well–constructed hull can defy any sea!" This submersible was no resisting rock that waves could demolish; it was a steel spindle, obediently in motion, without rigging or masting, and able to brave their fury with impunity.

Meanwhile I was carefully examining these unleashed breakers. They measured up to fifteen meters in height over a length of 150 to 175 meters, and the speed of their propagation (half that of the wind) was fifteen meters per second. Their volume and power increased with the depth of the waters. I then understood the role played by these waves, which trap air in their flanks and release it in the depths of the sea where its oxygen brings life. Their utmost pressure—it has been calculated—can build to 3,000 kilograms on every square foot of surface they strike. It was such waves in the Hebrides that repositioned a stone block weighing 84,000 pounds. It was their relatives in the tidal wave on December 23, 1854, that toppled part of the Japanese city of Tokyo, then went that same day at 700 kilometers per hour to break on the beaches of America.

After nightfall the storm grew in intensity. As in the 1860 cyclone on Réunion Island, the barometer fell to 710 millimeters. At the close of day, I saw a big ship passing on the horizon, struggling painfully. It lay to at half steam in an effort to hold steady on the waves. It must have been a steamer on one of those lines out of New York to Liverpool or Le Havre. It soon vanished into the shadows.

At ten o'clock in the evening, the skies caught on fire. The air was streaked with violent flashes of lightning. I couldn't stand this brightness, but Captain Nemo stared straight at it, as if to inhale the spirit of the storm. A dreadful noise filled the air, a complicated noise made up of the roar of crashing breakers, the howl of the wind, claps of thunder. The wind shifted to every point of the horizon, and the cyclone left the east to return there after passing through north, west, and south, moving in the opposite direction of revolving storms in the southern hemisphere.

Oh, that Gulf Stream! It truly lives up to its nickname, the Lord of Storms! All by itself it creates these fearsome cyclones through the difference in temperature between its currents and the superimposed layers of air.

The rain was followed by a downpour of fire. Droplets of water changed into exploding tufts. You would have thought Captain Nemo was courting a death worthy of himself, seeking to be struck by lightning. In one hideous pitching movement, the *Nautilus* reared its steel spur into the air like a lightning rod, and I saw long sparks shoot down it.

Shattered, at the end of my strength, I slid flat on my belly to the hatch. I opened it and went below to the lounge. By then the storm had reached its maximum intensity. It was impossible to stand upright inside the *Nautilus*.

Captain Nemo re-entered near midnight. I could hear the ballast tanks filling little by little, and the *Nautilus* sank gently beneath the surface of the waves.

Through the lounge's open windows, I saw large, frightened fish passing like phantoms in the fiery waters. Some were struck by lightning right before my eyes!

The *Nautilus* kept descending. I thought it would find calm again at fifteen meters down. No. The upper strata were too violently agitated. It needed to sink to fifty meters, searching for a resting place in the bowels of the sea.

But once there, what tranquility we found, what silence, what peace all around us! Who would have known that a dreadful hurricane was then unleashed on the surface of this ocean?

# CHAPTER 20

In Latitude 47° 24' and Longitude 17° 28'

IN THE AFTERMATH of this storm, we were thrown back to the east. Away went any hope of escaping to the landing places of New York or the St. Lawrence. In despair, poor Ned went into seclusion like Captain Nemo. Conseil and I no longer left each other.

As I said, the *Nautilus* veered to the east. To be more accurate, I should have said to the northeast. Sometimes on the surface of the waves, sometimes beneath them, the ship wandered for days amid these mists so feared by navigators. These are caused chiefly by melting ice, which keeps the air extremely damp. How many ships have perished in these waterways as they tried to get directions from the hazy lights on the coast! How many casualties have been caused by these opaque mists! How many collisions have occurred with these reefs, where the breaking surf is covered by the noise of the wind! How many vessels have rammed each other, despite their running lights, despite the warnings given by their bosun's pipes and alarm bells!

So the floor of this sea had the appearance of a battlefield where every ship defeated by the ocean still lay, some already old and encrusted, others newer and reflecting our beacon light on their ironwork and copper undersides. Among these vessels, how many went down with all hands, with their crews and hosts of immigrants, at these trouble spots so prominent in the statistics: Cape Race, St. Paul Island, the Strait of Belle Isle, the St. Lawrence estuary! And in only a few years, how many victims have been furnished to the obituary notices by the Royal Mail, Inman, and Montreal lines; by vessels named the *Solway*, the *Isis*, the *Paramatta*, the *Hungarian*, the *Canadian*, the *Anglo-Saxon*, the *Humboldt*, and the *United States*, all run aground; by the *Arctic* and the *Lyonnais*, sunk in collisions; by the *President*, the *Pacific*, and the *City of Glasgow*, lost for reasons unknown; in the midst of their gloomy rubble, the *Nautilus* navigated as if passing the dead in review!

By May 15 we were off the southern tip of the Grand Banks of Newfoundland. These banks are the result of marine sedimentation, an extensive accumulation of organic waste brought either from the equator by the Gulf Stream's current, or from the North Pole by the countercurrent of cold water that skirts the American coast. Here, too, erratically drifting chunks collect from the ice breakup. Here a huge boneyard forms from fish, mollusks, and zoophytes dying over it by the billions.

The sea is of no great depth at the Grand Banks. A few hundred fathoms at best. But to the south there is a deep, suddenly occurring depression, a 3,000-meter pit. Here the Gulf Stream widens. Its waters come to full bloom. It loses its speed and temperature, but it turns into a sea.

Among the fish that the *Nautilus* startled on its way, I'll mention a one-meter lumpfish, blackish on top with orange on the belly and rare among its brethren in that it practices monogamy, a good-sized eelpout, a type of emerald moray whose flavor is excellent, wolffish with big eyes in a head somewhat resembling a canine's, viviparous blennies whose eggs hatch inside their bodies like those of snakes, bloated gobio (or black gudgeon) measuring two decimeters, grenadiers with long tails and gleaming with a silvery glow, speedy fish venturing far from their High Arctic seas.

Our nets also hauled in a bold, daring, vigorous, and

muscular fish armed with prickles on its head and stings on its fins, a real scorpion measuring two to three meters, the ruthless enemy of cod, blennies, and salmon; it was the bullhead of the northerly seas, a fish with red fins and a brown body covered with nodules. The *Nautilus's* fishermen had some trouble getting a grip on this animal, which, thanks to the formation of its gill covers, can protect its respiratory organs from any parching contact with the air and can live out of water for a good while.

And I'll mention—for the record—some little banded blennies that follow ships into the northernmost seas, sharp-snouted carp exclusive to the north Atlantic, scorpionfish, and lastly the gadoid family, chiefly the cod species, which I detected in their waters of choice over these inexhaustible Grand Banks.

Because Newfoundland is simply an underwater peak, you could call these cod mountain fish. While the *Nautilus* was clearing a path through their tight ranks, Conseil couldn't refrain from making this comment:

"Mercy, look at these cod!" he said. "Why, I thought cod were flat, like dab or sole!"

"Innocent boy!" I exclaimed. "Cod are flat only at the grocery store, where they're cut open and spread out on display. But in the water they're like mullet, spindle-shaped and perfectly built for speed."

"I can easily believe Master," Conseil replied. "But what crowds of them! What swarms!"

"Bah! My friend, there'd be many more without their enemies, scorpionfish and human beings! Do you know how many eggs have been counted in a single female?"

"I'll go all out," Conseil replied. "500,000."

"11,000,000, my friend."

"11,000,000! I refuse to accept that until I count them myself."

TWENTY THOUSAND LEAGUES UNDER THE SEA     473

"So count them, Conseil. But it would be less work to believe me. Besides, Frenchmen, Englishmen, Americans, Danes, and Norwegians catch these cod by the thousands. They're eaten in prodigious quantities, and without the astonishing fertility of these fish, the seas would soon be depopulated of them. Accordingly, in England and America alone, 5,000 ships manned by 75,000 seamen go after cod. Each ship brings back an average catch of 4,400 fish, making 22,000,000. Off the coast of Norway, the total is the same."

"Fine," Conseil replied, "I'll take Master's word for it. I won't count them."

"Count what?"

"Those 11,000,000 eggs. But I'll make one comment."

"What's that?"

"If all their eggs hatched, just four codfish could feed England, America, and Norway."

As we skimmed the depths of the Grand Banks, I could see perfectly those long fishing lines, each armed with 200 hooks, that every boat dangled by the dozens. The lower end of each line dragged the bottom by means of a small grappling iron, and at the surface it was secured to the buoy–rope of a cork float. The *Nautilus* had to maneuver shrewdly in the midst of this underwater spiderweb.

But the ship didn't stay long in these heavily traveled waterways. It went up to about latitude 42°. This brought it abreast of St. John's in Newfoundland and Heart's Content, where the Atlantic Cable reaches its end point.

Instead of continuing north, the *Nautilus* took an easterly heading, as if to go along this plateau on which the telegraph cable rests, where multiple soundings have given the contours of the terrain with the utmost accuracy.

It was on May 17, about 500 miles from Heart's Content and 2,800 meters down, that I spotted this cable lying on the seafloor. Conseil, whom I hadn't alerted, mistook it at first for a gigantic sea snake and was gearing up to classify it in his best manner. But I enlightened the fine lad and let him down gently by giving him various details on the laying of this cable.

The first cable was put down during the years 1857–1858; but after transmitting about 400 telegrams, it went dead. In 1863 engineers built a new cable that measured 3,400 kilometers, weighed 4,500 metric tons, and was shipped aboard the *Great Eastern*. This attempt also failed.

Now then, on May 25 while submerged to a depth of 3,836 meters, the *Nautilus* lay in precisely the locality where this second cable suffered the rupture that ruined the undertaking. It happened 638 miles from the coast of Ireland. At around two o'clock in the afternoon, all contact with Europe broke off. The electricians on board decided to cut the cable before fishing it up, and by eleven o'clock that evening they had retrieved the damaged part. They repaired the joint and its splice; then the cable was resubmerged. But a few days later it snapped again and couldn't be recovered from the ocean depths.

These Americans refused to give up. The daring Cyrus Field, who had risked his whole fortune to promote this undertaking, called for a new bond issue. It sold out immediately. Another cable was put down under better conditions. Its sheaves of conducting wire were insulated within a gutta–percha covering, which was protected by a padding of textile material enclosed in a metal sheath. The *Great Eastern* put back to sea on July 13, 1866.

The operation proceeded apace. Yet there was one hitch. As they gradually unrolled this third cable, the electricians observed on several occasions that someone had recently driven nails into it, trying to damage its core. Captain Anderson, his officers, and the engineers put their heads together, then posted a warning that if the culprit were detected, he would be thrown overboard without a trial. After that, these villainous attempts were not repeated.

By July 23 the *Great Eastern* was lying no farther than 800 kilometers from Newfoundland when it received telegraphed news from Ireland of an armistice signed between Prussia and Austria after the Battle of Sadova. Through the mists on the 27th, it sighted the port of Heart's Content. The undertaking had ended happily, and in its first dispatch, young America addressed old Europe with these wise words so rarely understood: "Glory to God in the highest, and peace on earth to men of good will."

I didn't expect to find this electric cable in mint condition, as it looked on leaving its place of manufacture. The long snake was covered with seashell rubble and bristling with foraminifera; a crust of caked gravel protected it from any mollusks that might bore into it. It rested serenely, sheltered from the sea's motions, under a pressure favorable to the transmission of that electric spark that goes from America to Europe in 32/100 of a second. This cable will no doubt last indefinitely because, as observers note, its gutta–percha casing is improved by a stay in salt water.

Besides, on this well–chosen plateau, the cable never lies at depths that could cause a break. The *Nautilus* followed it to its lowest reaches, located 4,431 meters down, and even there it rested without any stress or strain. Then we returned to the locality where the 1863 accident had taken place.

There the ocean floor formed a valley 120 kilometers wide, into which you could fit Mt. Blanc without its summit poking above the surface of the waves. This valley is closed off to the east by a sheer wall 2,000 meters high. We arrived there on May 28, and the *Nautilus* lay no farther than 150 kilometers from Ireland.

Would Captain Nemo head up north and beach us on the British Isles? No. Much to my surprise, he went back down south and returned to European seas. As we swung around the Emerald Isle, I spotted Cape Clear for an instant, plus the lighthouse on Fastnet Rock that guides all those thousands of ships setting out from Glasgow or Liverpool.

An important question then popped into my head. Would the *Nautilus* dare to tackle the English Channel? Ned Land (who promptly reappeared after we hugged shore) never stopped questioning me. What could I answer him? Captain Nemo remained invisible. After giving the Canadian a glimpse of American shores, was he about to show me the coast of France?

But the *Nautilus* kept gravitating southward. On May 30, in sight of Land's End, it passed between the lowermost tip of England and the Scilly Islands, which it left behind to starboard.

If it was going to enter the English Channel, it clearly needed to head east. It did not.

All day long on May 31, the *Nautilus* swept around the sea in a series of circles that had me deeply puzzled. It seemed to be searching for a locality that it had some trouble finding. At noon Captain Nemo himself came to take our bearings. He didn't address a word to me. He looked gloomier than ever. What was filling him with such sadness? Was it our proximity to these European shores? Was he reliving his memories of that country he had left behind? If so, what did he feel? Remorse or regret? For a good while these thoughts occupied my mind, and I had a hunch that fate would soon give away the captain's secrets.

The next day, June 1, the *Nautilus* kept to the same tack. It was obviously trying to locate some precise spot in the ocean. Just as on the day before, Captain Nemo came to take the altitude of the sun. The sea was smooth, the skies clear. Eight miles to the east, a big steamship was visible on the horizon line. No flag was flapping from the gaff of its fore-and-aft sail, and I couldn't tell its nationality.

A few minutes before the sun passed its zenith, Captain

Nemo raised his sextant and took his sights with the utmost precision. The absolute calm of the waves facilitated this operation. The *Nautilus* lay motionless, neither rolling nor pitching.

I was on the platform just then. After determining our position, the captain pronounced only these words:

"It's right here!"

He went down the hatch. Had he seen that vessel change course and seemingly head toward us? I'm unable to say.

I returned to the lounge. The hatch closed, and I heard water hissing in the ballast tanks. The *Nautilus* began to sink on a vertical line, because its propeller was in check and no longer furnished any forward motion.

Some minutes later it stopped at a depth of 833 meters and came to rest on the seafloor.

The ceiling lights in the lounge then went out, the panels opened, and through the windows I saw, for a half–mile radius, the sea brightly lit by the beacon's rays.

I looked to port and saw nothing but the immenseness of these tranquil waters.

To starboard, a prominent bulge on the sea bottom caught my attention. You would have thought it was some ruin enshrouded in a crust of whitened seashells, as if under a mantle of snow. Carefully examining this mass, I could identify the swollen outlines of a ship shorn of its masts, which must have sunk bow first. This casualty certainly dated from some far–off time. To be so caked with the limestone of these waters, this wreckage must have spent many a year on the ocean floor.

What ship was this? Why had the *Nautilus* come to visit its grave? Was it something other than a maritime accident that had dragged this craft under the waters?

I wasn't sure what to think, but next to me I heard Captain Nemo's voice slowly say:

"Originally this ship was christened the *Marseillais*. It

carried seventy-four cannons and was launched in 1762. On August 13, 1778, commanded by La Poype-Vertrieux, it fought valiantly against the *Preston*. On July 4, 1779, as a member of the squadron under Admiral d'Estaing, it assisted in the capture of the island of Grenada. On September 5, 1781, under the Count de Grasse, it took part in the Battle of Chesapeake Bay. In 1794 the new Republic of France changed the name of this ship. On April 16 of that same year, it joined the squadron at Brest under Rear Admiral Villaret de Joyeuse, who was entrusted with escorting a convoy of wheat coming from America under the command of Admiral Van Stabel. In this second year of the French Revolutionary Calendar, on the 11th and 12th days in the Month of Pasture, this squadron fought an encounter with English vessels. Sir, today is June 1, 1868, or the 13th day in the Month of Pasture. Seventy-four years ago to the day, at this very spot in latitude 47° 24' and longitude 17° 28', this ship sank after a heroic battle; its three masts gone, water in its hold, a third of its crew out of action, it preferred to go to the bottom with its 356 seamen rather than surrender; and with its flag nailed up on the afterdeck, it disappeared beneath the waves to shouts of 'Long live the Republic!'"

"This is the *Avenger*!" I exclaimed.

"Yes, sir! The *Avenger*! A splendid name!" Captain Nemo murmured, crossing his arms.

# CHAPTER 21

## A Mass Execution

THE WAY HE SAID THIS, the unexpectedness of this scene, first the biography of this patriotic ship, then the excitement with which this eccentric individual pronounced these last words—the name *Avenger* whose significance could not escape me—all this, taken together, had a profound impact on my mind. My eyes never left the captain. Hands outstretched toward the sea, he contemplated the proud wreck with blazing eyes. Perhaps I would never learn who he was, where he came from or where he was heading, but more and more I could see a distinction between the man and the scientist. It was no ordinary misanthropy that kept Captain Nemo and his companions sequestered inside the *Nautilus's* plating, but a hate so monstrous or so sublime that the passing years could never weaken it.

Did this hate also hunger for vengeance? Time would soon tell.

Meanwhile the *Nautilus* rose slowly to the surface of the sea, and I watched the *Avenger's* murky shape disappearing little by little. Soon a gentle rolling told me that we were afloat in the open air.

Just then a hollow explosion was audible. I looked at the captain. The captain did not stir.

"Captain?" I said.

He didn't reply.

I left him and climbed onto the platform. Conseil and the

Canadian were already there.

"What caused that explosion?" I asked.

"A cannon going off," Ned Land replied.

I stared in the direction of the ship I had spotted. It was heading toward the *Nautilus*, and you could tell it had put on steam. Six miles separated it from us.

"What sort of craft is it, Ned?"

"From its rigging and its low masts," the Canadian replied, "I bet it's a warship. Here's hoping it pulls up and sinks this damned *Nautilus*!"

"Ned my friend," Conseil replied, "what harm could it do the *Nautilus*? Will it attack us under the waves? Will it cannonade us at the bottom of the sea?"

"Tell me, Ned," I asked, "can you make out the nationality of that craft?"

Creasing his brow, lowering his lids, and puckering the corners of his eyes, the Canadian focused the full power of his gaze on the ship for a short while.

"No, sir," he replied. "I can't make out what nation it's from. It's flying no flag. But I'll swear it's a warship, because there's a long pennant streaming from the peak of its mainmast."

For a quarter of an hour, we continued to watch the craft bearing down on us. But it was inconceivable to me that it had discovered the *Nautilus* at such a distance, still less that it knew what this underwater machine really was.

Soon the Canadian announced that the craft was a big battleship, a double–decker ironclad complete with ram. Dark, dense smoke burst from its two funnels. Its furled sails merged with the lines of its yardarms. The gaff of its fore–and–aft sail flew no flag. Its distance still kept us from distinguishing the colors of its pennant, which was fluttering like a thin ribbon.

It was coming on fast. If Captain Nemo let it approach, a chance for salvation might be available to us.

"Sir," Ned Land told me, "if that boat gets within a mile of us, I'm jumping overboard, and I suggest you follow suit."

I didn't reply to the Canadian's proposition but kept watching the ship, which was looming larger on the horizon. Whether it was English, French, American, or Russian, it would surely welcome us aboard if we could just get to it.

"Master may recall," Conseil then said, "that we have some experience with swimming. He can rely on me to tow him to that vessel, if he's agreeable to going with our friend Ned."

Before I could reply, white smoke streamed from the battleship's bow. Then, a few seconds later, the waters splashed astern of the *Nautilus*, disturbed by the fall of a heavy object. Soon after, an explosion struck my ears.

"What's this? They're firing at us!" I exclaimed.

"Good lads!" the Canadian muttered.

"That means they don't see us as castaways clinging to some wreckage!"

"With all due respect to Master—gracious!" Conseil put in, shaking off the water that had sprayed over him from another shell. "With all due respect to master, they've discovered the narwhale and they're cannonading the same."

"But it must be clear to them," I exclaimed, "that they're dealing with human beings."

"Maybe that's why!" Ned Land replied, staring hard at me.

The full truth dawned on me. Undoubtedly people now knew where they stood on the existence of this so-called monster. Undoubtedly the latter's encounter with the *Abraham Lincoln*, when the Canadian hit it with his harpoon, had led Commander Farragut to recognize the narwhale as actually an underwater boat, more dangerous than any unearthly cetacean!

Yes, this had to be the case, and undoubtedly they were now chasing this dreadful engine of destruction on every sea!

Dreadful indeed, if, as we could assume, Captain Nemo had been using the *Nautilus* in works of vengeance! That night in the middle of the Indian Ocean, when he imprisoned us in the cell, hadn't he attacked some ship? That man now buried in the coral cemetery, wasn't he the victim of some collision caused by the *Nautilus*? Yes, I repeat: this had to be the case. One part of Captain Nemo's secret life had been unveiled. And now, even though his identity was still unknown, at least the nations allied against him knew they were no longer hunting some fairy-tale monster, but a man who had sworn an implacable hate toward them!

This whole fearsome sequence of events appeared in my mind's eye. Instead of encountering friends on this approaching ship, we would find only pitiless enemies.

Meanwhile shells fell around us in increasing numbers. Some, meeting the liquid surface, would ricochet and vanish into the sea at considerable distances. But none of them reached the *Nautilus*.

By then the ironclad was no more than three miles off. Despite its violent cannonade, Captain Nemo hadn't appeared on the platform. And yet if one of those conical shells had scored a routine hit on the *Nautilus's* hull, it could have been fatal to him.

The Canadian then told me:

"Sir, we've got to do everything we can to get out of this jam! Let's signal them! Damnation! Maybe they'll realize we're decent people!"

Ned Land pulled out his handkerchief to wave it in the air. But he had barely unfolded it when he was felled by an iron fist, and despite his great strength, he tumbled to the deck.

"Scum!" the captain shouted. "Do you want to be nailed to the *Nautilus's* spur before it charges that ship?"

Dreadful to hear, Captain Nemo was even more dreadful to see. His face was pale from some spasm of his heart, which must have stopped beating for an instant. His pupils were hideously contracted. His voice was no longer speaking, it was bellowing. Bending from the waist, he shook the Canadian by the shoulders.

Then, dropping Ned and turning to the battleship, whose shells were showering around him:

"O ship of an accursed nation, you know who I am!" he shouted in his powerful voice. "And I don't need your colors to recognize you! Look! I'll show you mine!"

And in the bow of the platform, Captain Nemo unfurled a black flag, like the one he had left planted at the South Pole.

Just then a shell hit the *Nautilus's* hull obliquely, failed to breach it, ricocheted near the captain, and vanished into the sea.

Captain Nemo shrugged his shoulders. Then, addressing me:

"Go below!" he told me in a curt tone. "You and your companions, go below!"

"Sir," I exclaimed, "are you going to attack this ship?"

"Sir, I'm going to sink it."

"You wouldn't!"

"I will," Captain Nemo replied icily. "You're ill-advised to pass judgment on me, sir. Fate has shown you what you weren't meant to see. The attack has come. Our reply will be dreadful. Get back inside!"

"From what country is that ship?"

"You don't know? Fine, so much the better! At least its nationality will remain a secret to you. Go below!"

The Canadian, Conseil, and I could only obey. Some fifteen of the *Nautilus's* seamen surrounded their captain and stared with a feeling of implacable hate at the ship bearing down on them. You could feel the same spirit of vengeance enkindling their every soul.

I went below just as another projectile scraped the *Nautilus's* hull, and I heard the captain exclaim:

"Shoot, you demented vessel! Shower your futile shells!

You won't escape the *Nautilus's* spur! But this isn't the place where you'll perish! I don't want your wreckage mingling with that of the *Avenger!*"

I repaired to my stateroom. The captain and his chief officer stayed on the platform. The propeller was set in motion. The *Nautilus* swiftly retreated, putting us outside the range of the vessel's shells. But the chase continued, and Captain Nemo was content to keep his distance.

Near four o'clock in the afternoon, unable to control the impatience and uneasiness devouring me, I went back to the central companionway. The hatch was open. I ventured onto the platform. The captain was still strolling there, his steps agitated. He stared at the ship, which stayed to his leeward five or six miles off. He was circling it like a wild beast, drawing it eastward, letting it chase after him. Yet he didn't attack. Was he, perhaps, still undecided?

I tried to intervene one last time. But I had barely queried Captain Nemo when the latter silenced me:

"I'm the law, I'm the tribunal! I'm the oppressed, and there are my oppressors! Thanks to them, I've witnessed the destruction of everything I loved, cherished, and venerated— homeland, wife, children, father, and mother! There lies everything I hate! Not another word out of you!"

I took a last look at the battleship, which was putting on steam. Then I rejoined Ned and Conseil.

"We'll escape!" I exclaimed.

"Good," Ned put in. "Where's that ship from?"

"I've no idea. But wherever it's from, it will sink before nightfall. In any event, it's better to perish with it than be accomplices in some act of revenge whose merits we can't gauge."

"That's my feeling," Ned Land replied coolly. "Let's wait for nightfall."

Night fell. A profound silence reigned on board. The

compass indicated that the *Nautilus* hadn't changed direction.
I could hear the beat of its propeller, churning the waves with
steady speed. Staying on the surface of the water, it rolled
gently, sometimes to one side, sometimes to the other.

My companions and I had decided to escape as soon as the
vessel came close enough for us to be heard—or seen, because
the moon would wax full in three days and was shining
brightly. Once we were aboard that ship, if we couldn't ward off
the blow that threatened it, at least we could do everything that
circumstances permitted. Several times I thought the *Nautilus*
was about to attack. But it was content to let its adversary
approach, and then it would quickly resume its retreating ways.

Part of the night passed without incident. We kept watch
for an opportunity to take action. We talked little, being too
keyed up. Ned Land was all for jumping overboard. I forced
him to wait. As I saw it, the *Nautilus* would attack the double-
decker on the surface of the waves, and then it would be not
only possible but easy to escape.

At three o'clock in the morning, full of uneasiness, I climbed
onto the platform. Captain Nemo hadn't left it. He stood in the
bow next to his flag, which a mild breeze was unfurling above
his head. His eyes never left that vessel. The extraordinary
intensity of his gaze seemed to attract it, beguile it, and draw it
more surely than if he had it in tow!

The moon then passed its zenith. Jupiter was rising in the
east. In the midst of this placid natural setting, sky and ocean
competed with each other in tranquility, and the sea offered
the orb of night the loveliest mirror ever to reflect its image.

And when I compared this deep calm of the elements with
all the fury seething inside the plating of this barely perceptible
*Nautilus*, I shivered all over.

The vessel was two miles off. It drew nearer, always moving
toward the phosphorescent glow that signaled the *Nautilus's*
presence. I saw its green and red running lights, plus the

white lantern hanging from the large stay of its foremast. Hazy flickerings were reflected on its rigging and indicated that its furnaces were pushed to the limit. Showers of sparks and cinders of flaming coal escaped from its funnels, spangling the air with stars.

I stood there until six o'clock in the morning, Captain Nemo never seeming to notice me. The vessel lay a mile and a half off, and with the first glimmers of daylight, it resumed its cannonade. The time couldn't be far away when the *Nautilus* would attack its adversary, and my companions and I would leave forever this man I dared not judge.

I was about to go below to alert them, when the chief officer climbed onto the platform. Several seamen were with him. Captain Nemo didn't see them, or didn't want to see them. They carried out certain procedures that, on the *Nautilus*, you could call "clearing the decks for action." They were quite simple. The manropes that formed a handrail around the platform were lowered. Likewise the pilothouse and the beacon housing were withdrawn into the hull until they lay exactly flush with it. The surface of this long sheet–iron cigar no longer offered a single protrusion that could hamper its maneuvers.

I returned to the lounge. The *Nautilus* still emerged above the surface. A few morning gleams infiltrated the liquid strata. Beneath the undulations of the billows, the windows were enlivened by the blushing of the rising sun. That dreadful day of June 2 had dawned.

At seven o'clock the log told me that the *Nautilus* had reduced speed. I realized that it was letting the warship approach. Moreover, the explosions grew more intensely audible. Shells furrowed the water around us, drilling through it with an odd hissing sound.

"My friends," I said, "it's time. Let's shake hands, and may God be with us!"

Ned Land was determined, Conseil calm, I myself nervous

and barely in control.

We went into the library. Just as I pushed open the door leading to the well of the central companionway, I heard the hatch close sharply overhead.

The Canadian leaped up the steps, but I stopped him. A well–known hissing told me that water was entering the ship's ballast tanks. Indeed, in a few moments the *Nautilus* had submerged some meters below the surface of the waves.

I understood this maneuver. It was too late to take action. The *Nautilus* wasn't going to strike the double–decker where it was clad in impenetrable iron armor, but below its waterline, where the metal carapace no longer protected its planking.

We were prisoners once more, unwilling spectators at the performance of this gruesome drama. But we barely had time to think. Taking refuge in my stateroom, we stared at each other without pronouncing a word. My mind was in a total daze. My mental processes came to a dead stop. I hovered in that painful state that predominates during the period of anticipation before some frightful explosion. I waited, I listened, I lived only through my sense of hearing!

Meanwhile the *Nautilus's* speed had increased appreciably. So it was gathering momentum. Its entire hull was vibrating.

Suddenly I let out a yell. There had been a collision, but it was comparatively mild. I could feel the penetrating force of the steel spur. I could hear scratchings and scrapings. Carried away with its driving power, the *Nautilus* had passed through the vessel's mass like a sailmaker's needle through canvas!

I couldn't hold still. Frantic, going insane, I leaped out of my stateroom and rushed into the lounge.

Captain Nemo was there. Mute, gloomy, implacable, he was staring through the port panel.

An enormous mass was sinking beneath the waters, and the *Nautilus*, missing none of its death throes, was descending into the depths with it. Ten meters away, I could see its gaping hull, into which water was rushing with a sound of thunder, then its double rows of cannons and railings. Its deck was covered with dark, quivering shadows.

The water was rising. Those poor men leaped up into the shrouds, clung to the masts, writhed beneath the waters. It was a human anthill that an invading sea had caught by surprise!

Paralyzed, rigid with anguish, my hair standing on end, my eyes popping out of my head, short of breath, suffocating, speechless, I stared—I too! I was glued to the window by an irresistible allure!

The enormous vessel settled slowly. Following it down, the *Nautilus* kept watch on its every movement. Suddenly there was an eruption. The air compressed inside the craft sent its decks flying, as if the powder stores had been ignited. The thrust of the waters was so great, the *Nautilus* swerved away.

The poor ship then sank more swiftly. Its mastheads appeared, laden with victims, then its crosstrees bending under clusters of men, finally the peak of its mainmast. Then the dark mass disappeared, and with it a crew of corpses dragged under by fearsome eddies. . . .

I turned to Captain Nemo. This dreadful executioner, this true archangel of hate, was still staring. When it was all over, Captain Nemo headed to the door of his stateroom, opened it, and entered. I followed him with my eyes.

On the rear paneling, beneath the portraits of his heroes, I saw the portrait of a still–youthful woman with two little children. Captain Nemo stared at them for a few moments, stretched out his arms to them, sank to his knees, and melted into sobs.

# CHAPTER 22

### The Last Words of Captain Nemo

THE PANELS CLOSED over this frightful view, but the lights didn't go on in the lounge. Inside the *Nautilus* all was gloom and silence. It left this place of devastation with prodigious speed, 100 feet beneath the waters. Where was it going? North or south? Where would the man flee after this horrible act of revenge?

I re-entered my stateroom, where Ned and Conseil were waiting silently. Captain Nemo filled me with insurmountable horror. Whatever he had once suffered at the hands of humanity, he had no right to mete out such punishment. He had made me, if not an accomplice, at least an eyewitness to his vengeance! Even this was intolerable.

At eleven o'clock the electric lights came back on. I went into the lounge. It was deserted. I consulted the various instruments. The *Nautilus* was fleeing northward at a speed of twenty–five miles per hour, sometimes on the surface of the sea, sometimes thirty feet beneath it.

After our position had been marked on the chart, I saw that we were passing into the mouth of the English Channel, that our heading would take us to the northernmost seas with incomparable speed.

I could barely glimpse the swift passing of longnose sharks, hammerhead sharks, spotted dogfish that frequent these waters, big eagle rays, swarms of seahorse looking like knights on a chessboard, eels quivering like fireworks serpents, armies of crab that fled obliquely by crossing their pincers over their carapaces, finally schools of porpoise that held contests of speed with the *Nautilus*. But by this point observing, studying, and classifying were out of the question.

By evening we had cleared 200 leagues up the Atlantic. Shadows gathered and gloom overran the sea until the moon came up.

I repaired to my stateroom. I couldn't sleep. I was assaulted by nightmares. That horrible scene of destruction kept repeating in my mind's eye.

From that day forward, who knows where the *Nautilus* took us in the north Atlantic basin? Always at incalculable speed! Always amid the High Arctic mists! Did it call at the capes of Spitzbergen or the shores of Novaya Zemlya? Did it visit such uncharted seas as the White Sea, the Kara Sea, the Gulf of Ob, the Lyakhov Islands, or those unknown beaches on the Siberian coast? I'm unable to say. I lost track of the passing hours. Time was in abeyance on the ship's clocks. As happens in the polar regions, it seemed that night and day no longer followed their normal sequence. I felt myself being drawn into that strange domain where the overwrought imagination of Edgar Allan Poe was at home. Like his fabled Arthur Gordon Pym, I expected any moment to see that "shrouded human figure, very far larger in its proportions than any dweller among men," thrown across the cataract that protects the outskirts of the pole!

I estimate—but perhaps I'm mistaken—that the *Nautilus's* haphazard course continued for fifteen or twenty days, and I'm not sure how long this would have gone on without the catastrophe that ended our voyage. As for Captain Nemo, he was no longer in the picture. As for his chief officer, the same applied. Not one crewman was visible for a single instant. The *Nautilus* cruised beneath the waters almost continuously. When it rose briefly to the surface to renew our air, the hatches opened and closed as if automated. No more positions were reported on the world map. I didn't know where we were.

I'll also mention that the Canadian, at the end of his strength and patience, made no further appearances. Conseil couldn't coax a single word out of him and feared that, in a fit of delirium while under the sway of a ghastly homesickness, Ned would kill himself. So he kept a devoted watch on his friend every instant.

You can appreciate that under these conditions, our situation had become untenable.

One morning—whose date I'm unable to specify—I was slumbering near the first hours of daylight, a painful, sickly slumber. Waking up, I saw Ned Land leaning over me, and I heard him tell me in a low voice:

"We're going to escape!"

I sat up.

"When?" I asked.

"Tonight. There doesn't seem to be any supervision left on the *Nautilus*. You'd think a total daze was reigning on board. Will you be ready, sir?"

"Yes. Where are we?"

"In sight of land. I saw it through the mists just this morning, twenty miles to the east."

"What land is it?"

"I've no idea, but whatever it is, there we'll take refuge."

"Yes, Ned! We'll escape tonight even if the sea swallows us up!"

"The sea's rough, the wind's blowing hard, but a twenty–mile run in the *Nautilus's* nimble longboat doesn't scare me. Unknown to the crew, I've stowed some food and flasks of water inside."

"I'm with you."

"What's more," the Canadian added, "if they catch me, I'll defend myself, I'll fight to the death."

"Then we'll die together, Ned my friend."

My mind was made up. The Canadian left me. I went out on the platform, where I could barely stand upright against the jolts of the billows. The skies were threatening, but land lay inside those dense mists, and we had to escape. Not a single day, or even a single hour, could we afford to lose.

I returned to the lounge, dreading yet desiring an encounter with Captain Nemo, wanting yet not wanting to see him. What would I say to him? How could I hide the involuntary horror he inspired in me? No! It was best not to meet him face to face! Best to try and forget him! And yet . . . !

How long that day seemed, the last I would spend aboard the *Nautilus*! I was left to myself. Ned Land and Conseil avoided speaking to me, afraid they would give themselves away.

At six o'clock I ate supper, but I had no appetite. Despite my revulsion, I forced it down, wanting to keep my strength up.

At 6:30 Ned Land entered my stateroom. He told me:

"We won't see each other again before we go. At ten o'clock the moon won't be up yet. We'll take advantage of the darkness. Come to the skiff. Conseil and I will be inside waiting for you."

The Canadian left without giving me time to answer him.

I wanted to verify the *Nautilus's* heading. I made my way to the lounge. We were racing north–northeast with frightful speed, fifty meters down.

I took one last look at the natural wonders and artistic treasures amassed in the museum, this unrivaled collection doomed to perish someday in the depths of the seas, together with its curator. I wanted to establish one supreme impression in my mind. I stayed there an hour, basking in the aura of the ceiling lights, passing in review the treasures shining in their glass cases. Then I returned to my stateroom.

There I dressed in sturdy seafaring clothes. I gathered my notes and packed them tenderly about my person. My heart was pounding mightily. I couldn't curb its pulsations. My anxiety and agitation would certainly have given me away if Captain Nemo had seen me.

What was he doing just then? I listened at the door to his stateroom. I heard the sound of footsteps. Captain Nemo was inside. He hadn't gone to bed. With his every movement I imagined he would appear and ask me why I wanted to escape! I felt in a perpetual state of alarm. My imagination magnified this sensation. The feeling became so acute, I wondered whether it wouldn't be better to enter the captain's stateroom, dare him face to face, brave it out with word and deed!

It was an insane idea. Fortunately I controlled myself and stretched out on the bed to soothe my bodily agitation. My nerves calmed a little, but with my brain so aroused, I did a swift review of my whole existence aboard the *Nautilus*, every pleasant or unpleasant incident that had crossed my path since I went overboard from the *Abraham Lincoln*: the underwater hunting trip, the Torres Strait, our running aground, the savages of Papua, the coral cemetery, the Suez passageway, the island of Santorini, the Cretan diver, the Bay of Vigo, Atlantis, the Ice Bank, the South Pole, our imprisonment in the ice, the battle with the devilfish, the storm in the Gulf Stream, the *Avenger*, and that horrible scene of the vessel sinking with its crew . . . ! All these events passed before my eyes like backdrops unrolling upstage in a theater. In this strange setting Captain Nemo then grew fantastically. His features were accentuated, taking on superhuman proportions. He was no longer my equal, he was the Man of the Waters, the Spirit of the Seas.

By then it was 9:30. I held my head in both hands to keep it from bursting. I closed my eyes. I no longer wanted to think. A half hour still to wait! A half hour of nightmares that could drive me insane!

Just then I heard indistinct chords from the organ, melancholy harmonies from some undefinable hymn, actual pleadings from a soul trying to sever its earthly ties. I listened with all my senses at once, barely breathing, immersed like Captain Nemo in this musical trance that was drawing him beyond the bounds of this world.

Then a sudden thought terrified me. Captain Nemo had left his stateroom. He was in the same lounge I had to cross in order to escape. There I would encounter him one last time. He would see me, perhaps speak to me! One gesture from him could obliterate me, a single word shackle me to his vessel!

Even so, ten o'clock was about to strike. It was time to leave my stateroom and rejoin my companions.

I dared not hesitate, even if Captain Nemo stood before me. I opened the door cautiously, but as it swung on its hinges, it seemed to make a frightful noise. This noise existed, perhaps, only in my imagination!

I crept forward through the *Nautilus's* dark gangways, pausing after each step to curb the pounding of my heart.

I arrived at the corner door of the lounge. I opened it gently. The lounge was plunged in profound darkness. Chords from the organ were reverberating faintly. Captain Nemo was there. He didn't see me. Even in broad daylight I doubt that he would have noticed me, so completely was he immersed in his trance.

I inched over the carpet, avoiding the tiniest bump whose noise might give me away. It took me five minutes to reach the door at the far end, which led into the library.

I was about to open it when a gasp from Captain Nemo nailed me to the spot. I realized that he was standing up. I even got a glimpse of him because some rays of light from the library had filtered into the lounge. He was coming toward me, arms crossed, silent, not walking but gliding like a ghost. His chest was heaving, swelling with sobs. And I heard him murmur these words, the last of his to reach my ears:

"O almighty God! Enough! Enough!"

Was it a vow of repentance that had just escaped from this man's conscience . . . ?

Frantic, I rushed into the library. I climbed the central companionway, and going along the upper gangway, I arrived at the skiff. I went through the opening that had already given access to my two companions.

"Let's go, let's go!" I exclaimed.

"Right away!" the Canadian replied.

First, Ned Land closed and bolted the opening cut into the *Nautilus's* sheet iron, using the monkey wrench he had with him. After likewise closing the opening in the skiff, the Canadian began to unscrew the nuts still bolting us to the underwater boat.

Suddenly a noise from the ship's interior became audible. Voices were answering each other hurriedly. What was it? Had they spotted our escape? I felt Ned Land sliding a dagger into my hand.

"Yes," I muttered, "we know how to die!"

The Canadian paused in his work. But one word twenty times repeated, one dreadful word, told me the reason for the agitation spreading aboard the *Nautilus*. We weren't the cause of the crew's concern.

"Maelstrom! Maelstrom!" they were shouting.

The Maelstrom! Could a more frightening name have rung in our ears under more frightening circumstances? Were we lying in the dangerous waterways off the Norwegian coast? Was the *Nautilus* being dragged into this whirlpool just as the skiff was about to detach from its plating?

As you know, at the turn of the tide, the waters confined between the Faroe and Lofoten Islands rush out with irresistible violence. They form a vortex from which no ship has ever been able to escape. Monstrous waves race together from every point of the horizon. They form a whirlpool aptly called "the ocean's navel," whose attracting power extends a distance of fifteen kilometers. It can suck down not only ships but whales, and even polar bears from the northernmost regions.

This was where the *Nautilus* had been sent accidentally—or perhaps deliberately—by its captain. It was sweeping around in a spiral whose radius kept growing smaller and smaller. The skiff, still attached to the ship's plating, was likewise carried around at dizzying speed. I could feel us whirling. I was experiencing that accompanying nausea that follows such continuous spinning motions. We were in dread, in the last stages of sheer horror, our blood frozen in our veins, our nerves numb, drenched in cold sweat as if from the throes of dying! And what a noise around our frail skiff! What roars echoing from several miles away! What crashes from the waters breaking against sharp rocks on the seafloor, where the hardest objects are smashed, where tree trunks are worn down and worked into "a shaggy fur," as Norwegians express it!

What a predicament! We were rocking frightfully. The *Nautilus* defended itself like a human being. Its steel muscles were cracking. Sometimes it stood on end, the three of us along with it!

"We've got to hold on tight," Ned said, "and screw the nuts down again! If we can stay attached to the *Nautilus*, we can still make it . . . !"

He hadn't finished speaking when a cracking sound occurred. The nuts gave way, and ripped out of its socket, the skiff was hurled like a stone from a sling into the midst of the vortex.

My head struck against an iron timber, and with this violent shock I lost consciousness.

# CHAPTER 23

## Conclusion

WE COME TO the conclusion of this voyage under the seas. What happened that night, how the skiff escaped from the Maelstrom's fearsome eddies, how Ned Land, Conseil, and I got out of that whirlpool, I'm unable to say. But when I regained consciousness, I was lying in a fisherman's hut on one of the Lofoten Islands. My two companions, safe and sound, were at my bedside clasping my hands. We embraced each other heartily.

Just now we can't even dream of returning to France. Travel between upper Norway and the south is limited. So I have to wait for the arrival of a steamboat that provides bimonthly service from North Cape.

So it is here, among these gallant people who have taken us in, that I'm reviewing my narrative of these adventures. It is accurate. Not a fact has been omitted, not a detail has been exaggerated. It's the faithful record of this inconceivable expedition into an element now beyond human reach, but where progress will someday make great inroads.

Will anyone believe me? I don't know. Ultimately it's unimportant. What I can now assert is that I've earned the right to speak of these seas, beneath which in less than ten months, I've cleared 20,000 leagues in this underwater tour of the world that has shown me so many wonders across the Pacific, the Indian Ocean, the Red Sea, the Mediterranean, the Atlantic, the southernmost and northernmost seas!

But what happened to the *Nautilus*? Did it withstand the Maelstrom's clutches? Is Captain Nemo alive? Is he still under the ocean pursuing his frightful program of revenge, or did he stop after that latest mass execution? Will the waves someday deliver that manuscript that contains his full life story? Will I finally learn the man's name? Will the nationality of the stricken warship tell us the nationality of Captain Nemo?

I hope so. I likewise hope that his powerful submersible has defeated the sea inside its most dreadful whirlpool, that the *Nautilus* has survived where so many ships have perished! If this is the case and Captain Nemo still inhabits the ocean—his adopted country—may the hate be appeased in that fierce heart! May the contemplation of so many wonders extinguish the spirit of vengeance in him! May the executioner pass away, and the scientist continue his peaceful exploration of the seas! If his destiny is strange, it's also sublime. Haven't I encompassed it myself? Didn't I lead ten months of this otherworldly existence? Thus to that question asked 6,000 years ago in the Book of Ecclesiastes—"Who can fathom the soundless depths?"—two men out of all humanity have now earned the right to reply. Captain Nemo and I.